JACK FOUR

NEAL
ASHER
JACK FOUR

TOR

First published 2021 by Tor
an imprint of Pan Macmillan
The Smithson, 6 Briset Street, London EC1M 5NR
EU representative: Macmillan Publishers Ireland Limited,
Mallard Lodge, Lansdowne Village, Dublin 4
Associated companies throughout the world
www.panmacmillan.com

ISBN 978-1-5290-4997-8

1 3 5 7 9 8 6 4 2

A CIP catalogue record for this book is available from the British Library.

Typeset in Plantin by Palimpsest Book Production Limited, Falkirk, Stirlingshire
Printed and bound by CPI Group (UK) Ltd, Croydon, CR0 4YY

Visit **www.panmacmillan.com** to read more about all our books
and to buy them. You will also find features, author interviews and
news of any author events, and you can sign up for e-newsletters
so that you're always first to hear about our new releases.

In this time of Covid-19, bitter elections and general political throat-tearing, it's difficult to step outside my cynicism to find anyone to dedicate this book to, so instead I'll dedicate it to the island of Crete – for my garden in the calm of Papagiannades where I grow chillies, for the mountains that provide me with energy even after trudging through them for miles, for the Libyan Sea where, while out in my kayak, I can find a quiet mind.

Thank you, Crete.

Acknowledgements

My thanks to those who have helped bring this novel to your e-reader, smartphone, computer screen and to that old-fashioned mass of wood pulp called a book. At Macmillan these include Bella Pagan (editor), Georgia Summers (assistant editor), Samantha Fletcher (desk editor), Neil Lang (jacket designer) and Eleanor Bailey (marketing); also freelancers Jessica Cuthbert-Smith (copy-editor), Robert Clark (proofreader), Steve Stone (jacket illustrator) and Jamie-Lee Nardone (publicity); and others whose names I simply don't know.

Though at times they irk me with their demands to see more from this character or that in my previous books, further thanks are due to the fans I chat with on social media. I may not end up doing what they want, but they do spark some things off. It's pleasing to know that they get joy from the same things as me, but then, I was a fan myself before I tentatively pushed down a key on my father's old manual typewriter!

Glossary

Atheter (The): A highly advanced space-faring race who during their time encountered the civilization-destroying Jain technology. Eventually, to escape this technology, they committed a form of racial suicide by sacrificing their civilization and intelligence. Their animal descendants still exist on the planet Masada. They are gabbleducks – creatures that speak nonsense and whose behaviour is always strange.

Augmented: To be 'augmented' is to have taken advantage of one or more of the many available cybernetic devices, mechanical additions and, distinctly, cerebral augmentations. In the last case we have, of course, the ubiquitous 'aug' and such backformations as 'auged', 'auging-in' and the execrable 'all auged up'. But it does not stop there: the word 'aug' has now become confused with auger and augur – which is understandable considering the way an aug connects and the information that then becomes available. So now you can 'auger' information from the AI net, and a prediction made by an aug prognostic subprogram can be called an augury.
                    – From 'Quince Guide' compiled by humans

First- and second-children: Male prador, chemically maintained in adolescence, enslaved by pheromones emitted by their fathers and acting as crew on their ships or as soldiers. Prador adults also use their surgically removed ganglions (brains) as navigational computers in their ships and to control war machines.

Hardfield: A flat force field capable of stopping missiles and energy beams. The impact or heat energy is transformed and dissipated by its projector. Overload of that projector usually results in its catastrophic breakdown, at which point it is ejected from the vessel containing it. Hardfields of any other format were supposed to be impossible; however, it has now been revealed that they can be made spherical and almost impenetrable . . .

Hooders: The devolved descendants of Atheter biomech war machines. Creatures that look like giant centipedes, they retain some of their war machine past in that they are rugged, tough, vicious and very difficult to kill with conventional weapons.

Hooper: A human from the oceanic world of Spatterjay who has been infected with the Spatterjay virus. Commonly passed on through a leech bite, this virus makes its host inhumanly strong, dangerous and long-lived.

Jain technology: A technology spanning all scientific disciplines, created by one of the dead races – the Jain. Its apparent sum purpose is to spread through civilizations and annihilate them.

King of the prador: The king who ruled the prador when they attacked the Polity was usurped by another prador who had been infected with the Spatterjay virus. The new king, and his family, have been highly mutated by this, resulting in extreme body changes and increased intelligence.

Nanosuite: A suite of nanomachines most human beings have inside them. These self-propagating machines act as a secondary immune system, repairing and adjusting the body. Each suite can be altered to suit the individual and his or her circumstances.

Polity: A human/AI dominion extending across many star systems, occupying a spherical space spanning the thickness of the galaxy and centred on Earth. It is ruled over by the AIs who took control of human affairs in what has been called, because of its very low casualty rate, the Quiet War. The top AI is called Earth Central (EC) and resides in a building on the shore of Lake Geneva, while planetary AIs, lower down in the hierarchy, rule over other worlds. The Polity is a highly technical civilization but its weakness was its reliance on travel by 'runcible' – instantaneous matter transmission gates.

Prador: A highly xenophobic race of giant crablike aliens ruled by a king and his family. Hostility is implicit in their biology and, upon encountering the Polity, they immediately attacked it. They originally had an advantage in the prador/human war in that they did not use runcibles (such devices needed the intelligence of AIs to control them and the prador are also hostile to any form of artificial intelligence) and as a result had developed their spaceship technology, and the metallurgy involved, beyond that of the Polity. They attacked with near-indestructible ships, but in the end the humans and AIs adapted, their war factories out-manufactured the prador and they began to win. They did not complete the victory, however, because the old king was usurped and the new king made an uneasy peace with the Polity.

Quantum crystals: Can be used to store masses of data in a distributed fashion throughout any system, including the human body. This form of storage is being experimented with by the Polity and can take the place of a memplant – a device used to record a human mind.

Reaver: A huge golden ship shaped like an extended teardrop and one of the feared vessels of the prador King's Guard.

Runcible: Instantaneous matter transmission gates, allowing transportation through underspace.

U-space: Underspace is the continuum spaceships enter (or U-jump into), rather like submarines submerging, to travel faster than light. It is also the continuum that can be crossed by using runcible gates, making travel between worlds linked by such gates all but instantaneous.

1

When the cold coffin opened, only the body of a human male existed. It had a bald skull, dark complexion and hazel eyes. The brain which sat inside its skull was a blank slate, though one formatted along standard lines. It would not, for example, need to be instructed how to keep its heart beating; autonomics ran as they should. The shape of a human mentality was sketched through the grey and white matter, but there was no sentient person there.

The body lacked all the bolt-on advantages of current humanity, such as nanosuites, boosting, cerebral augs, gridlinks or motorized paraphernalia. It was in fact one of a vanishingly small number of humans not to be a cyborg. It did, however, have its genetic modifications, since the superfluous had been removed, ensuring it would suffer no inherited diseases. Without intervention, it had a good chance of living for a hundred and fifty years solstan. Right now, it seemed highly unlikely it would make it into its teens.

Microwave heating raised the body's temperature and particular chemical processes kicked into motion, but in all these activities there was no tendency, yet, towards decay. Mitochondria stayed on hold, awaiting their trigger. Pads folded around the skull. These injected a host of nanofibres and tubules into the head, which began making connections throughout, injecting neurochem and jump-starting nerve impulses. Other pads touched here and there over the body, injecting more neuro-chem, a required microbiome, complex proteins and sugars, as well as carbon fibres into the heart muscle and spine. Everything was starting to reach readiness as the body rose to optimum temperature. Enzyme keys to turn on the mitochondria flooded the heart and it soon began beating, spreading that key throughout the body in the blood. Following this, the organs started up in a steady cascade. The complex chemical factory of the liver began its work, while in the skull the fibres and tubules laid down data in moving patterns that would allow the brain to function, to understand some of its environment and to respond to simple orders.

I opened my eyes.

The cold coffin had popped open and I lay gazing up at a shiny aseptic surface, flinching as connections pulled out of my sore limbs, my mind all but vacant. I then felt something buzz against the side of my neck and an impulse driving me. I sat up and looked around, seeing further coffins protruding from other walls and their occupants also sitting up. I even felt a little sick, but didn't realize then that my body didn't possess the alterations to the inner ear most modern humans possessed.

'Proceed to the exit,' said a voice.

I understood the words perfectly, even though I had never heard nor spoken words before. It gave me context, a sense of place and what 'exit' would mean, and with that a growing sense of self. I felt an urgency to obey them, but also some confusion about where an exit might be. Others started hauling themselves out of their coffins and moving in a direction I labelled 'down' in relation to my position in the coffin, while the idea of 'cold coffin' lodged in my mind, but with language associations I did not understand. I watched the first of my fellows pull herself through a circular hatch. Understanding of shapes intruded on my thoughts, along with 'hatch', its only association, for a second, to the 'lid' of my coffin, but then came ideas of doors and other movable items that might block my progress. I noted then that all the females looked the same as each other, as did the males. The concept of human sex differences had surfaced in my thoughts as a kind of 'by the way'. Light flashed in my skull, then jagged lines crawled across my vision. I couldn't identify this for a moment, until I came to understand these were the visual effect of a migraine headache – an ancient human condition. I next questioned my impulse to follow the others. Little did I realize this was the first moment I strayed from design, and that things were already happening in my mind which weren't in the others'. Again I felt a buzzing against the side of my neck and my urgency to obey increased. I reached up and felt some solid lump attached there just below my ear. A further intense buzz drove shooting pains throughout my body and propelled me out of the coffin after the others.

I was the last through and floated into an area where some unknown force then grabbed me and pulled me down. *Gravity*, I realized, grasping the concept even as I fell beside one of the women, thumping into her. She looked at me blank-eyed, a stream of drool issuing from the side of her mouth. I noted the clamshell of technology attached to the side of her neck. The migraine lights flashed in my mind again and I recognized this thing as a slaver unit, based on prador thrall technology, which used the same nanowires and neural meshes as a cerebral augmentation to key into the brain and nervous system. I was wearing one too. The slavers could quickly impart complex instructions through it, which I'd be unable to disobey, as well as knowledge they felt it necessary for me to know, such as the effect of gravity. I also began to understand that my knowledge of this device hadn't actually come from the thing itself, but was is some way related to the migraine lights.

'Move into ranks,' said the voice.

Images rose in my mind of soldiers standing in a row, and marching. Associations blossomed through my consciousness, including positions in organizations and societies, the relative importance of individuals and the smell of something foul. This surge of connecting thoughts, along with the sudden change in perspective and pull of gravity, made me retch for a moment and I spat green bile. I felt my flesh sagging on my bones as I stood up. Self-awareness of my human body and its constituents came upon me then – bones and organs and muscles. A positioning instruction fell into my mind and I walked unsteadily to my assigned place amidst the rest. I had a number and it was four; I knew the numbers of the others too and where I should be. I stood in the front row with five other men. Five more were behind us while two rows of five women stood behind them. I turned my head as a door opened to one side and two big ugly men walked in. I watched them but then noticed my fellows weren't doing the same and so faced forwards again.

Knowledge, accompanied by a brief flash of jagged lines, arose from somewhere deep within me. I understood there'd be danger in revealing it and that I had to be like the others, to blend in. The two men were clad in heavy combat armour. Both their suits possessed a segmented insect look and were coloured black and white, as well as strewn with decals and insignia. I didn't know what any of this meant and could only read 'Strato-GZ' on a decal. One guy's armour was plain but bulky, while the other man seemed to have a taste for the baroque – his possessed ornate spikes and decorated plates to give it a barbarian look. Both had big pulse guns at their hips, while the one in the barbarian outfit also carried an ionic stun baton tucked into a belt, and a wide machete sheathed down his hip. Schematics of how these suits and the pulse guns worked bled into my perception, along with formulae of chemistry and physics, knowledge of materials technology and power supplies. My skull ached as all these details established themselves. It seemed as though thousands of windows had opened in my mind to endless progressions of data. The less ornate one then dropped a large plasmesh sack on the floor and kicked it over to my fellow at the end of our row.

'Hand these out, Jack,' said the man. I now understood that my fellow was Jack One while I was Jack Four, knowledge that came from a combination of initial loading and the *other* rising in my skull. Jack One stooped and took packages out of the bag, then handed them to the others. I accepted mine, as did the rest, and like them just stood there holding it, even though I recognized it as wire-toughened plasmesh overalls and slippers, which I would doubtless be told to put on. The instruction arrived shortly from the slaver unit on the side of my neck, with all the detail concerned with dressing – which I already knew. This made it clear to me that I wasn't supposed to possess the growing body of information somehow being impressed in my consciousness.

'I don't see why she thinks clothing is necessary,' said the man in barbarian gear, waving his stun baton at us. 'It's not like they even know they're naked.' My internal perception analysed the baton: its power supply and simple electromechanical action, and its effects.

'All part of the deal, Brack,' replied the other.

'Maybe it's to stop 'em fucking each other,' said Brack. 'But I doubt they've even got the minds for that.'

'No,' said the other. 'The overalls are protective, to prevent damage. It's dangerous for soft clones in there. Anyway, we're

SGZ and do what we're told. If you wanna argue it with her, Brack, then be my guest.'

Soft clones . . .

I was a clone. Greater detail of human biology suddenly rose up for my inspection. I pulled on the overalls and slippers, careful to ape Jack Three next to me. Meanwhile I began to understand that I wouldn't forget this Brack, for I was becoming aware, somehow, of everything I experienced being indelibly imprinted in my memory, and I understood too that this wasn't *normal*. I wondered about the style of armour they wore, which seemed more than just military. What exactly did SGZ mean and who was the woman, obviously their boss? I wanted to see her and find out her name too.

'Jill Eleven, stop dressing and come here,' said Brack.

'Come on, Brack, not now,' said the other.

'Hell, Frey, if you don't try, you don't fly.'

Frey: that name imprinted on my memory too.

The woman moved out of our ranks. She had pulled her overalls on up to her waist but now just held them bunched there as she came to stand before Brack.

'Take them off,' he said.

She obeyed, soon standing naked.

'You fucking damage the product and Suzeal will have your balls for earrings,' said Frey.

'This ain't damage,' said Brack, as I ran through his previous words again. *Suzeal*, I thought. *I will find out who you are.*

Brack pulled the Jill off to one side and through a doorway I hadn't seen before. As I put on my slippers and stood upright I watched carefully out of the corner of my eye, seeing the door close, and noting that my companions weren't even glancing that way.

After a short time I heard muffled sounds from behind the

door, but didn't know if they were of pain or pleasure or from whom. This didn't last long and ended with a guttural shouting from Brack. The flickering lights in my mind imparted the knowledge that he had been swearing in a form of Anglic slang that had taken hold in parts of the Graveyard, a borderland of space between the Kingdom of the alien prador and the human Polity. Implicit with this came more information about the two realms, of a war between them that had ended in an uneasy truce. Images of horrifying warfare flicked through my mind. They were second-hand, I understood, but how could they be there if I was a newly created clone?

'Put your clothes on and get back into the ranks,' said Brack, leading the Jill back out again.

She obeyed and as she walked over I could see blood coming down her legs. I felt a brief sick lurch of something inside I only recognized later as anger.

'When you've quite finished down there,' came a woman's voice over an intercom. 'We're going in now, so get them fed – I don't want any of them collapsing before we make the exchange.' Then after a pause, 'And Brack, you forget your position in the SGZ. If there are any problems with that Jill Eleven you lose half of your cut.'

Brack and Frey stood perfectly still, then Frey headed over to one of the walls and opened a hatch there. 'Jack Four, come here and distribute these.'

'The bitch was watching,' said Brack.

'And probably still is, and listening,' said Frey, adding bitterly, 'no talk of demotion for you, though. But one day you'll push too far, Brack.'

I felt a surge of panic. I wasn't at the end of the row nearest Frey, so why had he called me? The instructions for the physical actions arrived in my mind. The slaver units possessed sufficient computing to translate verbal orders into actions, yet again I hadn't needed them. I stepped out of my line and walked over to the cupboard. From there I took out blocks of a dark brown substance and drinks bottles and handed them to each of my fellows individually. This wasn't the most efficient way, because I could have handed them to those nearest me, for them to pass along. But I followed the instructions to the letter. Jill Eleven, I noticed, was standing awkwardly and blood now pooled around her ankle.

'Let's take a look,' said Frey.

'Sure,' Brack replied, seeming a bit subdued now. He turned to the wall directly opposite us, then reached up to the grey metal slug of an aug behind his right ear. Touching the thing was unnecessary since the cerebral augmentation didn't need physical operation. Knowledge about the schematic for it unfolded in my mind: it had nanofibres which penetrated his brain, neural meshes, neurochem and optics and light-operated switches in their millions, as well as its laminar crystal computing, bionic power supply and bone anchors. Next came further detail on layered coding languages: whole edifices of data. I wanted to throw up again and bit down on it. The wall ahead of us flickered, almost in tune with the jags across my vision, and I realized it had been painted with nanobond screen paint. I tried to encompass the detail on it and only belatedly heard the 'Eat your food and drink your drinks' from Frey.

I took a bite from the block, tasting all the vitamins and proteins and thought it rather like pork and apple, while the cold drink tasted of blackberries. I still didn't know how I could possibly make such comparisons. Memory analogues, much like those from an aug, were loading to my mind, but their source remained a mystery.

The wall now lit up as a screen, giving me a full view of

vacuum scattered with stars. An immense vessel sat out there which I recognized at once – knowledge already acquired. The column-like thing measured fifty miles from top to bottom with a large off-centre disc at the top. At the bottom, which was then out of our sight range, I knew there were two massive ion drives like giant, cored olives. This was the King's Ship – home to the ruler of the Prador Kingdom. And this must be where the vessel we were aboard was heading.

The great ship loomed and, from what was visible, it seemed we were approaching the base of a giant tower. As we drew closer and closer I discerned the spines of great docks and our vessel soon turned towards one of them. The thing looked small at first, but as perspective altered I saw it was miles long and hundreds of yards wide. We came up beside its golden curved wall and it extruded a smaller moving dock which, with its array of clamps at the end, bore a horrible resemblance to a giant rag worm – a comparative my mind dredged up from what had already loaded. The thing snaked out and landed with a thump, just below our point of view. Our vessel halted and vapour puffed out in vacuum as the dock made its connection.

'Big ugly fucker, isn't it?' said Brack.

I just managed to stop myself replying to him. With my mind moving faster, it was hard to keep my self-control rigid, but I had to banish my confusion. I needed to accept the knowledge pouring into and establishing itself in my mind and not keep puzzling about the source. For now, it was about survival. I was alive, feeling more so every minute, and wanted to stay that way. I was clearly a clone being delivered by some very nasty types to some even nastier ones: the prador. I had to escape somehow and . . . well, I was angry. I realized it had been rising up inside me slowly, gathering pace then taking a leap forwards when Brack raped Jill Eleven. However, the slaver unit on the side of my neck meant I could do nothing but obey those keyed into it as my overseers. The best thing would be to escape before I was transferred aboard that monstrous ship, but that seemed impossible. I'd therefore have to bide my time and seize any opportunities once I was on there.

'Okay, take them through,' Suzeal commanded.

Brack walked up to the screen wall and palmed it, hitting a door control. A wide door opened, giving the illusion of us walking straight into the body of the King's Ship.

'In threes, follow me,' he said and stepped through.

The instruction for physical movement arrived in my skull via the slaver unit. Falling in behind the first three, I stuffed the rest of the food in my mouth and drained the bottle, while around me the others simply dropped theirs. I thought it a risk worth taking. Brack led us through a short corridor which, judging by the structure of the walls, sloped down in relation to the rest of the ship. But it wasn't noticeable since the corridor had grav-plates in the floor. This then opened into a disc-shaped room where others of Brack and Frey's kind waited, all heavily armed. I noted Polity-issue pulse rifles, one large hermaphrodite lugging a particle cannon, while on either side were shielded Gatling cannons with figures in control seats behind the shields. These pointed towards the wide door at the end. The detailed knowledge I had of these weapons concerned me, as did my tendency to assess what might happen here should they be used. I noted too that those who wore armour or envirosuits with the same decals and decoration as Brack and Frey seemed to take precedence over others in more standard attire.

A woman stepped forwards. She wore a heavy, armoured exoskeleton in gold and black with those decals and other orna-mentation. So this was the voice in command over them? She stood over seven feet tall and had a strong jaw, with long ginger hair in a plait swept down over one shoulder. She moved out to inspect us as we came to a halt.

'They're all good?' she asked.

'Stats seem optimal,' said Frey. 'Just some . . . things.'

'What?' she shot at him.

'Well . . . Jill Eleven had a bleed but it's stopped now. It hasn't weakened her too much. Jill Seventeen seems to be loaded with recessives, but no problem for our purposes.'

'The Jacks?'

'Just something odd about Jack Four. Getting some weird feedback through the slave unit. Probably just an IQ anomaly.'

She walked down the line of us on one side, then back up the other, turning to face me. I continued looking straight ahead, but every feature of her face impressed itself in my mind. She gave an odd smile and moved on.

'Right, here's how it goes. We take them through to where a guide sphere is due to collect them. Our diamond slate should be waiting in exchange.'

Diamond slate was currency, though 'guide sphere' I only understood from context.

'And if it's not and they shaft us?' asked Brack.

She gazed at him steadily.

'Then we're dead,' she said simply. 'But you should have some faith in the trajectory of what we are doing.'

'Yeah, right,' said Brack, obviously not a believer.

She frowned, glanced at the others in the room, then said, 'Let's do this.'

The circular lock ahead lay twenty feet across. It now irised open to reveal a diagonally divided oval behind – a prador door. With a crack, that division parted and I felt the rush of air against my face as the pressures equalized. Suzeal's people crouched behind the deck-mounted Gatling cannons and heavy armoured shields floating on grav-motors, with all their weapons pointed towards that opening door. As its two sections rumbled and revolved back, it soon revealed the tube leading back into the main dock was empty. After a moment Suzeal stepped out of cover.

'Fuck,' she said succinctly.

'No guide sphere and no diamond slate,' said Frey noncommittally.

Suzeal sighed and then said, 'Okay, four of you with me. It could all simply be a matter of translation. I was told that they would be waiting for us in the dock. That might not necessarily mean here in this docking tube.' She turned to us. 'You, follow.'

Suzeal, Brack, Frey and two others launched into the docking tube, which had zero gravity, and we followed. I copied Suzeal and the others by slamming my hands against the dock walls and propelling myself along, but then damned myself for doing so. My fellows struggled with it until instructions arrived via their slaver units, and Suzeal looked back at me speculatively. Soon we moved into the huge main docking tunnel where artificial gravity brought us crashing down to the floor. Landing perfectly upright, Suzeal again swore.

'They're fucking pulling us in,' said Brack.

'Stow it, Brack,' she snarled. 'Understand that they don't need to pull us in – if they want to fuck us then we are royally fucked already.'

He grinned and turned away. I sensed there might be more to the relationship between the two of them than was first apparent. This keyed in with Frey's resentment at the man not being 'demoted'.

A sweaty jog brought us up to the doors into the main

ship and here sat two crates on top of a grav-sled. A stony sphere about the size of my head lay beside the sled.

'There, you see,' said Suzeal. She stepped over to the sphere. 'You have the coding for the slave units?' Meanwhile Brack and Frey had popped open one of the crates. Inside, I could see the gleaming slabs of diamond slate – a natural gemstone valued all across occupied space.

'I have the coding,' the sphere confirmed, voice flat and, well, stony.

Brack and Frey checked the other crate, then Frey took up a control from the sled and lifted it from the floor. The thing was ready to follow him.

'Let's get the fuck out of here,' he said.

'One moment.' Suzeal held up a hand and then walked over to us. 'I can't tell you what will happen to you all here and, really, most of you wouldn't understand if I could.' She then walked over to me, pushing the one ahead of me out of the way. She faced me directly. 'Except you, of course. You might under-stand.' I said nothing, just kept my face blank. She continued, 'Are you in there, Jack? Is the real Jack in there?' She then hit me, throwing me against the Jack behind and we both went down. I had the overpowering urge to retaliate but knew that might be the death of me. Instead I focused on the positional data from my slave unit, stood up and moved back into my place, even though she stood in the way. I kept pushing against her as if mindlessly trying to return in line. She blocked me for a while longer, then snorted in disgust and stepped out of the way. I reassumed my position.

'Come on, Suzeal – let's blow this place,' said Brack.

'Okay.' She walked past me, and all the others went too, the sled obediently following Frey. I listened to them drawing away and wondered if I could now make some sort of escape – maybe run off and hide somewhere aboard this giant ship, then find my way onto another craft docked to it and leave.

'Follow,' said the voice of the sphere, and I could do nothing but obey.

The prador-scale tunnel was oval in section and consisted of yard-wide hexagonal panels set in an alloy grid. The panels looked like granite but I *knew* they were actually polystyrene-light airform stone. On the floor nearby, I noted a creature and felt some confusion at the sight of the thing. Jags appeared in my vision again and I then recognized it as a ship louse – quite a standard life form in a prador vessel. But this one was a cyborg, its head a complex sensor array, while the alternate segments of its body were chromed metal. It scuttled away noisily and disappeared through the gaps in a barred hole near the floor. I felt a gust of air as we passed this and understood it to be an air vent. I looked back, now feeling that I didn't need to be so careful about my movements, and noted the large bolts holding the grating in place. They were made for prador claws and I wondered if I'd have the strength to undo them.

At length an order arrived in my mind to halt and I did so along with the others. A weird tingling started on my scalp and, as I reached up to scrub at it, it began to transit down my body. I stood still, realizing we were being scanned. The sensation reached my feet and then cut out. I was about to move on again when a pillar rose out of the floor ahead of us and it became clear we had only experienced a basic scan and now the real thing was coming. The hooded head on top of the pillar dipped and the air hazed between us and it. My feet grew hot and then the heat travelled all the way up my body. By the time it had departed the top of my head, sweat was trickling into my eyes. I wiped it away, noting that the others did not have the sense to do the same. The sphere then started rolling again, circumventing the pillar sinking back into the floor.

We trudged on through the bowels of the King's Ship, stopping for a further scan. I felt grubby and sticky, and my skin had reddened as if with sun burn. I really hoped that two scans were enough to satisfy prador paranoia. I had become aware, with the jagged lights now muted and sliding to my peripheral vision, that I probably didn't have the usual immunity-boosting nanosuite which humans had within their bodies, and my risk of genetic damage and cancers had now climbed through the roof. A corridor, like the partially flattened gut of a tapeworm, curved round and, with a degree of irritation, I started pushing my mind, seeking further data about my surroundings. This distracted me from a growing feeling I finally understood as I came face to face with my first prador: we had been sold to monsters.

The thing rounded the bend up ahead of us and hurtled down the corridor at great speed. It was small for its kind but almost certainly one of the king's family, one of the Guard. I wanted to dodge to one side to let it past, but the slave unit instruction merely halted us all in place. It turned and skidded to a stop too. Comparatives arose in my mind. The thing seemed like the by-blow of a giant fiddler crab and a wolf spider. Its body had the shape of a vertically flattened pear – the narrower top section being its visual turret, pushed to the fore of its main body, with two stalked eyes sticking up above an array of red eyes behind a visor. It had six legs, two claws and underslung manipulators I could just about see. All of these were clad in blue metallic armour that perfectly matched its form, even its grinding mandibles. But something about this assessment nagged at me and the lights flashed again. Further updates revealed that the inner form of members of the Guard did not necessarily match the outer appearance of their armour. These creatures were mutated.

Behind its head turret it carried a heavy pack which gurgled as it moved – seemingly some tank of liquid attached to a large power supply. From this, tubes and power cables fed down to objects attached to the underside of its claws. These looked like guns (though that might have been more my expectation of prador), but protruded glassy tubes. I reassessed: perhaps some kind of spray-cleaning device? I also recognized my feeling of vulnerability.

'You are to follow me now,' said the prador in perfect Anglic. It directed its stalked eyes towards the guide sphere and, as if being admonished, the thing abruptly shot away.

The prador turned to head in the same direction as the ball, its words propelling us after it too. For a moment there I'd thought I might be free of my unit's influence, but it seemed this prador could also control us. As we moved into a jog to keep up with the creature, I wondered what had happened. Its arrival had been hurried and something had changed. Again reviewing what I knew about the King's Ship and pushing my mind for more, I felt knowledge surfacing.

Weapons development occupied the lower areas, but nothing that might damage the ship itself. It was mostly small arms made there – carried by individual prador. Higher up, biotech weapons laboratories were rumoured to be operating. However, none of these, no matter what might go wrong, required an apparently armed prador to take over accompanying us. Above this my knowledge grew vague until nearing the top. Up there the king experimented with his own children and himself in an effort to learn more about something called the Spatterjay virus and its effects upon him and his family. It also seemed likely that the king's breeding programme exclusively occupied the whole floor below his sanctum – being almost completely infertile himself, he was physically incapable of mating with prador females without killing them.

The mass of data opening in my mind brought on a headache. Yet again, I wondered where all this was coming from because, this time, I realized that the average Polity citizen would not have had access to this stuff. I next considered scenarios that required us having a personal guard, the most likely being that something, high up, had escaped. The prador led us all the way along the corridor to a chamber surrounded with access points to a series of dropshafts. Here other heavily armed prador were arrayed, facing the shafts.

'Wait here,' said the guard, pointing down at the floor with one claw.

It headed over to the others, whom I studied. They were mostly wearing white armour which matched their aseptic surroundings. But many of them had decorated this with even, multicoloured patterns, and some had almost outrageously colourful armour. This indicated the psychological changes on the part of the Guard, since normal prador tended to wear bland utility armour whose only concession to colour was when they activated outer meta-material camouflage. The Guard showed an artistic bent which was highly unusual for the species. Even as I thought this, I understood the information had its uses to Earth Central – the AI ruler of the Polity. Such knowledge was used by it and its subordinate AIs to penetrate the Kingdom and drive change with subtle forms of psychological warfare.

I began sweating again and this had nothing to do with the scans I'd received. My expanding knowledge now scared me and my nascent sense of self was becoming confused within it. I was a clone, but who was I? The information settling in my mind possessed a quality I could only describe as personal experience.

The prador clattered and bubbled for a while and I tried to listen. In a panicky surge, I realized I understood prador speech, but they were using a version of it I didn't know. I extrapolated, presuming some kind of slang used by the Guard. My panic increased as I began to comprehend some morphemes and knew that, given long enough, I would get what they were saying. But the speaking stopped and the blue-armoured prador returned, gesturing to the dropshafts. Compelled by our slave units, we followed it over to them. It waved us ahead at the mouth of one shaft and without hesitation we stepped in. The irised gravity field took hold and accelerated us upwards. I peered down, seeing my fellows tumbling behind, with our guard close after them, then found I couldn't move my head. The field tightened around us and I realized, from how fast the walls of the shaft shot by, that our acceleration had increased. After a moment, I couldn't breathe. It was the nature of the fields in such shafts that, below a certain level, acceleration couldn't be felt, but we had gone beyond that. The field protected us from acceleration damage, but in so doing might yet kill us.

The shaft diverted twice and I felt the changes of trajectory as a wrench throughout my entire body. Then we slowed and the pressure finally eased. I took a breath, just before the shaft ejected us into a short corridor. We went in too fast and as my feet hit the floor, I flung myself into a roll. The others were not so lucky and crashed in messily. Coming upright, I dodged aside as the guard came in hard behind, feet skidding across the floor and peeling up metal, slamming into the crowded mass of the others. I saw a Jill ripped open and smeared across the floor under one of its feet, leaving a line of guts, with the sound of bones snapping too. Numb horror arose in me, but alongside this was a cold analysis: there was definitely a problem here, otherwise the prador would not have risked destroying the product they had paid for.

The guard skittered aside and turned to look at the mess. Instructions arrived to bring us to our feet and move back into ranks. The Jack next to me was bleeding from a head wound, while one behind kept trying to stand on broken legs. The guard moved over to the injured Jill as she shivered against the floor. It reached down and casually snipped off her head, the thing thudding across the floor in a spray of blood. It then moved to us and I felt a surge of fear as it loomed directly over me. But it plucked out the Jack behind with the broken legs and discarded him to one side in two pieces. I tried to quell my horror but couldn't stop myself shaking. The creature then backed up and peered closely at me. I felt surges of data in my slaver unit, that buzzing sensation, and a sense of alien inquiry. Then it stopped.

'Move fast,' the prador instructed, suddenly racing off.

The corridor terminated at a round chamber where a ridged ramp rose up and curved round. It took me a moment to recognize the prador version of stairs. Why no grav here? Why the necessity to climb?

'Move!' said the prador.

I realized I'd been hesitating while the others swept past me.

We followed it up the ramp, the wide uneven steps difficult for the others but not me. After perhaps half a mile, we arrived in another corridor, where the prador gestured us ahead until our group came to some large doors. These ground open, revealing a wide room filled with upright glass cylinders. Many of them were empty, but I was shaken to see that others contained naked humans floating in amniote, with life-support devices attached. A second prador stepped into view and my fellow clones moved forwards, each positioning themselves beside an empty cylinder. I watched as a complex grab, like a Polity spiderbot, reached down and hoisted one of them up, attached a face mask and inserted various tubes, then dropped her into the tube. It began to fill with amniote as other grabs came down too. Panic seized me, and I still hadn't moved to take a position beside one of the tubes. I had to run now or I would never get out of this place. Even as I turned, a huge armoured claw closed about my neck.

'You will come,' said the guard.

It now clattered prador speech at the other prador, who was clad in dirty white armour and was as small as what my errant mind classified as a second-child. This one headed over and peered at me closely. A further exchange followed, during which I picked up the morphemes for 'anomalous', 'unprogrammed' and something that I thought, by context, must be 'behaviour'.

I couldn't move and didn't dare struggle. The claw had closed just enough to hold me but not choke me, and I'd already seen how easily this creature discarded clones.

Further morphemes became clear: 'experiment', 'danger below' and 'escaped'. I was pretty sure these didn't relate to any threat from me but could be connected to there being a problem, as I'd suspected earlier. The two then turned to me and, after another brief exchange I didn't understand, I heard, 'our father' and 'the king'.

Abruptly the guard tossed me out into the corridor. I kicked out against the wall then came down on my feet. I was about to run when the slave unit took firm hold and waves of data washed through my mind, as the doors closed on my fellows.

'Why do you have a mind?' the guard asked.

I considered playing dumb but realized this wouldn't be my best option. If this creature believed I *was* dumb then I would probably end up in one of those cylinders.

'I don't know,' I replied, my voice catching because this was the first time, in my life, I had used my vocal cords.

The guard waved a claw towards the stairs. 'Go.'

I began climbing again, having no ability to do otherwise with the slave unit vibrating against my neck.

'Do you have a name?' the guard asked.

'Jack Four.'

'You have memories,' it stated.

'I don't know where they come from,' I replied.

The prador fell silent behind me until we reached a level floor. Here corridors led off while the stairs continued over to one side. My unit slammed me to a halt and the guard moved past me, clattering in prador speech. This time I understood perfectly.

'The escaped experiment has moved higher up?' it asked, then after a pause, 'I will guard the junction. Our father will not be pleased.'

It moved ahead, then faced me. 'Keep going. The king waits.' It waved a claw towards the stairs and turned back to look down the corridor and held its station, claws pointing forwards and the power supply on its back whining. I wanted to pose a few questions but knew I would get no answers. The unit compelled me on, and I began to climb again.

I was alone now but the grip of the slave unit felt tighter than ever. I could do nothing, when all I wanted was to run, to find some way out of this nightmare, as well as answers to the puzzle that was me. What felt like a burn in my guts started building, a need to pay back those who had delivered me and my fellows into this.

The stairs, after numerous switchbacks, finally terminated at a diagonally divided prador door. The thing was closed and I noted scratches and damage on it. Up closer, I saw the kind of marks that might have been made by human fingernails but for the fact that they were gouged into hard metal. From down below came the sudden roar of what sounded like a gas torch igniting, then a loud crash and a chittering. It didn't take much for me to realize the prador there had just used its weapon, and I was grateful when the door in front of me abruptly ground open. I moved into a painfully white corridor, unusually rectangular rather than oval. But as the door began to close again behind me, it started making a grinding sound and with a huge effort I looked back to see the door control showering sparks. My slave unit then delivered a simple concise instruction: Run.

2

I ran, dodging through corridors and frequently changing direction. In darkened rooms I glimpsed more chain-glass tubes containing organic monstrosities, a normal prador partially dismembered on a huge polished table, and a great mass of old-style spherical Polity incubators linked in series. In one place there were amniotic tanks containing vaguely human forms, horribly distorted. Then I heard another crash, and the sounds of skittering movement. I changed direction and ran into a circular chamber, nearly colliding with a prador female. I knew at once that, all instinct and aggression, she would try to kill me. The slave unit slid to a different setting with a more generalized instruction to give leeway for action: Survive.

She crouched before me but immediately rose up and hissed, extra-long mandibles extending. I dived to one side, rolled and came upright again, then moved to go past her, just as something slammed into her and sent her skidding backwards.

The figure was that of a vaguely human man, but huge. His head jutted forwards on a long neck and resembled a baboon's, with the lower part extended into predatory jaws and hardware buried in his skull. The female grabbed him with her mandibles and slammed him down on the floor, but then didn't seem to know what to do. As she shifted her grip, he grabbed a mandible with his ridiculously long, clawed fingers. They struggled against each other, the female abruptly rolling, until he suddenly broke free and tore off the mandible. He then drove his other hand right down into her mouth, grabbing and pulling till he ripped out something fat and glistening. The female emitted a high keening and skittered away. She hesitated for just a second before turning and disappearing into a nearby corridor. He stood there, gasping and shuddering, and finally abandoned the mandible. Big tears in his torso weren't bleeding, but just leaked a clear jelly-like fluid.

Then I understood.

Putting together all I knew about this place with all I'd seen, I came to the conclusion that here must be the escaped experiment the prador had seemed so concerned about. And it was pissed off. I just stared, human biology holding me frozen to the spot while my rational mind told me to run. The man shuddered and swung his predator's head around until he located me, making noises that sounded suspiciously like an attempt at speech, but which transformed into a snarl. Pulling back his lips from sharp canines, and exposing a long black tongue, he stalked towards me.

I realized that I was probably about to die and stared at the weirdly mutated man as he came closer. Running was no longer an option – I had seen how fast this individual could move.

'Who are you?' I asked suddenly.

This gave him pause, and he tilted his head. Only then did something else about this erstwhile human impinge: he was blue. From head to foot he was a deep royal blue with just a few patches of diseased-looking skin, white and pink with a speckling of black. Most of that skin had a fibrous appearance. My mind, or whatever supplied it, provided the answer. Here was a human deeply infected with the Spatterjay virus – the same virus that had mutated the king and his Guard, his children. For him to have changed so drastically, the man must have been deprived of the nutrition needed to hinder the virus, or been subjected to constant stress. Very few hoopers – the name given to those living on the world of Spatterjay where the virus came from – got this bad. Though I knew some had undergone monstrous mutations like this.

'Are you conscious?' I asked.

The man responded again, shaking his head, then snarled again. It didn't matter what he had been: right now he was a dangerous creature prone to attacking anyone or anything. So it was with hoopers who'd been heavily mutated by the Spatterjay virus.

He abruptly crouched and seemed about to leap, but the gas-torch roar exploded into life and two streams of flame struck him. With a horrible squealing, he tumbled through the air, fibrous skin peeling up from his body and burning. Yet he still hit the ground on his feet and accelerated straight into the flame. Looking to the source, I saw the blue-armoured prador, the flame issuing from the nozzles on its claws. *Run now?* I thought, but instead I backed up towards the wall and watched.

The man dodged to one side and leapt, coming down onto the prador's back and there tore away tubes and cables, shutting down the twinned flamethrower. This action, along with what he'd done to the door mechanism and his attempt at speech, bespoke intelligence. Whoever the prador had been experimenting on was not a clone like my fellows, nor was he a human blank – one of the hooper humans enslaved by coring and thralling. Again I felt a rush of panic about the activity in my mind, as the explanatory ideas and harrowing images surrounding this arose clearly. The virus infected humans and made them unreasonably tough and rugged. In the past, during the war long ago, some piratical humans had 'cored' these infected humans, removing the brain and spinal cord from each and replacing them with a thrall – a device on which my slave unit was based. The thrall effectively turned them into humanoid robots. Those villains had then sold this product on to the prador.

The man next dropped down in front of the prador and grabbed one claw, but though he'd prevailed against the unarmoured female, this one wore a motorized suit. It picked him up with its other claw and flung him away. He hit a nearby wall upside down, then peeled off and fell, yet again coming down on his feet and leaping back towards the prador. Landing on top of the thing, he wrapped his legs around its visual turret and gripped its armoured eye stalks as if intent on steering the thing. Unbelievably he tore one away, then used it as a club to smash the creature's visor. As the visor cracked, the prador shrieked and shot across the room, tipping itself at the last moment to slam him against the wall. It backed up as he fell, then snatched him up and sent him skidding across the floor. Starting to advance on him again, it abruptly halted and backed up. I wasn't sure why.

The man stood, moving more slowly now. Burned lengths of stringy flesh and skin hung in tatters, but even as I watched they were writhing back into place on him, turning pale and pink as they healed.

'What the fucking hell are you?' I wondered aloud.

He snarled at me again, almost casually, and continued to move towards the prador, but halted too, head swinging to peer to one side. Something was there. I looked over as a nightmare head appeared ten feet up from a nearby corridor. Great mandibles clattered then shimmered along their inner edges as shearfields activated. A large complex foot came down heavily on the floor and the giant, louse-like form stepped out.

I recognized the king of the prador at once.

His body was scattered with scars and technological additions.

His foreclaws were long, like a langoustine's, and oddly he possessed none of the weapons prador usually sported. The man-thing surged towards him and leapt, but the king moved horribly fast, snatching him from the air with one claw and slamming him to the floor. There was a whine of overloaded shearfields, followed by a crack. The man rolled clear of a claw which had been broken open, a great chunk of fibrous flesh hanging from his hip, black ribs exposed and a length of blue intestine trailing. The other claw struck him in the chest, sending him arcing across the chamber, with the king surging after him. As the man-thing rose yet again, the king grabbed him up in his mandibles and shook him like a dog killing a rabbit before crunching him down onto the floor. He stamped heavily on the man's back and ripped up one arm, nearly detaching it, but it clung on with a strew of fibres. He then stabbed down with the undamaged claw and closed it round his saurian neck just below the head. Again I heard the whine of shearfields struggling to cut through. The head mostly came away but still remained attached by fibres. And the man kept fighting, even as the king bowed down with his mandibles and tore at him.

Finally it was over: the Spatterjay-virus-mutated man lay spread across a ten-foot area in a disjointed mess, yet was still *connected* and moving weakly. Just then, further armoured prador from below streamed into the room, towing a grav-sled. They crowded to one side and, at some unheard order, surged forwards to begin snatching up the still-moving and fibrously connected pieces, loading them onto the sled. I noted they arranged the body parts in their position before dismemberment and couldn't think why. The king, meanwhile, turned my way and walked over, looming above me.

'You come with me,' he said, his Anglic slurred as if by the pleasure of the kill.

* * *

I followed even though I hadn't been compelled by the slave unit. With prador everywhere, running now seemed likely to result only in my dismemberment too. The king led me through the way he had entered, bringing us out to a curved gallery beside a panoramic window that looked out into vacuum. Out there other prador ships called reavers milled around, like hunting barracuda.

'Who was he?' I asked, suddenly brave.

The king closed up his damaged claw with a crackling sound. I could see the broken carapace there but none of the usual green prador blood. The fact that I knew their blood was usually green was just another piece of the information constantly surfacing in my mind. Fibrous flesh had bulged through the cracks and now appeared to be hardening. Suddenly he spun about and closed a long claw around me, then hoisted me up from the floor, bringing me in towards his nightmare head and studying me with blood-red eyes.

'Suzeal was to provide all but mindless clones,' he said. 'What are you?'

'I don't know,' I managed. 'Data is entering my mind all the time.'

'I should dispose of you.'

'I am no danger.'

'You do not know that.'

He was right. I had no idea what I was or what purpose I might serve. I stayed silent in agreement. The king emitted a disconcertingly human sigh and released me. I landed in a crouch as he turned away and settled down on the floor. He almost seemed jaded and bored – I had interested him for only a moment.

'Suzeal,' I said abruptly. 'Who is she?'

He swung back to look at me, then obviously decided to

engage. 'Her organization is semi-religious, military, its people inducted from mercenary humans in the Graveyard. They have been difficult to locate.'

I didn't know what to make of that and could think of no reply. But I frantically searched for something to say – some way to keep him engaged, for his boredom might mean the end of me.

A hint of movement over to one side drew my eye as robots scuttled out. These things, each a foot long, resembled rhinoceros beetles forged out of magnesium alloy and white porcelain. I recognized the Polity tech.

'Multi-purpose,' I stated, nodding to them, 'combining the function of autodocs and maintenance bots.'

He shifted round to study me again as the bots streamed up over his long louse-like body and set to work, cutting into carapace and tough flesh to remove nodules and areas that simply did not look right, spraying in collagen foam and layering on pieces of artificial carapace, rerouting optics and fluid tubes, as well as tending to various other devices connected to his body.

'Who was the man who attacked you?' I asked again quickly.

The king paused once more, considering, then with what looked like a bored shrug, began, 'As I understand it, he was a human involved with Suzeal's trade in human beings. A trade which is now illegal under our agreements with the Polity, but it continues. He had fallen out of favour with her and been sold to an Old Family father-captain to be prepared for coring and thralling.'

Sweating again, I felt a now-familiar panic at what was arising in my mind. I realized I needed it because while I kept the king interested, I stayed alive. A limited objective, but there it was.

I *knew* that 'Old Family' meant a normal prador descended from the line of the previous king. There was something wrong about that and I strained for information until something clicked and I 'remembered' – if that's the correct term. It had been believed that all those descendants were exterminated by the new regime.

'Interesting to know they're still around,' I said. When the king made no reply I groped around for something to keep the exchange going. 'And what happened to the father-captain?'

'He, and his children, are in cells two floors below.' The king swung his head away from me to inspect the work of the bots on his body. 'They will be useful in further investigations of prador biology.'

'So,' I said, 'you captured a human and ran experiments on him? I don't know the source of the knowledge in my mind, but I'm pretty sure there was something about that in Polity agreements.'

The king swung his nightmare head back and gazed at me with that array of glaring red eyes. 'Because of course the Polity never experiments with any prador that fall into its hands . . .'

My conscious mind lacked information on this, even though I tried to force it to the surface. I saw a brief image of a prador in heavy restraints in some laboratory, its carapace hinged over like a lid while human technicians delved inside. It was whistling and clattering its mandibles. Confused, I realized that the image arose not from reality but a wargame virtuality.

The king turned away again as robots scuttled down to his mandibles and began making repairs there. 'It has come to my attention that the mutation the Spatterjay virus causes is highly influenced by the nature and mind of the one who's infected. In some cases the mutation can cause extreme changes and ultimately produce a very dangerous creature. The pirate, Jay Hoop, was one such individual. Our experiments have produced another.'

'Jay Hoop,' I repeated, struggling to find something, my head aching.

'Probably in the DNA,' said the king.

'The virus DNA? What?' I was confused.

'No, the DNA Suzeal used to create you.' The king pondered on this, not looking at me. 'DNA itself can be a good storage medium for data besides that used to grow your body, but I suspect otherwise. The Polity AIs have been experimenting with distributed quantum crystal memplants.' Now he did swing back towards me. 'Curiously, one of your fellow clones which my children have already examined had neither, nor did she possess the kind of knowledge you evidently do.'

One of the armoured prador from earlier moved into view and crouched, waiting. Suddenly my sense of danger increased.

'You are saying I have the memories of someone?' I was desperate to keep this going.

'I would say that you are the original sample while they were multiplied from what created you, so without the quantum crystals. It will be necessary to examine you.'

There it was. I was damned sure I would not survive any examination here.

'You will go with my child here.' The king gestured towards the prador.

The slave unit turned me and set me marching. The prador stood and moved ahead, and I could do nothing but follow.

'It is impossible for you to disobey instructions from the slave unit while it remains on your neck,' said the king as I departed. 'But, of course, you do not have to obey instructions it does not give.'

I didn't know then and I do not know now why the king said that. Perhaps he was just bored and wanted to see what I would do. Perhaps he liked throwing a spanner in the works of his ship and testing his own children. Or perhaps he saw in me a reflection of his own need to survive.

Whatever his reasons, he had shown me the way.

The prador led me out of the king's quarters. I noted its stalked eyes facing back towards me while it navigated with its forward eyes. I trudged along obediently, down the stairs and to the junction I had seen earlier. The wall was still smoking. Here numerous corridors speared off into the ship and the next stop further down would be where my fellows had gone. I had no doubt the small prador in dirty white armour would conduct its examination of me there too. But the king had hinted to me how I might escape. His unexpected last words had made abundantly clear that I only had to obey direct instructions from the slave unit while it was on my neck. But this didn't mean I could do nothing else. As soon as the prador's stalked eyes started checking the surrounding corridors and no longer focused on me, I reached up, dug my fingers in around the unit and tore it away. Then I ran.

I had reached fifty yards down one corridor when a bubbling shriek issued from behind me. I saw a corner and turned, just as a weapon filled the corridor with flying metal. My neck hurt badly. I assumed some of the fibres the slaver unit injected were larger than nanoscopic and I had ripped them out. But I just kept going, feeling blood running down and glimpsing it spattering on my shoulder. I took another turn and another, then beside me saw a row of smaller tunnels and ran into the third one along. Luckily it was too small for my erstwhile escort. I took two more turnings, until slowing to a walk just as something loomed into view ahead.

A small second-child prador appeared sans artificial armour. Its narrow carapace terminated in a tail, its legs were unusually long and it only had one claw, a triclaw. For a second I was tempted to turn round and run again, but then reasoned that the King's Ship would have its complement of human blanks and the thing might well disregard me. As it drew closer, I moved to the side of the tunnel and stood perfectly still. It watched me with one stalked eye. Here was one of the king's children, a second-child, mutated by the Spatterjay virus, in the process of growing up and yet to attain either the size or status required for it to have its own suit of artificial armour. As it moved on past, ignoring me, I started to breathe more easily.

I carried on, scanning along the wall of the tunnel. I'd been lucky so far, but this couldn't last in the main prador corridors. Finally reaching a barred vent, the same as the ones I'd noticed earlier, I tried to turn one of the bolts securing it. The thing wouldn't budge. An epiphany came when I pushed and it sank a little way before springing out again. Prador engineering and their physiology. I had been assuming it was a threaded bolt but such fixings weren't so easy for a race whose main manipulators were claws; they did the more delicate stuff by touch with their underslung manipulators. I pushed the bolt down, turned to release it, and it sprang out a few inches. I went round them all and soon each one was hanging out. Then I spotted the second-child running back towards me, eerily silent but intent.

I heaved the grating out, expecting it to be heavy but discovering otherwise, turned with it as the second-child arrived, and hit the creature's reaching claw as hard as I could. The prador squealed and rattled deformed mandibles, its body slamming me to one side and turning. I pushed forwards and hit it again, this time catching it across its visual turret, its claw snipping just inches from my face. I didn't let up. I just kept on hitting the thing until it retreated. I drove it back a few yards, tossed the grating at it and then dived through the hole in the wall. The air vent was a yard across and I scrambled along it fast, just avoiding the claw that came questing after me. The pull of grav slid to one side, screwing my perception of 'down' and making me nauseous. Further along, the second-child had begun unbolting another grating and it hissed and clattered at me as I went past. A turning offered itself, taking me away from the corridor I'd been in. It felt almost as if I was climbing a steep slope, as the grav from the corridor fell behind me. It also grew steadily darker, since the only light issued from the vents.

I continued to crawl along these vent tubes for ages, and I lost myself in there. Establishing some sense of direction was nearly impossible. Besides the dark, the tubes were not grav-plated but influenced by whatever areas they served, so I crawled up apparent slopes then down into areas where grav waned to nothing. One downslope seemed to grow steeper and I turned off before I ended up falling through what turned into a 'down' shaft.

Finally I found a spacious area at a junction with grav below me, light coming from a vent in the floor, and settled down with my back against the wall. I couldn't spend all my time just running: I needed a plan. I visualized the ship, with my position in the top tilted disc, while all the vessels clung below it on the column extending 'down' towards the engines, or on jutting spine docks. They were quite far beneath – I reckoned about ten miles. I remembered the tube that had turned into a down shaft, the image just repeating in my mind with nothing coherent attached, when sleep fell on me like a black wall.

Pain in my leg.

I woke with a start and kicked away a ship louse trying to chew through the tough fabric of my overalls. This one was no cyborg and after a moment it came back. Thumping my fist on its head end made it squeal but only seemed to make it more determined to chew on me. I hit it again, then again. Rage rose up inside and I found myself hammering at the thing.

'Die, you fucking bastard!' I bellowed. 'Fucking die!'

It did eventually, and I started to calm down. I stared at the thing, the migraine lights flashing as I thought about biology. The creatures, just like the prador, were alien and possessed a genome with some very different bases to Earth, but they did produce protein and other digestible parts. The trick was to avoid the internal organs and stick to the muscles. I picked it up, pulled off a leg and cracked it open with my teeth, then sucked and chewed out the glutinous amber flesh. It tasted foul but I felt better afterwards. Okay, food supply secured. I also needed water, which I could search for as I headed downwards. I didn't allow myself to think too hard about what lay ahead; or how little chance I had of stealing a spaceship, let alone getting it away from the King's Ship and out of the Prador Kingdom.

'How do you eat an elephant?' asked Drasden Pike.

'I don't know,' I replied tiredly.

'Why, one bite at a time!' he declared delightedly.

A thrumming echoed in my head as the jagged lights came back. I stared at the remains of the ship louse, trying to reclaim more, but only knowledge and experience surfaced without any other flashes of memory. The king had claimed I could have quantum crystals inside me – that they formed a memplant. Such devices stored the mind of a human being, yet, thus far, all I'd experienced was the knowledge one might acquire from an educational upload. That brief fragment of memory had felt utterly alien and it had simply not been me. I pushed myself up and crawled into a tunnel. The first thing I needed to do was determine my position within the ship. One bite at a time.

Through the grating I saw a small room packed with containers. A series of rails ran along the ceiling, and a claw hung from a motorized unit that could traverse them. While I watched, the unit whined into motion and shifted along, casting shadows from dim round light panels. It took a turn and lowered the claw to one of the cylindrical containers, picking this up and shifting it to the side of the room, then inserted it into a hatch. I reached through the grating and undid the bolts. My arms ached by the time I had got the last of the stubborn things out and I just caught the grating before it fell into the room, turning it to pull it in through the hole, and rested it beside me in the tube. The stubborn fixings were a good sign – with luck it meant no prador had been in here recently with an oil can. Sticking my head through to get a better look around, I didn't see a door to this automated supply chamber. I assessed further and, being reassured that I'd be able to stack up some of the containers to gain access back into the vent again, I dropped inside.

Immediately stepping over to a container, I tried to figure out how to open it. It seemed to be made of compressed fibre and I struggled with it. In the end I dug at the thing with my fingernails to make a hole, easily tearing it open after that. A heavy object rested inside, surrounded by aerogel packing. I pulled the thing out and just for a second wildly hoped for a weapon. Stripping off a thin layer of plastic revealed a thick rod about a yard long with a ring of blocky mechanisms about its centre. I hefted it. Well, it would serve as a club. Moving back out of the way as the grab claw above shifted again, I sat between containers and examined my find more closely.

I waited for something to surface in my mind as I examined the object, but nothing occurred. Discarding the thing in disgust, I opened more containers but found the contents the same. So, a club it must be.

I stacked up some cylinders to get back into the vent tube and crawled on, dragging my makeshift weapon with me. Eventually I entered a tube that apparently sloped down, becoming steeper as I traversed it. Luck stayed with me, though, with the rod turning out to be just the right length to wedge wall to wall, aiding my descent as the tube steadily transformed into a down shaft. I edged down for some time into pitch dark, passing two side tubes I found by feel, until tiredness and the presence of light attracted me into the third. I slept in there and, as had become usual, my breakfast woke me by trying to gnaw on some part of my body. I learned to sleep lightly, sitting upright in any area with conventional grav, because lying down had lost me a chunk out of my ear. I also learned to sleep with my arms folded, keeping my bare hands away from the floor. After hollowing out another ship louse, I descended again to reach a vent junction at the bottom of the shaft. Then I halted to think hard about what I was doing.

When Suzeal and her crew had approached the King's Ship, it'd stood like a tower to my perspective. In essence it was very much like a tower in its construction, with the king's living area right at the top. Grav-plates did not have the reach of planetary gravity because, to my limited knowledge on that subject, they simply did not operate in the same way – theirs was some principle involving the amplification of molecular binding forces. However, it made sense to place them facing in the same direction because their influence did reach far enough for them to interfere with each other. So 'down' would be down to my original perspective . . . probably. Different construction might

37

have been used beneath where the king lived. I really needed to locate myself. I decided to head in one direction, as best I could, in the hope of reaching the ship's hull and finding one of the numerous magnifier ports there – those ports were another stray piece of information which had surfaced in my mind. I set off, aware I still needed to find water too – the moisture from my disgusting diet wasn't going to be enough.

The prador ran in my direction and bounced off the wall right beside the air vent grating I was peering through, and for a second I thought my presence was the cause. Surely it could not see me in the shadows, so had it smelled me? No, a prador's sense of smell wasn't much better than that of a human. They had evolved in water and their equivalent of smell worked best in that medium. And, like humans, their evolution towards intelligence had sacrificed much of that. The thing moved back over to the other side of the room, rattled its feet against the floor and bashed its claw against the wall. Some kind of fit, or had something irritated it? Being careful to stay back in the shadows, I inspected its accommodation.

Deep shelves ran along every wall, loaded with equipment. A trumpet-shaped device protruding from one wall was its toilet, while over to another side stood an array of hexagonal screens. A saddle sat in front of them and there were pit controls in the floor for the creature's main claws, as well as others on its surface for its underhands. I found all of this interesting but focused mainly on the pool and the array of spigots protruding around its rim. It had never occurred to me that these creatures might like to bathe but, considering their nature, I shouldn't have been surprised. I licked my lips and settled down to wait.

With a crump and a hiss the prador's armour separated around its equator. The top half, along with the visual turret, rose up on chromed rods, then it detached from the forward ones and hinged over on the back ones. Further cracks separated the armour on its legs and claws. I spied the diseased-looking organics within, pink and speckled black. Something from below then shoved the creature up and out of its armour, and, as it caught one edge with a triclaw to vault over, I saw that in no way did this thing resemble its artificial outer covering. It was one of the Guard – an older, heavily mutated king's child and maybe one of those that had been aboard his original ship when he came from Spatterjay. Even as I thought this, I realized only a select few Polity citizens knew about that. It led me to speculate on something else. Had Suzeal taken my source DNA from someone called Jack, whom she'd killed? And this Jack, who I'll call Jack Zero, had he worked for Earth Central Security? Quite possibly he'd been one of the legendary Polity agents. It was a nice fantasy.

The prador looked like a giant copepod with its segmented back, but one with overly long limbs and a distinct, fleshy look. Once out of its armour, it collapsed for a moment as if its limbs struggled to support it. I noted its resemblance to the king but only until, with a sucking sound, its head detached from its body and extended on a neck of pink corded muscle. After a time, it finally heaved itself up and perambulated shakily over to the equipment racks and began selecting various tools with which it then returned to its armour. It set to work, rapidly disassembling and reassembling things, making adjustments. I moved closer to the grating to get a better look, then dodged back when its head snapped round. I lay there, keeping as still as possible. It probably couldn't see me because I was black with filth. It returned to its work, doubtless dismissing anything it had heard or otherwise sensed as a ship louse which, I certainly knew now, occupied these vent pipes in their thousands.

After a while I began to understand the creature's objective. It had grown and needed to make its armour fit better by expanding parts and sections, adjusting internal supports and pads inside and ratchetting out sliding plates to make the legs longer. Perhaps its discomfort had been the reason for its irritation when I first saw it. I moved back out of sight. At some point, this thing would leave its accommodation and I'd be able to access that pool. I folded my arms, rested back and a second later fell asleep.

Pain again.

Without even opening my eyes I raised my metal rod and brought it down hard beside my leg. Crunch clang. I opened my eyes wide and felt a surge of panic. The action had been automatic, performed throughout numerous sleeps, but I'd forgotten I was resting right next to a prador's living quarters. I flipped the expiring louse away and kept still, listening. From the living quarters I could hear the clattering of prador speech, the bubbling and hissing. I then heard human speech too and had no idea why. I crawled back to the grating and peered through cautiously.

The prador sat on its saddle control facing away from me, manipulating pit controls with its foreclaws. It'd put on its armour. The speech came from the array of screens in front of it. Each showed different things: other prador, scenes out in space, prador glyphs scrolling diagonally, while one or two displayed either Polity broadcasts or recordings. Did it understand and interact with everything there? No, my knowledge told me, not all, but it could look at different things with its variety of eyes. I started to move back out of sight, but noticed further movement in the vent tube. I turned, ready to scoot off another ship louse, then froze.

Wider than my leg, the thing's centipede body occupied at least ten feet of the tube, and its goat-like eyes surrounded a hollow mouth. I could see movement deep inside that cavity and abruptly shuffled back past the vent grating as it extruded a long yellow tongue ending in hinged pincers. It grabbed the louse I'd killed and sucked it up, regarded me for a second and then surged forwards fast. I raised my club ready to hit the thing but it just crawled over my leg and kept going. I sat there, shaking.

After a time, I moved back to the grating. The prador spent ages with its screens and pit controls and it brought to mind social media addicts of a different age. I killed another louse, as quietly as possible, and this time ate what I could of it, throwing its remains far down the tube in the direction the centipede thing had gone. Eventually the prador heaved itself off its saddle control, went over to its racks and began attaching equipment to its armour. Once fully loaded, it opened the door with a stab of a claw into the pit control beside it and departed. Off to work or to a prador party? I had no idea. I waited a little while longer, just in case it had forgotten something, then decided the doors opened slowly enough to give me time to get back into the ventilation system before it could do anything about me.

The bolts came out easily and I shifted the grating to one side, ready to be grabbed and pulled back when I needed to exit. I went over to the pool and stuck my face in it for a drink, only to spit it straight out. The stuff was brine. Working the various spigots required a bar jammed into small pit controls behind them and each emitted strangely coloured and smelly fluids. The prador equivalent of bubble bath? But none of them produced fresh water. I debated drinking from them, until I spotted another tap with a dependent hose above the trumpet-shaped wall toilet. This at last rewarded me with a stream of cold fresh water – the best thing I had tasted . . . in my whole life.

I filled myself to bursting then checked the equipment racks for a container. A row of plastic tubes, each about six inches across and two feet long, contained eel-like creatures in fluid, with large caps on the end suitable for prador claws. Some delicacy, perhaps? At the end of the row I found a couple of empties and saw that a button at the end of each cap collapsed a seal around the insert – they were watertight. I filled the tubes with water and capped them, then put them in the air vent, adding one with its eel-like contents too. It would maybe taste better than ship lice, though it could poison me – I decided to take the risk. Now for the pool.

I jumped in and, fearing the prador's return, quickly sluiced off the black filth. Immediately feeling better, I decided to take a risk. Testing spigots provided soapy fluid full of grit – but of course, why wouldn't a technological species use a substance to break down the surface tension of water for washing, and why wouldn't they use grit for scouring? I stripped off the overalls and washed them and myself properly, pausing in my ablutions to feel the stubble growing on my previously bald head and wondering what colour it would be. I eventually got out and dressed, and began to inspect the equipment shelves further.

Many of the items were just too unwieldy. A Gatling cannon rested on one of them, with reels of ammunition beside it, but I could hardly lift up the cluster of barrels. A mass of hand tools lay there, every one made of heavy metal, then opening a toolbox revealed a smaller and more delicate variety that prador must employ with their underhands. Screwdrivers and wrenches were handy, but I hit the jackpot with a small atomic shear. A slide button pushed out an end cap and, between it and the body of the device, extended a shimmering wire. I tried it against the edge of the shelf and with a whine it sliced off a lump of composite. Everything useful I piled into the vent tube, keeping the shear in my pocket. Next I needed something in which to transport my haul. I returned to the Gatling cannon and from behind it pulled out a sheet of material much like canvas. It even had a string running through eyelets, and pulling this tight turned it into a sack. Enough. I pissed in the prador's pool, drank my fill again from the freshwater spigot, then returned to the ventilation system. I had what I needed to survive – now to find my way out to a ship.

3

Darkness followed, then far ahead I saw a light flashing like an arc welder and heard something thrashing about in the tunnel. A vent into the corridor running from the prador's quarters provided enough illumination for me to see the centipede thing lying there. It wasn't moving; smoke, along with the smell of burned fish, filled the tube. I only paused in going past the creature to note its head had been charcoaled. My choice of transit was now becoming increasingly dangerous.

The robot, when I saw it, blocked the tube like a waiting spider. I stopped crawling and began to back up, but the thing shot forwards, its numerous arms running treads against the walls. A flash came as I shoved my sack behind me, then hot pain down my side from armpit to hip. I smashed my bar into its sensor head, also knocking aside a groping claw. The flash came again and this time I saw the laser stabbing through the smoke issuing from me. I struck it wildly, knocking down legs, and the thing dropped, its laser burning into the bottom of the tube. Finally I broke enough of its legs to stop it targeting me any longer.

I had never known such pain. In the illumination from a nearby vent, I inspected a long burn down my side. The laser had seared away the plasmesh but left the strengthening wires of my overalls intact. Those wires had to be a highly conductive alloy. Had I been naked, the laser would probably have burned deep inside me and killed me. But it'd still seared a foot-long black line in my skin, and red plasma now leaked from the cracks. I had to get away from here. I'd managed to defeat this robot because it was designed only to hunt down creatures like the centipede behind me, but almost certainly it linked into some system and would broadcast a fault code. I grabbed my sack and climbed over the thing. But when I reached the next vent I hesitated, then dumped my sack and crawled back, taking hold of the robot and pulling it to the vent to inspect it.

Six legs extended from a central body which contained a power supply, a primitive mind perhaps not much different from that of its prey, a radar sensor head and below that its swivel-mounted laser. My pain had now increased and I just wanted to crawl off somewhere and rest, but it also seemed to focus my mind. I could not miss the opportunity here. Laying out my tools, I set to work, though it turned out I hardly needed them. The power supply detached easily from the robot's body, spring clips freeing it. I pulled it out, found the leads that supplied power to its limbs and detached them all, at both ends, then put them in my sack. I sliced the laser from its mount and examined its connections further. Power ran straight from the supply to it, while optics ran to its guide motor and into its brain. I needed to replace that with a trigger, but couldn't do that here. I put the laser and power supply in my sack, then stripped out anything else useful and took that too. Perhaps more from the limbs? No, I could hear a prador coming down the corridor so moved on as quickly and quietly as I could.

I don't know how long I pushed on for, maybe hours in the dark and through areas of varying grav. At one point I just stopped and cried with pain, then had it increase when a ship louse found my wound attractive. I moved on towards a thrumming sound and entered an area where the tube widened out, but then came up against a cage behind which a huge fan turned. Light penetrated from a large chamber packed with machinery beyond the fan, amidst which I could see tool-laden prador working. Too tired and uncomfortable to do anything about my haul, I rested and uncapped the container holding the eel thing. The tough and rubbery flesh tasted wonderful. I ate half of it and immediately afterwards weariness hit me like a club. I jammed the sack against the wound in my side to try and keep the ship lice away, then fell into a sleep as deep as death.

Waking, it seemed, would always be a painful process for me. My side hurt, not because of lice chewing on it, but the burn. My guts then cramped up agonizingly. I felt the desperate need to shit and managed to hold off until my overalls were down. Diarrhoea squirted but gave me no relief and I puked, bringing up chewed flesh and watery bile. This went on and on for hours and I grew sure I was going to die. That no lice paid me a visit seemed small recompense. In my fevered state, I realized that, long being resident aboard prador ships, the creatures probably kept well clear of moving parts such as the fan I lay beside. After a time, I began shaking – one moment the breeze from the fan felt too cold, another moment it prevented my skin from catching fire. Sticky pools spread around me. I hallucinated, seeing a future in which all that would be left would be an empty skin surrounded by this miasma. I tried to quell a terrible thirst, and threw up again immediately. It just went on and on.

Time passed, as it does.

Eventually I fell into another exhausted sleep. I woke shivering still and moved away from the stinking mess I'd left, towing my belongings with me. A stream of diarrhoea and vomit had run along the tube for as far as I could see. Terribly thirsty again, I opened a water tube, but was then too scared to drink from it and just sat there feeling beaten from head to foot. As I put the water tube back, I saw the one containing the remains of the eel thing and said out loud, my voice rough, 'Maybe stick to eating the lice.' This gave me a fit of the giggles, until I cried again.

Later, something thunked in my skull, flooding it with a hard lucidity. I took out the water tube and drank from it this time, retching a little but managing to keep it down. It made me feel a lot better. I inspected my now raw and hideous burn, but could do nothing about that, so just cleaned myself with a little more water as best I could, then put my overalls back on. I next killed a louse and ate what I could of it. Weak and shaky, I moved on, entering a side tunnel and taking a turn which brought me back to another fan. Here I laid out my tools and all the parts from the robot.

Carving away metal with the shear turned the support bracket of the laser into a handle. I dismantled the radar and accessed the robot's mind, puzzling over it all for some time, until I saw the schematics of it in my skull. I discarded the mind, radar and much else, and discovered that detaching all the optics and pulling out a small processor fired up the laser continuously. In the end I worked out the best way to operate it: the power supply went into my pocket, while the power cord was extended with a couple of those stripped from the robot's motor. A simple relay, tied to the handle with a strip of material from my overalls, acted as a trigger. The laser went into my other pocket. As I finished, I understood perfectly that my other self – Jack Zero from whom I had been cloned and whose knowledge continued to surface in my skull – must have been adept at this sort of thing.

I continued heading as best I could in one direction, still hoping to reach the hull of the ship. But the changes in grav confused me, and I realized that if any of the vent tubes had a slight curve,

I probably wouldn't detect it. In a tube with high air flow, thinking it might be a main one, I followed the air blast. This tube went on for miles, until I saw light ahead and eventually reached its source. A ring ran around the end of the vent tube where it opened out into a spacious area, and there was a row of baffles directing the air blast through the gratings below. The light was issuing up through those gratings. As I drew close to the ring, a laser snapped at me from one of four inset eyes and burned a hole through my overall sleeve into my forearm. I backed up quickly, then checked where the proximity detector operated by extending one of the water tubes in front of me. The laser covered a space of about a yard in front of the ring. It must have been put there to keep ship lice out and now I really wanted to see what lay ahead.

My original club served a useful purpose here. I emptied the sack and wrapped it around my hands and arms, gripped the length of alloy, then moved forwards and bashed one of the eyes. Luckily the laser only hit the alloy, raising a red glow on it. The eye fizzled and emitted a dispersed light as I went for the next one. After destroying all three, I refilled the sack and crawled through. Initially, the view down in front of the baffles only revealed a wall hung with pipes and protruding pit controls, but when I climbed over the baffles, I peered down at something familiar.

The grated ceiling hung over a laboratory, and I recognized the prador immediately below me. Abandoning my sack under one of the baffles, I moved stealthily in pursuit of this small prador in dirty white armour and was soon looking into a part of the laboratory I'd seen before. Feed tubes, optics and shielded cables were strewn over the grating where I crouched, while below, my fellow clones floated in cylindrical tanks. One of the mechanisms evenly scattered on the underside of the grating was set into motion and it lowered its spiderbot claw to haul a clone out of her tank, removing all the feed and breather pipes, and depositing her on the floor.

'Follow me,' said the prador in Anglic.

She stumped along after him, seemingly unaware of the dripping wounds all over her body which, I noted, were not bleeding as much as they should have been. I watched in frustration as he took her into a smaller room. I had my laser, after all. Shouldn't I make some daring rescue attempt? But the laser would have no effect on that armour, and even if it did, what then? What could I do with her or the others even if I managed to get them out of there and into the vents? Would they even follow my instructions? No, they would probably sit in a vent pipe mindlessly while lice chewed them down to the bone. I had to be practical – helping the clones was completely beyond my abilities and would just get me killed. It was a sour and bitter concession and the impossibilities aggravated me keenly.

'Remove your garment and lie down,' the prador instructed and, when she lay down on the low slab, he closed clamps over her wrists and ankles.

What happened next confused me utterly. He clambered over her, so his body now blocked my view of most of hers, though I could still see her head. Horrible crunching and sizzling sounds ensued and, shaking her head from side to side, she opened and closed her mouth like a fish. He had positioned himself so he could employ his underhands and whatever tools he was using. I gripped the bars of the ceiling grating for fear I might do something stupid and closed my eyes. Really, I could do nothing, so why did I feel so helpless and ashamed? I had to remember no real mind existed inside that woman's head, but it felt like cowardly self-justification.

The prador now began clattering and bubbling in his language, some of which I understood, much of which I recognized as a scientific vocabulary. 'The virus had established' in the 'test subject' apparently. Finally he backed off to reveal he had split open her arms and legs down to the bone, as well as opened up her torso from neck to groin. She should have been pouring with blood but only clear fluids leaked out as she writhed, exposing fibrous growths with a bluish tint within. The Spatterjay virus was growing there and my knowledge told me it had developed unreasonably fast. Even as I watched, her wounds were starting to close.

'Test subject optimal,' said the prador in his own language.

He reached over and with one claw began roughly pinching the wounds closed, holding them this way for a moment each time. When he took his claw away, they had all but sealed. Her writhing diminished and he undid the clamps, flipping her over onto her face, then secured them again. Next he introduced a new clamp that closed rams on either side of her head just ahead of the ears, and in one quick movement tore off the slaver unit on the back of her neck. With a whine, the slab tilted and he pulled over what looked like a Polity pedestal-mounted auto-surgeon, which then ran its program. I could see little of what it did, just heard the buzz of a saw, and the whickering of chain-glass scalpels. The autosurgeon then rose and shifted to one side, exposing its work. The thing had taken off the back of her skull, opened out her neck vertebrae, and extracted the contents. With a soggy thunk, the surgeon deposited them on a platen that swung aside. There lay her brain, along with a tail of spinal cord. She was now as good as dead.

I gazed in horror as the surgeon stretched gleaming limbs to a nearby rack and removed an item I had never seen before but recognized at once. Silvery spider legs surrounded a squat cylinder from which also extended its own segmented tail. I glimpsed the surgeon inserting this into the skull cavity, the tail sitting comfortably in the row of open vertebrae. Then came the sound of bone and cell welders, and it blocked my view for a while. When it next moved away, it had closed the vertebrae, while movement down the spine revealed gleaming microfibres spreading to make connections. The cylinder part sat centrally in her skull, while its legs pressed against the interior to hold it in place. Here the surgeon paused, because the prador wanted to make a closer inspection. He chuntered to himself, but my mind was too numb to translate. As the surgeon returned to its work, he reached out and picked up the brain with the attached piece of spinal cord and inserted it into his armoured mandibles and thence into his mouth. No chewing required for something so soft, I assumed. It seemed the ultimate insult.

This woman's skull no longer contained a human mind. I had just seen someone cored and thralled and turned into a human blank.

My numbness remained as the surgeon sealed up the Jill's skull and withdrew, following which the prador undid all the clamps. I watched him head over to another rack, take out a hexagonal device and insert the spike on its underside into a socket on the upper section of his armour, beside his turret. He shuddered, banging one claw against the floor, while I noted the hole had been one in a row, with another row present on the other side of his turret too. The woman raised her head, clumsily got her arms underneath her and rolled off the slab to fall on the floor. She lay there jerking her limbs randomly then, finally, it seemed the prador accustomed himself to the control unit he had just installed, and she stood up. She moved back and sat on the slab with her hands on her knees. The prador then moved away, seeming to lose interest.

Feeling cold and stunned, I followed him back into the other part of the laboratory. There he moved over to an array of pit controls and inserted a claw to twist and manipulate. Movement in the tanks caught my eye as snakish forms entered them all. They attached to the bodies inside, which began to thrash in agony. Spatterjay leeches – the usual vector of transmission for the virus. These clones too, when ready, would be cored and thralled, becoming simply organic extensions of the controlling prador's mind. Again I reminded myself that any efforts I made on their behalf would be futile and I'd probably end up the same way as them. I had to look to my own survival and nothing else. But I still sat there in a daze, until the anger boiled up in me once more.

Undoubtedly prador were vicious creatures, but humans had provided these test subjects. I reviewed the faces and names of the suppliers: Suzeal, Brack and Frey. My purpose started to become clearer to me. I not only wanted revenge, I needed to get out of this place and . . . stop them. This aim hardened in my thoughts, though I realized bitterly it was also driven by my guilt at not being able to do anything here.

Returning for my sack, I headed across the grated ceiling to the far side, over partitioned parts of the laboratory in which more tanks contained gross distortions of humanity and others that had once been prador. Airflow now feathered from below. It came in the way I had come, was directed down by the baffles, sweeping around the laboratory then up again. Shortly it blew from behind me too, sucked through a filter system which looked like a wall of intricately tangled wires. A mote of dust struck this as I watched and flared like a mosquito hitting the grid of an electric zapper, so I kept well away and walked along parallel to it. I assumed this system was to destroy dangerous biologicals, which didn't bode well for my health should I remain here for any time. Then, as I walked along beside the filter wall, something below riveted my attention, and I peered through.

Another Polity autosurgeon was standing over to one side of a slab on which the man-thing had been reassembled. Numerous staples marked where the body pieces had been joined together again, while massive clamps secured his arms, legs and torso. I'd assumed his remains were scheduled for disposal, but it seemed that merely being torn apart by the king of the prador hadn't been enough to kill him. The legendary hooper humans were famed for their ruggedness because they could survive the most appalling injuries, but this seemed beyond ridiculous. As I gazed at him shifting on the slab, constantly testing his bonds, he opened his eyes and grew still. He had spotted me.

The horror of everything I'd witnessed redoubled. In his gaze I saw intelligence, and an understanding the others lacked, as well as rage – plenty of that. Though not one of the clones, his physical transformation showed what might become of them. Seeing this earlier experiment, I thought more closely about events here. From the information I had, I knew that the prador had cored and thralled virus-infected humans throughout the war with the Polity, so the technique had been long established. But this procedure being conducted here, in a laboratory, had to be something new. The virus had established quickly in the clones, so I suspected a much faster-growing, mutated form of it. Could they have tried it on this man first, without coring him, to study the effects? Perhaps he'd not been cored subsequently because this faster-growing virus hampered the process at a later stage. I didn't know. I turned away and headed back to the baffles, climbed over and destroyed the vermin lasers on another ring and then returned to the ventilation system. Always on the move, searching for the skin of the ship, sleeping, and eating the lice that woke me every time. Forcing myself to forget what that human might be enduring.

★   ★   ★

When I finally found the first window I'd come across in my long wanderings, it revealed the good news that I'd managed to travel down into the stalk of the King's Ship. The air vent opened into a wide corridor with oval ports slightly above head height. Rough walls like stacked slate were easy to climb up so I could peer through. I gazed first on starlit space with a stab of agoraphobia, then at the underside of the upper disc of the ship, and down towards some docks, just visible, with clinging ships. Darting back into the vent, I had the grating back in place by the time a party of noisy prador came past, loaded with tools and towing grav-sleds stacked with machinery. I headed in the same direction, the vent tube tracking the corridor, hoping for some shaft going down close to the hull, because I didn't want to get lost again.

I caught up with the prador just a little while later and stopped to observe them working. Here the corridor was smooth but for a huge hole in the wall. I could see into this, into the layers and cavities of the ship's outer armour, as complex as skin. It revealed superconducting meshes, impact foams and laminated metamaterials, but also a cavity between layers which was braced by shock absorbers like hair cells. One of the prador climbed into the hole to install something in a pipe which, judging by the air blast as the creature uncapped it, extended to vacuum. The prador quickly shoved in a sliding bung, then a long complicated mechanism went in after it which might have been a weapon or a detector. The prador and its fellows connected this up to the power and optic system running through the armour. Once they'd finished and left, I made a decision: there lay my route down.

Preparations now needed to be made. I found a route away from the corridor and traversed this until reaching a junction. Here I spilled out the remains of the eel thing, then shifted back and waited. As ever, the ship lice came. I killed the first and ate it, and intended to catch a good load of them to keep as a food supply. I could put them in the now empty container . . . but the idea abruptly panicked me. Whatever had poisoned me might still be in the container, and I didn't know how long it would be before the meat from a ship louse spoiled. I changed my plans, caught and killed four more of the creatures and ate what I could of them too. That would have to be enough. I then returned to the vent tube beside the corridor.

Here I took out the laser again and began tinkering with it. After a while I found the adjustment I wanted: a simple ring to turn and a slider to push down to the bottom. Now when I triggered the thing it produced a defused white light rather than a deep purple beam. I had a torch. Next I used the shear to make two pairs of slices in my sack – the intervening material between each pair of cuts serving as straps. Shrugging on this backpack, I went through the vent grating.

The gap between armour layers stood four feet wide, braced across at intervals by the shock absorbers. I pointed my torch down and didn't see an end to the space. Lines marked the edges of huge alloy construction slabs forming its outer wall, and each rectangle, as far as I could see, extended lengthwise down the pillar of the ship. The edges of these would have to be my guide once alterations in grav lost me my present perspective. I climbed in and, using the shock absorbers as climbing aids, descended.

Gravity changed as I worked my way nominally 'down' through this gap yet, when I flashed my torch at the slab lines, I found this was no longer affecting my sense of direction. Food supply turned out not to be a problem, since the lice occupied this space too. This also confirmed that it lay open to the ship's air supply. Such gaps in Polity ships were often filled with inert gas, but that was unlikely to be used aboard a prador vessel – being armoured and tough enough to survive in vacuum for an appreciable time, the prador considered seals and atmosphere security the province of weak creatures like humans.

I stopped to sleep in areas where grav pulled me against the inner wall, always scribing an arrow into the other wall to tell me what direction I had been going. The lice here were particularly aggressive, and the reason for this I soon found out to be clusters of eggs clinging to the bases of shock absorbers. Close inspection with the laser torch revealed translucent globules with small lice inside. At one point I observed a youngster hatching with the mother in attendance, one of the cybernetic lice I'd noticed on first boarding the ship. It had stuck itself to the wall with a glassy exudate and its young crawled all over it. Mother love? The cybernetic remains of one I later found beside a hatched-out batch of eggs provided the answer. As with some terran spiders and insects, the mother obviously became her young's food source. This struck me as a predictable nastiness in this place, then further knowledge of their biology surfaced in my mind. They had three sexes, so I wasn't sure if the one serving itself up like this could be called 'mother'.

After a time which I could only measure by my number of sleeps, which was three, the scenery changed. I came down on a wide pipe, sure to be an airlock leading outside, then further pipes loomed out of the dark. One of them, for no immediately apparent reason, possessed numerous windows of a crystalline yellow substance. I could see enough inside to confirm my conjecture: it was another massive tunnel, probably leading to one of the huge docks. Ships were near, but how the hell would I get to one? Well, I needed to eat the elephant. First I had to get out of the hull armour.

I began to explore, now not concerning myself with sense of direction, and eventually glimpsed a distant glow. As I moved towards it, I saw movement that resolved into prador at work in another hole made in the armour from the inside. I took a position on one of the docking pipes and watched for hours. Eventually, when it seemed the activity had ceased, I went over. Here they had opened a hole much larger than the one above, perhaps for a new dock or airlock. I risked going right up to the workings to peer into the huge corridor lying beyond. Spotting one of the ubiquitous vents, I adjusted the laser back to its kill setting, despite the certainty it wouldn't touch a prador in armour, and took out the shear. Soon standing in the corridor, I looked along it to see prador perambulating towards me. It was too late to hide now so I crossed, used the shear on the grating bolts and dived into the vent. A flash of blue fire ignited behind me and, crawling up the tube, I glanced back to see a glowing hole in the wall. If I had chosen to turn left rather than right I'd be dead now. I scuttled on, took the first turning away from the corridor and found a place to rest and consider my next moves.

I explored, noting an increase in the louse population and assumed that, being mutualistic life forms, the higher prador population in this part of the ship had attracted them. More of their predators were evident too, but they ignored me. When, as seemed inevitable, one of the vermin-killing robots surged towards me, I hit it with the laser and the thing slumped in smoking ruin. Even though I was aware the things had been designed to kill just vermin, and had no armouring, I felt unreasonably happy with this victory.

Vent tubes once again became my world. With my sack turned into a backpack, I could move a lot more quickly and damned my stupidity for not doing it before. The lightness of the pack was another reason I could travel faster, since I had run out of water some while ago. I eventually came to a vent overlooking a huge internal space, where a crew of five prador were moving stacks of supplies and feed umbilicals around a ship. Small for a prador vessel, the thing measured about a mile long, with fusion engines to the rear, blisters for faster-than-light U-space engines and a rounded-off nose. It looked a bit like a gravestone and this suddenly triggered a familiarity for me. This was no prador vessel but an old Polity wartime supply ship, obviously adapted for the prador. At the far end I noted castellated doors and became excited as I realized these, and the ship, could be my means of escape from this place. Then something else drew my attention.

Nine figures walked into the area in two rows of four with a familiar form in the lead. The man-thing wore a frame like a primitive exoskeleton that ended at his knees and elbows. It ran in segments up his spine to cup the back of his skull, while here and there over his body other hardware disappeared into healing slits. He showed no signs of wanting to attack anyone. The eight clones were as obedient and docile as ever but, seeing what had happened to one of them, I assumed they had all been cored and thralled and were under the thorough control of the prador in the dirty white armour walking behind. I wondered what had been done with the others. Had they been treated the same? Had they died during their procedures or failed in some other way? Or were they all still writhing in their tanks back in the laboratory? As they proceeded up the ramp into the ship, their serendipitous arrival seemed to confirm that I had to get aboard too. I hurried along, looking for a way down.

A brief stop in another smaller prador accommodation provided more water and a chance to clean myself. The place seemed Spartan and hadn't been used in a while. With no belongings evident, I deduced it must be temporary accommodation for visiting crews. From there I found my way to a vent at ground level. I watched, soon realizing I could not simply walk aboard, and turned my attention to the nearest pallet of supplies. It lay just ten feet from the vent and I had to take the risk. The grating came away easily and I rested it back in place without tightening the bolts, so I could dart back in if one of the prador here spotted me. Then I ran over to hide behind the stack. Made of compressed fibre like those I had seen in the supply room, the boxes had actual lids which peeled off molecular seals. Three of them sat in a row before me, and a larger box kept me concealed while I opened one. Inside rested a series of cylinders filled with chunks of meat under an oily fluid. The box had room for me, but not with these inside.

One after another, I transported the heavy cylinders back to the vent and rolled them inside. Even though it was apparently prador food in them, my stomach grumbled, and I feared being heard. But I made each journey to the vent only when the loading crew were moving the next load of supplies up the ramp. As soon as I'd made enough room, I slung in my backpack and climbed in after it, pulling the lid closed above.

It took only a little time before the fears kicked in. What if they loaded this cargo into a hold without atmosphere? Maybe they'd empty the boxes of their contents for storage? I tried to persuade myself that if I was really a clone of a Polity agent, I should be braver than this, but my mind meanly reminded me that I apparently only possessed the genome and knowledge of whoever had been my source. I'd all but persuaded myself to return to the ventilation system, where I could survive and watch and wait for a better opportunity. But even as I thought this, I heard prador nearby and then the maglev pallet rose and set into motion.

Too late now.

I felt it when the pallet went up the ramp. Other sounds impinged from within the ship: the crackle of a cutting laser and the drone and susurration of a matter printer, prador crashing about, their clattering and bubbling language. The pallet turned, turned again, then dropped with a crash to the floor. My small hide shuddered then jerked sideways, rose up and came down. A moment later, a crump from above sounded as another box went on top of mine.

I fumbled in the darkness for a tool out of my pack and used it to bore a hole in one side of the box. As the tool broke through, it hit another surface, so I tried the other sides and, on the last go, light shone in. I widened the hole just enough to get my eye to it, only in time to see a prador lifting another box into place and blocking my view. I sighed, made myself comfortable and just listened. I heard what must be the ramp close up and much later the fusion engines roaring into life. I didn't even notice the vessel actually leaving the King's Ship and guessed it had used maglev or grav to take it through the doors and outside. These were either not noticeable, or compensated for by internal grav. The roar of the fusion engines continued for some time and was certainly compensated for, because I didn't feel any motion. Listening, I drifted off for a while, then woke with a start. I panicked at the sense of something missing, then realized I'd woken without a ship louse trying to take a chunk out of me.

The time had come for me to get out of this box and reconnoitre. I pushed up against the lid and felt something shifting above. Then, suddenly, I wasn't sure where 'above' was as my entire existence seemed to twist off in a direction I couldn't point to. Panic returned and I shoved harder. The weight above fell away and I heard an awful crashing that somehow, in my mind, translated into flashes of light. I stood up, swaying in the darkness. Belatedly, even as it faded, I realized my perceptual distortion was due to the ship entering underspace. Its journey had properly commenced. Activating the laser torch, I looked down from a mountain of boxes at one split open on the floor, cylinders rolling and some open and spilling their contents. I needed to make a swift departure in case a prador came to investigate the racket. I just hoped they would blame the fallen box on it having been inadequately stacked.

The small human construction hold had a prador door installed, taking up most of one wall. Operating my torch intermittently to save power, I studied the diagonally divided heavy slabs and then the pit control to one side. Maybe I could operate it with the bar in my backpack, but did I really want to wander about in the prador section that lay beyond? I needed to find something like the ventilation system of the King's Ship but the human-scale system here would be too small to crawl through. I also needed to see if I could find anything useful before leaving this place. I began opening boxes, again being careful about the power usage of my torch as I looked inside each.

Many of the boxes contained prador food. Useful knowledge surfacing as ever told me the steaks in fluid were from mudfish, while a large box contained whole carcases of reaverfish wrapped in transparent plastic. Then I found a box containing recognizably human food. Blocks of the stuff I had first eaten aboard Suzeal's ship were stacked like bricks wrapped in thin tissue paper. Certainly packed with all the vitamins, proteins and fats a human body required, just the sight of them started me salivating even though I was dehydrated. The smell then hit me and it took all my will not to snatch one of them up and gobble it right away. If I took just one or two the prador might notice them missing, so instead I took the whole upper layer and put it into my pack, hoping this would go undetected.

I opened more boxes, still fighting the urge to eat, but intending to only when I'd got somewhere safe. They contained more food items and demijohns of fluid I didn't recognize. I walked around the stack, noting that a net lay rolled up to one side ready to

61

secure the load, and I guessed this had been forgotten. The prador might return to spread it over the boxes and tighten it down. I hurriedly scanned the walls looking for a vent cover, and instead found a human-sized door of the original vessel.

The holds of such ships were of a modular construction for atmosphere security. The door had no power running to it but as a security feature had a manual wheel. It turned easily enough but the door was jammed and I guessed this was the result of alterations distorting the internal structure here. My bar came in useful again, first inserted in the wheel as a lever, then in the side of the door as a crowbar.

Another hold lay beyond, where the netting had been spread over heavy cases. Having struggled to close the first door behind me, I found another on the further side and went over to try it. This one was jammed too, but I didn't need to use the bar. Beyond it a diffuse light penetrated. A short corridor terminated at a curved metal wall with a yard-wide pipe running along it horizontally, while the light came through a join between two sections of that wall. I walked in, flashed my torch into a space to the left and lit the entrance to a dropshaft. At the curved wall, I peered through the gap into a prador-sized corridor with the kind of ridged floor their feet preferred. It seemed they had only torn out what they needed to install their own infrastructure and not bothered to remove the rest. Stepping back, I gazed at the pipe. It had not been familiar to me; even though I had seen a lot of them, that had only been from the inside. Despite my earlier doubts, this ship did in fact have a prador ventilation system. I returned to the hold, leaving the door open – my exit.

A simple button slackened a cable coming up out of the floor, and at its end a hook pulled the net down taut. I released a few of these to get to a large case with a lid secured by the same bolts used for the ventilation gratings in the King's Ship. Inside, packed in expanded foam, lay a particle cannon. I found it almost painful to close and seal the lid on such a destructive weapon, but I had to be practical – it was too heavy for me even to pick up. Its presence excited me, however, because it indicated what other things might be here. I ignored further cases of a similar size and moved on to a smaller one. The familiar shape of a Polity armaments case revealed itself under the laser torch, the lid secured by a lock whose code needed to be input through a panel on the side. Reading what had been printed on the surface gave me pause: ENERG 4.2MW AL-PULSE. As I studied this the lights abruptly came on. No time. In panic I pulled the netting back down and secured it even as the door-locking mechanism clonked in the wall. I went through the open human door and closed it just as the prador door ground open.

In the short corridor I sat down, quietly, with my back against the wall. Grav was low here, the pull from the plates in the hold giving me the illusion of sitting on a slope. Almost without thinking I took out a food block and started eating, too fast, because I bit my tongue. I forced calm and ate more slowly, speculating on what I had seen.

So, they had human weapons aboard – that case had contained military-issue pulse rifles. The only humans aboard, as far as I knew, were the clones and, arguably, the reconstructed man-thing. There had to be more going on here than grotesque experiments involving the Spatterjay virus. It looked as though the prador had used it to toughen up a group of humans and were now transporting them somewhere, along with weapons for their use. *They* were a weapon. Why would the prador need them? Perhaps a furtive attack on a human installation, I surmised. Prador trying to penetrate such a place would be spotted at once. Unreasonably strong, rugged and apparently human troops could move in such an environment with ease and cause serious mayhem. The beginning of an attack on the Polity? I thought not. The clones were simply too small a force for that and, anyway, this ship would have no chance of passing the watch stations along the border. That left one likelihood for where we were going: the Graveyard.

4

The Graveyard buffer zone lay between the Polity and the Prador Kingdom, a no-man's land scattered with settlements of humans and prador. In this lawless place those from both sides had found a home. The likes of Suzeal and her crew operated there, and prador who disagreed with the truce their king had agreed to had found refuge in it too. But everyone conducted all sorts of covert and black operations in this place. Both sides sought control there, while being careful not to break truces or inadvertently push the two realms into full-blown war again.

As I listened to movement in the nearby hold, I ran through my analysis. It all seemed to make perfect sense, but I realized no normal human citizen would have the strategic knowledge to think this way. It seemed, yet again, to be the reasoning of some kind of agent. Also, though it would surely mean more violence to come, I felt grim satisfaction in drawing nearer to my goal. I'd got out of the King's Ship, would soon be out of the Kingdom and in the area of space where I might eventually find Suzeal and her crew. But that was supposing I managed to survive aboard this ship, and all it might entail to escape it. Seeing the larger picture didn't presuppose I would achieve my current objectives, such as simply finding something to drink.

I stood up, headed for the dropshaft and peered into its darkness.

Up or down? It didn't really matter. I had to explore, find water, and other secure places to hide, as well as acquire the tools to help me survive. Yet, as I reached out and grasped one of the rungs and began to descend, I felt happy. Only a moment's thought told me why. Yes, I advanced towards my ultimate goal, but the happiness arose from being in a place where I could simply stand upright without any immediate fear of ending up blown to pieces by a prador Gatling cannon, and where I might be able to wake up without my ship louse alarm clock.

The drag of grav dropped to zero as I descended, then for a little while it pulled me to one side before zeroing once more. It climbed again until I came down on the upper surface of a newly installed prador corridor. That was it: a dead end at the bottom. I ascended, quickly passing my entry point to come opposite another entrance, and shone my light in it. Here there was a corridor with doors down one side and sliced off at its end by a new wall. Rather than explore there, I continued climbing, grav waxing and waning all the way. The shaft terminated. I experienced the odd dislocation I had felt just before I broke out of my box, and realized the shielding from the effects of U-space wasn't as good here, so perhaps I was near the hull. I took the side tunnel presented. Low grav again – the plates were probably only powered by a fading backup.

On the right-hand side of the tunnel stood a ladder with a tall cabinet beside it. I climbed to a circular atmosphere door, wiped dust off a small window and peered up into an airlock. I had reached the hull. Dropping back down, I walked on to a bulkhead door at the end. The door opened towards me – I would not have been able to open it if vacuum had lain beyond. Another ladder led up into a small circular room, where I discovered that, as well as not removing a lot of the infrastructure of the ship, the prador had failed to remove all of the crew.

A black dome capped this area – I assumed it was reactive laminated chain-glass blocking a view into a continuum said to drive humans insane. Panels lined the low wall, many of them pulled off to reveal the packed paraphernalia of electronics. An acceleration chair was positioned inside a horseshoe console and in the chair sat the corpse of what I assumed to be a man. Distinguishing sex wasn't possible with the body's state of mummification. I made the assumption 'him' due to size but, considering the size of Suzeal, it might well have been a false one. I inspected the hollow eyes and exposed teeth, the pale cropped hair and the metal aug stuck behind his ear. I reached out to touch the device but quickly snatched my hand back. There was no sign of how he had died so a bioweapon could have killed him, and its spores, or whatever, might still be active.

Studying the console, I saw screens and hologram projectors but not much in the way of manual controls. I assumed he had auglinked into the system before him to control . . . whatever he had controlled. Again scanning my surroundings, I didn't see much of use to me and returned my attention to him. I studied him for a long moment, then transferred that inspection to myself. The overalls which Suzeal and her crew had provided me with had a slice down the side, with the laser wound underneath still healing. It was filthy, stained and worn through to the strengthening wires, while my slippers were falling apart. I decided that if a bioweapon had killed him I had probably already breathed in the dust of its remains anyway, and hauled him out of his chair.

He had on an envirosuit with heavy boots, gloves tucked into pockets in the sleeves, a fabric hood concertinaed to form the back collar and a transparent visor similarly folded down at the front. I took my time stripping it off, finding an absorbent undersuit beneath that had soaked up most of the exudate of decay. There wasn't much of it so he had clearly been vacuum-dried here. Perhaps vacuum had killed him, though I would have thought, if this place had been losing air, he'd have had time to close up his suit. When I tried to take off his boots I found that the press of a button loosened them, showing that the suit still had some power. As I finally pulled him free of the thing, certain anatomical features confirmed my previous supposition. I tore off the least stained piece of his undersuit and wiped out the interior of the envirosuit, then stripped and put the thing on. Some adjustments at shoulders, knees and waist with thread motors had it fitting perfectly, while the boots adjusted and tightened automatically.

'Thank you,' I said to him hoarsely. 'And I'm sorry.'

Suddenly the place had the quiet feeling of a crypt and I wanted to get out of there. I turned to head for the door. But I suddenly felt the dislocation of transition from U-space and, a moment later, the black glass dome cleared.

Blue stars gleamed across hard vacuum, and a huge ship out there drew my attention. I recognized it at once. I had seen its like scattered distantly around the King's Ship and, of course, knowledge of old-style prador dreadnoughts resided in my mind. We were not yet in the Graveyard, for such a ship's presence there would be a truce breaker. Stretching miles across, the thing resembled the body of an adult prador, a bridge on top much like such a creature's visual turret, but the body below was more spread out, giving it the look of a fat manta ray. The bridge wouldn't contain this vessel's father-captain – he'd be deep inside in an armoured sanctum – but it would contain a lot of the ship's sensors and perhaps a crew of his children. A red light issuing from ports there gave the impression of eyes, looking at me. Perhaps they were. I quickly went over and sat in the chair. Any queries from there about a human underneath a bubble on this ship's hull would be answered with a dismissal: just one of the previous human crew, dead of course.

While I watched, a port opened under one of the side wings and objects began to stream out – a swarm of wasps leaving a nest. They glinted in reflected sunlight from a sun I could not see. As they swirled closer, I soon identified them as prador, all heavily armed and clad in armour of a uniform khaki. These were not King's Guard but the unmutated kind; utterly vicious and lacking in even an ounce of empathy. Continuing with my previous speculations, I reckoned the clones were the initial assault force, whose purpose would be to go in, to open the way for the main force: these prador.

The bulk of these alien troops arrived in an ordered stream, the vessel shuddering as they boarded. But others patrolled at a distance, commanders perhaps. I froze in place with my head tilted back while a shadow crossed the hull outside as one came to hover directly over me. I hoped the exterior was mirrored and that it could not see inside, or that it wouldn't be able to tell the difference between me and the corpse on the floor. I then panicked about that corpse. What if the prador reported two humans up here? It drew closer and closer, glare reflecting off its armour as the nearby sun rose over the ship, which had begun to turn. Missiles sat on the creature's back and it had a Gatling cannon attached on the underside of a claw. The tip of one jaw on its other claw hinged down to expose a shiny throat. It could see inside, and now it had readied its other weapon too. It drew closer still, then tapped on the glass with its cannon. I remained immobile. After an interminable pause, thrusters fired from its armour and it swept away.

I started shaking, then reached up and wiped away the sweat beaded on my forehead. Heaving out of the chair, I considered putting the envirosuit back on the corpse and returning it to its place. But my filthy overalls luckily nearly matched the colour of the envirosuit, so I hurriedly dressed the corpse in that and returned him to his chair. About to head out, I noticed something on the hull nearby. There stood a weapons turret with a particle cannon protruding in the middle and missile clusters on either side. So the man here had controlled that. With all its missiles still in place, I guessed the thing hadn't been much help. I got out of there and back into the dropshaft.

Whenever I touched a corridor wall I could feel the rumbling vibration from the movement of the new prador aboard. By the time I reached out to the first door in the unexplored corridor it had settled a little and I assumed they were now quartered.

The door opened into a standard cabin, the light coming on then fading to a dull glow. I quickly stepped over another corpse lying on the floor and went directly to the sanitary unit, took out one of my water containers and put it under the shower head, punching the start panel. Water came out for just a short time, then turned dirty and stopped. Despite the stuff having turned dirty brown, I drank it all and found it delicious. I headed out quickly, closing the door so the light would go off. Power here was obviously low – maybe in a battery backup – and I didn't know how long it would last. In each of the cabins I went straight to the shower, nearly filling both containers, and in the last I had to do this hurriedly because of the stink. Time now for a more leisurely inspection.

The woman on the floor in the first cabin had mummified and not vacuum-dried like the man above – a large stain had spread out on the carpet around her. I could still smell a hint of putrefaction. I searched lockers inset in one wall, finding her clothing which, at a stretch, would be useful to me, but I left it since others had occupied other cabins. I tried not to let the sad remains of a life affect me, but they did. She had a personal unit that powered up but was coded to DNA scan. Maybe it would work if I put her finger against it, but did I want to read her personal musings and look at pictures of her family and acquaintances? I found a bottle of rum and slab of chocolate frosted with age and put them on the bed. Next I dragged out a large toolbox from a low locker and opened it. Plenty of human tools, many with working power supplies, and I guessed her to be a ship's engineer. Everything in her cabin would have been very useful to me when I'd been in the ventilation tubes of the King's Ship, but now I needed to be selective. I moved on to the next cabin.

This man had died in his bed. I found useful clothing, stripped off my envirosuit and put on a fresh clean undersuit. I also found a stash of etched sapphires and New Carth shillings. I added these to my haul because at some point I hoped to be venturing into the human world. I also added a pack of jerky and some glassy sweets. The next cabin stood empty – no one home and no belongings. I swallowed bile and prepared myself for the last one.

The two in there had survived much longer than the rest, hence their delayed state of decay. They had tubed their enviro-suits to a single oxygen bottle, and emptied it. A container of water sat beside them, half full, while a few food wrappers scattered the floor. As I picked up the pulse gun lying beside the woman, I studied their wounds. It looked as if she had shot the man through the side of his head before turning the weapon on herself. But what had chewed up their envirosuits? When one of them moved, I jerked back, pointing the gun at them, then saw a familiar creature move out from behind the man. The louse had obviously eaten its fill because it scuttled straight along the bottom of the wall then up it and through a broken plastic vent cover. I tracked its course with the gun, for a moment considering testing the weapon on it, then turned away and inserted the thing into a convenient loop on my envirosuit belt. Oddly, despite having had the things try to feed on me and having fed on them, I felt no urge to kill it.

As I searched the cabin further I wondered how it had all gone down here. The prador would have been after the ship intact, so would not have employed their usual method of either blowing it to pieces, or cutting a hole to get inside and gutting the place with personal weapons that could stand in for human artillery. I reckoned on an electromagnetic pulse or warfare beam to disable the vessel, but how then did they turn off the air supply?

Human troops, I thought.

The clones and I were not the first in the King's Ship. Likely this kidnapping and experimentation had been going on during and since the war. Certainly the man-thing had been infected with the Spatterjay virus earlier than the clones. Perhaps he had come in here and shut down their air, though it would have been more his style to tear them all limb from limb. But I had only seen this small portion of the ship. Outside of the holds was room for a much larger crew, and the ship could have been retrofitting for passengers too. In fact, that seemed quite likely, since it probably came from the Graveyard where no runcible network stood available to transport people instantly from world to world through underspace. There had certainly been more people here and I had strong suspicions about their fate.

Along with the gun I found two extra combined power and aluminium powder clips that inserted into the handle, as well as some more luxury items of food and drink, clothing and another toolbox – this one with the facility to levitate over grav-plates – and a rucksack to replace my adapted one. I shifted all these useful items into the empty room, first ensuring the vent cover in there was intact. I used the toilet in the woman's room, since none of them flushed and I wouldn't be leaving my shit and piss behind me in a vent tube. I ate some of the chocolate and another block of clone food, washed down with mucky water, then slept in a bed for the first time in my life. It took me some while to drift off even though I was bone weary. Lying down to sleep on something soft was so unfamiliar to me.

In that half-sleep before waking I felt the ship slide into U-space again and found myself slipping into weird nightmares of travelling through an infinite vent tube folded back upon itself like a Klein bottle. I woke with a new urgency to make preparations for when the ship arrived at its destination, which could happen at any time. I needed to ascertain the prador plans so I could make an effort to foil them. It would be no good to me arriving at some human colony or installation which was in the process of being obliterated or taken over by them. I ate, drank and filled my pack with the tools that might be useful. I felt a bit of a wrench leaving the laser behind, but I no longer needed it since both toolboxes had contained powerful torches, and the gun at my hip served the other purpose.

Via the dropshaft, I returned to the short length of corridor terminating against a prador corridor with a vent tube running along beside it. A small diamond-head vibro-shear sliced easily through the tube metal and soon I lowered a plate of it to the floor. I ducked inside and shone my new torch in either direction. The vent tube curved out of sight both ways. I chose a direction and climbed in, moving with fast familiarity. At the first turning, I used a luminescent marker to draw an arrow back to where I'd entered and, after a hesitation, added more information: how many vent gratings passed, approximate distances.

The new tube took me past more vents, doglegged right past another opening into a small prador sanctum, then terminated at an original dropshaft leading up and down. I turned round and headed back to the junction, adding another arrow there with a brief note on what I'd found. The sanctum I would return to for water when needed, the shaft I'd take a look at later. My steady exploration brought me back to the start. The main tube lay in a ring with many spurs leading off to various holds, the large maintenance section before the fusion engines, a couple of generator chambers, the ventilation fans and filters, and other essential items of the ship's infrastructure. One spur gave me views through vents with motorized atmosphere-sealable louvres into a hold where prador worked in and around an old Polity shuttle. Another spur revealed a newly installed shuttle bay in which sat a large prador war boat. Guns protruded all over from its thick armour, and on its nose a war dock jutted out that could drill its way through the hull of other ships, or through the tegument of a space station.

During my exploration, I had seen only one sanctum and I guessed who would be in there. I had yet to see where the prador troops were billeted, and still had to think of any way to foil their plans, beyond an attempt at sabotaging the shuttle and the war boat. Prador had been busy around both vessels and any plan I made could not be reliant on the chance they might leave it unattended. I needed something solid. After food, water and a short sleep I set out again. Leaving an empty water container by the vent into the sanctum, which was now, as I had thought, occupied by the small prador in dirty white armour, I moved on to the dropshaft. The climb down brought me to where it connected to another prador vent tube – they were using the shaft as part of the system. Shining my torch along it showed it running to vanishing points in both directions. The ship was a mile long and it would take me hours to explore along here. And I was no further ahead with a plan.

Higher up, the shaft opened into a human corridor, three cabins lying along one side. Human remains lay scattered here, dismembered. It gave me no satisfaction to have my earlier hypothesis proven. The same disarray lay in the cabins, with weapons burns and punctures on the walls. These luxurious cabins had dark ports on their far walls, so obviously sat at the hull with a view into space when permitted. I found another weapon that clearly hadn't helped its owner – a QC laser carbine with extra screw-on energy canisters. With this, I no longer felt any need to return to the case of pulse rifles, and I killed the temptation to search further. I had the necessary stuff now; I just needed that plan.

The corridor terminated against a new prador wall, openings on either side into vent tubes – like the shaft, they were using this corridor as part of the ventilation system. I moved along one of these and finally gazed through a grating at prador, one upon another in zero gravity. Checking further vents revealed more of the same and, after the fourth, I needed to see no more. A large chamber had been carved out in the middle of the ship and the prador were stacked in there like army ants.

As I headed back, I realized the war boat wasn't big enough to take all the soldiers I'd seen. So, how was this attack going to run? I'd already surmised the target could be a large ship, space station or inhabited asteroid or moon. It struck me as likely it was something the inhabitants wouldn't want a ship of this size to go near. The clones and the man-thing were an initial strike force, to be sent over in that small shuttle. Their mission would surely be to disable defences, whereupon the war boat – much faster and more manoeuvrable than the ship itself – could head over. Perhaps this would be to establish a beach head to allow the ship to dock, or perhaps the prador would just cross over through vacuum in their armour. This last point didn't matter. The shuttle and the clones were the key because without them the attack would fail – their presence here presupposed that.

A glance into the shuttle bay showed me prador scattered around in there. Was this because of the clones now present in that place? I saw they were sitting on the floor in one area, eating food blocks and passing round one of those demijohns. Meanwhile, the man-thing sat separately from them, a huge collar around his neck connected to a heavy chain bolted to the floor. Perhaps they didn't trust the technology installed on his body. Perhaps he'd just escaped the same thing when I first saw him. But no, I doubted the prador were there as guards, for they seemed as somnolent as those earlier, while the clones and the man-thing appeared completely under control. Here was as good a place as any for the prador to wait, either entertaining themselves with systems in their armour, sleeping or in a drugged torpor – whatever prador did in such situations. I moved away to take another look at the war boat. I managed to see inside through an open ramp and prador were packed in there too. I headed away, still with no idea what to do.

What was my main aim? I had to get off this ship, away from the prador and back into human society. But if my deductions were correct, the prador were probably about to attack a human installation. I realized I needed to go back to my main aim of escape and work from there. And I knew where I needed to look if I was to have some hope of achieving this limited goal.

Just minutes later I arrived at the corridor leading to the emplacement where I'd found my envirosuit. Such suits were excellent technology and, as the two bodies below had demonstrated, it was possible to survive in airless places in one. However, anyone working out in vacuum, like out on the hull of a ship, would want something more substantial. Radiation would still be a factor, because even though the electromagnetic diverter field of a ship extended some way from its hull, it still let stuff through that was usually dealt with by the metamaterial layers in the hull itself. Exterior maintenance also involved tools like laser cutters, atomic shears and other power tools that could easily hole an envirosuit. No, a heavy suit was needed for that, one with perhaps a monitoring and a doctor system that could save a life or even put someone into emergency suspension.

I stood below the circular airlock and then turned towards the big cabinet. I had thought little of it at the time, being more intent on the door at the end, but now its purpose seemed obvious. I studied the palm lock for the cabinet, found the nearest door edge and ran an atomic shear down it, hearing its thrum increase and feeling it tug a couple of times. I ran the thing along the bottom and the top to be sure, slicing some more locking bars there. A thump against the door and it swung open on hinges. I nodded on seeing the contents and tried not to feel smug. So, I had my spacesuit, and a way off this ship.

Back in my selected cabin, I woke to the sound of rattling and scrabbling and immediately knew it issued from the air vent. I looked up at it, saw it still intact, drank the remainder of my water and started in on one of the food blocks. I felt tired and miserable. I'd worked out an escape off the ship, but it just didn't seem to be enough. However, my subconscious had apparently been chewing the problem over. I needed to go to war.

I sat up and the cabin light came on as it had before – much duller now with the power supply continuing to wane. I had first thought that the prador must have used an electromagnetic weapon of some kind when they attacked this ship. But I was clearly wrong as all the electronic personal items and tools I'd found in these cabins still worked. Their only problem was that they'd been cut off from the main power supply as the prador installed their own infrastructure. They were on battery backup, though, and I'd found the batteries, taking those out of the other cabins too and using them here. The same applied to the weapons emplacement I'd seen above. It was low grav there, as here, and a glimmer of power in the horseshoe console indicated a fading backup.

I walked over and picked up the three batteries I'd taken from the other cabins and studied them. Each was a slab six inches by three and a couple thick. Though called batteries, they were actually packed with hundreds of square metres of layered meta-materials and were a combination of ultra-capacitor and battery. I put them down again and made a selection of tools from the two boxes, putting them in the rucksack. I tossed in a couple of adaptive chargers with universal bayonet plugs and, after a further hesitation, picked up the laser carbine – an awkward item to carry but one I was reluctant to leave behind.

Having got used to moving about in my territory, it now only took minutes to reach the hull corridor leading into the weapons emplacement. I paused at the spacesuit and checked a readout on the back of one heavy gauntlet. The thing had power and a full air supply – no reason why it shouldn't since there had been no drain on it. I entered the area under the dome; the glass there was still black because we were still in U-space. I first took off the covers on the lower part of the console. Nothing there. Next I turned to the panels and before I'd even got started I saw where one of them stood open, revealing a cube ten inches on its side. Obviously the battery backup here needed to be larger than for the cabins. The moment I disconnected the cube the lights died and the grav shortly afterwards. I clipped my torch to a shoulder mount on the envirosuit and pulled on the battery. At first I thought I'd missed some fixings, then it began to move. It had a hell of a lot of inertia which meant it would be unreasonably heavy once I got over gravplates again. I'd have to be very careful. I loaded it in the rucksack, put that on and headed for the door.

Moving a heavy weight in a rucksack in variable grav was no easy task. I also damned my decision to bring the carbine as it kept getting in the way. Every time I halted in zero grav the battery tried to tug me along my course. A sideways pull had me clinging to the rungs of the dropshaft until switching to rungs on the other side, where it shoved me against the wall. By the time I entered the ventilation system, I was sheathed in sweat and my back ached. But I persevered, finally coming to the grating which opened into the prador sanctum, the battery trying to crush me into the floor of the tube. It looked as if no one was home. Quickly undoing the grating bolts, I entered, leaving the carbine behind in the tube. My first job was to charge the battery. Struggling under the weight of it, I rounded a murky pool in the centre and managed to put the battery down, still in the rucksack.

I caught a breather. After studying the row of sockets in the wall, I took out one of the chargers and clipped it on top of the battery. This freed a thin s-con power cable and bayonet plug, and I quickly inserted it. The charger's screen lit up as it automatically adapted to both power source and battery, then a charging bar appeared. I sighed and stepped back, then immediately headed over to the vent to fetch the water container I'd stashed there. Only then did I see an archway, opening into another area which I'd not been able to see from the vent. Damning myself for not taking more precautions in entering here, I drew my pulse gun and walked over. I didn't expect problems, though, since if the prador had been here it would surely have heard me and reacted by now.

I stepped through the arch and froze. The prador was here.

I gaped at the dirty white armoured shape crouching against one wall. The creature seemed an awful lot bigger now it stood right before me; the pulse gun utterly ineffectual against this thing. I started to back out, but halted as I noticed, either side of its visual turret, the rows of units it used to control the clones. A surge of anger ran through me. Then I realized I wasn't seeing the whole picture. The prador hadn't made a move; surely it should have attacked me by now? Perhaps it was asleep? Perhaps it was in some other state of somnolence like those prador packed in the centre space of the ship? Walking quietly, I headed back out and over to the charging battery. I had to keep my nerve. The battery, heavy and difficult to move, needed to be repositioned for a faster escape. Unwinding all of the power cable gave me ten metres of shielded s-con. Thankfully the charger had not been made with a less conductive cable or there would have been much less of it. Trailing the cable, I dragged the rucksack with the battery still inside over to the vent, then heaved the thing up to put it inside, sliding it along so I could get in there quickly. By now the charging bar indicated the thing had reached a quarter charge. But as I turned back I saw them: two stalked eyes coming up out of that murky pool, watching me.

I pointed the pulse gun at the eyes, but for some reason couldn't bring myself to pull the trigger. It must have been this prador's armour I'd seen through the archway. It was the one who had done terrible things and would probably do more in the future. It had sliced open one of my fellow clones and allowed Spatterjay leeches into the tanks of the others. Yet, still I could not fire and my fury of a moment ago waned. It wasn't the knowledge that it would be difficult to kill, having been virally mutated, or that the moment I fired it would probably attack. I felt the same reluctance as I had with the ship louse I'd found feeding on the human corpses: a fellow feeling, empathy, for here was a creature like any, who wanted to live as much as me. The eyes sank away. I decided to leave it be. It might be that I had the knowledge of a distinctly capable Polity agent, but that didn't mean I had either the instinct or the training to be a killer. I would charge the battery and then get away from here just as fast as I could. Still, best to be prepared. I began groping behind me for the carbine, whereupon the creature took the decision out of my hands.

Throwing a wave ahead, it surged out of the water, revealing its heavy mutations. Diseased pink and black in coloration, it seemed fleshy and resembled a giant octopus rather than a creature with a carapace. Even its claws didn't look as if they could shear anything, being more like the claw flesh of a cooked crab extracted from its shell. But it rose up on the edge of the pool and threw itself towards me. So I opened fire.

The pulse gun had little recoil and I managed three shots into its body, below two vertical rows of bony plates that had once been mandibles, before diving aside. It slammed into the wall beside the vent and turned, its bony plates clattering and a wet squeal issuing from deep inside it. I now saw the technology interwoven in its body and the interface plates either side of its head. The control units on its armour plugged into those and at the sight of them my anger resurged. I came up on one knee and fired again, hitting distorted limbs whose jointed sections bowed under its weight. It turned towards me and its visual turret, which I had thought firmly attached, rose up on a ribbed neck and it squealed again. I just kept firing as it came at me, then ran past it to leap over the pool. Its claw hit me in mid-flight and I came down on my shoulder, then rolled upright and continued firing.

My shots were hurting it, but didn't seem to be slowing it down. I glimpsed the gun's readout – twelve shots left. It took the shortest route around the pool after me, which luckily drew it away from the vent hole. I aimed carefully, hitting its head and the array of pink eyes there. It lurched back, then abruptly forwards, into the pool and then out again, sprawling where I had been a moment before. But by then I was back at the vent.

With the gun pointed at it, I kept the trigger pressed, while glancing in the vent, and with my other hand I grabbed the carbine. I had the weapon out just as the mutated prador slammed into me. The slick weight of the thing pinned me, and one of the claws closed around my chest. It wasn't hard, it had no carapace, but it closed tightly and I simply couldn't breathe. I felt something break, probably a rib, as the thing tried to draw me towards its bony plates, which were now moving like the teeth of a chainsaw, yellow drool spattering from them. I triggered the carbine.

A deep thrum came from between us, followed by sizzling and a puff of steam. The creature shuddered and its weight fell off me. In an explosion of rank black smoke, the beam exited its back. It howled, soaking me with saliva and gobbets of green, then rolled away, coming down on its back, legs waving in the air. I crawled free and fired again, sweeping the beam across. Two of its legs came away, but it flipped and began crawling towards the archway. I hit it again and again, punching burning holes through its body. It tried to heave up but something inside it had been pushed past breaking point and organs prolapsed out of a hole in its underside. Clouds of smoke and steam now filled the sanctum as it finally moved through the arch. I followed, slicing off the remaining legs on one side. But still it kept moving until it had reached its armour. It touched one of the armoured claws with its own fleshy one and the armour parted horizontally with a thunk, the top half rising on polished rods. No, I could not allow this. I moved round, burning off one of its claws and then the other. It was almost immobile now, but stretched up with its head, extending its neck as if it might use this to pull itself into its armour. I burned through the neck, sliced off remaining limbs, then began to cut the body in half even as the carbine flashed a warning and its beam died.

I felt sick and wanted to throw up, but my body quelled that. In the steaming remains I saw movement: an exposed organ pulsing, fibrous muscle quivering, the stumps of legs shifting up and down. A pool of liquid had spread out around the thing, but it was clear and contained only a few green jelly gobbets of what presumably was left of its blood. I had chopped it into pieces yet still it seemed to be alive. I remembered then the man-thing the king had torn apart and how that humanoid was now perfectly intact again. He'd been reassembled straight afterwards, however, while this mutated prador remained in pieces. Could it recover from such appalling injuries? I looked down at one disconnected leg from which a fibrous tendril oozed slowly across the floor towards the main body, and knew that it could. I kicked all the legs far away from the body and when I did the same with the head, the bony plates snapped at me. I threw it back into the pool in the other room. Irrational really, since a prador's main ganglion – its brain – resided inside its body. I considered cutting into the thing to destroy that brain, but couldn't bring myself to. I went over to the bayonet plug of the charger, which had been dislodged during the combat, and inserted it back into its socket.

In the same way that my embedded knowledge had told me that normal Polity citizens weren't aware of the Spatterjay mutation of the king and his family, I also understood that normal prador didn't know this either. Those that had come aboard from the other ship had been 'normal', so I concluded it highly unlikely the prador in the dirty white armour would have allowed them access to its sanctum. Even if any of them did break in, they'd be utterly baffled by what they found. Some strange sea creature dismembered in the cabin; perhaps the remains of the resident's last meal? What I didn't know was whether any more of the king's children were aboard, but I needed to act as if that was the case. The prador would be found and then the ship would be searched.

I lugged the battery back up to the weapons emplacement and slotted it back in place. Grav came on fully this time, but to save power I sought out the relevant cables and disconnected them. When my efforts had me floating off the floor, I activated the gecko function in my envirosuit boots and walked round as if on glue. Everything on the console lit and it threw up a holographic screen above it, crosshairs in the middle and options listed down the side. The particle cannon was out – not enough power for that – but the missiles could be launched. A warning appeared at the bottom informing me AUGLINK DISCON. I reached out, putting my finger into the screen, and banished it off to one side. Now it seemed I could select other options.

I chose one, then powered down the console and got out of there.

Back in my hideaway I paced around, thinking hard. If I was lucky, it might be that the dismembered prador wouldn't be discovered until the ship reached its destination, as only then would it be needed to control the clones and the man-thing. I decided I must move. It took three journeys to haul my acquisitions up to the weapons emplacement. I loaded my rucksack with food, tools and water and screwed another energy canister on the carbine. From one of the toolboxes I removed a deposition welder and put it over by the bulkhead door into the dropshaft, but decided not to seal it just yet. Then I waited, and waited, ready to act.

5

Just because I felt ready for the ship to reach its destination didn't mean it would oblige. Eventually returning to the humdrum necessities of my existence, I ate and drank and, after closing and locking the shaft door, slept for a while. Motion sickness later woke me – sleeping in zero gravity wasn't great. I sorted cables and managed to turn on two grav-plates in the corridor, but at very low power, then ventured down to my previous hideaway, grabbed a mattress and heat sheet and installed them on the two plates. But I still felt I had to do more, be as prepared as I could. So I went to check on the spacesuit.

After stripping off my envirosuit, I backed into the cabinet, stepping into the boots and closing the spacesuit up around me. Though bulkier than the previous garment, its motors made it easy to move. As I stepped out of the cabinet the concertinaed helmet folded over my head and a visor slid up to seal against it, its head-up display lighting. Touching the controls on one gauntlet, I searched through the HUD to call up the needed controls. Crosshairs appeared, and the link established to the emplacement on the hull. It worked – the weapons turret would be on the move trying to track where the crosshairs pointed, so I quickly shut it down. I checked other options and familiarized myself with controls that had been common to a previous version of me. Backing into the cabinet again, I opened the suit and stepped out. It was stupid to waste power on such exercises. I didn't really want to lug the battery, which supplied everything around me and charged the suit, back to that sanctum again.

That sanctum . . .

No, I didn't want to go there. Though I feared the discovery of the prador's remains and what would ensue, I was reluctant to have that fear confirmed. Instead, back in my envirosuit with the carbine strapped across my back, I ventured to the tubes of the ventilation system again to look in on the main force of the prador. They had now cleared a space to work in. Racks had been set up to take Gatling cannons which, it appeared, were undergoing maintenance. Behind these, prador stood one on another in a sheer wall rising fifty feet. Since all their visual turrets pointed towards me, I moved slowly back from the grating and out of sight. Did this indicate our imminent arrival at their target?

I headed to the bay containing the war boat. The prador there were now crowded outside it, running through similar checks, and after a while, in dribs and drabs, began to return aboard. The old shuttle next. The smell hit me even as I approached the vent. The clones and the man-thing were still in the same place and, apparently, had been using the floor for their sanitary arrangements. Then something else froze me in place. Two prador stood in the bay studying the clones and neither were wearing the same kind of armour as their fellows. One's was polished chrome with a pattern on it like a purple Rorschach blot, while the other was clad in bright yellow with zebra stripes. So there *were* other members of the Guard aboard; the king's family. This meant others with the same mutation as White-Armour, and who might check on his sanctum at any time if he'd been out of communication for a while. I realized I had to overcome my reluctance and go to check on that sanctum myself.

Hurrying through the system, I came to the relevant grating

and peered inside. Little seemed to have changed so I unbolted it and stepped in, further scanning the interior. My gaze fell upon the laser burns. Any prador coming in here would know there had been a fight. I scrubbed at one with my boot but couldn't erase it. Then I noticed something swimming in the pool. When I walked over and peered in it disappeared into the murk. I'd kicked the creature's head in there, and now contemplated the effects the Spatterjay virus could have on organisms. With its eclectic collection of genomes from many creatures, it mutated its host to optimize its survival. I wasn't aware that it did the same for pieces of said creatures, but this appeared to be the case here. Readying the carbine, I headed cautiously into the nearby room.

The erstwhile prador had consolidated. The main body I'd come close to cutting in half had healed into one large slug-like lump, also producing a head turret either side of which it had sprouted tentacles. I suspected the genome the virus had used to do this must be from a whelk of the Spatterjay world. It had shed most of the tech grafted to its body, which lay in tangles all around, and was currently gripping one of its own severed limbs, feeding on it with the plug-cutting mouth of a Spatterjay leech. It turned its turret head towards me, attempting to focus with two eyes resembling those of the centipede things aboard the King's Ship, then just continued eating. My gaze strayed to a number of empty food cylinders lying on the floor, obviously pulled from a rack behind. Looking back into the main part of the sanctum, I realized it had collected up the severed legs and brought them in here to eat.

I aimed the carbine at it. Its head sank down and it stopped eating, quivering. Something else I remembered about the virus. Those infected by it, and then heavily damaged, turned into mindless animals and this was what shivered before me now.

They could be returned to themselves with correct feeding and antivirals, but the process took some time. Its reaction to my carbine could only be due to some vague memory of pain, surely? I lowered the weapon.

If others of the king's children came here, it would be some time before they got a coherent explanation from it of what had happened. Most likely their first assumption would be that one of the normal prador had come in and, seeing its real form, attacked it. How would this affect their mission? Had I removed their only control of the clones and thus prevented the prador initiating the attack they intended to make? No, control units were merely hardware, and it would just be a matter of another prador using the right coding to take over. I doubted this prador had been allowed to keep that coding secret, this undoubtedly being a mission instigated by the king. I turned away to head back into the ventilation shaft, but I couldn't catch a breath because a clattering alarm sounded and the main door to the sanctum started to open.

The two members of the Guard I had seen earlier down in the shuttle bay came in cautiously, even as I tightened the last bolt on the grating and withdrew my arm. They looked around, clattered and bubbled at each other, then simultaneously a clonk sounded as the tips of the lower jaws on their right-side claws hinged down to expose particle cannons. I had no doubt they were reacting to those laser burns.

One of them walked over to the pool, stabbed a claw in and snared what had once been the head of the sanctum's occupant. It still had its eyes, but had now sprouted flippers which flailed ineffectually. The Guard dropped this back into the pool then followed its fellow into the other room. A short while later they both backed out and one waved a claw at the other, who rapidly departed. The remaining prador perambulated round the sanctum inspecting the laser burns, before returning to the other room. It came out with a container that must have come from some storage I'd missed, but then I'd been rather busy at the time. Setting this down to one side, it returned to the pool, grabbed the head again and with one quick sweep, tossed it into the other room. Squeaking ensued, terminated by a squelchy crunch. The Guard clattered something, and I felt sure whatever had just happened in there had amused it.

Suddenly feeling vulnerable, I moved back from the grating and settled with my back against the wall, the carbine across my lap. The prador also settled down to wait. Perhaps an hour passed before the other one returned, towing a grav-sled piled with equipment. Again there was some exchange between them, and this time I concentrated, picking up a little of it. It had something to do with a 'command program' and 'initiation'. There also seemed to be some debate about allocation of tasks. They finally settled this as they unloaded the equipment. One opened the container and picked out thrall units, obviously taken from the armour in the other room. These it inserted into sockets on the underside of its fellow's armour, who then departed. Did I feel smug that my assumptions had been confirmed? Not really, since so many of my speculations also included the very high likelihood of my ending up dead.

The remaining prador now began to set up a big framework, almost like a gimbal, but with numerous extra struts and all sorts of adjustable clamps and pincers. I had no idea what this could be for until the prador ventured into the other room and dragged the remains of its squealing and honking fellow creature back into the main sanctum. It then forced the thing into the framework and began tightening the clamps and pincers, finally all but immobilizing it. While it looked as if this might be a method of torture, I assumed otherwise. The armoured prador began setting up tanks around the creature and stabbing drip feeds into its body. It also inserted a large tube into its leech mouth, tightening a clamp around it, and next connecting it to a pump and larger tank on the floor. The pump started to propel something into the leech mouth. Of course, the prador was filling his unfortunate brother full of the correct nutrients, perhaps viral inhibitors and other stuff to aid his recovery. As I moved away, I wondered how long it would be before they started hunting me down.

More waiting. I slept four times and made further inroads into my food and drink supplies, venturing to the cabins below for toilet visits and swiftly departing because of the growing stink. On the third journey for this, my world turned inside out and I nearly lost my grip on the rungs in the dropshaft. The ship had just surfaced from U-space. A surge of adrenalin drove me up to the emplacement and through my gecko-stick boots I could feel the rumbling of movement throughout the ship.

The dome had cleared again and now the holographic display showed a truncated system map with possible targets highlighted. In iconic form it showed a sun, numerous asteroids scattered around it, and a large planet orbited by numerous moons close by. Touching the icons brought up explanatory labels. The star was a K-class orange dwarf while the asteroids were, apparently, the remains of a world called Hamlin. The large planet bore the name Trallion and had breathable air, apparently the result of terraforming, as well as manageable gravity. But installations on the surface were sealed because of 'hostile environmental factors', which seemed decidedly vague. I felt it likely to be as much a casualty of the war as the tumbling remains of Hamlin. The Graveyard, stretching across the border between the Polity and the Prador Kingdom, had been the location of much devastation:

worlds had been destroyed or depopulated, fleets annihilated, space stations turned into floating scrap.

It seemed highly unlikely Trallion was the prador target. If they wanted control of it, they could just bombard the installations from orbit and then set up their own. No, it was something else. I touched another icon and read about the station Stratogaster, sitting in orbit of that world. A spinning wheel measuring fifty miles across, its separate spaceship dock extended from a moonlet which was in a matched orbit nearby, and its central docking hub sported a still-operational, massive wartime railgun. Here floated a survivor of the war, and it had to be the prize the prador sought. I expected they wanted to establish a larger base in the Graveyard and, rather than build their own, intended to take one over. I looked up, but could see none of these places yet, just a diffuse orange glow issuing from somewhere out of sight.

The independent kingdom of Stratogaster was a Graveyard trading hub ruled by the Stratogaster Trimor family. I could have read much more about it but was running out of time. The rumbling within the ship had increased and different sounds were now impinging: the thrum of atmosphere pumps, and deep clonks surely the docking clamps disconnecting. Then other sounds issued from nearby. Back in the corridor leading into this emplacement, I headed over to the bulkhead door that opened into the dropshaft, and peered down. Nothing was visible, but I could hear metal-on-metal movement down there. A second later a blast low down momentarily blinded me. The shockwave blew me back, and chunks of hot metal zinged up the shaft, one of them landing on my envirosuit and burning until I knocked it away. It was time to get rid of the thing anyway.

I stripped off and backed into the cabinet again, securing the spacesuit around me, its helmet closing and HUD activating. Exterior audio remained available so I immediately heard the movement in the shaft and stepped over. A familiar shape scrambled up towards me. Either the dismembered prador had managed to communicate my attack on him, or the others had simply surmised an enemy was aboard and, of course, had sent the perfect hound to hunt that one down. The man-thing halted his scramble up the shaft rungs and glared at me, then opened his carnivore mouth to show black teeth in what might have been a grin. I slammed the bulkhead door and locked it, took up the matter deposition welder and began to seal around the edge. I was halfway round when he crashed into it, and I finished the job just as he put a dent in the door with one heavy thump. Maybe it would hold him for long enough.

I grabbed my prepared rucksack, took the carbine too and launched up for the airlock. In a moment I was inside, manually closing its door, as the bulkhead door below bent in at one edge and a clawed hand reached through. As the air drained from the airlock, I only just heard the scrabbling below me before it faded. The man-thing certainly hadn't ceased its efforts, but no air remained to transmit the sound. Opening the outer door, I hauled myself up and stepped out onto the hull of the ship, gecko function engaging automatically, and breathed a sigh of relief – surely the creature couldn't follow me out here.

Now the ship was turning and the whole panorama swept into view. The world of Trallion rose over the metal horizon, swirled green and orange, with continents visible. Something glimmered in my new sky which I assumed to be the Stratogaster station, while the spaceship dock extending from the moonlet lay clearly visible: an immense scaffold of habitations and tunnels scattered with ships of various designs. Also appearing, nosing out from below my perspective, came the old shuttle. It seemed the clones had already been sent without their companion. Everything was happening as expected and now I just had to do my part. I'd agonized over this for some time, but again had to accept that the clones were mindless human blanks – organic robots programmed to kill.

With the HUD activated, the weapons turret beside me stirred as I moved my head, tracking those crosshairs. I simply faced directly towards the departing shuttle and held the crosshairs on it. The display outlined the vehicle and queried ACQUIRE? I hit the relevant section of the touchpad and the outline started to blink. Now, when I turned my head, the crosshairs shifted across my visor, tracking the shuttle, while the turret stabilized, pointing its load of missiles directly at the thing. FIRE? the HUD asked me, and now I hesitated. Again my reluctance to kill held me back until I remembered other details about Stratogaster – its population in the hundreds of thousands – and fired a missile. Beside me, in utter silence, one of the missiles shot away, ignited its burner and accelerated. It struck the shuttle to the rear, the flash darkening my HUD for a second. When my view cleared, I saw that I'd blown a chunk out of the back of the thing, putting out probably half of its fusion drive, while burning debris strewed away from it. I fired again and, to be sure, a third time.

The missiles streaked in. The second struck amidships and ricocheted off, exploding nearby, its blast tilting the thing up to my perspective, just right for the third one to hit it again in the middle, the blast cutting right through and out the other side. As the HUD cleared again, I saw burning human shapes amidst the debris. The shuttle tumbled dead through vacuum, before another part of its hull blew away, this time due to explosive bolts. The prador I'd seen take on the clone control units jetted out, shedding fire from its armour and trying to stabilize with thrusters. I acquired it and fired a fourth missile, clearly having overcome my initial reluctance to kill. The missile struck it in the side. Legs exploded away, steam boiling out into vacuum from a hole in its armour.

The prador had now lost their initial strike force, and those on Stratogaster would be aware of something seriously wrong. But would they realize the real danger? The possibility remained that the prador might manage to explain this event away and still get a force to the station in that war boat, while the other force could launch an assault along a wide front. I targeted Stratogaster itself. Here the risk of killing innocent people dropped me into a world of indecision. It had seemed like a good idea before, when I calculated I could fire on the station and the defences would pick up on the missiles and destroy them before anything happened. Thereafter the station would respond strongly and fire on this ship. I resolved to do it; my previous self, I was sure, would not have hesitated. Still struggling with the idea, I called up details in my HUD of the spacesuit's thruster system, since I planned on being as far away as possible from the ship when the station fired on it. But I'd hesitated too long, and the man-thing suddenly appeared, crashing into me from the side and trapping me against the weapons turret.

His fist slammed into my spacesuit and it threw up damage warnings, but nothing critical yet. Vapour poured from his mouth, his skin was writhing and bubbling and eyes bulging. My fist landed with a satisfying motor-driven impact that blew more vapour from his mouth. One of his eyes burst, while the other bulged even more, then began to shrink again as vapour issued in a stream from its side. If I could only get him away from me it would be the end of him, but his grip on my arm felt solid. I hit him again and again. He bowed down, I thought from the damage, but he grabbed a rung in the hull with his free hand and tried to pull me after him. When that didn't work, he released his hold and struck my other arm with the edge of one clawed hand, attempting to break my hold on the turret. He then gripped the rung again and, following a row of them, started dragging me back to the airlock. Air began jetting from a crack between my gauntlet and sleeve, then sealed as breach sealant mushroomed from it. Subliminally I saw another departure from the ship – the war boat. He continued to drag me, his clawed feet also gripping the rungs, and no matter how hard I struck him I couldn't break his hold. I tried for my carbine, but just couldn't reach it. Stupid to have tied it to my pack, but I hadn't expected to need it out here. Still, there was something I could do. I turned and targeted the war boat, firing four missiles at once. I didn't see where they struck, though, before he reached the airlock and began to pull me inside.

Others were now departing the ship: the swarm of armoured prador. The ship surged, fusion drives igniting a sun glare on its horizon and small explosions cut across the hull towards me. A hit slammed me down, with fire exploding all around me, and I was freed from his grip. I glimpsed the man-thing still clinging to the airlock as I tumbled away through vacuum. FATAL BREACH the HUD told me, while my suit spewed breach sealant from numerous cracks. Pain surged and I wondered if my body had received a fatal breach too. His claw still clung onto my arm, his arm sheared off at the elbow. I pulled it off and discarded it, also banishing the scrolling list of warnings and crosshairs to call up SUIT MANV. Thruster jets at the ankles and waist stilled my tumble relative to the ship, but kept blasting to try and match acceleration. Meanwhile prador drew closer to me, so it wouldn't be long before one of them took another shot. I directed my course back down towards the passing hull. My landing was going to be hard.

As I descended, an icon blinked up in the corner of my visor. Knowledge not my own again surfaced: a com laser was on me. I looked at the icon directly and blinked deliberately, activating the connection. Vacuum glared as, at the same moment, the ship blasted with side thrusters to change course. Fortunately, or perhaps not, this turned it towards me and a moment later I bounced along the hull, my suit thrusters driving me back after each bounce. I was surely becoming one large bruise with shattered bones inside my suit.

'Who are you?' asked a female voice that sounded familiar.

'Jack Four,' I replied, as I finally fetched up against a communications array pylon jutting from the hull. Catching a breath, I noted oxygen was now down to two per cent, my calculated survival time with the leaks being just twelve minutes. I then noticed an unexpected reaction from whoever had spoken to me: she was laughing.

'Was it you who fired those missiles?' she eventually asked, once her hilarity had passed.

'I did.'

I could see a human airlock twenty yards ahead of me, and forced myself into motion. Body screaming, and with boots on spotty gecko function, I began to clump towards it, groaning in pain.

'Are you hurt, Jack Four?'

'Probably,' I managed tightly.

'Well, I guess I owe you at least this: Get yourself away from that ship,' she said.

'I can't. My suit's breached and I have about twelve minutes.'

She said something, but interference mashed it. Armoured prador swarmed above, some flaring out at the terminus of stabs of particle-beam fire, others throwing up hardfield defences. The hull jerked down, snapping away from my boots. Light blazed towards the nose and a giant spray of debris and fire reached out at an angle and spread on lines of smoke. A large chunk of the ship's nose had just disappeared.

'Are you still alive?' the woman enquired, not sounding particularly concerned. I realized the suit com device would have another function and studied my gauntlet touchpad. After a moment I found the cam activation and used it. Her face appeared up in the top right corner of my visor. Recognition hit me at once, while she studied me for a second, biting her lip in mild amusement. I stared at her face dumbfounded, perhaps too overloaded with adrenalin to find any other reaction, but I also felt my hopes of rescue die.

'It was my intention to destroy that ship.' She grinned.

'Oh really,' I replied, first discovering my capacity for sarcasm, then deciding I'd pretend I didn't know her, this being an advantage I might be able to play.

'It tried to get to the space dock but wouldn't have survived the particle weapons there. It certainly wouldn't survive another railgun strike.'

'Uh-huh.' I reached the airlock and operated the manual control. The hinged lid blasted over, ejecting the lock's content of air, and slammed on the hull. I used my suit thrusters to bring me back down to the hull again, feeling as if my shoulder had been dislocated.

'However, it does seem likely that their follow-up strike force will get there – they're more dispersed so harder to target. I've ordered evacuation.'

Strange but nice of her to keep me updated on the current battle, but I was more concerned about other things. 'You *were* going to destroy the ship?'

She had turned away from me, perhaps studying some instrument panel, and replied distractedly, 'Oh they recognized the targeting limitations of my railgun and are running in the only direction available to them. They know they stand little chance of taking this station without first disabling the railgun.'

'And I saved you from that,' I noted.

She turned back to me. 'My shot took out their U-drive and they cannot run out-system. I expected them to take a course to hide behind the planet but, if our vector calculations are correct, they're aiming to land on the surface. Seems a foolish move to me since they must know what's down there.' I noted that she hadn't acknowledged my last comment.

'The planet,' I repeated, as I inserted myself in the airlock.

'The ship may survive re-entry and landing,' she informed me. 'And you may, as well.'

'Well thanks for that.' Sarcasm had its merits.

'But I'd advise you to get away from the crash site as soon as possible.'

I caught her expression and saw how all this amused her.

The hull began splintering in a line towards me. One of the prador had clearly decided to do something about me.

'Why?'

'It will attract unwanted attention. The—'

I cut her off, slamming the airlock hatch just as Gatling slugs punched a line of deep dents across it.

A leak from the upper door of the airlock, caused by the Gatling slugs, meant it was refusing to charge with air, until I smashed my fist into the control panel. Manually opening the lower door, I managed to push hard enough to hinge it down off its seal against the air pressure. Finally enough air had entered, though still escaping above, for me to push it all the way down and go through. Closing it behind, I looked around with no idea where I was.

The airlock had given me access to a human-scale corridor that extended for quite a distance. Items fell through the air towards me and I shifted to one wall to bat them aside. Chunks of engineering tumbled past, tools, numerous photoelectric scales the size of a palm and as black as midnight, and a vacuum-dried human skull. Resting briefly, I felt hopeless. I had come so far and made it to the very place I was ultimately aiming for. The woman communicating to me from the Stratogaster station had been Suzeal. Was her full name Suzeal Stratogaster Trimor? My plan for escaping this ship had been to undermine the prador attack plan and, having abandoned the ship, then – with luck – be picked up by the grateful residents of that station. It just wasn't going to happen now. Even if I did survive out there against the prador soldiers, Suzeal would most likely just laugh while she watched my suit's air run out. And now I was caught on a ship that seemed likely to crash-land on a hostile world.

I chose the direction all the stuff was falling from and began to trudge that way. My suit indicated breathable exterior air, though it contained an unhealthy number of toxins. I felt no inclination to take it off since it offered protection, and the gecko boots. I also wasn't sure I would be able to move about without its motors. I felt raw from head to foot, had a terrible pain in my side below my ribcage, and visions of my undersuit soaked with blood.

A bulkhead door opened into another corridor running diagonally across this one. It terminated to my right against the wall of a prador corridor. On the left, a door stood open to a room with consoles along one wall, and a single acceleration chair running on rails to get to all of them. Inevitably the chair remained occupied with another human corpse – headless this time. I was about to walk in there when a side surge of ship's thrusters threw me in headfirst instead. I bounced off the floor, then came up as acceleration slammed me into the wall above the consoles. I pushed away from it and realized it was transparent – a screen – and I could see into a large open area. I hurriedly pushed away and down beside the consoles, peering over them into an engineering section.

A ceiling braced by webs of scaffold speared across above the screen. Down below, a gantry, almost hidden by pipes and power feeds, ran along behind a row of high-pressure water tanks, beyond which then lay massive injector assemblies. I appeared to be in some sort of control room for the fusion engines. However, the prador down below had set up their own saddle controls and other means of accessing the drive while everything in here was dead. I thought the gantry must have grav until one of them propelled himself from it and rose up, then with the stab of a thruster settled on one of the tanks. Dropping lower, I pulled myself along to the chair, reached up to undo a safety harness, pulled the corpse down with me and towed it along – envirosuits seemed to have been standard dress aboard this ship.

Past the end of the screen, another bulkhead door stood open. A further short stretch of corridor terminated against the outside wall of another prador addition. I opened the only door here, just as another deceleration threw me against the wall beside it. Something crashed to my right. Pulling against the edge of the door, I peered round to see that the screen – one sheet of tough chain-glass – had been knocked into the space behind, with the prador lodged there and scrabbling to pull itself out again. I pushed on into the cabin and left the door open, hoping it hadn't seen me, and painfully slowly unstrapped the carbine from my back. The scrabbling sounds continued until, a moment later when I peered out again, the prador made it back into the engineering area.

The headless corpse had now settled against one wall. I searched the cabin, glad to find a new envirosuit rather than having to don grave garments. After a long struggle, I managed to get out of the spacesuit, parts of it falling to pieces even as I removed them. Some spots of blood had soaked into my under-garment here and there but on inspection I saw they were from old wounds probably aggravated by limited areas of decompression. Breach sealant had also stuck to the garment in clumps so I abandoned it and hunted down another. Amazingly I could find no broken bones but I did see plenty of red tender areas that would probably bruise. Finally dressed in the envirosuit, I opened my pack. No water remained in the single container I had left – the fight had popped off the lid, while the food blocks had developed a hard vacuum-dried crust. I wasn't hungry anyway. Another surge flipped me across the cabin, so I pulled down on the bed and found straps to secure me there. And the manoeuvres continued.

A steady roar grew and grew, transforming into a vibration and then a violent shuddering. We had entered atmosphere, I was sure of it. Had the railgun shot disabled the grav-engines? It seemed so, as the shuddering threw me again and again against the straps. The noise increased to painful levels and I managed to close up the hood and visor of the suit, which filtered it a little. Great jolts then ensued and a crack snaked along the ceiling of the cabin. The whole room fell with a crash and I saw it had torn away from the corridor outside. Fire wafted across out there, then dispersed into webs, while smoke boiled up from below. Another jolt threw the cabin up, then it crashed down again. I closed my eyes and just hoped to live. And then, finally, it was over.

I unstrapped to the sound of things collapsing, booming, and settling with deep ominous creaks. Gravity had returned at an angle to the floor and I knew it wasn't from any floor plates. It seemed to have more substance, though that could have been because it was half above terran standard, as the readout on the world of Trallion had told me. I'd been used to a quarter above – that being the grav prador preferred. It emphasized all my aches and pains and seemed to be trying to drag my organs out of my body. I slid to the door and peered down a hundred feet into the tangled infrastructure of the ship, before hauling myself up into the corridor. This too had become a slope and I manually set gecko function on my boots to get up it. Beyond the tilted screen, the area behind the engines was gone. The water tanks were now close enough to touch, buried amidst tangled beams, pipes and warped sheets of bubble-metal. There was no sign of the prador. They were certainly buried in that mess but, in their armour, probably unhurt, despite the glares of fires I could see.

The next human corridor, leading to the airlock where I had entered, had snapped off. I peered over the end which swayed in mid-air above a drop of fifty feet down to canted gratings. A skein of optics still connected across the gap to the other part of the corridor. I tugged on it a few times to ensure it wouldn't break, but wondered if I had the strength to cross. I had to. Body screaming, I pulled myself up, got my legs around it and slowly shuttled to the next section of corridor. Dropping to the floor there, I rested for a second, then opened my hood and visor to throw up. What came out had blood in it, which didn't bode well. I noticed a smell of burning and all sorts of other complex odours. There was nothing I could identify because, though I possessed the knowledge of another human being, very little of it seemed to include what things smelled of. Then, belatedly, the flashing migraine lights returned. I smelled something like burning vegetation, but not quite the same, then complex odorants, perfumes and esters – the constituents of life but with a twist that made them, of course, alien.

The airlock, surprisingly undamaged, let me out onto the hull. I felt suddenly buoyant and light-headed and realized the air must have high oxygen content. A great plain of metal sloped down towards fires which were worming through a black tangle, streaked with purple and green and shots of eye-aching red. Here the front of the ship had mounded up plant growth and earth. All around hung a fog of smoke and steam, through which embers and other bits tumbled. I headed across this slope, finally reaching the edge. A breeze now picked up as if the world around me had decided to assert itself once again. The smoke cleared, revealing purple and green jungle, fading to red umber in the distance, where mountains humped up like giant hippos wading through the foliage. The sky was yellow while the sun, dropping down behind those mountains, glared orange. I walked along the edge of the ship. Fires burned below but not as many as to the fore. I hoped for a ladder but it seemed this vessel had never been made for planetary landing. However, the ship had snapped nearly in two and the break offered a way down.

Beam tangles and skeins of optics took me part of the way to the ground, a slope of hardened crash foam crunched underfoot for a few hundred yards, then an edge of hull offered a path just a foot wide. Finally I came to a point where I could use the ship no more, but directly opposite me thick branches of dark wood jutted out and were scattered with globular blue objects. I stared at them because they made no sense. Focusing on my second-hand knowledge of biology, I then recognized a banyan of a world called Circe. Why was this tree here on this alien world? I jumped, landing on a thick limb, and dropped along it as pain shot down my side. A long crawl brought me to the crown of the tree, then I climbed down using the crevices of its interwoven trunk. And finally I stood on the earth of this alien world.

6

Remembering that Suzeal had advised me to move away from the ship as soon as it crashed, I did so, even though her general amusement at my situation hadn't indicated concern for my safety. My enviroboots immediately sank into the soft earth of the planet and I only thought to turn off their gecko function after they'd quickly caked with organic debris. To my right, fire silhouetted banyan trunks and every now and again smoke set me coughing, and that hurt. I closed up the hood and visor and small suit fans cleared it, then began to bring the internal temperature down. This would last for some time since the power supply ran through the fabric, constantly topped up by movement, temperature gradients and light.

After an hour of this I paused to rest, then wondered again if I was doing the right thing. Suzeal had told me to get away from the ship because it would attract unwanted attention but back there I could find food and water. Was I just playing into the hands of someone I couldn't trust to have my best interests in mind? Then I remembered something. From a low branch I plucked one of the blue globes, which were in fact leaves, not fruits, opened my visor and bit into it. The things had all the wrong sugars in them and provided little nutrition, but they did provide fluid. I ate a number of them then began to move on. Rounding the banyan trunk from which the branch hung, I halted abruptly at the sight before me.

Just for a second I thought I had somehow walked a circular course and come back to the ship's hull, but this hull was moving, and it had legs. A great mass, like a living monorail train, slid past. The portion moving past me looked like the spine of a giant, fashioned from heliotrope, being mainly green but red where each of the 'vertebrae' connected. Heavy insect legs protruded with flat feet terminating in hooks. This was a creature similar to the centipede things in the prador ventilation systems, but writ huge. My mind provided recognition and detail, and a moment later it provided fear. I ducked out of sight behind the tree trunk and tried to disappear inside it. The creature crashing through the jungle just yards from me was a Masadan hooder. I had no doubt of that, even though the colour was wrong. Towards its fore, it had a spoon-shaped head cupped to the ground in which its main eyes and incredibly complicated feeding apparatus resided, though the thing had sensors all down its body. Its main prey animal possessed black fats that released poison into its flesh upon its death, so the hooder dismembered the prey while it was still alive, preserving its life till it ate the last morsel. It also tended to use the same feeding technique on anything else it caught and, given the opportunity, that could be a human being. Death would be a protracted, agonizing affair.

I unshouldered my carbine and gazed at the useless thing as I realized I knew a lot more about hooders than most people. They were not naturally evolved creatures or, at least, in their present form they weren't. Masada had been the home world of the Atheter – one of the three ancient alien races the Polity had identified, whose *deliberately* devolved descendants – gabbleducks – lived on that world too. Hooders had been biomech war machines the Atheter had made – themselves devolved naturally over a couple of million years. These incredibly tough creatures were impervious to most energy weapons and projectiles.

Obviously, their ruggedness extended to environmental changes, since Masada was a world devoid of oxygen. Perhaps the atmosphere here accounted for their colour change? Irrelevant really. I now understood exactly what 'hostile environmental factors' meant, and why no colony had been established down here. I also understood Suzeal's little internal chuckle. She had no expectation I'd be able to survive either inside or outside the ship.

I looked up at the banyan, then turned to peer deeper into the jungle. Another tree stood nearby with plenty of side branches, and it reared much taller than others around it. I waited until the sounds of nearby movement drew away, then headed over, keeping a sharp eye on my surroundings.

The tree's side branches stuck out perfectly level, as if trimmed by an expert in bonsai. I reached for the lowest branch at head height with trepidation, then tensed and hauled myself up. My body screeched at me and I felt something pop in my chest. Once up on the branch, I moved in and leaned against the trunk, fighting the urge to cough and scared of what might detect it. A brief and quiet clearing of my throat only made the urge to cough even stronger. I clamped down on it, closed my visor and climbed as though ascending a ladder, so close and evenly spaced were the branches. As I got higher I could hear crashes and bangs and a sound like giant rasps being dragged over tin. Nearer the top, the branches were thinner and now their foliage lay close by. I paused and recognized the leaves of a genfactored tea oak grown on many worlds. Perhaps it was left over from a previous colony on this world.

Soon I had sight of the ship and realized I hadn't got far from it – perhaps half a mile at most. For a second I thought tree branches lay over it, until I saw them moving, and one tearing up a chunk of hull metal, then flowing inside. Hooders were crawling all over the ship, while the bangs and crashes I could hear issued from inside. Then I also heard the fast machine sound of a Gatling cannon firing and, in a storm of metal splinters, one of the creatures peeled off the hull and tumbled down into the jungle. A particle beam stabbed in, hitting another in the middle and it reared up like a snake prodded with a stick. The prador, five that I could see, rose up through a pall of smoke, their grav-rafts rising alongside them loaded with their supplies. They'd obviously decided their smaller weapons weren't enough, and missile streaks cut in from them, raising multiple explosions on the hull. The blasts knocked all the hooders back down into the jungle, but I only saw one of them substantially damaged – two missiles hitting it in the same place and cutting it in half. The prador moved in around a clear section of hull and continued firing down into the jungle. One of them swept onto the hull with a grav-raft slaved behind it. The creature was small, and its flight appeared erratic. I pulled closer to the trunk. It seemed my would-be nemesis had made enough of a recovery to be reinserted in his dirty white armour.

Shortly after the raft settled, a hatch swung open in the hull and figures scrambled out. Human figures. I wished I had binoculars because I felt sure their skin had a bluish hue. Hadn't I actually killed the clones? In perfect recall I saw the bodies tumbling through vacuum and knew I had destroyed the force given the task of the initial assault on Stratogaster. But it seemed that hadn't included all of them. The figures clambered onto the raft. Perhaps White-Armour didn't want to abandon his work. With all aboard, the raft rose into the air just as the first of the hooders came up over the edge through a storm of fire. The prador rose too. I had seen enough and needed to get away from here just as fast as I could. But as I began to descend, the tree above me disappeared in an explosion of splinters under Gatling fire.

I fell from my branch and landed stomach down on one below it and hung on there, groaning in pain, as part of the jungle down to my right also fragmented. Looking up, I could see the prador in dirty white armour heading unevenly towards me, but fast. Adrenalin surged now, and the pain disappeared. I scrambled down to another branch as a white streak cut across my vision. The missile struck below, the blast wave lifting me up as the tree tottered and then started to go over. It crashed down in a tangle of branches and vines, one of its branches pinning my leg to the ground. However, my view of the approaching prador remained unimpaired. It drew close enough that surely it couldn't miss, until a hooder suddenly rose up out of the jungle, its cowl striking the prador like a racket and sending it tumbling. Another emerged, and then another, trying to reach the prador, but the Guard I had seen in its sanctum swept in and snared it, fired up thrusters and pulled it away. I started to scrabble at the earth underneath my leg, but further missiles rained down, blowing the jungle all around me to shreds and hurling one of the hooders up into the air. I buried my head under my arms until it ended.

I was alive, unbelievably alive. I reckoned the white-armoured prador had emptied out its missile supply in my direction while its fellow dragged it away. Perhaps that fellow had thought his behaviour irrational and perhaps, in the circumstances, it was. All around me jungle lay smoking and boughs splintered. A couple of fires had started and began sweeping across with choking smoke. I started to cough, but found it easy to stop when something big shifted through the smoke nearby. Having finally freed my leg, I looked back at the ship, now visible from ground level, and began to move away from it, crawling at first, then standing and walking. Pure dumb luck stayed with me.

★   ★   ★

Utterly focused on my surroundings, I was ready to dive into hiding at the slightest sign of movement. I walked beyond the smoke, the sounds of the hooders' steady destruction of the ship receding behind me. The banyan trees became smaller and then an even band of tea oaks displaced them. I suspected them to be the remains of a planted grove. As I walked, my suit started buzzing at me intermittently from inside the helmet, but I assumed this was from some damage it had received and ignored it. When it eventually stopped, I found myself on a downslope, the plant life around me changing to something damper and greener including cycads, ferns and giant rhubarbs interspersed with oily patches of bubble grass. I noted how nothing around me was unknown to my earlier self, even though I hadn't read all the detail on this world. Had it been terraformed and planted with flora found all across the Polity?

As I speculated on all this, my diving-for-cover strategy was tested by movement up in the branches of a tree I was approaching. I threw myself to one side and crawled behind a cycad, peeking out after a moment. The oddly shaped tree had a trunk like a pear, and branches decorated with blue foliage spread like those of a baobab. From these hung brown snake-like objects which I'd been sure I'd seen moving. Then I recognized them: Spatterjay leeches.

'Oh great,' I muttered.

The tree was the pear trunk of that world. Some symbiosis meant that when any creature wandered beneath it, the tree shook its branches to drop leeches on it. I wasn't sure of the biology behind that. So, it seemed I not only had hooders to contend with but Spatterjay leeches, which could grow big enough, on land, to take a large chunk out of me, even leave me in two halves. I then reassessed. The big leeches weren't exactly speedy. Most likely, with so many hooders about, the leeches only grew until they wouldn't be ignored as prey. I stood, circumvented the tree, and kept a wary eye out for any more of its kind. But with my envirosuit closed I felt safe enough from the creatures, even if they were in other trees, for I doubted their mouthparts could penetrate the tough material.

The slope grew steeper and the vegetation changed further. Now tall grasses and reeds speared up between rocks cloaked in mosses and lichens. Still the life forms remained familiar to me, or rather, to my earlier self. Then a sound filtered through that I first equated to spigots in a prador sanctum but soon turned out to be a stream running between rocks. I went down to the edge and peered into the water at small diamond-shaped rays. I half expected to see leeches attached to them since on Spatterjay the leeches had filled just about every ecological niche, but they were clean. I sat there in silence for a moment, until the damned buzzing started again. I lowered my visor and collapsed the hood back into the neck ring, which dulled the sound, and squatted by the flowing water. It was much cooler here than up by the ship. Did I dare to drink? Despite the banyan 'leaves' I'd eaten earlier, I was incredibly thirsty. I decided to test my luck further, cupped some water in my hands and drank. It was wonderful. I took my pack off and got the water container out, rinsed it, filled it and drank my fill from that before filling it again and capping it. All this liquid around me then had its effect on my bladder, which I emptied, noting the blood in my urine – just one more thing to add to the list of potentially fatal hazards.

Trudging along the course of the stream, I began to feel horribly weary. The sun stood high above but that made no difference. I'd never in my life thus far been governed by day and night. A flat boulder overhanging a small beach made of miniature snail shells seemed a good spot. I closed up my hood and visor for extra protection, curled up there with my head on my pack, and sleep came down on me like the darkness of a hooder's spoon-shaped head.

I woke panicked by the buzzing in my suit again, not knowing where I was or remembering much at all. The sun lay out of sight, but darkness had yet to fall. I quickly collapsed the hood and opened the visor to kill the intrusive sound. Food and water first, then I stripped out of my envirosuit and cleaned it in the stream, scouring away old blood and dirt with handfuls of the miniature snail shells. With the suit cleaned and laid out to dry, I took a further risk and entered the water to wash myself. Plenty of bruises showed on my limbs now, and my torso from neck to waist was just one large bruise. The crusty scab over the laser burn grew soggy and peeled away to reveal clean scar tissue, however, and I considered that one small victory. My ribs still ached abominably but, despite my earlier coughing, I'd produced no blood so hadn't punctured my lung. And that was a victory too. Other aches and pains were also evident, but then I had been vigorously active on a world with gravity higher than I was accustomed to.

Once I'd dressed again, I headed out. The sun, as far as I could judge, lay behind me whereas when I had set out from the ship it lay ahead, so I assumed I was going in the right direction: away from the ship. Where that would take me I had no concern beyond it being away from the hooders. How long, I wondered, before the local hooders lost interest in that vehicle and spread out again, or had they already done so? Keeping a wary eye on my surroundings, I climbed the slope on the other side of the stream into a patch of stunted banyan. Then I found myself amongst briars, regularly punctuated by shoots like asparagus standing taller than me, and large patches of giant rhubarb with leaves ten feet across. As I walked on, all of these grew increasingly sparse, displaced by purple and red grasses. Then I came upon the skeleton.

The thing had vertebrae that were solid lumps of its version of bone, green and whorled like old wood. Their solidity told me no spinal cord had run through it. Its ribs were of a double diagonal arrangement, like a trellis, and what looked like organic rivets had held them together. The skull, mostly jaws and teeth, had sockets for six eyes – two large ones at the centre and smaller ones either side. Its claws looked as if they could slice through metal. I had no idea what it was, perhaps a siluroyne from Masada, or a trigon from Parsis, but I guessed it had not eaten vegetables. It had also clearly been no match for the thing that'd killed it, scouring its bones and leaving them laid out like something you might find on an archaeologist's table. I stood over what would become of me if I fell victim to a hooder.

'Well at least it's neat,' I said out loud.

The buzzing intruded again, even though I hadn't put up my hood or visor. Suddenly intensely irritated by the sound, I sat by the skeleton, found the clips that detached the collar with integral hood and visor, and took the thing off. A first visual inspection revealed nothing, but when I opened up the hood and looked inside I saw the even arrangements like a weave in the fabric, and two flat circles of metallic material at about the level of the ears. So that's what it was. Quickly snapping the thing back into place on my suit and closing it up, I said, 'Allow comlink – visual.'

'Ah, so you're alive,' said Suzeal after a short delay.

'Thus far.' I tried to be casual.

'You surprise me, but then perhaps you inherited certain characteristics,' she replied – again after a delay. 'The prador put their ship down in the most infested part of the planet. I counted at least twenty hooders on the thing.'

'You did warn me to get away from the ship . . .'

'Yes, because the hooders generally don't range out from the area they occupy – something about the cyanide compounds throughout that jungle helps them survive the high atmospheric oxygen. I didn't expect the ship to land right in the middle of that lot.'

It didn't escape my notice that I could take her reply in two ways: she wanted me away from the ship because hooders would be drawn to attack it, or she wanted me away from the ship where I'd be more vulnerable to an attack from them.

'I'm surprised to find such creatures here,' I said, suppressing my urge to reveal that I knew her name, that I remembered her exactly.

'He didn't expect even half of the creatures to survive when he put them down there. The prador had obliterated the colony with crust busters and the dust in the atmosphere shoved it into a brief Ice Age. But he had no choice – Polity forces shifted his station here and wanted it as a weapons platform and repair depot, while the prador were on their way back.'

'I'm sorry. Who is "he" and why did he keep hooders?'

'Oh I see.' After a long pause she explained, 'My great-great-grandfather Eric Stratogaster built this station to house his collection of creatures. They were taken from many worlds, usually the nastier kind, and this station was once called Stratogaster's Zoo. Anyway, he would have had to dump them out at some point. The armoured containment was losing against the hooders in their section, while the droons were steadily acid-burning their way out of theirs.' This, apparently, wasn't quite enough, because she continued, 'Sleers were in the air ducts too, mud snakes in the ground of the human park and a siluroyne sometimes preyed on occasional visitors.'

Finally information I'd learned earlier dropped into place.

The soldiers she surrounded herself with were the SGZ and their decals read 'Strato-GZ'.

'So your name is Stratogaster?' I asked.

'Well, I've confirmed that for you, and of course you know my first name,' she replied. So my attempt at ignorance hadn't fooled her.

I felt suddenly tired. 'Can you get me off this world?'

She smiled. 'Whatever makes you think I would want to do that, Jack Four?'

'Because I prevented the attack on your station.'

'Ah, but Jack, I knew about the quantum storage of your mind in the initial sample – I ensured everything I found was there. I knew you'd re-emerge into the hell of experimentation aboard the King's Ship. It amused me, and I found it satisfying that you would experience such a horrific death. But I must admit I didn't expect to see you again after I put you there.'

'I am not who you think I am,' I stated. 'I understand that the knowledge I have is unusual, possibly arising from a Polity agent of some kind, but all I have is his knowledge. I don't have his memories, I don't have his complete mind.'

She appeared unsettled by this, then said, 'And I'm to believe this after all you've done?'

I considered my reply for a long moment. 'Would the person whose corpse you took my genome from have prevented the prador from disabling your railgun?'

She stared at me, then repeated, 'Corpse.'

My mind leapt on that. I'd made an assumption which might not be true. Perhaps the original, Jack Zero, wasn't dead. But also, in making that assumption, I'd gone some way towards proving I wasn't a pure copy of him because, surely, I would have remembered dying.

'Very well, I accept that you might not be the Jack I knew, though it appears you operate with the same . . . flare.'

'I want to survive,' I replied. 'I have no memory of this past "Jack" nor any inclination to pursue his goals. I just have knowledge. Perhaps that knowledge could be useful to you . . .'

Her silence was telling, but finally she said, 'We have a problem here.'

'Please elaborate.' I wanted to laugh at her problem.

'The prador are dug in at the space dock and have set up railguns there, though admittedly of low power. We've managed to stop everything thus far and are preparing to make an assault, but otherwise nothing is flying – they took out every vessel that tried to depart.'

I now understood the short delay to her replies – she was still aboard the Stratogaster station and there was a transmission delay from there.

'I'll get to you as soon as I can,' she added.

I couldn't quite fathom the look on her face, perhaps wistful, perhaps annoyed.

'You may be too late.'

'Maybe . . . Look, night is falling where you are so I suggest you hide up somewhere till morning. Then head towards the sunrise. That'll take you up into the mountains where it's a bit safer. Keep going. If I don't get to you, you'll eventually reach one of our installations down there. I'll give you the code to get inside.'

'Right.' In the time we'd spent talking the sun must have dropped over the horizon and a hot red twilight ensued. 'How far is this place?'

'About four hundred miles.'

'Right.'

'I'll speak to you again tomorrow. Busy up here.'

A click signalled the end of the exchange. I nodded. Good, it seemed she was coming and, if I survived, this would take me one step closer to carrying through the promise I'd first made to myself aboard the King's Ship. Suzeal would pay for what she had done to me and my fellow clones, and I'd stop her horrific trade. Even as I thought this, I wondered if what I'd told her was entirely true. Perhaps I did now possess more than I thought of my original self.

Ahead of me, where the ground was more open, boulders were scattered here and there. They offered the only cover, however. Turning round, I retraced my course until I found another boulder drowned under thick briars. I crawled deep inside and made a nest, curled up and hoped I wouldn't be an even arrangement of bones on the ground come morning.

During the night a hooder came past my hideaway then turned and came back close on the other side. I remembered then that the sensors down the sides of their bodies detected complex molecules in the air, vibrations and infrared. I hurriedly sought out the controls for my suit's cooling system and shut it down, since it radiated excess heat through wires in the outer layer of the fabric, and lay there still and sweating. After a time, with no movement detected, I opened the visor and closed down the hood, imagining steam jetting out from inside the collar. This seemed to exasperate something else big out in the darkness, because it huffed cavernously. I held up my carbine in readiness but nothing happened.

Sleep came eventually, intermittently, broken by surges of panic. The possibility that I was developing an anxiety disorder was not unreasonable. Later on something whickered nearby and came closer with a sound like sandpaper over rocks. I hoped it was just passing by, but then it started to rip at the brambles. I pointed the carbine again and took out my torch, hoping to light a clear target. When I flashed the beam on, it revealed an utter horror. A thing like a giant scorpion, but with a long spike of a tail, mandibles like pickaxes and other eating cutlery such as jointed saws, was tearing its way towards me. It froze and whickered again, focused on the light with three compound eyes, then began pulling at the brambles more eagerly. I was about to fire when, with a sound like someone hawking up a gallon of phlegm, a sheet of white slewed out of the night and hit the creature. The sheet – a great mass of mucus – engulfed the thing and it froze again. Steam began to rise off it, with the mucus bubbling. The creature emitted a high hissing squeal and, when it turned, demonstrated a physiology that wasn't remotely terran. Its segments revolved independently to tumble it back out of the brambles. Something large and high up huffed as if in boredom and I only glimpsed the massive two-fingered claw that snatched the smaller creature away because by then I'd thought to turn off my torch. The hissing retreated and died. All movement stopped for a while and I smelled burned chicken. A short while later, I heard a sound as of someone huge sucking the dregs from a plastic cup with a straw. I closed my hood and visor and decided to bear the heat.

Morning twilight, red as blood, saw me awake and carefully crawling out of my hideaway. I scanned all around for movement, then began trudging towards the open ground. I soon found the remains of the creature from the night before, recognizable only by its pickaxe mandibles and some scraps of carapace. I moved out past the giant asparagus, then stopped under the shade of oversized rhubarb leaves to survey the terrain ahead. A plain now stretched for as far as I could see, scattered with occasional boulders. I waited and watched, feeling that with night being the most dangerous time, I would set out across there the moment

I saw the sun. I sat down with my back against a thick fibrous stem, collapsed my hood and closed down my visor, then turned on the suit's cooling system. Opening my pack, I took out one of two remaining food blocks and the water. I'd finished the block when a diamond ignited on the lip of the world and began to etch out a chunk of it. There lay the sun, and beyond those mountains the installation where I would be safe, supposedly. I packed my things, shouldered the pack, and held the carbine across my stomach. The hooder chose that moment to begin nosing into view from the jungle. It froze, raised its spoon-shaped head and swung towards me.

I ran, well aware that I had no chance of getting away from the thing. I'd reach one of those boulders and just try to use it for cover. Shoot the hooder. Even as this plan formed, a dry and cold part of me noted that I didn't have a missile launcher and the carbine could be put to a better use. No, I would not accept that. The dry narrator informed me that I would, once that hood began to come down on me. Yes, I admitted, but only then would I put the carbine under my chin and pull the trigger.

I reached a small boulder and stopped to catch a breath, glancing back. The hooder seemed hesitant and, having reached the stand of rhubarb, it advanced no further. Perhaps I could deter it? I aimed the carbine carefully at the hooded head presently hovering about five feet up, level with the ground, and fired. The beam stabbed across and struck its nose, splashing there. When I took my finger off the trigger I could see no damage to it, merely a fading hot spot. I'd really done the wrong thing, though. It suddenly reared, raising its spoon head fifty feet above the ground, and I could now get a good look at the underside. Comparisons arose. It had the appearance of a horseshoe crab, though there were tentacles there too, and two vertical rows of glinting red eyes. In eerie silence it came down again and began heading towards me, smooth as a swimming eel. I turned and ran, heading towards a larger boulder.

But that boulder began to rise into the air, the ground erupting all around it. Earth fell away, revealing a primary thorax with four limbs held close against it. I saw that what I had first taken to be a boulder bore the shape of a ziggurat. It was a head and when it opened the two distance eyes on its top tier, the earlier version of me found recognition.

A droon.

It rose up out of the ground on the four legs extending from its secondary thorax, reached up with one two-fingered hand to brush caked earth from the underside of its head, then opened its orange mouth just below the upper eyes, as if smiling. I halted, no idea how I could survive the hooder, let alone this monster.

It came clear of the earth now, lashing a long jointed tail behind, rising further than its previous thirty feet as if taking in a huge breath, mouths opening in every ridge of its head, which stretched and extended higher and higher. I dodged left, running for another boulder. I saw the monster track my course, before I nearly fell over a rock and so concentrated on where I was going. I heard the cavernous huff then a moment later the sound of it hawking up its acid phlegm. Perhaps my envirosuit would be resistant? I thought not: the enzymatic acid spat by a droon could eat through ceramal battle armour. I dived and rolled, then rolled again behind the rock, just in time to see its spit hurtle through the air, stretching out as it did so. But then it splashed on the hooder, just behind its head. The hooder flinched, its back humping up, then shook itself with a hard snapping sound. Some of the mucus flew away but most stayed in place, spreading out like an amoeba to engulf a whole segment of the creature as it began writhing with steam rising from it. Its struggles flung a boulder weighing tons into the air and it inadvertently struck it

121

on the way down again, shattering the thing. Its body scythed through the giant rhubarb, bringing the lot down. I gaped. It just didn't seem possible something so large could move so fast and violently. Then I returned my attention to the droon.

The monster now stood completely clear of the hole in which it had concealed itself. Its strange head swung towards me and rose, then pumped up and down like a bellows, emitting a sound like a faulty piston engine starting up. Impacts threw grit in the air in a line towards my rock and I ducked out of sight. One struck the rock and two more hit beyond it, the first just a few feet away from me. The splash there bubbled and turned black as it etched its way into the ground. I risked another look. Its tail thrashing, the droon had begun to advance on the hooder which, meanwhile, seemed to be coming apart at the point the acid had struck – sheets of carapace bubbling up and peeling. I considered my position for half a minute. It seemed the droon's attempt at me had been half-hearted and more of a dismissal than anything else. I rounded the rock, keeping well away from the acid, and ran away from the scene as fast as I could.

With my body aching and breath coming hard, I looked back. The droon and the hooder were a mile or more away now and still fighting in a chaotic tangle, a cloud of dust spreading around them. Even at this distance I knew I hadn't found safety, for both creatures could move fast and range far. But I took a drink and reduced my pace to a jog because I simply couldn't keep running at full pelt. I felt grateful then to my earlier self for being the source of my body. It had taken a great deal of punishment yet still kept going.

It soon became evident that the wasteland must be the droon's hunting ground, for I saw other remains of the thing that had visited me in the night scattered around. They were clearly not as uncommon as I would've liked. Piles of half-dissolved bones marked the site of one mass killing. The bones were pearly grey and flat like blades, ribcages interlocking like segmented carapace, while the skulls were small strange things with far too many holes. The remains of a smaller droon – mummified and untouched by acid – elicited further buried knowledge in my mind: droons were highly territorial and fought off interlopers of their own kind too. It seemed that for a while I would be safe from other droons, though not their prey which, apparently, included hooders.

Some while later I slowed to a walk. Looking back, I could no longer see the two combatants. I speculated on which I'd prefer to be the winner, that being dependent on how I preferred to die: slowly dissected in darkness or dissolved in acid. I hoped the droon had won because it looked slower than a hooder, but I also hoped it had been injured by its prey. Ahead, a band of vegetation stretched before the mountains and I wondered what horrors might await me there. Movement, just in front of this, had me ducking behind a boulder. Buzzing started from my collar again and I cursed it, then decided to allow the comlink.

'I'm trying to decide whether or not you are highly capable or unreasonably lucky,' said Suzeal.

'You can see me?'

'Oh yes. I have satellites all around that world. It has all been highly entertaining for us up here. I expected the sleer to drag you out of those brambles. Did you know the droon was there?'

Of course, if she had satellites they would likely be able to detect all sorts of radiations, so night wouldn't conceal me.

'Why do you ask?'

'Well, if you knew it was, you made a clever move in firing on the hooder to draw it over the territorial line. If you didn't, firing on the hooder was a dumb move.'

I could now see a herd of creatures moving out from the tree line, inevitably directly towards me. If I broke from cover they would spot me. If I stayed put they might not, depending on how close they came to the boulder. Then again, my thinking was just a bit too prosaic. They might not have eyes, but might be able to detect my breath in the air, or sense my heart beat.

'So what's happening up there?' I whispered, also aware of just how good many creatures' hearing was.

'The assault is under way. We managed to destroy their rail-guns with missile strikes but they're still dug in and heavily armed. The assault force is preparing now, but we'll send a test ship first to see if we missed any railguns.'

'Then you'll come and get me?'

'Oh, I don't know. I may yet leave you there just for the entertainment value.' She added, 'And you didn't answer my question.'

'I didn't know the droon was there,' I replied.

'Well now, that could mean you've been telling the truth because your other self would not have been so stupid. Then again, your other self would also have been smart enough to lie about it.'

'What about the prador down here?'

'Up in the mountains ahead of you.'

'Where you directed me.'

'Easy enough for you to circumvent them and advisable that you do so. What did you do to annoy Vrasan so much? His response to you was . . . excessive.'

'Vrasan?'

'A small prador in white armour – the one I conducted my negotiations with. I'm still wondering what to do about him.' Her voice had gone utterly flat. Good to remember how she sounded when angry.

'You mean, besides preventing his attack on you?'

'Yes, besides that.'

'I got into his sanctum and sliced him up with a laser carbine.'

'Really? He survived? Why didn't you finish the job?'

'Perhaps because I am not a Polity agent,' I replied, noting that she clearly didn't know about the Spatterjay mutation of the king's children.

The creatures drew closer. They looked like ruminants, but for the six legs and mouthparts like trumpets. They seemed to be hoovering the ground with these as they advanced, then stopping occasionally to spit out something from an orifice below that trumpet. Glancing aside, I focused on a scattering of balled-up lumps of grit nearby.

'I would say it's a shame you didn't kill him, but still, the fact you didn't now gives me an opportunity to do something more interesting with him.'

It seemed the approaching creatures were not predators. This of course made sense. How could the monsters here survive if all they had to eat was each other? Still, herd animals could be just as dangerous as any predator. I realized then that in talking to Suzeal and not acting, my only remaining option was to hide and hope the things passed by on the other side of this boulder.

'So what happened between you and him?' I asked. 'What's this all about?'

'Prador politics, I think.' She thought about that then added, 'The involvement of your erstwhile self was coincidental, though Polity pressure does help drive the issue.'

'I don't understand.'

'We'd only traded with Old Family prador until Vrasan made his offer. The money was . . . a lot. The king supposedly wanted the clones for experimentation. Vrasan even gave us some detail on the new form of Spatterjay virus they were using – all of it looked completely plausible. Then we found the locator beacon in the diamond slate.'

She seemed chatty and I hadn't expected such a full answer but, of course, it didn't matter to her how much I knew. From her perspective she was talking to someone likely to end up dead.

'Locator?' I wondered. I began to see the shape of what had been happening, but lost it in too many complications. I felt tired as I tried to sort it all out in my head, and the migraine lights began flashing again.

'They won't attack you, you know,' she said after I'd fallen silent.

'What?'

'The rock suckers. They stay in the forest overnight then come out in the day to graze on the fungus growing in the grit of the plain. It contains something they need. They usually lose one or two of their number to sleers or the droon when he's out and about in the day, but their fast breeding accounts for the losses. Completely harmless unless you surprise them, then they'll kick out your spine.' She smiled, perhaps at the prospect of this happening to me.

I stood up, then damned myself for taking any notice of what she'd said. Two of the nearest creatures raised their heads and gazed at me with four blank green eyes each. The rest just carried on hoovering past.

'You said something about a locator?'

'Oh yes, where was I? You see, ECS frowned on our trade across the border into the Kingdom but wasn't able to do anything about it. They came close with your previous self, but still weren't able to locate us. They were certainly putting pressure on the king about it, but my guess is he acted out of self-interest. I'd say his main aim wasn't to shut down the trade, but to find out who the Old Family recipients were. He made it illegal in the Kingdom so, if he can get evidence on which families are involved, he can deal with them without too much objection from the others.'

ECS, I thought. Earth Central Security comprised the military, police, special forces and spies of the Polity. It seemed I had final confirmation of who my previous self had been.

'As in, put them on trial?' I suggested wryly.

She laughed so hard she started coughing.

'You still have your previous self's sense of humour,' she finally managed.

'I try, but my situation is lacking in reasons for laughter.'

She nodded. 'Quite.' Her attention seemed to be wandering, but before she cut the link I managed to nail something else bothering me about her explanation.

'I don't understand why the king needed a locator to find your station.'

'History,' she replied. 'A lot of information was lost during this king's usurpation of the last. The Polity moved the station here during the war before they dumped the creatures down there. It wasn't called Stratogaster station when they were using it, either.'

'But surely the king has his agents in the Graveyard and there would be those prepared to sell the information?'

'This is true. The king's interest in this place is a recent thing, else he would have learned its location long ago.' She paused contemplatively. 'I'm still not sure why his interest was suddenly sparked now. We've been trading for a long time and the Polity has been putting on pressure for a long time. I'm sure there's something I'm missing.'

'Maybe that pressure peaked?'

'Maybe.' She looked doubtful, then dropped the subject. 'Ahead of you in the mountains there are later-stage sleers but your weapon should be enough to deal with them. Stay alert. That being said, a bigger problem seems to be on your trail.'

I looked round sharply. 'The hooder?'

'Oh no. It limped back into the jungle to nurse its wounds and now the boundaries are once again established. And not the droon either – it's back in its hole regrowing a couple of legs.'

'Then what?'

'I'll give you a clue: he looks marginally like a man but for the nerve-impulse control frame grafted on, and his skin is very blue. Another one of Vrasan's toys.'

She started laughing again, then cut the connection.

7

Suzeal didn't care whether I lived or died and no doubt thought the latter more likely. It seemed I was an entertainment – a passing distraction – and maybe, being a walking dead man, someone she could safely talk to. Thereafter I was perhaps a source of useful data from my old self. The fact that I existed proved she'd had some nasty interaction with him, and she had as much as told me he worked for ECS.

After the last of the rock suckers moved past, I continued towards the tree line, the landscape gaining a few lumps, then a final upslope taking me towards the vegetation. Vines cloaked the ground, sporting low flat leaves and sausage pods that exploded when touched and sprayed me with wet seeds. They looked terran, but no part of me recognized them. Finally I got a closer look at the trees. They were organisms like by-blows of pines and cycads, their trunks and branches heavily scaled and sprouting masses of needles and globular cones. The vines faded away under these, displaced by spreads of bracket fungus and patches of what were perhaps yellow dead nettles. I stopped to sit on one of the fungi then got up hurriedly when white insects with doubled thoraxes, much like those of a droon, crawled out of holes in the upper surface. I found a fallen trunk and sat on that instead, watching carefully for a while before relaxing.

So, presuming Suzeal was telling the truth, the man-thing I'd fought aboard the ship was following me. He had survived being vacuum-dried – probably pulling himself back through that airlock. I presumed that the 'nerve-impulse control frame' she'd mentioned grafted to his body was a better or easier option to control him than coring and thralling, considering his advanced viral mutation. But why was he following me? It could just be some perverted instinct or the continuation of the program that had originally set him upon me. I had visions of him grabbing and dragging me all the way back to the ship. It might also be that Vrasan had a linked control unit and was directing him. The prador still had a score to settle with me.

What the hell could I do about this? Looking back along my course, I saw my footprints clearly visible in the earth and now in the needle mulch. Was he following my tracks? I cut a branch and tried smearing them out, but this only turned over an orange mycelium, probably of the fungus, and made a trail more visible. Instead, I walked all around the area to lay false trails, smeared them out at their terminus, then walked backwards in my previous footsteps. When I felt the issue confused enough, I stepped up onto one of the bracket fungi, then carefully from one to another, taking a course parallel to the tree line at first then gradually turning inwards. I left few marks as the things were as hard as old wood. I just hoped the disturbed insect things would shortly return to their burrows. Thereafter I watched where I walked and took every opportunity to conceal my trail: walking along a log, and at one point climbing from tree to tree until a branch snapped and dumped me on my backside.

Soon the vegetation began to change, with the trees becoming squatter, the fungus sparse and displaced by clumps of white flowers around which bee-like things buzzed. The slope grew steeper and finally a spine of rock, with scree on either side, took me up out of the trees. Thereafter I chose to walk on rock wherever I could and no longer concealed my trail elsewhere as I picked up my pace. I'd spent enough time at that; it would either work or it wouldn't.

I continued up into the mountains keeping the sun ahead, estimating the direction I should take when it moved overhead, then following the course of a stream ever upwards. I drank again and topped up my water container, reckoning I was past worrying about what bugs I might be picking up. Fish swam in some of the pools, but I wasn't yet hungry enough to risk the same thing happening to me as when I had tried the prador food. It grew colder and I turned off the cooling in my suit. The sun shifted down the sky behind and revealed that the stream had taken me off course. Climbing a steep rocky slope out of the valley it had been carving, I then trudged higher and higher via snaking paths made by some three-toed animal. Eventually, high up, a jutting slab gave me a view down the winding curve of the stream to the lower tree line, the plain beyond and the hazy jungle beyond that. There I saw a shape stepping out of the trees, a man shadow cast blackly behind it. Annoyingly he seemed to be walking up the spine of rock I had negotiated earlier, so my previous attempts to hide my trail hadn't put him off. Closer still, coming up the course of the stream, came something larger and, in appearance at least, nastier.

Suzeal had mentioned sleers. Now this information, plus the sight of the thing coming up the stream course, propelled something I already knew into my consciousness. Sleers had an interesting life cycle with many stages. At the beginning they were mostly cave hunters, possessed of a feeding head with grinding mandibles and extensible antlers, ten legs attached in pairs on independently rotating body segments, and though quite capable of killing a man, they never grew larger than a metre in length. After a few years, they encysted in the ground and there transformed to the second stage. The front segment would fold up and meld into the feeding head, the two legs attached turning into carapace saws for dealing with larger prey outside the sand caves – prey they could see with a triad of compound eyes. They also grew an ovipositor drill which they used to inject paralytic. These were a form of adult that split itself for mating: each half moving on four legs. The rear section would go off to mate with the rear sections of other sleers, while the feeding or hunting end continued about its business – the two sections still communicating by low-frequency bioradio. Once reconnected after mating, the whole creature would then lay eggs in a cave or burrow in which to dump paralysed prey, their nymphs hatching out and feeding on this preserved food.

I now realized the thing that had tried to get to me in the brambles had been such an adult. It seemed likely that had it not eaten me on the spot, I would have served as such preserved food for its young. I shuddered at the thought of that. Then, thinking about all the monsters here, I wondered at my second-hand knowledge of them and what that might tell me about my previous self's fascination with alien killers. Perhaps to him they were just something he needed to be aware of when conducting his missions on strange planets.

The second-stagers grew to about two metres in length, which was about the size of the one I'd encountered. But their weird life cycle did not end there. After many years the things encysted again and transformed into the third stage. These laid eggs in a similar manner, but out of them hatched second-stage sleers. The biological imperative for this remained vague to me. These creatures inevitably grew bigger – up to four metres long. Their carapace was dark grey, rather than bearing the usual sand-coloured camouflage of their younger brethren, perhaps for night hunting. Another pair of legs would ride up beside their head to form pincer arms like inwardly turned pickaxes, complementing their carapace saws which, of course, were much bigger too. The things would run on six legs. Other transformations and stages ensued and apparently the question remained open about how many there actually were. I didn't need to know about those, at least not yet. The thing coming up the course of the stream was a third-stage sleer. All that remained to me was to try not to panic and figure out what the hell I could do about it.

I watched for a while longer, vague ideas about my response surfacing in my mind. Both the sleer and the man-thing were on my trail. Both were moving at a fast walking pace and were about a mile apart. I closed my eyes and mined further knowledge about sleers. They weren't particularly intelligent, though, apparently, they did get brighter the older they got. They were tough – their carapaces as hard as a prador's, and they were fast, but energy weapons were effective against them. The people living on the world of Cull, where they were to be found, could kill them with primitive guns, but also drove them with fire. Like any animal, they didn't like fire. Okay. My plan was beginning to take shape.

Suzeal had told me my carbine could handle a sleer, but I didn't want to handle it, I wanted to drive it. Also, though my carbine was a powerful weapon, I had no faith in it against a Spatterjay-virus-mutated human. I'd seen what he was capable of surviving and, it seemed evident, I would not be able to stay ahead of him perpetually. Eventually he'd catch up because I felt certain he didn't suffer the unadjusted human need for sleep. However, he wasn't armed so would have as much trouble against a creature with a carapace as he had with the prador. Well, at least enough trouble to slow him down. Factor in the carbine too . . . I abruptly picked up my things and began heading back along my route up here. I calculated it would be about twenty minutes before I came face to face with the sleer.

I kept time with a clock in the control screen of my suit and, after fifteen minutes, found a rock to crouch behind, putting out my pulse gun and all the spare energy canisters on its surface. Even as I put down the last of these, the monstrous thing came into sight below me. It looked even bigger now and a lot more formidable. I watched it pause and snap its pickaxe pincers at the air, black antlers shooting out from holes in its head like the fronds of a tubeworm, then it came on.

I took careful aim at a rock ahead of it and fired, the beam screeing through the air, barely visible only where it reflected off water vapour and incinerated floating dust. It splashed on the rock, which exploded satisfactorily, throwing smoking splinters in every direction. The sleer halted and shifted sideways with a weird rotation of body segments. I fired again hitting another rock in front of it, then another and another. It snapped at the smoking fragments, then I saw a wisp of smoke from its head and it backed up rapidly. A shard had landed in one of its three compound eyes. Another shot set a low tangle of herbage smoking and burning, and yet another in the stream next to it blasted boiling water over it. In one revolving segment motion, it turned and headed fast back the way it had come. I picked up energy canisters and inserted them in various pockets, the pulse gun going into my belt. My hands were shaking as I set out after it.

Now, loping from rock to rock, I began to see a flaw in my plan. I had no guarantee the sleer would attack my other pursuer, or that he might attack it. Maybe he'd just jump out of its path and the thing would keep going and I would end up facing him alone. I hesitated, but then forced myself on. I was committed now.

A few hundred yards down, the creature slowed, then abruptly spun round, antlers fully extended and pincers snapping. It had sensed me. It began to move towards me, but I fired again putting a smoking crater right in front of it and kept moving towards it. The thing surged over the crater so I fired again and again with less accuracy. It dodged about in sprays of rock splinters and clouds of steam, but then one of my shots hit a forelimb, the thing bursting open and spewing oily fire from the cracks. The sleer emitted a shrill hiss, hesitated, then reluctantly turned and headed away from me again. I waited a while, letting it get further ahead so my presence didn't become so much of a temptation again, then followed just as it was about to move out of sight. When it slowed I put another shot into the stream behind it. The thing accelerated but as I drew closer, I saw that it wasn't the shot that now drove it.

The man-thing had been down on all four limbs, moving like a dog chasing a scent. He froze for a long moment then abruptly scuttled aside and leapt up onto a boulder beside the stream and began climbing a muddy cliff towards overhanging vines. The sleer, obviously seriously miffed about being turned away from one prey, was having none of this. It revolved to one side, sinking its limbs in the same cliff further up the course of the stream, and went along this as if gravity didn't matter. Its pickaxe mandibles clashed closed on the man's torso, one of them going through, its spike coming out of his back below his collarbone. He punched it with his remaining fist and I heard the impact. Both of them fell from the cliff in a blur of limbs, the smack of further impacts like gunshots. The sleer turned its ovipositor tail in and stabbed repeatedly, while the man flailed at it with both arms. Drawing closer, I noted that where one hand had been severed away now grew another, small and folded up.

They bounced off the surface of the boulder then down into the stream, kicking up a spray as they fought. I drew close enough to ensure the accuracy of my shots, settled behind a boulder and braced the carbine across the top of it. I felt a sudden reluctance, similar to earlier, to fire on something nominally human. I remembered how he had behaved aboard the King's Ship, the intelligence I'd seen in his eyes, and that the frame attached to his body controlled his subsequent actions. But then I fired anyway.

My first shot hit him in the side and flamed there, peeling up smoking skin. I swore, aimed more carefully, then hit the control frame where it lay across his shoulders. The thing smoked, and further down his spine near the base of his back, one of the segments running down folded up on a small detonation. This sent him into a fit, which gave the sleer an advantage. It managed to force him down underneath it, its carapace saws cutting in, but slowly, on either side of his torso. He recovered, driving his fist up underneath its head with a shattering impact. I saw him tear away carapace and reach in to pull out something glutinous. The sleer began shuddering and they rolled. It continued stabbing with its ovipositor and I had clear shots again.

I hit the metallic device cupping the back of his head. Something blew inside it, knocking his head out of the thing to expose a hole in his skull via which numerous fibres entered. The cup then started to pull back in, but rather than continue his attack on the sleer he reached behind, closed his hand around those fibres and wrenched, tearing them out of his skull. His body convulsed hard, flinging him from the sleer's grip and tearing off one of the imbedded pincers. He landed beside the stream, now shuddering so hard and fast he was almost a blur, while the sleer coiled up, shaking. I waited. Eventually the convulsions ceased and he collapsed on his face. The sleer began to uncoil, looking around as if confused about what had happened to it. Stepping out from behind the boulder, I walked over. I didn't feel at all good about what I had done, and what I intended to do.

Standing over him, I fired into each of the segments down his back in turn, punching molten holes through. Next, putting the carbine barrel into the hole in his head, I grabbed the cup device and pulled. It tore up, the section below seeming alive and trying to cling on with numerous hooked limbs, then one of the lower segments broke away. I pulled it up, long fibres coming out of his body, and the piece of technology writhing. I tossed it aside and fried it until it stopped moving. More movement came from the sleer. I aimed at its head but watched it steadily collapse. It was no Spatterjay-virus-infected creature and couldn't sustain the damage he had inflicted. Its head dipped down into the stream, the water bubbling for a moment and then the bubbles died.

I returned my attention to the man, reached down and heaved him over onto his back. He just lay there staring up at the sky. Despite the pincer through his body and the burns on his back from where I'd destroyed the control frame, he was still breathing. The sensible thing for me to do now would have been to cut him into pieces with the carbine and scatter them, or perhaps burn them all down to ash. If what the king had told me was true – that he'd been involved in the coring and thralling trade – he certainly deserved to die. But I doubted much remained of the original in there, and I wasn't the man from whom I'd been created. After a moment he blinked, and his eyes focused on me, head twitching, lips folding back from those carnivore teeth. There was no movement from his limbs, so I reckoned the spinal damage had shut him down, at least for now. And with the unit gone, the prador could no longer control him.

'I'm sorry for what happened to you,' I said, shouldered my carbine and walked away.

'I've just watched the recordings,' said Suzeal.

She had opened communications as I was sitting outside a cave I'd found, trying to decide whether to spend the night there or not. I wasn't sure it was a good idea to cut off options for retreat and it also looked like something had been living in there or, rather, feeding. Pieces of sleer were scattered on the cave floor.

'Really? What recordings?'

'Of your recent . . . encounter. Good idea to drive that sleer into him, but surely you're aware that the damage you inflicted isn't enough to stop him?'

'I'm aware of the effects of the Spatterjay virus.'

'So why didn't you destroy his body?'

'Because I am not a murderer.'

'It would have been appropriate self-defence.'

'I stopped him as far as I needed to. I destroyed the control hardware and without either Vrasan or an earlier program directing him, he shouldn't have any further motivation to come after me.'

'Yes, you may be right. They're little more than animals in that condition.'

I contemplated that. As she didn't know the truth about the king and his children, she didn't realize that despite their extreme mutation, they still retained their intelligence. She also hadn't seen the man-thing attempting to talk, or the strategic nature of his attack against the king. It then occurred to me that I shouldn't be so confident he wouldn't come after me. Who knew what might drive him, whether it was just the commands or that he now held a grudge against me?

'How far am I from this installation now?' I asked.

'You've covered little more than twenty miles, and I suspect you won't be reaching it anyway.'

I was learning that Suzeal enjoyed taunting me, but this still sparked my anger anyway. 'I've managed to survive thus far.'

'Yes, and against some ferocious creatures. Nevertheless they were just animals.'

'And your point is?'

'Do you understand how prador thrall technology works?'

I raked through my mind for knowledge on the subject and found it was extensive. Why did she want me to prove it to her, though? I decided to play along, to see what it would get out of her. 'The thralled creature runs mostly on programs that are sub-AI but complex. These programs direct autonomics and all the complexities of physical movement, so the prador in control just gives his orders and the program responds. Those who're cored and thralled are capable of obeying complex instructions but are essentially mindless, while those only thralled retain their mind, which allows them to follow even more complex instructions. But they're still incapable of disobeying.'

'Correct. Now what do you know of the recording facility?'

I felt a flash of anger because I knew she was playing some game, but I continued anyway. 'A lot is recorded through the slave's senses so the programs running it can make adjustments for efficiency. So, if the slave loses a limb, for example, then alterations must be made for that. This isn't the case for a slave that's retained its mind, though.'

'You do know a lot.' She smiled. Nastily. 'Of course the recording resides both in the thrall and in its control unit. What do you think would happen if a slave went offline or was otherwise disconnected?'

I sat there considering that and then felt my back creeping.

'I don't think you'll last the night,' she added, then cut the link.

I stood up, then abruptly ducked down and ran for the nearest cover, which was a mass of bushes covered with white berries. From there I looked up at the sky. Stars were out with wraiths of reddish cloud strewn across them. A moon had risen, like an iron-coloured apple with a bite taken out of it. But nothing else was visible up there. No prador, as yet. Suzeal was right, the prador controlling the man-thing would've been aware the moment his thrall hardware – the frame I'd destroyed – went offline. The next thing it would've done was look at the recording, seen me and at once known my location. But was the one with the control units Vrasan? Maybe the others didn't yet consider him stable enough for that. And if so, could it also be that whoever'd been in control didn't consider hunting me down a priority?

No, I was kidding myself. The prador might be stuck down here but that didn't make them any less vengeful and aggressive. So why hadn't they come yet? Perhaps they were otherwise occupied at present, but they did have their hounds. I moved round behind the bushes. The mountain slope here had terminated at the base of a tall cliff – the one in which I had found the cave. I'd spent some time working my way along it trying to find a way either up or around it to put me back on course. I continued along below it, eventually finding myself again on one of the animal tracks and just kept going, hoping to survive till morning. I might then have more chance of seeing the hunters I felt sure were out here.

Nothing much happened for a long time, then suddenly a figure loomed out of the moonlit night, three red eyes gleaming at me. I backed off quickly and leapt to one side, slipping over, then sliding partway down the slope on damp vegetation before coming up against a tussock of the stuff. Shouldering my carbine, I pointed it at the creature, which had turned to watch me fall. Large horns curved inward above the eyes, with another jutting up behind. A long thick tongue protruded from its tube-like mouth and parted. As the two halves rubbed against each other, the noise was like a knife being drawn. It then dipped its head and pulled up a clump of vegetation with that tongue, drawing the mass inside, and grinding it with a sound like a wood saw. It gazed at me contemplatively then moved on. I could now see its low six-legged termite body and hooked tail with what looked like a morning star on the end. A line of smaller versions of the creature – without horns or tails – followed, and even smaller creatures scuttled along below them. A male with his harem of females and brood of children? That was too prosaic again and centred on terran biology. The idea of male and female might not be relevant, with more than one sex or no sex at all. The smaller creatures could even be the adults, or a herded food source.

Once they'd drawn past, I climbed back onto the path and moved on. I started to relax and, perhaps as a consequence of that, to feel tired. Trudging along, I sank into a fugue and wasn't completely aware of my surroundings. A sound behind snapped me out of it, panic surging. I squatted and turned, the carbine levelled. I then recognized the sound of falling stones and saw them tumbling down the cliff face and bouncing on the slope below. From above came another sound: a groaning, a hiss and then an 'Oh!' that sounded suspiciously human. The fall of stones ceased and it all went quiet for a moment, then a large object fell down through the night, hitting the slope to bounce and sprawl. For a second I thought it might be the man-thing, but in the moonlight I saw a naked woman. I couldn't see the colour of her skin, but she still moved, despite being headless, and was clearly one of the clones: a Jill.

Stepping away from the path, and partway down the slope, I scanned the cliff above. Sheer rock rose a hundred feet, nothing else. I headed over to have a look at the body and found her twitching and shifting like someone having a nightmare. I stepped round and studied her neck. Her head hadn't been severed but torn off and I could see no signs of thrall hardware in the stub

141

of her neck vertebrae, just a hollow slowly filling with glistening fluid. I stared for a while longer, wondering what to do. Should I burn her up? No, that might attract unwanted attention and she'd ceased to be a danger to me. As I trudged back up the slope I reckoned the virus inside her was advanced enough and had enough materials to work with. She would grow a leech mouth with which to feed, as well as some kind of brain or ganglion, from the virus's eclectic collection of genomes, to guide the body, and then join the host of monsters here.

I felt no more danger of drifting into fugue as I walked. The clones were out and about, almost certainly hunting me, and something, perhaps a sleer, had torn the head off one of them. But an inconsistency kept nagging at me as I progressed. Then, as I rounded a corner and saw that the cliff had collapsed ahead, I realized what it was: her clothing. She'd been naked yet the clones I'd seen were still wearing the overalls we'd put on aboard Suzeal's ship. Why would the prador have ordered them to strip naked? Because their garments were white and easily seen? Perhaps, though the last time I saw the clones their overalls had been filthy and no easier to see than their skin. Perhaps the metal in them could be detected by some of the animals here? Perhaps during her fight with a sleer, or whatever had got her, they'd been torn away? The more I thought about it the more puzzled I became, then I reached the rubble pile and put such thoughts aside.

This rock collapse offered me a route upwards, but if I climbed here, would I end up running into more clones? The woman had been up there and perhaps the others were too. I decided to climb anyway. Most likely they had been spread out to cover a wide area and, by climbing here, I would be heading somewhere that only the woman was meant to have been searching. I heaved myself up onto a tilted slab, scrambled up a scree pile above it, then decided to avoid the scree when it slid down, making a racket as it went. I stepped from rock to rock and walked where the steep slope seemed more stable. Weariness hit again and I ached from head to foot. A gap where slabs lay tilted against each other beckoned to me, and a quick flash of my torch showed it empty of anything nasty. I crawled inside to a corner and flashed the torch again, finding nothing, then put up my hood and visor and curled up out of sight of the entrance. Each time I started to drift into sleep a surge of panic dragged me back out of it. I thought I would never sleep, then it seemed just a moment later I woke to full daylight.

Screw you, Suzeal – I had survived the night.

I lay in my hideaway feeling logy and disinclined to do anything at all. My body was leaden and the prospect of fighting for survival for another day held no appeal. Finally, a full bladder, the need for a shit, and hunger and thirst drove me upright. I moved deeper into the hide to piss and then detached my envirosuit trousers and squatted. I'd just finished that business and was looking up to clear sky through a gap in the rocks a few feet away, when a slippered foot came down to block the view. One of the clones. As carefully and quietly as possible, I pulled up my trousers and moved back to where I'd left my pack and carbine. I hoped to hell the one out there wouldn't be able to identify the smell, because it was foul. What should I do now?

I could continue to hide and look out for danger as I journeyed but the clones would always be about. One of them could ambush me at any moment whereas, right now, I had the advantage. As I moved carefully towards the entrance, carbine ready and pulse gun in my belt, I understood how easy it was to make the small step from self-defence to killer. I moved out, slow and careful again, not making the slightest noise. She stood thirty feet downslope from me: another Jill. Her back was to me, a pulse rifle braced across her stomach while she scanned the slope below, her head turning from side to side with robotic regularity. I took aim across the top of a rock, carbine firmly braced. And I fired without hesitation. No second thoughts and no momentary guilt.

My shot hit her squarely on the back of her neck, burning away skin and then flames flaring. She stood for a moment longer than she should have, reaction time with the thrall running a longer circuit than the human nervous system, then was propelled into action. She flung herself down in utter silence, turning and firing upslope as she did so. I moved out fast, leaping up and firing at her again. With her arm flaming, her pulse rifle dropped, clattering to the rocks as she scrambled towards me, horribly fast. I fired and kept firing, punching burning craters in her tough body as she kept coming at me like a running cat. The beam just wasn't penetrating and didn't slow her at all. She covered twenty feet and I concentrated on my aim, the beam travelling up her torso and into her face, then I jumped aside. Blind, she careered past me until her leg went down into a crevice. I turned as she struggled to pull free and fired into the back of her neck and then her skull. Her movements became frenetic and then disjointed. The stem of her thrall hooped out of the ruin of her neck, then snapped free, flicking like a tail. I kept the beam on the back of her skull until something blew away some of the charred bone. Trailing smoke and fire, she bowed her forehead to the stone and just stayed in that position twitching, as if being electrocuted.

I shut down the carbine, noting its low charge and that only one energy canister remained. I stared at her, just for a second feeling sick about what I'd done, but that quickly cleared.

Controlled by another, her purpose had been either to kill me or to drag me back to the prador for a harsher death. Survival instinct kicked in and I ducked down, scanning my surroundings because she might not have been alone. When no one else showed themselves, I immediately grabbed up her pulse rifle and checked its controls to be sure I knew how to use it. Shouldering the strap, I moved back over to her to use the butt of my carbine against the back of her skull, which broke open easily, being so charred. I grabbed the still-slowly-moving tail of the thrall and pulled. The whole thing came out with a sucking crack. The legs around the cylinder which had been in her skull still flexed in and out as they tried to find the inner skull to brace against. I threw the thing as hard as I could downslope, and then searched her.

She wore a belt around her waist with a sidearm and three reloads for the rifle. These contained the combined energy and metallic dust packs and slotted into the weapon like bullet clips in ancient projectile assault rifles. There were also five small spheres along a strip. Of course my earlier self, having had much interest in such things, recognized the grenades at once. I touched one of them and the number '1' appeared on its surface, then on the surfaces of all the others. Running my finger down the side of it set the count higher. I took it to '4' and left it at that. Detonation would be four seconds after I detached a grenade from the strip. I then pulled the sidearm out of its holster and inspected it. The thing was a pepper-pot stun gun which fired a cloud of beads filled with a neurotoxin that would paralyse a man. The sight of it sickened me because I now knew the intention of the prador directing these clones. I was to be brought to them.

She had nothing else on her I could use. I had hoped for food and water but supposed that the prador just let them forage, or didn't bother feeding them until it became an absolute necessity. Her twitching had died now, but she still moved slightly. I picked up my pack and got away from there just as fast as I could.

Above the cliff, a flat plain extended for about a mile to another upslope. As I had discovered already walking in these mountains, the top was always higher than expected. I set out at a jog across it, the sun again shining in my face, my visor automatically polarizing to deal with it. What looked like dry grass lay underfoot, along with the dried-out remains of flying arthropods that floated up like confetti whenever I kicked one. I saw a snake, a genuine terran snake, and stopped to inspect it. The creature studied me back, jetted out its tongue briefly, then headed away as if embarrassed by the encounter.

Soon reaching the next slope, I cut across it diagonally. It seemed ludicrous to keep going up over every mountain. I would circumvent what I could and keep generally towards the sunrise. Suzeal could correct my course once I got over the mountains, if she really intended to rescue me from this world. And if, the stray thought arrived, these mountains did actually come to an end in a few hundred miles. But I had little choice but to keep going – in fact, no other choice. And whatever Suzeal's intent, getting to a human installation on this world seemed like a good idea.

On this particular mountain I was very high up, though not into the snowline which I could see at its peak. As I rounded it, the vista opened out before me and my guts sank. Perhaps she'd been lying completely about the installation and how far I would have to go to reach it. Ahead was a mountain range that disappeared into orange haze. Valleys lay in between, packed with forests or jungles or whatever terms applied. Waterfalls glinted on a couple of slopes too, and silhouetted against the sky were flocks of birds . . . or flying creatures. Yet, even though the prospect was daunting, and it was highly likely Suzeal had been lying to me, my mood began to lift. Despite the danger, I could take pleasure in this beautiful view. I was about to move on when the coms unit buzzed.

'My, you are a survivor,' she began. She didn't look happy, but whether about me surviving or some other matter. I wasn't sure.

'They're not trying to kill me, just capture,' I replied.

'Yes, the resolution from my satellites is quite good. I saw the stun gun. I expect Vrasan wants to play with you. Of course, he wouldn't try to core and thrall you since you're not infected with the virus – the procedure would kill you.'

'Where are the prador in relation to me now?' I asked, wondering if she might like to see how I would survive up against Vrasan.

'I see that the other clones moved in on where you killed that Jill. They are of course heading after you but are still a little way behind.'

'The prador?' I asked again.

'Keep heading towards the sunrise and you should be good. I'll warn you if you go off course. You're doing very well.'

So she wasn't going to tell me where the prador were. But I'd get as much more as I could from her.

'And how are things up there?'

She grimaced. 'They're still dug in. They had another railgun. It'll be more difficult to remove them than we thought.'

Failure, then.

'So you won't be coming for me just yet.'

'You seem able enough to survive.'

'Something killed one of the Jills,' I stated.

She waved a hand airily. 'A sleer, I expect, judging by the injuries. I didn't see the actual event.'

'Okay.' This time, I wondered if my suspicions of her lies came from my own instinct or knowledge from my previous self. I kept trudging, trying to figure out why she might do so. She was playing games with me, that was clear, but why? What was in it for her? When I said nothing more, she disconnected.

Rounding the mountain, I headed down towards a valley that would take me nominally in the right direction. As I descended, it got warmer. Soon I found myself slipping on strews of bubble grass and, from where this grew, gazed down into a packed mass of the cycad-like trees, where vines tangled intervening spaces. I headed across the slope, aiming to walk along above and alongside this mass. A hoped-for path failed to materialize in the steep valley sides; however, further along the vegetation below thinned out and I glimpsed an area clear of trees around a waterfall. I had emptied my water container some time before and also finished my food. Perhaps the time had come for me to risk foraging because I wouldn't reach my destination on an empty stomach, especially labouring against a gravity here for which evolution had not designed me.

Moving through a combination of trees like the ones I'd seen before, including a banyan from which I ate unsatisfactory 'leaves', and a pear trunk tree devoid of leeches, I came to an area scattered with actual cycads protruding pink fleshy-looking flower spikes. Underfoot, mosses squelched and slimy things like long leaves writhed when I stepped on them. I came to a mass of blue reeds throwing up twenty-foot-tall papyrus heads and heard a river beyond. Although I couldn't see it, I followed its course. The sun had moved up overhead, then steadily behind when I saw something glittering on a slab of rock.

The thrall unit had been smashed with a heavy stone lying beside it, while the burned remains of a Jack's head lay next to it. I stared. The deliberate use of a rock to do this, and the burned state of the remains, told me at once a person had killed this clone. For a second I wondered if another had become fully conscious like me, then felt stupid because, if it had been cored, that wasn't possible. I squatted down and scanned my surroundings but could detect no movement. Who would kill one of these? The prador had no reason to and I couldn't think of anyone else. But maybe my assumption that only the prador, the clones and I were here had been a mistake. With the right equipment, it would be easy enough to survive. Suzeal had directed me to a human installation. Why were they here? Were they occupied? Perhaps she'd sent someone out to look for me. Even as I thought this, a cynical side dismissed the idea, both as a threat or a hope of rescue. There was little to no chance Suzeal, or any of those she ruled, would put themselves at risk to help me. And there were dangers enough here that Suzeal wouldn't need to send someone against me. I noted a trail leading from the rock back between the cycads and cautiously followed the writhing green to its source, crouching beside one of the cycads. Someone was here!

No.

A small droon looked up. Just for a second it had seemed human, but when it shifted I saw the rest of its doubled thorax. It huffed its head but showed no inclination to attack. Instead, it jetted out a series of wormish pipes from the lower tier of its head and began sucking at the mess of bubbling fluid in front of it, which issued from the side of the half-dissolved corpse. Were they intelligent? My knowledge told me yes, about as bright as a dog. Maybe it had removed the thrall and smashed it because it'd writhed like the one I'd removed, while the burns I'd seen on the remains of the head were from acid.

I backed away, pulse rifle pointed at the thing and then, when far enough away, turned and ran. Despite the boggy ground, I set a good pace and just kept going until I began to feel weary, slackening to a jog and then a walk. A clearing to my left revealed a bank beside the river, slow-moving at this point and deep. I went over, filled my water container and studied the water. Not seeing any fish, let alone having any idea how to catch them if I did, I moved on. Then I heard something running through the vegetation behind, sounding as though it had too many legs. I turned and squatted, raising the pulse rifle, not sure whether the carbine might have been a better choice. But I had no time to change as the droon came into sight moving fast, bouncing off the side of a cycad as it altered its course towards me.

When the stream of white pulses punctuated a line to its head, I thought I'd fired, but then two more joined it. The droon crashed down, limbs all askew, most of its head and part of its upper thorax blasted away. It flailed, smoke and fire rising from it, as another shot came in – a small missile. The thing flew apart on a hot blast, raining fragments all around me. I turned, trying to locate the source of the shots. A Jack stepped out from behind a tree holding up a weapon and its shot slapped my chest, as well as stinging my right cheek and forehead. I fell on my backside and wasn't sure why. The side of my face had gone numb and weird coloured lights rotated in my right eye. I tried to raise the rifle but my right arm was dead too. I fumbled with it until a boot slammed into my chest, knocking me down on my back. He reached down, ripped open the front of my envirosuit and fired another shot from his stun gun into my chest. And then the world went away.

8

They had tied me with wire to a travois made out of branches and one of them was towing it. As I became fully cognizant of my surroundings, the events that had led me to this point returned in a disjointed fashion. It was as if my brain had been programmed to record events but hadn't allowed them into my consciousness while they were happening. One of the clones had picked me up and slung me over his shoulder and they'd proceeded thus for a while. Somebody had said something, over to one side in the trees, words that didn't make any sense, and gunfire had ensued. They'd run for a while, then stopped and made the travois. I reckoned it was so the one now pulling me could have his hands free to use his weapon. Five of them surrounded me, as far as I could see: three Jacks and two Jills.

All of their actions could be construed as those of intelligent people. They'd reacted to a situation in a logical manner. But I knew that the logic lay some distance away from here in the mind of the controlling prador, probably Vrasan. From the travois, where I still lay paralysed, I could see the four walking behind. They were robots. They walked with steady monotonous precision, their heads turning regularly as they scanned their surroundings and their eyes blinking with the same regularity. One of them stumbled on a rock and an appreciable delay followed before he righted himself. He showed no reaction to the obstacle, didn't even look. Another had lost her slipper, but it made no difference to her pace. The state of one of the Jacks really brought home to me their lack of sentience. Something had taken a bite out of the side of his head. A chunk the size of a fist was missing, taking with it one eye and the bone in that area, and I could see the silvery legs of his thrall braced inside. But he carried on, regardless.

The paralytic had waned just enough now for me to be able to blink and move my head slightly, while my limbs felt like lead. I wondered if, once I could move them, one of the clones would step over and put another stun shot in me, or whether the controlling prador thought my bonds enough, so I didn't try. I just lay there, trying to decipher some way out of this and trying to ignore that there might not be one. Then I heard it again: that nonsense voice in the vegetation.

'Umber stroobergak-fraggle,' it said.

It sent shivers down my spine. It made absolutely no sense yet seemed as though it ought to. It didn't sound quite human and my adopted knowledge finally provided an answer. It was the gabble. Creatures from many other worlds had been dumped here from Stratogaster's Zoo. Hooders, and Suzeal had mentioned mud snakes, as well as a siluroyne. These were all vicious dangerous predators from the world of Masada, but other nasty things came from there too and it seemed one of them might be trailing us. The gabbleducks were the devolved descendants of the ancient alien Atheter. They spoke like the thing I was hearing, in pseudo-Anglic, and nobody knew why. Often they just seemed wrapped up in their own concerns and ignored any humans that came within their compass. But they were still predators and did kill people on that world. Sometimes they took it into their heads to pursue particular victims over hundreds of miles and would even try to break through township defences there to get to them. They'd tear them apart, chewing on the remains, but not swallowing anything. Or sometimes they pursued people for miles, caught them, only to lose interest afterwards.

My mouth regained some feeling and at last I could summon up enough saliva to moisten it. Maybe I could speak, but what would be the point? The Jack who'd lost part of his head carried my pack and weapons. Why was he bothering? Perhaps Vrasan was curious about me and wanted to examine my belongings. I took this as a good thing. If I got the chance to escape, I might be able to get them back. I certainly wouldn't be able to survive without them. And perhaps this indicated Vrasan's intentions weren't only to give me a hard death. Maybe he wanted to question me – wanted information. I grimaced. Prador never asked nicely. Whichever way this went, I'd have to be ruthless and take any opportunity to escape as fast as possible. Cynical me opined that I was unlikely to be given a chance, I was as good as dead.

I had no sense of how much time had passed, and it came as a surprise when the vegetation faded around me and I found myself being towed across a flat plain scattered with boulders the size of buildings, blue-silver in the light of a moon I'd not seen before. The clones didn't stop and I drifted off, then jerked awake to the sound of pulse rifle fire and the sound of a gabble-duck grumbling nonsense. It then retreated behind a mass of contorted stone decorated with trees like saucer-shaped spreads of foliage. I lay utterly still, hoping none of the clones had seen me jerk, because I could now move my limbs. Despite that, however, my bonds gave me little freedom of movement. The night proceeded with no further sign of the gabbleduck.

Dawn twilight revealed the loom of mountains all around us as the clones dragged me down a scree slope onto an animal track winding down into yet another valley. The sun burned a lump out of the horizon to my left, just before we entered the shade of growths which were either plants or fungi. Branches from their pure white trunks spread grey masses, like a cross between fungus brackets and lichen, but sprouting small red globes on short stalks. No memories of these rose for my inspection, just comparisons. I wondered if they were something else from Stratogaster's Zoo. Besides prey animals, he had also kept native flora to complement his vicious fauna. Or just maybe these were part of the original life on this world, presuming it had had any in the first place.

As we passed underneath them, I felt something land on my face, with others pattering on my envirosuit and a rain of them all around. The clone directly behind me, the Jack with a big gap in his skull, walked along oblivious to a white segmented worm stuck to his head. The thing seemed to possess a pincer head at each end and writhed through the ginger stubble of his hair and into the cavity, disappearing out of sight. I tilted my head slightly, seeing similar creatures worming their way up my suit towards my face. Meanwhile, one that had actually landed there started probing the edge of my mouth, then using its pincers on my lip. The horror of it overwhelmed me. Would the Jacks just continue walking while this thing tore at my mouth and finally wormed its way inside? I groaned out loud.

The Jacks remained oblivious as blood ran down my chin and my neck. I yelled and the thing took the opportunity to shove between my teeth. I bit down, crunching, acrid fluid flooding my mouth to suck the moisture from my tongue. I spat it out, but even then another reached my collar. I shrieked and fought against my bonds, managing to dislodge one of the things lower down. This was no good. I needed the clones to act.

'Do you want me alive or not?' I bellowed. 'These fucking things will eat me!'

The clones did nothing for a long while. I saw one worm force its way into a Jill's mouth, while another had begun chewing at the orbit of a Jack's eye. Perhaps this last motivated the prador, for he wouldn't want his slaves to start losing their senses. All at once, they started to brush the creatures off themselves. The Jill reached up to pull at the one in her mouth, which had a grip on her tongue. It snapped in half, and she reached inside to tug out the rest of it. The Jack who now had one within his skull only got rid of those on his clothing or head. I supposed he couldn't reach the one inside, or the controlling prador wasn't aware of it. Another worm at my neck crawled up the side of my face, and I shook my head, shouting as I tried to dislodge it. The thing decided my ear might be a nice place to be and started chewing there to widen the gap. I yelled again, and at last one of the clones stepped forwards.

She stood over me and inspected me from head to foot. Even as I yelled and struggled, she removed all the worms that had fallen on me or the travois, starting from the feet upwards. This more than anything expressed her lack of awareness, or perhaps it showed an amused cruelty on the part of the prador. Finally she took hold of the thing boring into my ear, pulled it out and discarded it. I lay there sobbing. Such horrible pain from such small creatures, and just a fraction of what might be in store for me.

As we progressed under the strange plants or fungi, more kept falling and the clones continued to brush the things away. The Jill stayed attentive, plucking them off me even as they landed. Soon, banyan, and then the occasional pear trunk, displaced those growths and leeches were the things that dropped when we passed under the latter. They probed the clones for only a moment then fell away. Perhaps they found their flesh too tough or perhaps, controlled by the virus and finding their potential host already occupied, they knew to seek elsewhere. One landed on me, down on my leg, and stabbed ineffectually with its wad-cutter mouth. Then inevitably it began to crawl up towards my face, but the Jill plucked it away too. I felt conflicted about this, as I knew the leech bite infected its recipient with the virus. So, if I was bitten, I would in time become as rugged and strong as the clones. But did I want the kind of resilience it imparted, when being taken to the prador, as this would also facilitate being cored and thralled?

A stream lay at the bottom of this valley too, running between wide slabs of rock below a cliff made up of similar slabs, and in which I could see occasional caves. I briefly thought the day must be ending because, coming clear of the trees, we entered twilight. I panicked when something else pattered against my envirosuit, until I realized the twilight was due to thick cloud and it had begun to rain. This seemed suitable weather for my situation. As we travelled further, I saw the first sign that the prador encampment might be near. A slab lay bare as we approached, yet something faded into existence on it as we passed. Sitting atop it was a tripod, riveted into the stone, supporting a blocky device that turned with the same regularity as the clones surveying their surroundings. My mind found recognition: the chameleonware device had of course first hidden itself, until we moved inside its field. I noted the cloudy sky had taken on a metallic tint while occasional ripples of iridescence passed over the surrounding rocks. And I recognized what might be another of Suzeal's lies.

She'd told me the clones were some distance behind me. She'd also implied, right from the start, that she knew the location of the prador base, despite being evasive with me when I asked where they were. But the fact that the prador used chameleonware indicated otherwise. The prador wouldn't have started using 'ware just to cover a location in the hope she hadn't tracked their course. They would've either started using it straightaway, as they departed the ship, or at some point soon afterwards while on the move. I reckoned she only had a vague idea that they might be in these mountains – they were ideal for concealment – but not exactly where. This now brought me around to her other lie.

She had wanted me to be captured or killed. I could think of any number of reasons for the latter, including her entertainment, but the former was more interesting. I had no doubt she'd been watching from her satellites as the clones took me, and had followed their course through the mountains. But now we'd passed under a chameleonware shield, she wouldn't be able to see us. Perhaps by allowing me to be captured, and knowing the clones would take me back to the prador, she hoped to locate them. It seemed logical, until you factored in that the prador didn't want to be found. They wouldn't lead those eyes in the sky directly back towards them. Chameleonware shields could cover wide areas, and be scattered where there was no other useful concealment, as well as blurred and laid along various courses. They could also work electronic chaff, projecting images of the prador encampment, or even the clones themselves, in the wrong locations. A short while after I'd pondered on this, the clones proved me right.

They halted for a bit, just standing around, perhaps while the prador updated their programming, then abruptly crossed the stream. Up on the other side, they worked their way along parallel to the cliff, then used projecting slabs as steps to go higher, two of them now carrying my travois. And then they entered a cave. It grew steadily darker as we moved inside, then the lights came on. Beads of luminescence stuck haphazardly on the ceiling and walls made it almost painfully bright in there. These were shells of light-emitting meta-material, wrapped round a power supply that was activated by the presence of people – a Polity invention.

Stalactites hung above, long and spindly in the higher gravity and scattered with crystals like amethyst and ruby. At first the clones walked on a mud floor, and I wondered how the mud had extended so deep. A side cave, which was particularly full of the stuff, revealed the source. It was shit. A loud clattering and cheeping started up. *Bats*, I thought, but the creatures that flew out I immediately identified as the flying insects whose papery corpses I had seen when crossing a previous mountain top. They had two sets of wings, wide heads bearing ugly-looking mandibles and numerous legs which hung from doubled thoraxes like a droon. I assumed them to be life from the same world, but didn't recognize them.

Deeper inside, I began to see signs of recent cutting: boulders sliced through, disintegrated to rubble and pushed to one side, as well as the regular marks of other cutting on some walls. And for a stretch, a whole tunnel had been bored through. All of this hadn't been done to widen the cave for the clones, but for something larger. The prador had come this way, probably using intense geological scanning, and with a destination in mind. They had almost certainly scanned this world previously too, as the ship came down, and then retained that information. The journey went on and on. Sliding into a state halfway between sleep and waking, I lost track. My hunger, which had risen a couple of times, had now waned to a tight clench in my guts. I'd pay for this in terms of energy, since I'd been free of fat when I was first delivered to the prador and hadn't subsequently had a chance to accrue any. My injured mouth felt horribly sore, as though burned, and virulent too, as if something might be incubating in my lips. When at one point small white worms issued from the hole in the injured Jack's skull, I got the horrors. Then I must have slipped into complete sleep.

I awoke when the travois thumped against the ground. The sky roiled umber above me, while heavy rain splashed in the churned soil and granite slabs all around. It soaked my face but I was grateful for its coolness – I felt hot and my lips were burning. I just lay there for a moment, then raised my head to look around. I'd been abandoned just outside the cave, where it entered a shallow valley. The ground lay nominally level but hadn't been that way before. At the end I could see a heap of rocks, earth and shattered banyan, with further untouched banyan lying beyond it. The five clones had moved over to my right and sat in the shade of an overhanging slab, eating food blocks with metronomic efficiency. The prador I'd seen escaping the ship were ahead of me, two of them installed in large machines. One seemed to be sitting at a thing like a large piano, but metallic, with a conveyor underneath and other machines clustered around. From there came the sizzle and hum of a matter printer. Another operated a scoop arm to hoist glittery rubble from a pile and drop it into a hopper. I assumed the rest of the equipment he controlled consisted of a furnace, forges, casting beds and other items for the production of technological items. Further equipment lay scattered here and there, including the grav-barges, particle cannons and other partially assembled weapons, and stacks of supplies. The Guard who had rescued Vrasan crouched behind one of the barges, setting up a missile launcher, but I couldn't see any sign of Vrasan himself.

Movement came in the corner of my eye, and the sound of rattling metal.

I strained my neck to look round to my left and felt an immediate surge of panic. Here rested an item I'd really not expected to see. Under a protruding slab lay a hooder, fully a hundred feet long. It moved again, straining against massive chains riveted in place along its carapace at one end and bolted into the rock below at the other. The top of the spoon-shaped head of the thing had been opened, with a shield-shaped chunk of carapace discarded on the ground nearby. Heavy composite clamps secured the head immovably to the stone. In the head cavity lay purple wetness, but also the silvery glint of metallic items. I now noticed the segmented metalwork running all the way down its back. Vrasan bobbed up into sight behind the head, holding a large gleaming object like a metallized jellyfish – a hemisphere from which hung numerous tentacles and other protrusions. The tentacles were moving as he lowered it into place, eager to seek out their targets. The hooder shuddered as they went in, its feet scraping against the stone frenetically with a sound like numerous engines starting up. Vrasan ignored this as he next took up a deposition welder and sealed the hemisphere in place.

He was thralling a hooder. I stared in disbelief. How the hell had they captured the thing? I guessed some form of stun – probably something that would kill or blow apart a normal creature. And what could they possibly want to do with it?

When Vrasan had finished his work, he moved round from behind the creature and stalked over towards me. Even as he drew close, two of the clones appeared beside me and began undoing the wires securing me to the travois. They hauled me upright and the passing thought I'd had about trying to run was crushed as they had to support me. They all but carried me over to a frame rooted in the ground, and manacles clicked around my wrists, holding my arms above my head by chains to a crossbar. As I slumped, the manacles dug in, so I tried to force some life into my legs and stand, shakily. The rain pummelled down on me and I thought I would die here.

Vrasan moved up to stand before me. His armour now bore camouflage stripes of black, grey and green. The eyes behind the visor didn't match the creature underneath . . . this was supposing he had returned to his original form. He clattered and bubbled at me, then prodded me in the guts with one claw, driving the

wind out of me. I understood a little of it. I expected him to be
happy to have captured me and relishing the prospect of what
was to come, but his speech included phonemes for 'aberrant
behaviour', 'fascination' and 'I need to understand'. He clattered
for a moment longer, a deep buzzing ensued, then he spoke in
Anglic through a translator maybe linked to his mind, for his
mandibles grew still.

'Your behaviour was not expected. You should have been
incapable of the things you did, so what are you?' he asked.

'A human being,' I replied.

'Insufficient answer. Further insufficient answers will be
punished.'

I thought hard about my reply, seeking advantage, and only
answered when he advanced towards me threateningly.

'Knowledge began loading to my mind from when I woke up
aboard Suzeal's ship.'

I kept the answer brief because that would elicit other
questions from him and the longer we kept talking the longer it
would be before he did something nasty to me.

'Suzeal put an implant inside you,' he stated.

'She did not.'

'How do you know this?'

'Because I believe I know the source of that knowledge.'

He watched me for a long silent moment then said, 'You will
tell me the source of this knowledge and you will make your
answer elaborate and detailed. If your answer is brief I will remove
your foot.'

'Okay, no need to be so pushy. I've had a traumatic life thus
far and it's difficult to get my thoughts in order.' He began to
reach down towards my foot so I continued hurriedly, 'As far
as I understand it, Suzeal used the DNA of a Polity agent
whose name was Jack. I call him Jack Zero. She copied the

sample to produce the other clones but used the original to make me.' Now I began to see something to my advantage. 'When I met your king he told me that the Polity is using quantum processing crystals in its human agents to record data – just like memplants. He told me this before sending me away, but also revealed to me how to escape the slave unit attached to my neck.'

Vrasan withdrew his claw sharply. 'So you are effectively this Polity agent?'

'No.' I shook my head. 'It has been my experience that I don't have that agent's memories, just his knowledge. I know much of what he knew, but I have no idea how he knew what he did. I know, for example, that hooders are devolved war machines, and understand some of their biology, the way they behave and how resistant they are to most weapons. I don't know when or how Jack Zero learned this – whether through experience or mental upload. This is why, incidentally, I'm curious about how you managed to subdue that beast – it must have been quite a feat.' I nodded towards the hooder.

Vrasan shuffled round and looked back towards the hooder. 'I lured it here because I knew it could not be subdued for long. We hit it with sonic stun grenades on every segment, while simultaneously blowing EMPs underneath it. It had to be timed perfectly to generate a neural surge through its spinal cortex – the blasts starting at the tail and working their way up. This effectively knocked it out for three minutes, in which time we moved and secured it with bonds already prepared. The spine frame went on next, set to generate further surges to suppress it and prevent it tearing free.'

Good, I had sparked his ego and he liked to talk about his work. Perhaps it was the white armour, but I now had an impression of him as the prador equivalent of the white-coated scientist working in his laboratory. Probably brilliant, and maybe a bit unstable.

He swung back towards me. 'The king told you how to escape?'

'My mind wasn't as functional then as it is now. I didn't realize that the slave unit only forced me to comply with orders and didn't stop me from doing anything else, like tear the thing off.'

'And you claim the king told you this?'

'He didn't tell me to tear it off, but he did inform me that I had independent action outside of its orders. Perhaps it was a whim – he seemed bored.'

Vrasan made a strange bubbling sound suspiciously like a sigh. He moved forwards and reached out with one claw. I tried to get away but he closed its tips hard on either side of my skull, but then gently turned my head. No doubt he was inspecting the scar on my neck.

'I don't see what use a hooder could be to you down here,' I risked, hoping to provoke him to tell me more.

He released my head. 'The hooders are incorrectly described in the Polity as devolved war machines. They were converted from their original wild form into biomechs. When the Atheter chose their cowardly retreat from civilization, they shut them down and also returned their facility to breed. Thereafter, over two million years, they did not devolve but evolved, adapting as wild creatures do to their environment. However, like all life, their ancestry is written into their genome. This includes their biomech component, which is still in there in recessive genes or alleles. They were formidable weapons, capable of manipulating matter and energies to a level seen neither in the Kingdom nor in the Polity. In their old form, they would be easily capable of flight from the surface of a world, and disabling the weaponry of an old Polity station.'

I sagged a bit on my chains. This seemed utterly insane yet

the things I'd seen and experienced pointed to the truth of it. 'You intend to commission this hooder?' I asked weakly.

'The process has already begun,' Vrasan stated. 'The thrall submits it to my control while, inside, it is re-expressing its ancestral phenotype.'

I forced some strength back into my legs and stood straight. 'You seem to know a great deal about hooders. I'm not sure this is something even a Polity AI would attempt.'

'How do you know Polity AIs have not attempted or are attempting it?'

I didn't really, I just wanted to keep the talk going. 'You're correct. My knowledge of what they do is limited.' My head sagged again and it seemed, with my reserves depleted, I had hit a low ebb. I snapped it upright when one of the clones moved up beside me, desperate to find something more to say. 'But you won't destroy the station, at least at first, because you want to know which Old Families Suzeal has been trading with,' I babbled. 'I also expect that returning to the king with such a war machine will be . . . helpful.'

The clone undid the manacle on my right wrist, then slid the chain attached to the other manacle along the crossbar and down a side post. I collapsed on my backside into the mud, glad to rest, and relieved Vrasan hadn't yet decided to start any prador games.

'You have an interesting mind,' he said, peering down at me.

'You wish to stop the trade in human blanks out of Stratogaster and catch the culprits they are being sold to. Why did the king not take Suzeal and her ship when she came to you?'

'Her greed and the possibility of greatly expanded trade drew her to us personally. But she warned us that she would destroy herself, her compatriots and her ship if any attempt was made to seize them. We expected this.'

'It all seems very just, and perhaps altruistic. Yet you cored and thralled living human beings to reach your goal.' I regretted saying that at once.

Vrasan showed no reaction for a moment, then waved a claw at the two clones. 'They were merely human shells – no more sentient than a mudfish with some extra programming laid down in its brain. Humans have a curious attachment and attitude to their flesh despite being quite capable of leaving it.'

'What are you going to do with me? I am a sentient human being.'

'You may possess useful data. I will remove the quantum storage inside you and study it and, if feasible, record it. I can make the search and removal process painless, but your attack on me and your interference in our plans requires a response, so I will not.'

'I only shot you to survive – you attacked me.'

'But you had no need to disrupt our attack on Stratogaster.'

'What chance did I have of survival if you'd occupied it? Of being rescued by my own kind?'

'You hoped for rescue?' he wondered, then abruptly moved away, the two clones following.

The rain was trickling down inside my suit so I put up my hood. I'd begun drinking from a nearby puddle, also probing my swollen lips, which seemed better now, when a clone walked over and dropped a food block beside me. I was about to say thank you but then felt stupid to be so inclined. Vrasan probably wanted to keep me healthy until he took me apart. I ate anyway, while inspecting the chain and manacle. And, sitting there, I thought of various things which didn't make sense.

These came to me as I watched the prador working the machines for a while, then I turned my attention to the hooder, studying the hardware along its body. Was it feasible, in the time that had passed, for the prador to hatch a plan, to commission an ancient alien biomech war machine and put it into action? My knowledge of the war and of prador society told me they were industrious, technically adept and could work very fast, but surely doing something like this required more than that? The schematic of the biomechanical component of this machine, written into its genome and an alien technology, needed to be reinitiated. This required deep knowledge, AI-level planning and calculation, highly specialized components and programs, and more I couldn't think of right then. Vrasan's brilliance? Possibly, but not without laboratory research and the support of lots of prador technology. Even the thrall itself had to have been heavily redesigned to incorporate alien biology. I didn't think it was something they could have designed and built in the days available. Was it likely that a few prador, with some equipment grabbed from a crashed ship under attack from hooders, could simply capture a hooder, slap on a thrall and then restart genome programs inside it that had been somnolent for two million years? No, it was not. Vrasan's actions here had required careful *preparation*.

Another thought now arose that seemed to confirm this. Suzeal had been puzzled by the prador setting their ship on course to land on the planet, when it would have been easier for them to hide behind it. This indicated that their purpose in coming here hadn't just been about shutting down the coring trade and getting evidence on the Old Families involved. It seemed an operation in two parts: seize the station and gather that evidence, then from there initiate phase two, which was to get hold of hooders and commission them. It made sense. The hooders of Masada were inaccessible to the prador since that planet lay in the Polity. But the prador would still have known about the hooders and learned about their ancestry. And the prador very much liked getting their claws on new weapons.

It was all irrelevant, really. Suzeal had allowed me to walk into an ambush, had in fact facilitated it, and when Vrasan had the time or inclination to spare from whatever tasks occupied him now, he would begin cutting me up and removing the quantum crystals inside me. I glanced at him. He'd gone over to one of the big sleds where the two clones were helping him mate some large device into a hole newly opened in his carapace armour. It looked much like a smaller version of the hemisphere he'd installed on the hooder and I reckoned it must be the control hardware. After a time, he returned to the creature and stood at its head, while it grew utterly still. Meanwhile the clones took up heavy tools and began boring out the rivets holding the chains to its carapace.

I studied my manacle – the thing was ceramal and impossible for me to cut or break. I could do with one of those tools, whatever they were. Further scanning of my surroundings revealed nothing I could use. My pack lay over where the clones had been eating, along with my weapons and theirs, but all unreachable. My gaze next strayed to the cave mouth, which I now noticed to be lit. The brightness of the light there brought home to me how dark it had become, so I reckoned night must be falling. I could see one of the clones squatted in there down by one wall. I had no idea why and dismissed it, turning elsewhere. Over on the far side of the valley stood one of the chameleonware devices. It lay too far away for me to throw a stone at it in the hope of knocking it out and, even if I did so, would that bring rescue? That bitch Suzeal. Did it amuse her, as it obviously had before, to think of a clone of Jack Zero, with whom she obviously had some history, subject to the vicious intentions of the prador? Even though she wouldn't see or know what happened, and the exact prador position would still be unclear to her?

My gaze still on the chameleonware elicited knowledge from Jack Zero. The devices were standard prador manufacture, nowhere near as efficient and complex as the Polity version. I understood now that some of my earlier thoughts on the thing had actually been about Polity tech and not these. They had to be carefully programmed to block signals in the EMR spectrum between those who were concealed behind their field. Their reactivity was limited because, unlike the Polity version, no AI or sub-AI ran them. They didn't have the backup circuits and, also because of that lack of reactivity, could be knocked out by any suitable EMR blast which was close enough. All of this still seemed no help to me, but something about it just kept niggling at my mind. Then it came to me in a hot flush down my back: *They had to be programmed to block the signals under their field.* So Suzeal *had* used me to find the prador. But it required action from me, and seemed likely could still result in my death. She was waiting. She was ready.

But if I was going to die in Suzeal's bombardment of the prador, then surely that was better than being taken apart by Vrasan? Yes, it was, and I might yet get some chance of escape. I leaned over to my collar.

'Open previous comlink,' I said.

'About bloody time,' Suzeal replied.

9

'What are you going to do?'

'Well I'm—'

The link fizzed out, detected and intercepted by the chameleonware, but tardily. I wondered if it had been enough, and I continued wondering as I sat there, the rain growing heavier. I looked up and speculated on what she'd do first if she had managed to locate me. Perhaps, even now, a satellite up there was inserting a missile into a tube and firing it. The thing would take some minutes to reach this place. There'd be a flash and then oblivion. Or maybe not. She had said she wanted to do something 'interesting' with Vrasan, and burning him up in nuclear fire didn't seem to be that. Surely, being the type she was, she would at least want him to know she was killing him? I began to shove at the post to which they'd secured me. While I did this, lights came on across the encampment, confirming my earlier thought about nightfall and, checking around to ensure I wasn't observed, I noticed him.

He had moved out from the cave and now crouched at the entrance. Even through the heavy rain and spray, and over my distance from the cave, I could see he didn't look like one of the clones now – bigger, a pack on his back and a pulse rifle braced across his stomach. I glanced over to the hooder and counted. All five clones were there. When I looked back, he'd moved over to the other side of the cave, concealing himself against the wall so as not to be seen by Vrasan or the clones at work around the hooder. There stood the man-thing, clad in overalls and carrying items he must have taken from one of those, I now guessed, whose head he had torn off.

But how could he be functioning like this? Yes, it was true that heavily virus-mutated prador like Vrasan could be intelligent, but prador were of an utterly different biology from humans and their mutation hadn't proceeded from injury but something else. My understanding was that humans who were mutated by the virus to this extent lost their minds, diminishing into no more than a beast. Yet, of course, I'd seen intelligent behaviour from him aboard the King's Ship, so why shouldn't he have regained that once he was free of his control frame? In retrospect, I realized that his previous behaviour hadn't aligned with my second-hand, embedded knowledge of such things. Perhaps I should be careful of being so reliant on it – a lot of my other assumptions and speculations could have been wrong too. But this didn't matter, what concerned me now was how his presence might affect my future – if I had one.

He peered past the edge of the cave wall then abruptly pulled back. Vrasan, who until that moment had remained still, swung around. The prador might have been facing away from the cave until then but that didn't mean he hadn't seen him. Prador used their forward eyes to focus on what they might presently be doing, but their stalked eyes were sentries, forever on the alert for danger. Vrasan began to move towards the cave, but with perfect timing a light streaked down through the roiling sky and hit just at the end of the valley. I glimpsed it as it came down and turned away as bright light flashed red through my closed eyelids. I waited to die, expecting the roar of a blast front to incinerate me. Instead the ground shuddered to an intense crackling. I looked back to see a wall of iridescence shoot along the valley and up its slabbed walls. A glance towards the smoking chameleonware device told me all I needed to know: Suzeal had taken down their 'ware and had yet to begin her real attack.

The prador burst into frenetic motion. The two working the machines suddenly rose out of them on grav – they probably hadn't been using it before since it was particularly difficult to conceal. Vrasan and the Guard clattered and bubbled loudly, their speech amplified by their armour, bellowing orders. The two descended again to shut down their machinery and rapidly disassemble it, while the Guard joined them, quickly and efficiently loading it all onto the grav-sleds. I watched Vrasan. He'd turned away from the cave and his full attention was on the hooder, which had raised its spoon-shaped head from the ground. I hoped the thing, now freed, would slam down on him, but it meekly swung out from the valley edge, lowered its head and entered the cave.

The man-thing had moved and, scanning around, I couldn't locate him. Vrasan shot out into the valley, his clones running to keep up. He had them helping with the loading, the operation so fast the clones must have been pre-programmed for it. I kept trying to locate the man-thing, then finally saw him squirming through the mud near where the clones had been sitting. He gathered up a couple of pulse rifles and my carbine, clips and food, and then took my pack to throw them inside. Once he'd done this, his head swung round and he looked straight towards me. Just then another crack like a thunderbolt split the sky and a streak cut down, straight on the carapace of one of the original prador. Fire exploded underneath the creature while the course of the projectile from above turned into a column of steam. The blast lifted the thing and sent it tumbling along the valley to come down on its back, legs utterly still. More shots came down, three of them hitting nothing but mud and fountaining it up in columns of fire, and a fourth hit the edge of a grav-sled, taking off the corner but not disabling it. Vrasan abruptly spun around and headed back to the cave, while the Guard directed a sled after him. Perhaps he'd simply forget about me.

A hand came down on my arm above the manacle, unfeasibly long fingers wrapping round it. I looked straight into the face of my erstwhile nemesis. He showed his teeth, then reached down with his other hand to tug at the chain securing me. I wondered if the chain was beyond even him. But no, he took hold of it in both hands and pulled. Nothing happened for a moment and I felt like shrieking at him to use the pulse rifles but then the chain snapped with a loud crack. Adrenalin surging, I jumped up and he held my pack out to me. Did he realize it was mine or was this more a case of sharing the load? I took out one pulse rifle and pulled the pack on. He gestured, pointed, and broke into a run towards the end of the valley.

I expected to be scythed down by Gatling fire at any moment. But it didn't come until we climbed the mound of debris. Hearing it, I dived down the other side as part of the mound behind exploded into splinters of wood and rock. Thankfully my companion had done the same. He showed those teeth again, gesturing ahead. I ignored him, though, and climbed back up a little way to peer over. The prador who'd fired was one of the originals and still continued to pursue us as another rain of what I presumed to be mini-railgun strikes exploded along the valley. One shot punched through a procession of three sleds heading for the cave, blowing half its load away and knocking out its grav so it dropped heavily on the fire underneath. I glanced to the cave and saw two clones run out – two Jacks – who then headed in our direction. I scrambled down again.

My new ally had waited. 'One prador and two clones coming after us,' I told him.

He hesitated, looking back up the rubble pile, then nodded and gestured into the banyan. We ran through the trees. A low drone from above, and glimpses of steering-thruster flashes, indicated the pursuing prador had taken to the air. But the foliage and branches were thick up there . . . I remembered all the detector equipment prador had and reckoned it could easily see us down on the ground. The thing confirmed this by opening fire. Gatling cannon slugs hammered into the trees above, shattering branches, and many slamming into the ground all around. I thought about throwing myself down but realized that I would present a larger target lying down, and it was best to keep running. A heavy thump threw my companion forwards. In the stuttering light of the cannon I saw his overall ripped open to reveal a groove carved down his back and a remaining thrall segment peeled up. He rolled and came upright again, keeping moving as if little of consequence had happened. As I came up beside him he suddenly reached out and dragged me to a wide trunk on one side. Here the branches above were thicker and closer together, and Gatling fire slammed into them, creating a rain of splinters and smoking cannon slugs. This pause afforded some protection but it couldn't last. The prador would either cut through with the cannon or use something else. He did the latter.

A particle beam lanced down, setting the tree ablaze. Branches exploded in the sudden heat and gaps emerged. Then other detonations started to occur all around us. These were strikes from above, marked by lines of vapour stretching up into the dark sky. The particle beam cut off and, shifting out a little way, I managed to see the prador hovering above. He hung there for a moment, wavered as if indecisive, then shot away. As he left I saw something fired by him streaking towards us.

'Run!' I shouted, even as I did so.

We got maybe ten paces before the tree exploded. The blast

picked me up in a wall of burning splinters, mauled me like an angry giant and deposited me at the foot of another tree. I lay there stunned for a moment, but the danger hadn't ended and we needed to move quickly. I stood, not even thinking about probable injuries, retrieved my pulse rifle and tried to orient myself. My companion came round the tree peeling splinters out of his neck and pointed. We ran on.

I briefly wondered about what had happened. I would've liked to believe that Suzeal had, after a transmission delay, seen our situation and tried to help out. But the likely explanation seemed to be that once viable targets had moved into the cave, Suzeal had switched to the prador after us. As we kept going and no clones came at us, I thought further. The first railgun shot, almost certainly from one of her satellites, had been very accurate, but those that came subsequently put the lie to that. Lucky shot, I guessed. Her hardware almost certainly wasn't controlled by AI, just like the big railgun she had on the station wasn't either, so that couldn't sufficiently account for atmospheric effects. It also had its spectrum of scan limited by the cloud, the darkness and perhaps by remaining chameleonware effect. Still, she had small weapons in orbit and when I'd encountered the hooder and the droon it had been a clear morning, with no 'ware active. She could've helped me then.

We ran on, but I began to lag and then bounced off a tree I'd simply not seen.

'I can't keep this pace,' I told him.

He glanced at me, hardly even breathing deeply, and slowed to a jog. After seeing that even this was becoming a struggle for me, he slowed to a walk. The fire in the trees was now receding behind us; it had also become difficult to see, even though the cloud above had begun to clear and moonlight beamed through occasional gaps. I listened intently, still expecting to hear the clones running up behind us. That they hadn't yet appeared I put down to the lack of light. They were rugged and tough like my new friend, but couldn't see in the dark any better than me.

'I don't suppose you can talk,' I said.

He shook his head once, then held up his fingers to his lips. I nodded understanding.

Wider gaps began to appear above, showing the cloud breaking up rapidly, perhaps due to the effect of the railgun missiles. They must have expended a huge amount of energy up there, but it was more likely to be the breeze I'd begun to feel, though that could've been an effect of the shots too. My companion abruptly halted and looked around. After a moment, he walked over to a nearby banyan trunk, reached out to take hold in a couple of places, then turned and nodded me over. He only began to climb once he'd seen me following. I wearily struggled to reach the crown of the thing until he leaned over and hauled me up as if I weighed nothing. The crown stood wide, small pools occupying gaps, moss, lichen and alien epiphytes and bromeliads growing in abundance. He reached out and grabbed my chin, directing my gaze elsewhere, then pointed and made a walking motion with two fingers. My thoughts leaden, it took me a moment to understand what he meant.

The tree we stood on was one trunk of a banyan but not the whole plant, which could cover an area of miles. Thick branches arced over to other trunks and I got the idea as he stepped onto one and began moving along it, heading towards the side of the valley. Going on hands and knees at first, I gained confidence, finally walking upright like him. Gecko function was a failure as my boots caked with moss, but the branches were plenty wide enough. It was, I reflected, this kind of growth that had saved us from being minced by railgun slugs.

We travelled in this manner for some time until he later turned and squatted, holding his finger up to his lips. I squatted too and heard movement below, then carefully risked a peek over the edge. Expecting to see one of the clones down there, it took me a moment to identify something very different, as plated darkness flowed between the trees. It was about as wide as the branch we crouched on and roughly twenty feet long. A small hooder, perhaps an infant? I didn't know enough even to guess since my knowledge only covered their capabilities and durability. It was well to be reminded that the dangers here were not only from the prador. As the thing passed out of sight, my com device chose that moment to buzz a couple of times and my companion looked round at me hissing, teeth exposed in what was definitely not a grin. I tapped the control screen to turn it on, then quickly worked through it to turn off the communicator.

It soon became increasingly difficult to find branches which could support us as the trunks got smaller and the banyan steadily petered out, displaced by those white fungus trees whose residents had tried to eat my face. I didn't like the idea, but after we'd been forced to double back a couple of times, I whispered to attract his attention and pointed downwards. He nodded agreement and we descended.

Once we were under the fungus trees, I put up my hood and closed my visor. The horrible worms pattered down and tried to find access to me, but I brushed them away. My companion seemed oblivious to them and, not having much luck penetrating his skin, most fell away. Walking behind him, I noted some still clinging on around the now dry wound in his back and the remains of his thrall there. They were tenacious, but these too eventually fell away as we came to a slab-strewn slope at the edge of the valley. We climbed up this, into the bright moonlit night. This moon wasn't the one which looked like a half-bitten apple, but a larger orb, orange and smooth with its own small glittery ring system. I felt incredibly tired but, while scanning my surroundings, also incredibly alive.

As we trudged through the darkness, feeling this way buoyed me for a while, until the weariness took me into fugue, and I became only aware of walking and trying not to fall over. At one point I looked up and found myself alone. My companion reappeared a moment later and, grabbing my arm, towed me inside a small cave. I lay on the floor and the last thing I saw was him squatting, silhouetted by moonlight in the entrance.

I rose to consciousness with the daylight, feeling as if someone had cast me out of lead on the floor of the cave, and didn't want to move. Eventually forcing my eyes open, I stared up at the fossils, like tangles of bent spoons, on the ceiling, and I wondered if they were some ancestor of the hooders. As the ridiculous idea passed – wrong world – I came to full wakefulness and slowly sat up. No sign of my companion. I folded my visor and hood down, which I'd left closed last night, and noted my pack still resting beside me, so didn't think he'd abandoned me completely. I pulled it over and then noticed some of my tools lying on the floor, all damaged beyond use. Lying amidst them was the manacle from my wrist, which had been snapped open by someone very strong.

I saw only one pulse rifle pointing out of the pack, while a burned hole ran through the top and out the bottom. I couldn't see why my companion might have taken the missing pulse rifle and laser carbine, and thought I'd probably lost the weapons during our escape, since they hadn't been that secure. The hole was almost certainly from a Gatling slug. I'd been just an inch or two from dying. I opened up the pack, hoping the water container had stayed undamaged, but it was missing. My companion had obviously gone through the pack and had perhaps left to fill the container. I took out a piece from one of the broken food blocks, then looked up as a shadow blocked out the sun. He stood there with the water container under one arm and gestured, pointing at the food and indicating the pack. Apparently I wasn't to eat it, so I put it back. He ducked into the cave dragging something and deposited it on the floor.

As he sat down with his back to the wall, I got a better look at him. He seemed more human now, perhaps because he wasn't trying to kill me. No, on closer inspection his snout appeared shorter and his eyes weren't the complete black they'd been before, though this could have been due to the light. The most evident change was stubble on his previously bald head. He was wearing overalls which covered most of his body and so concealed any changes there; I looked down at his new hand. This was smaller than the other and the fingers not so long, but whether that was due to it not having attained full growth I didn't know. He reached out and dragged the deposited object closer and I inspected it.

He had killed a sleer and here, sans legs, lay one body segment. Digging claws in, he peeled up a chunk of carapace, exposing gelatinous green, then pushed this away to expose yellow flesh beneath. Using a chain-glass spatula he had taken from my pack, he carved a chunk and held it out to me. I took it and just held it, still remembering how sick I'd been aboard the King's Ship from eating the wrong thing. He gouged out some for himself and ate, and after a moment I ate too. The stuff tasted acidic – one of the disconnected pieces of knowledge surfaced and I recognized a taste like mango, but not as sweet. In silence, we steadily ate our way through most of it. When he'd finished, he pulled a belt around his waist that I'd only noted in passing. The thing was constructed from a vine, while the small sack attached he made from some kind of leaf with the consistency of fabric. The visible contents were recognizable at once: garlic bulbs. He ate two of them whole without offering me any, and with this, further knowledge came to me.

The Spatterjay virus mutated its host but its growth could be retarded. A range of Polity drugs did it. A substance extracted from the bile ducts of oceanic leeches – usually as big as whales – killed the virus. This was necessary for the large leeches because they had made the transition from plug feeders to eating whole prey which, by dint of the virus inside them, tended to not die simply by being ingested. The substance – sprine – enabled the leeches to digest such prey. Sprine in heavily diluted form was also used to retard viral growth in humans. But, because of the biology involved, some human food was also effective, and one of the best of these was garlic. He knew his problem and was doing something about it.

'Lucky to have found that here,' I said.

He nodded agreement, but of course the conversation stopped there.

'We need to find a way to communicate,' I added.

He tapped at his throat, shook his head then inserted another whole bulb of garlic and crunched it down. I returned my attention to the sleer flesh and ate some more. Who knew when I would get anything else to eat? It then occurred to me that he might also have been reserving the food in the bag for himself, for the same purpose as the garlic. When I could finally cram no more in, I snared the water container and drank, then moved to go outside.

'I need to take a shit.'

He nodded once and I went, my stomach bubbling and mouth-watering. I felt a bit sick, but managed to hold onto the meal. When I finally returned I sat and studied him as he tied up his stock of garlic.

'You know, I've been talking to someone on the station,' I said. I had his attention, very abruptly.

'Her name's Suzeal and—'

A second later he had me pinned against the wall of the cave by my throat, his mouth open in a snarl just inches from my face.

'Let . . . me . . . finish,' I managed to choke out.

He slackened his grip slightly.

'She's a bitch,' I said. 'She delivered me as a clone to the prador . . .' I told him my story briefly and tersely, and finished with, 'Like I said, she promised to rescue me, but I know she used me to locate the prador and I doubt my rescue was ever a serious consideration. But there's still a chance of that. I want to continue heading for the installation she told me about.'

He released me and moved back. Then he abruptly stooped and wrote in the dust: *she dangerous*.

'Yes, I know.' I shrugged. 'But what else can we do?'

He reached over and grabbed my wrist and with one sharp claw tried to work the console of my suit, but it wouldn't respond. Releasing me, he slammed his fist against the floor again and again, hissing as he did so, then abruptly backed up, slamming it against the wall so hard the stone splintered. From this I understood that, despite all his human behaviour, he was struggling for control. Finally it came to an end and he settled, knees up against his chest, folded in.

'Shall I talk to her again?' I asked.

He stared at me for a long while, then reached up and pointed to his ears.

'You want to hear.' This was what he'd been trying to do with the console but the suit, not recognizing him as its occupant, had not allowed it. I made the required alterations then said, 'Open previous comlink.'

Tumbleweed.

The comlink fizzed and I got nothing.

'Not there at the moment.'

He unfolded.

'What's your story?' I gestured at the floor.

He wrote, *too many words* then gestured eloquently before grabbing my pack and tossing it at me. Time to go.

'Where to?' I asked.

Instal, he wrote.

The sun breaking over the mountains greeted us.

'We head towards the sun until we're out of the mountains, then I hope to get further directions from her.'

He nodded once and led off.

Old vegetation cloaked the ground where it wasn't covered by slabs or buried in scree. The recent rain, however, had obviously been welcome because new growth had begun to appear. White furry things with ball heads were easing up, blue, orange and plastic-green spikes, the green nets of early bubble grass and bright toadstools like discarded buttons strewed the ground. At one point, my companion spotted some small green blades and set to uprooting them with his clawed hand, securing a mass of garlic bulbs, many of which he ate, the rest I ended up hauling in my pack.

An animal trail took us down and we skirted yet another valley. Having seen that hooder the previous night, I felt no urge to go down there for anything. My companion halted me, then held up his hand to his ear. His hearing was good because it took me a moment to distinguish the sound from the susurration of the wind. Then I heard it: the sound of someone speaking words of which I could make no sense – the gabbling of an alien mind that had sacrificed intelligence for species survival.

'Gabbleduck?'

He nodded grimly.

'What's your name?' I asked.

He stared at me for a long time; eventually he brushed away some of the ground cover with his foot before squatting. I bent down too and watched him write *Marcus*, then scrub it out straight after with his foot.

I glanced up at the sky, thinking about Suzeal's satellites, and held out my hand. 'Pleased to meet you, Marcus.'

He hesitated again before grasping it, after which he abruptly turned away and moved on. I stared at his retreating back. He wasn't entirely human and, in reality, I had little true experience of human interaction. But I was sure he'd lied. It occurred to me, judging by his reaction to the mention of Suzeal, that he might not want her to know his name, should she come for us, and so hadn't told me the truth. But Marcus would have to do for now. I stepped after him, about to say something further, when pulse rifle fire cracked and sizzled through the air where I'd been standing.

I hit the ground as more shots ensued, then scrambled downslope, heading to the left since the shot had come from my right. Marcus was down, smoke rising from his body, but he kept moving at a speedy crawl towards some rocks. Then he leapt up and over them to the right, shots nailing his path and stone exploding in every direction. I kept going, down towards fungus trees since they offered the best concealment. I pulled away a worm on my face, got my visor down and hood up. The limb of a fungus tree fell, smoking, behind me, as I came upright and dodged between the things to get out of sight of the snipers. I squatted by one white trunk and pointed my rifle back the way I had come. A hand closed on my shoulder like a vice, hauled me up and threw me, slamming into another tree that showered worms. Still holding onto my rifle, I fired even as I slid down the thing. The rifle the Jack in front of me had begun to aim exploded. He stood there with the remnants of the thing burning in his hands, then his programming caught up and he discarded it. I saw the blast had taken away half his right hand. I kept firing, his chest flaming, and I tried to correct my aim to his face as he surged forwards. He snatched the weapon and twisted it from my grip, grabbed for my throat, but got just a handful of overalls.

Time seemed to slow.

Migraine lights flashed as a whole slew of new data fell into my mind in one seemingly indigestible lump, but it began to dissolve and distribute. He was much stronger than me, so I had to incorporate that into my strategy. I brought my knees against his chest and threw myself backwards. We both went down. As my pack hit the ground, I caught him behind the neck and heaved with both legs, flipping him behind me. He still held onto my overalls as I drew my sidearm and fired at his face. His grip slackened and he rolled away. I rolled too, simultaneously shedding my pack and coming up on one knee to fire at him again as he rose, going for his eyes. He ducked, his program protecting his eyes, and ran at me, while I turned and thrust-kicked the side of his leg and bounced away, something in me baffled because I had not damaged his knee, but he did stumble and fall forwards. My next two shots I put precisely in the back of his neck, then as he turned, head smoking, I shot him in the face. With one eye now burned into a ruin, still he came on. Jumping up, I spun and snapped out another kick which struck him in the side, but it also put me off balance because I'd been aiming for his face, and had tried a kick my body could not yet manage.

Stumbling, I rolled forwards and came up, firing shots into his body, tracking up again to his vulnerable head. His overalls were now burning as he continued to charge at me relentlessly.

I leapt at him and threw myself into a dropkick, feet slamming into his chest and hurling him backwards, then came down feet first to jump past him. But his hand closed about my ankle. I rolled over and could see he was down on his chest with his head up, and so fired at his face again, putting out his other eye, while he continued to pull me towards him. At first I struggled to get away, but instantly realized this was the wrong thing to do and stopped. Instead I pushed myself towards him, folding the leg he held, then spun over and brought my other knee down on his back. Pressing the gun against the back of his neck, I held it there and kept firing, even though it felt as if my ankle was breaking, while his other hand closed on my thigh, fingers digging in. Through a haze of pain, I felt him shuddering, then the gun died.

I don't know how long I sat there until Marcus appeared and snapped away the clone's fingers. Even once free, I couldn't pull the gun away from the back of his head nor relinquish my grip on it. Marcus pulled my arm back and finally the tension started to leak out. I rolled clear, then started to probe my ankle. A crunch attracted my attention and I looked over to see Marcus had smashed the Jack's skull open with a rock. He grabbed the thrall and tore it out, its tail burned and melted where my shots had finally killed the thing. He tossed it over to land beside another he'd abandoned, obviously having killed the other Jack.

I finally stood, right leg leaden with pain at the thigh, left ankle feeling broken, though it wasn't. I limped over and picked up my pack, then moved a little deeper into the valley where the banyan grew, and opened my visor and hood there. I sank down by a trunk, pulled down my envirosuit trousers and inspected my hip. It was red and swollen and bloody where the mesh had broken the skin. Muscular damage only. I next took off my boot and checked my ankle properly. In the short time since I'd last felt it, the thing had swollen hugely and was also bloody from the mesh. Searching through the pack, I found a length of the webbing I'd used as a strap for my first iteration of a pack and bound up my ankle, using the atomic shear to split the end of the webbing so I could tie it securely. Marcus came to squat beside me.

'I won't be able to move very fast,' I said.

He waved a hand dismissively. Any urgency had passed with the two clones dead, unless Vrasan had sent some more. But I suspected the prador had other concerns right now and would be reluctant to lose the remainder of his clones.

Marcus pulled the pack over and took out a food block, which he held out to me. This made me smile. 'No – your need is greater,' I said.

He nodded, put it back, then picked up the shear and abruptly leapt up to climb the trunk. I heard him moving about up there as I rested, the thump of my heart steadily waning. Dry-mouthed, I reached out and took up the water container and drank. Shortly after, a strange stillness seemed to have descended around me. No more worms were falling from the fungus trees and the breeze had stilled. Marcus had stopped moving too. I thought this was all to do with my condition – the calm after the storm and other suitable analogies. Then it moved into sight, huge, over to my left and spoke.

'Ababa-herber scopolot,' it said.

I froze for a second, then looked round for a weapon. Marcus's pulse rifle lay propped against the tree, but if I reached for it the thing would see me move. I just stayed there being as small and inconsequential as possible.

An arcing array of emerald eyes crossed its domed head over a duck bill which, when it opened it to huff out vapour, revealed a tangle of white thorny teeth. The body behind bore some resemblance to that of a hippo, but humped along with a gait something like a huge fat caterpillar, smoothly though, and I knew they were able to move fast. It perambulated clear of the trees and then crouched, like some massively obese cat preparing to pounce.

'Ulbscabber,' it noted, then seemed to relax, and sauntered towards the still-shifting Jack lying there. Had it been attracted by carrion? This seemed likely.

The thing paused by the corpse and reached out with one large black claw to prod it. It walked round as if mildly puzzled, then heaved back to settle on its rump directly facing me. I now got a good look at those dimorphic forelimbs. They could separate at the forearm, the claws themselves dividing too, giving it effect-ively four forelimbs. Folded lower down against its belly were two smaller, stunted limbs and I didn't know whether this was usual or not. With a main forelimb it scratched at its belly contemplatively, while reaching down with the other to prod at the corpse again, before turning its attention to the two thralls. It picked one up and held it before its eyes. Intelligence? No – it then inserted the thing in its mouth and tried chewing it, before pulling it out, inspecting it again and discarding it.

I felt no fear. This could have been because the Jack had come close to killing me and I'd been overloaded with adrenalin. I certainly wasn't stupid enough not to know my extreme danger. But the creature was an enigma. Descended from the Atheter, these were the animals this spacefaring race had deliberately turned themselves into. The Atheter had been arguably more advanced than the Polity, but sacrificed their intelligence to escape the civilization-killing Jain technology whose effects lay scattered all over the galaxy, and most notably in the virus which had transformed the Jack now lying on the ground in front of this creature. Their history was an operatic tragedy. I felt awed and humbled to be near one, as well as sad. The feeling didn't last.

The gabbleduck, after considering the thrall, returned its attention to the Jack, reaching down and calmly tearing off an arm. It held this up for inspection before chewing on it contemplatively, then seemed to rather enjoy the taste and chewed more enthusiastically, stripping the tough flesh off the bone and swallowing a lump. As this went down, it abruptly froze and its eyes grew wide. A couple of seconds passed. It jerked, its claw snapping out and sending the arm spinning into the trees. It then hunched forwards and howled. I had never, in my brief life, heard anything like it, and felt in my core that my predecessor hadn't either. It dug right down inside me, flowing down my spine and pulling my guts into a knot. It seemed the essence of grief for the passing of civilization and it was angry, livid – there was so much rage there.

Hunching further forwards as the howl died, it opened its bill wide and heaved, ejecting from the back of its throat a jet of white bile and chunks of flesh, splashing onto the corpse. It grabbed up the corpse and tore it into pieces, hurling them off into the trees so hard they broke branches. Next it rippled forwards, horribly fast and came right up to me. I could smell its breath – carrion and something spicy – and white bile spattered my face, burning where it touched. I had no time to reach for the pulse rifle and thought I must be about to die. I stared into those emerald eyes and it seemed I could see star systems in their depths.

'Oogra blastic blastic,' it told me knowingly, then abruptly rounded the tree and went crashing off into the valley.

I lay there noting how close I'd come to defecating. My heart was thumping and I held out my hands to watch them shake. Hot and cold shivers ran through me. I don't know, I just don't know. This had been as dangerous to me as the encounter with the Jack because, in the end, I could have died. But I also had a sense of an encounter with something otherworldly, almost supernatural in its effect. I felt as if I'd never be able to stand, to go on, and that after this all striving had been sapped of meaning. The gabbleduck, I was sure, was no mere animal. Marcus came down the tree and silently handed me a walking staff he'd cut. My hands steadied on the thing and the shivering stilled. In a dreamlike state, I finally hauled myself to my feet while he took up the pack and his rifle. We collected my rifle on the way out of the valley – I wouldn't let him carry that.

Rationality returned and I wondered again about the creature we'd left behind. To say that its response to the Jack had been extreme was an understatement. Had it, in some way, sensed the Jain technology in his virus? Did enough of its intelligence remain for it to know it was in the presence of some part of the technology that had led to its kind abandoning their minds? Perhaps not. Perhaps some cellular mechanism deep inside the thing had identified it and caused it to eject it. But that howl. I don't know. I just don't know.

10

As the sun set we made camp in a bowl of rock high on the face of one mountain. Marcus had gone off ahead earlier, as I trudged along wincing with every step, and then returned with a load of sleer segments bound together with vine. The extra weight hadn't seemed to affect him at all. Once at our camp, he disappeared off again, breaking into a fast run down towards a nearby valley, and it was only then that my suit started buzzing.

After allowing the comlink, I said, 'What the fuck do you want?'

'Well that's not very friendly,' Suzeal replied.

Her voice came out loud because I'd set the comlink so that Marcus could hear too. I turned it down again, then closed up my hood and visor to see her face and study her reactions.

'You let me walk into an ambush and used me to get to the prador. I guess, because of that, I'm not feeling very friendly.'

'You were useful to me,' she stated flatly. 'Let us hope you may continue to be so, otherwise I see no reason to send a shuttle to pick you up.'

'And that might actually happen? Sure you haven't got further uses for me down here?'

'Tell me about the prador,' she said. 'The cloud and the chameleonware echoes made it difficult enough to hit anything, let alone gather data. They were making something and I'm sure I saw a hooder down there . . .'

I considered just telling her to fuck off, but she was still my only chance of rescue from this world, and I thought it would be interesting to see her reactions to what I had witnessed.

'Vrasan thralled a hooder.'

'The fuck!' she exclaimed. 'That's insane. How the hell did he do that?'

'I think his mission here had more than one objective and he came prepared. You were right, this wasn't all about those Old Families. He wanted to know who you were trading with and shut you down, sure, but I think the king wants hooders too.'

After a long pause she asked, 'Why?'

'Because they're ancient biomechs and it may be possible to return them to functionality. I don't need to tell you how much the prador like weapons.' I kept back from her Vrasan's hope that he could use a hooder to attack her station.

She fell silent again, then turned contemplative. 'Seems I've been missing a trade opportunity. I expect the king would pay well for living hooders.'

Was she amoral or immoral? I wondered. There was no thought there for how dangerous it would be to humanity if the prador reactivated Atheter war machines. But then, she traded in living humans. Why would I have expected any other response from her?

'How is the situation up there?'

'The prador are still rooted like beetles in a log. We can't get anything out of the station and they've been firing at any ships that arrive, driving them away. They also keep taking shots at us, trying to hit our railgun, but our laser and hardfield defences are preventing that.'

'So what do you intend to do?'

'It might be time to sacrifice the space dock,' she opined. 'The loss of infrastructure will be catastrophic and will take us years

190

to recover from. But we're losing a lot of trade and the dock isn't completely necessary for transfers.'

'Aren't there people in the dock?'

'A few thousand at last count, if they're still alive.'

I felt horrified by her callousness and tried to put myself in her position. Her biggest concern was the bottom line. While the prador occupied the dock, trade wouldn't recommence so I supposed she considered the loss of ships and traders on and in the dock a minor matter which she could blame on the prador.

'Can you talk to them?'

'Oh I've been talking. It seems they've backed themselves into a corner. They have their mission, and the member of the Guard I spoke to sees no way out but to stick to it unto death, which I'd have been happy to provide long ago if it wouldn't have caused so much damage to me.'

'Tell him,' I said.

'Tell him what?'

'Tell them that you will destroy the dock unless they stop firing on incoming and departing ships.'

'A threat I have already tried.'

I thought about that for a moment. 'He probably doesn't want you bringing in any assistance or further armament.' I thought for a bit longer. 'The king wants those Old Families. How important, relatively, is your space dock compared to your trade with them?'

'Interesting question.' She looked contemplative. 'The dock is probably more important now I know the king is moving against those families. That exchange has a limited life and it would be good to start trading with the king and his family instead. I'd certainly need the dock if I started moving hooders.'

'Give them something in exchange for a ceasefire,' I said, but then instantly felt bad about encouraging her to sign the death sentence of those Old Families. I added, 'Of course, the king doesn't know which families are involved so you don't have to give them all. You should also factor in that not destroying his prador here will put you in a better position with the king.'

She stared at me hard. 'And you are a clone only a few months old,' she said.

'With the knowledge of a Polity agent integrating in my mind.'

'Yes. Physical aspects too, it would seem.'

I knew exactly what she meant. 'Skills, it seems, are also a part of that knowledge. I didn't know I could fight like that until pressed to do so.'

'And who knows what else you may discover? Now tell me about your interesting companion. I've never seen a mutation so advanced, with the human retaining that level of intelligence.'

I felt wary of her interest, and trod carefully. 'There's little to tell. By freeing him from his thrall, I released the prador control of his mind and he was obviously grateful for that.'

'You must have some detail about him.'

'Very little. He can only communicate by scribbling in the dust. I know his name and little beyond that. We haven't really had time to get fully acquainted.'

'And that name is?'

I didn't want to tell her, and she probably hadn't been able to see what he'd scribbled in the dirt. But it struck me that she'd see it as implausible I hadn't asked it, and I also still felt sure Marcus wasn't his real name.

'Marcus is all he told me. I've tried getting other information but I'm not sure he understands. He may have retained some intelligence but I think, through the mutation, he's lost a lot of his memories. His scribblings are hardly legible.' Even as I finished speaking, I realized this was the first time in my life I'd told a direct lie, even though I'd been evasive with Suzeal on certain things before. But then, for the larger portion of my life, I hadn't been speaking to anyone.

'Very well, we'll speak again.'

'Wait! Are you going to negotiate with the prador? Might you be able to come for us soon?'

'I will consider it.'

'And are we still heading in the right direction for that installation?'

She hesitated, looking at something to one side. 'Head about ten degrees to the right of the sunrise now.'

'How far away are we?'

'Your journey to the prador base covered a lot of the distance. You're now two hundred and sixty miles from the installation. In another hundred, you'll be out of the mountains.' She clicked off the link.

I closed down the visor and hood then looked over at Marcus, who was now squatting at the edge of the bowl with a pile of wood on the ground in front of him.

'She obviously wanted to talk while you weren't here,' I told him. 'Still problems up there, so no pick-up for us. I told her as little as possible about you, in fact said you are brain-damaged, which I suspect is what you prefer.'

He nodded once and picked up the wood, bringing it over, piling it carefully and using one pulse shot to set it burning. That evening we roasted the sleer flesh and it tasted better. The anachronism of a campfire brought comfort – something deeply rooted in the human psyche. It also brought a sleer to investigate, but it paused at the edge of the light, then headed off again. I wondered how much fire would put off the other monsters here, and if it really was a good idea, then drifted to sleep on the stone.

★   ★   ★

The first day had been hard, the second day harder still. On the fifth morning the swelling had gone down around my ankle and I tightened the binding. I ate some of the human food Marcus offered me and felt an extreme hunger for it, despite having gorged on sleer flesh over the previous days. Some nutrient was obviously missing. Our communications were brief while I struggled to walk, briefer still while we saw to the necessities of survival. I tried, but he seemed disinclined to share much, especially when I wanted to learn more about his past. Perhaps he was ashamed or reluctant to share, if what the king had said was true about him having been involved in the coring and thralling trade. Or perhaps he feared I'd pass on information to Suzeal. I promised that during my next communication with her, I'd ensure his presence, but it had been a few days since we last spoke and I was beginning to feel concerned. Every evening I'd tried to reopen communication with her, but had just got a fizzing sound.

'Perhaps something's happened up there,' I said. 'Suzeal has been quiet.'

We'd camped in the lea of a rock in twilight. Marcus stared at me, but of course said nothing. His face had regained some more humanity, so I could just about read his expression. It seemed the essence of, 'Yeah, whatever'. Suzeal could have become bored with us now since all we'd been doing was plodding through the mountains. Or maybe, no longer serving her purposes, I'd become irrelevant.

Days and nights followed in quick succession. We fell into a routine of Marcus heading off during the day to hunt and gather while I plodded on, and evenings of fire and food. On the tenth evening we stopped lighting a fire after we spotted a hooder in the moonlight heading out of a nearby valley. We fled into the night and saw it reach the fire and scatter it in a shower of sparks, then travelled on in fear of it coming after us. But it didn't. The following day we continued walking and, even after this, my ankle and thigh were a lot better that evening, though covered in deep black bruises. A repast of cold sleer preceded sleep, and the day after we finally got a view from the mountains of rolling hills and a plain lying beyond. It was sitting under a haze so it wasn't clear, but I could see circular areas dotted it which seemed likely to be banyans.

As we descended to the hills, we found that the simple terran grass had won the battle against alien flora and had cloaked the stretches of ground lying between copses of banyan and other trees. A herd of animals, like those on the droon's hunting ground, grazed on the grass, which surprised me, but then, cellulose is cellulose. A muddy heap punctured with holes revealed other animals resembling a cross between meerkats and rabbits, and the grass in the surrounding area was cropped down like a lawn. They disappeared when a shadow passed over the ground of a flying creature which seemed to be the by-blow of a crab and a beetle. As the hills began to flatten out, I got a closer look at the plain ahead and saw reed-like plants rippling in the breeze, cut through with glistening channels. At this lower elevation, the circular areas I'd seen earlier were no longer visible. As we drew nearer I began to hear what sounded like eerie music and understood that ahead lay a landscape much like that of Masada. The plants were flute grasses, the stems of which, when they shed their side shoots, turned into musical instruments played by the wind. I was surprised, since Masada had a very different environment, what with its lack of breathable air. I would've thought the high oxygen content here would poison if not inhibit these plants. Instead the dumping of Stratogaster's Zoo had clearly created a unique environment which had attained a balance. Polity ecologists would have been fascinated.

Soon we reached ground dotted with flute grass shoots – red

and purple and sharp – and more knowledge came to me. On Masada the Theocracy once punished people by pegging them out over such growth, so they died in agony as the shoots penetrated and grew through their bodies. Of course, my earlier self would have known something like this, as his interests always seemed slanted towards death and destruction. The ground started to get boggy, but tightly bound with flute grass rhizomes. It moved as we walked but we didn't sink. We next had to round old growths of stems, still standing stripped of side shoots, while new growth came through and put out wiry tangles dotted with buds. Finally we came to a wall of the stuff and my heart sank. This would slow us considerably, but Marcus moved into the lead, parting and crushing down the grasses with relentless strength. I was glad to have retained my walking staff because the grasses made the surface difficult. We trudged on as the sun fell down the sky and set in the mountains behind. As it began to grow dark, Marcus halted and pointed at the ground, then walked a spiral, crushing down grasses. This would be our camp for the night.

'You cannot write in the dust here,' I said.

He nodded agreeably and tore open a sleer segment. We ate in silence, drank some of the remaining water, then I curled up and had no problem drifting into sleep.

Pure starlit night was strewn with stars above us. Marcus had said something, I was sure, and that was what had woken me.

'What—' I began, then stopped when he held his finger up against my visor. I sat up carefully, wincing at the crackling of the grass beneath me, then opened my visor and hood, pushing them down into the neck ring. Distantly, something big was pushing through the grasses, and then it uttered familiar nonsense phrases that sounded like someone grumbling. That a gabbleduck

moved through the grasses nearby was bad enough, but worse
was that I couldn't shake the conviction it was the same one
we'd seen up in the mountains. Had it followed us?

The thing continued to move off, its mutterings growing
increasingly difficult to hear. I leaned back and looked up at the
sky. Plenty of stars were evident and then, by its slow progress
across the firmament, I picked out a small moon. Lights flashed
around this object and, between it and a point off to one side,
a blue-orange line flashed briefly into being. I suddenly realized
I was seeing the docking moon and the Stratogaster station,
though the latter was an indistinct dot. A particle beam had
obviously just been fired, but whether from the moon or the
station I didn't know. It struck me as likely Suzeal hadn't followed
my advice to begin negotiations with the prador. I touched
Marcus's arm – he had his head tilted, still listening – and when
I had his attention, pointed up at the moon. We watched for a
while and the beam flashed again, this time between the moon
and another point, which flared and died. It was the prador doing
the shooting. Perhaps they'd just taken out another arriving ship.
Marcus hissed, then bowed his head between his knees and
became somnolent. This seemed his preferred sleeping position,
if sleep he did. I lay down again and drifted off.

A wind began blasting with morning twilight, pulling me awake
to the cries of the damned and the musical instruments of hell.
The sound was certainly different to the gentle fluting of yesterday.
We didn't eat, simply got up and started pushing through the
grasses. An hour or so later, the sun broke above and Marcus
altered our course as Suzeal had directed. During the long slog
throughout the morning, I'd noted a flickering on the control
console of my suit. An inspection of this revealed automatic
adjustments had been made to its fitting around my arms and

legs. I was putting on muscle and had apparently reached some fitting threshold.

We eventually came to one of the channels. It stood about six feet wide and three deep before reaching water. The rhizome mat at ground level lay six inches thick – a tangle of tubers like massed brown snakes interspersed with off-white balls the size of a fist. Below this, metallic grey mud reached down to the water and formed the bed. What seemed to be fishes swam there, but when one of them reared its plug-cutting mouth out of the water I realized they were Spatterjay leeches. Marcus jumped the channel first. Following him, I nearly fell back into it because of standing grasses, until he caught and dragged me from the brink. I gazed down at the leeches and this triggered my speculation.

The virus infected just about all humans resident on Spatterjay, but not only humans. Imported animals – livestock and pets – also became infected. Surely the same rule would apply here. The virus made humans and animals tough, rugged, practically immortal and, if not held in check, it could also turn all of them into monsters. What if droons, hooders or even gabbleducks were bitten by leeches? A moment's thought made me realize that with their carapace armour, it was probably not possible for droons or hooders to be bitten. A leech might be able to bore through a gabbleduck's tough skin but, having seen the previous gabbleduck's reaction to the Jack, I wondered if their bodies might reject the virus. Still, the virus vector wasn't only via the leeches. It could survive in the stomach, so any hooder or droon eating an infected animal, or even one of the leeches themselves, might become infected. The idea gave me the horrors until something else grabbed my attention.

The wind parted the grass to reveal a low curve directly ahead. At first it looked to be some atmospheric effect, maybe a bank of cloud rising over the horizon, but as it loomed higher I recognized something solid. Closer still, the outline became clear as a shallow dome. My first thought was that Suzeal must have been lying about the position of the installation, because this looked artificial. Next, I could see that a line underscored it and this gradually revealed itself to be a jagged slab of composite, fifteen feet above the ground. It was supported by I-beams of punched-out bubble-metal, evenly spaced in X patterns, and crowding a dark space under the composite. At ground level in one or two places, the beams were attached to a lower slab of composite. It looked like a piece of space port landing slab, with a dome structure on top of it. I realized it had to be one of the circular areas I'd seen from afar, mistaking them for banyans. We halted there.

'We should go up on top,' I said, but Marcus walked into the twilight underneath. 'Wait, there might be something useful up there.'

He gestured peremptorily for me to follow. Feeling no urge to go my own way, I did so. As we moved steadily inwards, he kept inspecting the ceiling. He halted and pointed. A stubby cylinder, about a metre wide and half again as long, protruded from above, beside one of the Xs. He walked over with me at his shoulder and, dumping his load of sleer flesh, rapidly climbed the X to reach the cylinder. Smashing his fist into its lower corner, he bent it in, got hold of an edge and tore the cylinder down. With a thunk, what turned out to be a hatch popped out. He shoved it down on a hinge, reached inside and pulled. The contents of the cylinder slid out like an insect from a chrysalis and thumped down beside me. The legs wrapped in close to the body certainly looked insectile. The body, however, was a short cylinder while its head consisted of folded tool arms and scanning gear: A maintenance robot of some kind. I looked up again to see Marcus had inserted his top half into the cylinder. He scrabbled at something inside for a while, then came out. Climbing higher, he braced against the I-beam and kicked at the cylinder, bending it to one side and finally tearing it away from the composite. Obviously there had not been enough room for him to manoeuvre inside it. This revealed another hatch, which he thumped hard until it hinged up and crashed over to let in daylight. I struggled to follow him up, passing up the segments of sleer and then the pack.

Flute grass detritus scattered the upper surface of the composite slab and had piled up against the snapped-off bases of pylons. Ahead lay the domed building, with walls about thirty feet tall and the dome on top of that. Large rectangular chain-glass windows ran round at two levels, some of them popped out, their sheets lying on the composite. There were doors at the lower level and up higher, with the remains of ripped-away steps running up the wall to them. We headed over and Marcus kicked open a door. Inside lay a short aisle then steps leading up; it seemed almost inevitable when we found a skeleton lying there. A woman I assumed, by the pink dress and high shoes. We climbed up further and found ourselves in a large apartment. Old and decaying furniture lay here, but numerous other items had been stripped out. Marcus walked over to a dusty mirror and wrote on it, *the war*, then began searching through the apartment. As I searched too, I thought about that.

Yes, this place looked centuries old. The skeleton below lay half crumbled, while the dress and shoes had survived by dint of being tough and resilient artificial fabric. I kicked at a low table and it collapsed in pieces, the wood almost rotten to dust. We found nothing of any real use, or at least, nothing worth carrying. A door led out into a corridor, with further doors leading off into other apartments. After fruitlessly searching a couple of them, we moved deeper into the structure. We found control rooms and small factory units, a small park in which terran plants still grew below a glass roof in the peak of the dome. There we gathered the remaining apples which clung to the gnarled branches of a tree and Marcus bagged them up in a plastic sheet. A shopping arcade got me hopeful, but all we found was a pack Marcus could use instead of the sheet. A few more corpses punctuated our progress, but usually only in hidden places we searched. Surviving residents must have abandoned this place with their belongings and the shopkeepers with their stock. As it began to grow dark, we returned to the park. Here we gathered wood and, without fear, lit a fire on which to roast our sleer.

'This place has been looted,' I opined.

Marcus nodded agreement.

'Perhaps more than once,' I added.

He wrote in the dirt *centuries* then reached up to pull at one of his canines. I thought he was trying to communicate something by this, but with a sucking crunch the tooth came out and he discarded it.

'You're losing your mutation,' I suggested.

He just dug into his diminishing supply of garlic and ate another bulb. This seemed answer enough.

In the morning we searched again, but in a more desultory fashion. It seemed to be getting on towards the time for our departure from the place, but I think both of us were reluctant to abandon this sanctuary. We walked into a gallery with mostly bare walls and some sculptures remaining – a large statue of some dignitary, rendered in iron and now rusty, had been left behind. Here and there screens must have once depicted something or other. Most were dead but one still ran a power supply and showed a repeating scene of a surfer. I had no idea why. One of the few paintings left showed an immense structure sitting on an ocean, scattered with low domes just like the one we were in. Marcus moved up to stand beside me.

'This was a raft city,' I said. 'Probably hit from orbit with a prador weapon and broken up, then washed inland by a tsunami from other blasts.' I shrugged. 'Or maybe where we are now was once under ocean – the war might have altered the geology.'

Marcus nodded.

'Time for us to move on,' I said.

He nodded again.

While heading out of the dome, we found a garage-cum-workshop with a long work area running to a door to the exterior. Tools lay scattered everywhere, probably not of sufficient value to take. Much had been stripped out but other things remained. A grav-car lay in pieces, heavily damaged and collapsed from a hydraulic lift, while at the end stood two skimmers. These too had been partially disassembled. I headed over, just a second after Marcus. I didn't hold out much hope because a working skimmer would surely have been taken, and these things had to be very old. The craft were ten feet long, their sides sloping inwards to central compartments behind curved screens. A forward seat sat at a steering column with four seats behind. Both skimmers had their panels down, revealing grav-motors and a tangle of pipes and power feeds, all tightly packed.

'Do you know anything about these?' I asked, gazing at him.

He made a sound now, either agreement or otherwise. After a moment he held up a hand and made a gesture I failed to interpret. I dredged my mind for data and realized I actually knew a lot about these things. I guessed maintenance of a vehicle was a necessary skill for a Polity agent. But again, they were ancient and the chances of doing anything with them meagre.

I studied the things further, taking in their state. Corrosion-resistant metal and composites in some places had decayed, but ceramal and meta-material components were built to last – while the grav-engines were also vacuum-sealed as units. This was old Polity tech but still tough and durable. Maybe there was a chance.

I stepped closer, thinking hard. If the grav-motors were shot, nothing could be done without specialized tools. If the grav-plane effect – basically steering – didn't work I might be able to do something. Power supply? It could be liquid hydrogen running to a capacitor-battery, in which case we would have no luck since it seemed very unlikely any hydrogen would remain. But it might be the kind of vehicle that ran pure water through a meta-material sieve to that battery, in which case we could get away with water less pure, at least for a while.

I quickly started pulling open inspection hatches and panels. Some were corroded in place but Marcus soon tore them off, since we wouldn't need them. It turned out that one ran on hydrogen and the other on water. After a while, I climbed up into the first and, just for the hell of it, tried the starter. A clattering sound issued from the back. The water pump should not have sounded like that, even without any water inside. But the fact it'd made a noise at all gave me hope. The other did nothing at all so I gestured to the one that ran on water.

'It would save a lot of time if we could get this running,' I said.

'Uh-huh,' he said – it seemed he could manage some throat vocalization now.

I stripped off my pack and took out my small collection of tools. I searched the garage, picking up other items that might be useful. Marcus went to the far end, I thought doing the same, until I heard a loud grating sound. He'd pushed the big sliding door halfway across, and then, with another heave, all the way to let in the daylight. I returned to the water-powered skimmer and made a further inspection. The panel over the pump already stood open and someone had debonded the pipe leading into the water tank. An old diagnostic device had been plugged in, but its screen was dead. The pump must have been the problem, I felt sure, and then wondered if the pump from the other car might be suitable. It was. It turned out the thing pumped liquid hydrogen at high pressure so its rating and seals were better. Water wouldn't be a problem for it, though adjustments would be required. I took out the diagnosticer, leaving its optic still in place, and pulled out its battery tab for inspection. The one from my atomic shear looked as if it might fit so I tried it. The screen came on.

'Yes!' I thumped the cowling.

Marcus, now standing behind me, took the thing out of my hand and peered at it. He carefully worked the touch screen with one hand, then handed it back. It seemed one diamond bearing had collapsed in the pump.

'The other one.' I pointed to the other skimmer.

We walked round and peered into the open cowling, but the pump had been removed.

'Fuck.'

We searched the garage for a while, recovering more useful tools, but found no pump. Marcus finally grunted something and shook his head in irritation. He abruptly reached down to grab my shoulder to tow me after him, walked me over to the door and pointed. Visible directly ahead, some miles away, stood another of the domes. He pointed to this and then to another even further away to the right, then turned my head to face him. He pointed two fingers at his eyes then pointed at the domes again.

'We go and look?'

He shook an admonishing finger, pointed to himself.

'You go and look?'

He nodded, then pointed to my eyes and made a circular motion with his hand to encompass this dome, then pointed to the water-powered skimmer. Okay, he'd go and see if he could find a pump, or perhaps a working skimmer. I'd search here and prepare the vehicle. I wasn't sure this was the best idea, but it was a plan, and he could certainly move faster over the terrain than I could.

'Find a pump if you can, and a power supply – we may need to jump-start the sieve and battery. And tools, and—' I clenched my fists in frustration. He patted me on the shoulder, then walked back with me to the skimmers. He dumped the contents of his pack and mine, taking both empty packs. With another squeeze of my shoulder, he simply jumped from the edge of the composite and disappeared at a fast run.

So, I had a diagnosticer, some tools and the knowledge in my mind. That knowledge covered the vehicle, because it was quite simple, as well as straying into esoteric stuff about grav-motors. Staying practical, I first removed the pump and then went round plugging the diagnosticer into every socket available to it. The grav-motor needed balancing but that couldn't be done without power. The device that drew accumulated rubbish from the sieve was itself full of rubbish. I took it out, increasing my collection of tools from the garage as I struggled with its fixings, then removed its clogged filters and replaced it. Without filters in the cleaning device, the sieve would shut down, but it'd take more than a few hundred miles before that happened. With all possible jobs done by mid-afternoon, I began to search the garage again meticulously. I found tools that would've been useful earlier and transported them back, as well as a collection of spares, but none for the skimmers. A storeroom was scattered with decaying boxes, mostly empty or containing parts for other vehicles, and there was a locked door at the back. I decided I needed to return to that door later, with the tools needed to open it, and then extended my search further.

Nearby were two more garages, all completely empty of hardware – we'd been lucky to stumble into the one we did first. Apartments nearby were much the same as others we'd ventured into: stripped of just about everything of value and use. A chamber had some equipment remaining in place, with two columns, one from the ceiling and one from the floor, extending platens with a gap between that had contained an AI. Nothing remaining was of much use to me, though, being far too specialized, so I returned to the locked door.

Numerous blows with a hammer exposed locking bars, which the shear went through easily enough once I'd returned its battery. But the thing began to falter on the last bar, and then died. I then felt very stupid because I'd used up the only battery available for the diagnosticer. Further hammer blows broke the bar, and the door led me into a stairwell which in turn went up to a door of decayed wood. I opened it with a kick. This gave into a small apartment, the ceiling being the low curve of the dome and a narrow window at one end admitting enough light to see by. Jackpot: the place hadn't been looted. Food in forever-seal plasmel packs, bottles of drink that looked cloudy and dubious, but also wine and a bottle of bourbon sat in the cupboards. A selection of glass knives from a rack, clothing still usable, an envirosuit, and more items in other cupboards and boxes caught my eye. But with the light waning, I decided to give the place a proper search in the morning. Piling the loot onto the floor, I used a corkscrew on one wine bottle, taking that and some food and a glass back down to the garage.

Sitting on the edge of the platform while the sun sank out of sight, I opened plasmel packs and feasted on sardines in tomato sauce and blue fruit in syrup, which the label told me was cerulean hogfruit. The strong flavours hurt my mouth, being so used to much blander fare. I drank some of the wine and didn't like the taste, but decided the effect might be enjoyable. After the first glass it tasted better. Halfway down the second glass I began to feel really spaced out, though, and poured the remainder back into the bottle. The combination of such rich food and alcohol seemed to suck the energy out of my body and I stood, nearly staggering off the edge of the platform, before managing to straighten up and walk inside. Lying down on the floor beside one of the skimmers, flat on my back, I watched the ceiling try to revolve. That was all I remembered until morning.

Thoroughly arid on waking, I drank water, ate some sleer and a couple of apples. As I walked out onto the platform, munching, I realized, by the shadow the structure was casting behind me, that I hadn't woken with the dawn. I idly wondered where Marcus was, then asked myself why I expected him to return. If what the king had said was true, he was undoubtedly a character as bad as those who worked for Suzeal. Yet he had saved my life when there had been no necessity for him to do so, and I found I trusted him on an almost visceral level.

What now? I returned to the hidden room to conduct another search. Food and drink I took down to the garage in a plastic crate, along with the envirosuit, knives and other useful items. The best and luckiest find, after my carelessness in getting through the door, was a selection of batteries, some of which fitted the diagnosticer and the shear. This find set me to work on the skimmer once more and I checked through everything again. Replacing a battery under the console enabled me to adjust grav-planing back to optimum, but it still didn't supply enough power to balance the grav-motor.

I thought about what else might be needed and walked out

to the edge of the composite slab, coming to a stop over one of the channels directly below me. The vehicle would need water – that is, if Marcus was able to return with a pump. I grabbed a plastic bucket from inside, attached it to a long optic, and then came back out to dunk it down into the channel. It came up with a leech stuck to the outside, which I knocked away, and the cloudy water had other things darting about in it. A further search inside resulted in some rough card and insulation fibre, which I set up in a funnel. The water dripped through this into another container, surprisingly clear. It removed the worst of the dirt, but the minerals and salts in it would still eventually cause problems in the engine.

While I was busy with this, I heard something thump outside on the platform: one of the packs. I walked over to open it and tried not to feel disappointed: plasmel packs of food. Peering over, I couldn't see any sign of Marcus, but he must have used one of the maintenance bot tubes underneath because a short while later he walked in from the back of the garage.

'Did you get something?' I asked.

He shrugged off the other pack, tight with items.

'Gok thing,' he managed, and squatted to open the pack.

Inside was a selection of pumps, obviously torn from various locations because parts of those locations were still attached. Marcus had made sure not to damage the things themselves. Looking at them, I realized, belatedly, that he hadn't needed to make the journey. All around us were other pumps to move water and fluids about this place. I selected a pump from an electric shower that seemed to have the right number of ports and pipes and took it over. It'd be a long job, because though I knew what needed doing, finding everything necessary would take some time. I pointed over to my haul from the hidden room.

'Food and drink there,' I said. 'And through that doorway is an apartment that hasn't been looted. I haven't searched it all.' I studied him, standing perhaps a foot taller than me. 'The envirosuit might fit,' I added.

He went over and started going through my haul while I set to work. Glancing at him occasionally, I saw him eat a lot, then try on the suit. It fitted at full extension as they were made to fit a variety of forms. He then headed off to the apartment. I stripped all the attachments off the pump, then thought to attach up a battery to see if it had any life in it. It worked but the power supply was wrong, something that would need adjusting once it was installed. Further scavenging around the garage, and from other pumps, yielded the required pipework and I fitted the pump in place. It was difficult, since the fixings weren't the same, but the torn-out fixings attached to the other pumps provided. In between times, I topped up the filter funnel, emptying the clean water into the tank of the skimmer.

'K – ore,' said Marcus, returning from the apartment and emptying out the crate I'd used earlier to add to our growing pile of supplies. He'd brought all the suspect food and drink, not having to worry about the kind of stomach complaints that I'd had aboard the King's Ship.

In time we began to lose the light and I did more work using the torch, then gave up. I collected up some sleer but, not liking the look of it now, instead took up a food block and the opened wine bottle and went out onto the slab. Marcus joined me a moment later with the bottle of bourbon and the dubious food and drink. He drank and he ate, then chugged bourbon straight from the bottle.

'It may work,' I said, though confident the skimmer would.

''oot,' he opined.

'Did you core and thrall people?' I asked, not for the first time.

''okitkate,' he informed me.

'Complicated?'

He nodded.

We sat there as it grew darker and he put aside the half-emptied bourbon, lying back. A moment later, I learned what snoring sounded like from his mutated face. I went back inside to sleep.

11

By mid-morning, I could think of nothing else to do to secure the pump. I went to the driver's seat, plugged the diagnosticer into the console and searched through to find the data on the pump there. A number of errors appeared but they concerned, as expected, power supply. With the voltage and amperage set as required, the errors went away. Pump power needed to be greater but the wiring, being highly conductive, could take it. Switching and other items also required adjustment, but in flight. I climbed out and went round closing up the covers that remained. As Marcus started putting our supplies in, I thought to tell him to wait, but then shrugged and got on with it.

Sitting in the driver's seat again, I hesitated over the controls, then swore and hit power up. The pump started with a nice steady hum, forcing water through the meta-material sieve. A screen came on and gave me a low power alert, but a bar steadily began to climb as the main battery-cum-super-capacitor rose to charge. I turned on the grav-motors. The skimmer jerked and then rose, tilting over to one side, and kept on rising. I ducked down as the thing crashed against the ceiling and focused on the plugged-in diagnosticer. Marcus was making a sound from below, which might have been laughter. A small adjustment brought the skimmer level, but the assumed ground level seemed a problem. Once it was reset manually, the thing dropped, levelling out about a yard from the floor. I realized I'd have to keep the diagnosticer plugged in to work this. The skimmer found its ground level with sensors, all of which were probably corroded.

Marcus was definitely laughing. I settled the vehicle to the floor and climbed out. We then threw in tools and further supplies and I added the other pumps, just in case.

'I think we're ready,' I said.

Marcus climbed in and took a back seat, while I got into the front and pulled an aged safety strap over my hips, but abandoned it when I couldn't plug the thing in. I brought the skimmer up and took it ahead. Once over the edge of the composite slab, it dropped as if I'd driven off a cliff, crashing down through the flute grasses, then slamming into the muddy ground. Thankfully the grasses cushioned the fall. The thing rose out of sucking mud to stabilize a few feet above it, still pressing down grass stems. Using the diagnosticer, I reset its level above ground. The thing had been programmed to fly over water and we needed to be higher than that. Once we'd adjusted, I directed it towards where the sun had risen earlier.

We seemed to hurtle along over the grasses and I felt an intense sense of achievement. When I checked our speed it was only forty miles an hour. Some sort of limiter, I had no doubt, but still a damned sight faster than walking, and safer. The dome receded behind and, as we came past one of those Marcus had ventured out to, a flock of what I now knew to be crab birds clattered up out of the grasses. They rose too abruptly for me to avoid them. One hit the cowling on the front while another slammed against the screen, leaving a green spatter as it bounced over and landed behind me. I heard it clattering there, then a crunch and a weird sucking cry, and looked back to see Marcus discarding the thing over the side.

'Perhaps I should go—' I began.

A hooder shot up out of the grasses, its cowl directly ahead, limbs rippling inside it and the two columns of red eyes seemingly glowing. I threw us to one side, but wasn't exactly driving on a surface with grip so the turn was slow. We sideswiped the cowl with a crash and its rim grated down the side of the skimmer, flicking up covers like scales from a fish. Bouncing away, the skimmer tipped and spun two full circles. Only by clinging onto the driving column did I manage not to be flung out as I fought to get it under control. Even as I did, the hooder turned and went for us again, just clipping the back end so the vehicle came out of it as if bouncing on springs. Then the monster just as quickly dropped out of sight. I got the skimmer controlled and checked readouts for damage reports.

'—iyah,' Marcus finished what I'd been saying for me.

Using the diagnosticer, I took the skimmer up another twenty feet. I'd been flying the thing as if we were in some inhabited area where height restrictions applied, which I didn't need to do. I assumed this had something to do with my inherited knowledge. I didn't want to take it too high either, though, because of the threat of it failing. Another hooder rose and tried to reach us just ten minutes after the first. This one was about the size of the thing Vrasan had slaved and luckily I saw it coming. I took the skimmer higher still, worried about the drop and keeping a wary eye on the readouts and the diagnosticer. Glancing back at Marcus, I saw him sprawled and enjoying the view, finishing off the bottle of bourbon. I guessed he could be relaxed about all this since a fall wouldn't hurt him as it would me.

As we continued on, I reckoned on about five hours of travel to cover the remaining distance to the installation. We passed over another dome and saw evidence there of what had destroyed the raft, for a great hole had been melted through it and the underlying composite. A particle beam strike, my weaponized mind told me. I began to relax and asked Marcus to pass me some food, while I searched for a cruise control. A simple locking button could set the joystick. I ensured it could be unlocked before using it, then opened a packet. Marcus passed another bottle of wine and corkscrew, but I didn't think that a great idea and took some water instead. My other self might have had a tolerance for alcohol but I certainly didn't.

The end of the flute grasses came into sight and near that edge stood a birdlike creature with a long neck terminating in a spike of a beak but no visible head. I took the skimmer lower and noted that the Masadan heroyne was smaller than it should be, as well as albino pale and sickly. I guessed some of the imports here didn't do so well. Beyond the grasses lay a plain, green and blue with regular rings of yellow. Taking the skimmer lower again brought into sight what looked like rings of toadstools. Hours slid by and Marcus started snoring again. The sun dropped down behind us and then my suit buzzed. I reached back and gave Marcus a shove, whereupon he emitted a comical snort before gazing at me blearily.

'Suzeal,' I said, raising my visor so I could see her face and allowing public address before answering, so Marcus could hear. Suddenly he was very awake and in his features, still regaining more humanity, I recognized something nasty.

'It's been a while since you communicated,' I observed.

'It may surprise you that your situation is not of prime importance to me,' she replied tartly.

'So what's happening up there now? I note that the prador have been using a particle beam weapon . . .'

'How do you know that?' Her expression filled with suspicion and I realized that games of 'I know things' were not a good idea.

'The moon your spaceship dock is sited on was visible in the sky a few nights back. I saw the particle beam flash.'

'Oh.' She looked briefly confused then continued, 'Yes, the bastards built a high-powered particle weapon and tried to punch through our defences. A ship arrived and they destroyed that.'

'And since then?'

She looked shifty. 'It was necessary to negotiate. I warned them that if they came close to penetrating my defences, I'd be forced to destroy the space dock. I made a further deal handing over the identities of two Old Families I trade with, in return for them allowing ships to dock with the station.' She looked annoyed about having done exactly as I'd suggested and hurriedly added, 'I pointed out to them that we have the manufacturing capability to make large weapons and that I'd not be able to bring in a significant number of troops, since they are simply not available in the Graveyard. We agreed on limitation in the size of ships docking and no war vessels.'

'That's very sensible of you.' I kept my face expressionless. 'It must have been difficult to be so restrained.'

She then cheered up, having got the nasty business of effect-ively telling me I was right out of the way. 'We have some supplies coming in now – not that we needed many – and I've opened negotiations, with a direct link to a king's envoy, concerning trade in hooders.'

'So things are looking up and, I hope, you'll be able to rescue us from this world.'

'You seem to be doing quite well. I wasn't aware there were functional skimmers down there. Those places have been stripped out many times, even in my lifetime.'

'We managed to scavenge enough parts to repair a water-powered one. Its working life will be limited by a lack of filtration, but should get us to the installation. Incidentally, are we on the right course?'

'Good enough.' She checked something beside her. 'At your present elevation you'll see it somewhere ahead of you – it's on the coast.'

'And then you'll come?'

Again a hesitation. 'I still have a lot to do up here and these negotiations are critical. You can gain access to the installation with this code.' A series of numbers appeared beneath her image. 'You'll need to record them if your suit has that facility.'

'No need,' I said. 'I'll remember them.'

'You always had that ability.' She paused for a second, replaying her words. 'I mean the man you were cloned from had that ability.'

I really didn't like that slip. Did she still believe me to be that man? And, if she did, what might she have in store for me considering she had sent clones of him to suffer in the King's Ship?

'That ability has enabled me to function as I have – it gives me perfect recall of the data I have from his mind, limited though it is.'

'Yes, quite . . . and your new friend? He continues to be stable?'

I glanced at Marcus as he worked free another of his carnivore's teeth. In the gap where he'd removed the other, I could see new white dentine.

'He seems so. Some aggression on occasion, but he doesn't show much in the way of intelligence and follows me about like a pet.'

Marcus looked at me sharply and made an obscene gesture involving his fist and his mouth, then pulled out the tooth and flicked it over the side.

'No further information on him?'

'Not really. All he does is eat and snore.'

'Very well . . . I'll be in contact again at a later time.'

'Good—'

She cut the link.

I looked round at Marcus and he shrugged.

The sea became visible through a low mist. The ground was rocky here with buttes sticking up, topped with vegetation, jagged hills on either side, and along the coast promontories stuck out and into the sea. Below, banyans had spread again like cancers in another forest that consisted of fungus trees, speared through with things similar to the leafless trunks of palms. I scanned along the coast looking for the installation but couldn't see it. At length, we finally slid out over the waves, which were low and rolling as if the sea were oily, but this was actually an effect of high gravity.

'Right or left?' I said, turning to Marcus. He shrugged, then pointed right.

We headed off along the coast over promontories and coves with yellow sand beaches. Seal-like creatures humped towards the waves as we passed. The second time we moved over some of these, closer inspection revealed their multiple long necks topped by parrot-like beaks. More monsters from Stratogaster's Zoo? About an hour later, we arrived at a point where the mountains dipped into the sea, and turned round there. With the sun now setting, I wondered what chance we had of seeing anything along the other stretch of coast.

'We'll get back to where we arrived then check the rest of the coast in the morning,' I suggested.

'Goo iea,' said Marcus, demonstrating that he could now use another consonant. His mouth probably hadn't yet achieved the right shape to pronounce the 'd'.

We kept looking for the installation as we went back, in case we'd missed it on the first pass. I had no idea what it looked like and, seeing the vegetation here, considered that it might be overgrown. Another hour later, we were, as far as I could see by the shape of the promontories jutting into the sea, back where we'd started. I began to worry about landing because the ground lay mostly in shadow. It would have to be one of the beaches and, having seen the creatures down there, the idea didn't appeal.

''ook,' said Marcus, pointing.

I peered across the shadowed landscape and saw a light glinting. It seemed to be a fire, although I couldn't think of a reason why there'd be one here. In all my travels, and despite this planet having an atmosphere with high oxygen content, I'd seen no signs of natural wildfires. In fact, when we'd lit a fire it had been surprisingly difficult to get going. I suspected even the apparently dry wood here was laden with moisture.

I directed the skimmer towards the light, finally slowing it to a stop above it. The fire down there silhouetted the regular structure of a downed pylon. A steady alteration through the diagnosticer took us lower and soon a tangle of fence pulled down by the same pylon came into view. At the top of the thing, in masses of smoking vines, lay what looked to be the mangled remains of some weapon. My brain worked too slowly and I'd just scrabbled to reset the diagnosticer to take us back up into the sky when the laser stabbed through the smoke. The skimmer jerked as if slapped, made some horrible metal-on-metal clattering sounds and slid sideways through the sky. It began to drop heavily, but it still had some grav-planing and I tried to direct it towards a beach I'd seen previously. We hit foliage that whipped against the craft, sideswiped one of the palm things and descended sharply. I pulled up the nose and we skidded through the sand, with it fountaining up on either side. Then the nose dropped with a bang. I slammed into the screen and found myself tumbling through the air, the screen skating off beside me. Instinct and perhaps inherited knowledge took over. I pulled in my arms and came down, briefly, on my feet, then rolled, shouldering the sand and tumbling end over end, folded into a ball. I hit a rock with my back and bounced up, slamming down, sprawled on my face, and wondering what had broken.

'—um,' said Marcus a moment later, reaching down and pulling at my shoulder. I tried to get up but my back hurt terribly and I groaned. He passed me a pulse rifle. I grabbed it and dropped it beside me. I saw he'd retrieved our two packs, having hurriedly stuffed them with supplies. I tried to rise again but simply couldn't move. Then something rose into the air inland and over to my right: prador.

'—um!' Marcus insisted, moving up the beach.

My legs felt numb and it seemed as if I'd lost my right foot. As I tried to move again, the pain grew suddenly intense and I just lay there, gritting my teeth. Marcus abruptly realized I wasn't following and ran back. He stooped over me and I could read the puzzlement in his half-human expression, but I wasn't going anywhere. He tried to pick me up and I screamed. After a moment I felt his hands on me, probing here and there, then finding something that blacked me out for a moment. When I came to, he was crouched before me with a small glass knife in his hand, gazing over towards the approaching prador. Was he going to put me out of my misery? He reached over and stabbed the tip of it into my thigh, just puncturing the fabric of my envirosuit. I felt nothing there.

'Fuck off,' I told him, because now I knew what had happened.

He hesitated, looked to the sky again.

'Just go,' I insisted, adding, 'You can rescue me later.'

Marcus gave one slow nod, then picked up my pulse rifle and rested it across my stomach. We both understood the situation perfectly.

''orry,' he said and, leaping to his feet, sprinted up the beach.

I watched the prador, not really caring about its approach, utterly stunned as my situation continued to sink in. It came in to hover over me and I felt the wash of its grav-engine, then it turned and, with a stab of thruster flames, headed inland. I'd felt no scan, but suspected there'd been one and it knew my condition. I tried to think clearly about its presence. Somehow the prador had made it here to the installation. I doubted they'd done so to intercept us, but for some other purpose. Had Suzeal known they were here? If so, why hadn't she warned us? Had she led me to them again deliberately? Was I again some foil in her plans? I simply couldn't find out without speaking to her and I really didn't feel like doing so just then because, really, nothing mattered anymore. I knew exactly what had happened to me. My pain had diminished and through it I could feel the damage. I'd broken my back and could no longer walk. I had told Marcus to go because, well, he couldn't carry me without me screaming. And even if we did get away, what then? He couldn't fix me and I'd be a burden, resulting in both of us likely getting killed or captured.

Now I would die, but what remained open to conjecture was how.

The prador would come back, or the clones would come, and they'd drag me screaming to their base. Whether to the installation, or elsewhere, I had no idea. Torture and death would ensue there. Or perhaps, seeing my injury and being busy, they'd dispose of me quickly? Yet, it wasn't death I feared, but being moved. Marcus's attempt to pick me up had been utterly agonizing. I lifted the pulse rifle and positioned it with the barrel under my chin and my finger on the trigger. But I couldn't yet pull the trigger. I wanted to hang onto the life that remained to me and do the deed when no other option remained.

'Open previous comlink,' I finally said.

'You're there,' said Suzeal immediately.

'Yes, we reached the installation, but guess who got here before us?'

'I don't have to. What happened?'

'You didn't see?'

'I can only see now and not very well. I'm working on cracking their chameleonware. The only reason I know where they are now is because of a grav spike. One of them is probably going to be in trouble with Vrasan for using the grav-engine in his armour.'

It all sounded perfectly plausible but just didn't matter. I found myself in a state of disconnection. All Suzeal's and Vrasan's machinations had become irrelevant to me.

'You didn't tell me what happened,' Suzeal reminded me when I made no reply.

'They hit the skimmer with a laser. We crash-landed on a beach.'

'You don't sound . . . right.' Was that actually concern I heard in her voice?

'Marcus has headed off and will probably evade capture – he's a lot tougher and more rugged than me. I hope so, anyway. Perhaps you can pick him up when you finally come here?'

'Are you hurt?'

'It was a hard crash and I got thrown out. I reckon I would've been okay if it wasn't for the rock.' I tried to shrug, then really wished I hadn't. 'I'm happy that I managed to survive this long. The chances were against it.'

'How are you hurt?' she asked stridently.

'Broke my back, so I won't be going anywhere. I have a pulse rifle so Vrasan won't be able to play any of his games with me.'

'Don't do anything hasty. A broken back can be repaired.'

'Yes, I know, but I don't think Vrasan will feel so inclined.'

She said nothing. What was there to say?

'I don't like what you do, Suzeal, and I hope your negotiations with the prador fail. You are either amoral or immoral and care little about the suffering of others. Goodbye now.'

'Wait!' she shrieked, but for the first time I cut her off.

I now just lay there listening. I heard the sound of a Gatling cannon further inland, then the crackle of a particle beam and light bloomed over in that direction. A little while later came the hiss and crump of the station railgun Suzeal had used to attack the previous prador encampment. The prador shot up and across, over the trees – probably running for cover. It grew quiet but for something buzzing as if in irritation. It drew close and then a beautiful blue beetle settled on my arm. I thought to brush it away, maybe crush it, but desisted. It deserved its life. As I watched it cleaning its mandibles, another sound impinged from the shoreline – something splashing in the water. I turned painfully and watched two parrot-like heads on the end of long necks rise into view out of the waves. I sighed. Perhaps the prador or the clones would never get to me. I pulled the pulse rifle from under my chin and took aim. That was when the stun round hit me.

I convulsed and sharp agony stabbed me in the back, but my vocal cords locked up and I couldn't scream. A Jill scrambled into view down the rocks, shouldering a pulse rifle, and fired on the creature coming out of the sea. Two accurate shots charcoaled the two heads, but the thing surged ashore, more of its heads rising from its long slug-like body. This was undoubtedly something from the zoo. She started pumping shots into the body, and a Jack ran in and opened fire. Finally, the thing thought better of it and retreated into the sea. I lay there in absolute terror of the two clones coming over to pick me up. They turned and stood looking at me, doubtless receiving further instructions from Vrasan. Eventually they walked over and hauled me up and the pain was just as bad as I'd expected. I fainted.

Consciousness slid back with its load of terror and expectation of pain. I travelled through the air, my back a ball of agony, but I somehow existed to one side of it. I slammed down on a hard surface under glaring lights, shortly occluded when Vrasan loomed over me, the manipulators usually folded against his underside now reaching forwards under his mandibles and gripping numerous gleaming implements.

'You deserve more, but at least this pain will serve as a re-minder never to interfere in my plans again,' he said in perfect Anglic.

He reached down and flipped me over onto my face and I shrieked. I felt something slice down my envirosuit and then he violently stripped it away, discarding it to the floor ahead of me. A clone walked over and picked it up. The only other thing I could see was a composite wall behind her. Vrasan buzzed and clattered above me and then came sharp agony as he sliced open my back. I tried to push myself up, tried to get some kind of relief. I realized I still must have some nerve connection to my lower body when I shit myself. Then the clone, who'd earlier picked up my envirosuit, stepped over and dragged my arms forwards and held them in a vice-like grip.

'You will not faint,' Vrasan told me. 'I have ensured this.'

Of course, the prador had become expert in torturing humans throughout the war. He cut and he sliced and he sizzled. The agony reached unbelievable heights. I wanted to die and in the hallucinatory madness of some red universe felt I might be able to, but it just went on and on. The screaming continued until I could scream no more, something seeming to break in my voice box. The pain was never-ending, and with it a horrible crunching and squelching in my back. I simply couldn't faint and there seemed no escape until, for the second time only in my life, a memory of my former self surfaced in my mind.

'Does it hurt, fucker?' asked Brack.

My head down, I could see the deep burns all down the front of my body, also the deep grooves where he'd used the grinding disc, some exposing bone. The agony wouldn't stop. It came in wave after wave and I just couldn't faint. Glancing aside, I saw where they'd riveted my left forearm to the wall and the drip feed there. Was it some sort of drug that prevented me sliding into unconsciousness? Yes, certainly that, and probably something they got from the prador. But I couldn't turn the pain off either, or displace into the hardware in my skull. So I knew then that the unfamiliar weight on the side of my skull, behind my ear, was an interrogation aug – keyed into my gridlink and shutting it down.

'Did you think we wouldn't find out?' *Frey enquired from where he leaned against the metal bench.*

'There's . . . nothing more,' *I managed.*

Brack smiled nastily and jabbed his machete straight into my burn. I shrieked and writhed.

'We know that,' *he said.* 'This is just for fun.'

'Suzeal,' *I said, mouth arid, broken teeth aching.*

'Do you really think she cares?'

He used the stun baton again. I screamed again. There was no advantage in not screaming.

'And you know what?' *he continued.* 'It's not going to end.'

I looked up and met his gaze.

'We got some real interesting plans for you.'

The pain rolled through me in waves, every one unbearable even at its lowest ebb. Eventually Vrasan ceased working on me. Incrementally the lowest ebbs of the pain began to give some relief. But always it came back. He picked me up, carried me to a wall and dumped me there, sending me back into hell for a while. Awareness of my surroundings stayed with me, but another kind of disconnect had happened which meant I couldn't recognize anything around me. Waves splashed and slowly my mind began to come back as the pain reached its lowest. I recognized the manacle around my wrist with a chain running from it to a staple in the floor. The tubes going into my arm and my chest came from a device also on the floor, filled with blood, probably artificial blood. The rhythmic sound of my groaning impinged and, after a time, stopped because it made no difference. I noted the pool of blood, urine and shit I sat naked in, then the wide circular chamber whose wall I lay against. The equipment here, under the glare of terran sun-lamps, was familiar from the prador camp, so too the hooder lying against the far wall. No . . . two hooders were there, both under the thrall.

In time the pain became all but bearable, although still intense. I started to feel other things, and something hard on my back sat between me and the wall. I wanted to reach round and touch it, but the chain didn't give me enough movement for that. I stared at my arm dully for a long time before remembering that I had another one. The long, loose tube moved with that arm, but I could move it no further when the pain came rolling back. So I just stayed still. Things around me were recognizable now, but I didn't have the mind to think about anything much beyond identification. Even surmising that artificial blood was going into me had taken a hard effort of will.

Time passed. Vrasan entered and left, then returned again. Other prador entered and left, and a clone came in through a human-scale door. Pulse rifle burns covered him and he'd lost his right arm. Vrasan and one of the other prador clattered and

225

bubbled at each other. The other one, by the looks of his armour, was one of the Guard. They were both angry, I realized, and belatedly picked up some of their speech. It seemed the clones had found Marcus and only this one had survived the experience. The Guard became adamant no more time should be wasted on hunting this erstwhile slave, and Vrasan finally agreed. I felt something then other than pain: satisfaction and just a hint of amusement.

By slow degrees I began to shift my tubed arm – testing the limits, searching out the least painful methods of movement. At length, I managed to feel the thing on my back. A hard plate sat right in the middle, a few centimetres wide and three times as long. All down the sides hard objects penetrated my flesh. Had Vrasan repaired my spine? This felt like some kind of splint. But the hard objects could also be the penetrating legs of a thrall. I tried to move my legs but they were dead. Surely, if he wanted to thrall me, he also wanted me functional? I just had no idea what he'd done.

I continued watching my surroundings, and now counted just two clones remaining. Vrasan headed with some equipment over to the slab on which he'd worked on me, and the clone without an arm climbed on. Vrasan set to work on him and a short while later the clone climbed off the slab with a new arm. It wasn't human, but a shorter version of a prador underslung manipulator rendered in brassy metal. It had two joints and the hand consisted of six fingers in rows of three, opposable. I guessed it was a spare for their armour and hollow so a real prador limb could fit inside. This was supposing the prador wasn't one of the king's children, who sometimes didn't have such limbs, or another normal prador who had lost a limb and controlled the armoured covering via a nerve shunt. I also guessed that Vrasan had no patience with waiting for the arm to grow back, or whatever a Spatterjay virus-mutated human might grow in its place.

The clone returned to duties, helping Vrasan and other prador at their manufacturing. I now eyed the neat piles of components they'd made. All of them were parts for hooder thralls, so it seemed Vrasan didn't intend to stop at two of them. The machine then stopped and the last components went into packaging, while the machine was rapidly dismantled by two prador. I noticed that activity had ramped up all around. Other machines were being quickly taken apart and loaded onto sleds, while over on the other side of the installation prador had hauled up a huge hatch in the floor. Prador tunnels again – it seemed they weren't staying. I watched this, wondering just what it meant for me. Eventually Vrasan came over again, and I sat there in terror of what he might be about to do.

'The agreement,' he said, 'is for an exchange.'

I stared at him blankly.

'You will say nothing of the work we do here,' he added.

'I don't understand,' I managed.

The manacle abruptly popped open and fell away from my wrist.

'You will stand up,' said Vrasan.

The most horrible, agonizing sensation ensued. Everything seemed to disappear and whatever he'd been using before must have ceased because I blacked out for a second. I felt my body still move independently of my mind, though. When consciousness returned, I was standing upright, but also found that I couldn't move any part of my body myself, not even to groan. I realized then that Vrasan's comment about me saying nothing had not been an instruction, but a statement of fact.

'In exchange for you, Suzeal will not attack this installation,' he said, turning from me. 'You will be unable to communicate what you know long enough for me to relocate. You may decide, should they have the technology to restore you, to continue saying nothing.'

This sounded crazy to me. Why would I want to keep his work here secret?

As he moved away, I started to walk. Every step was agony and the blackouts continued, but loss of consciousness didn't stop me moving. He marched over to a large door consisting of a cut-out slab of the wall composite provided with hinges. He pushed it open and walked out into daylight. There was nothing, I felt, more prone to undermine your sense of self, and personal ability to be effective, than having your body controlled by some other entity. I followed him out into a clearing beside the installation, then he cut the strings abruptly and I sprawled on the ground. I wanted to tell him Suzeal already knew he'd thralled a hooder, then I didn't want to tell him because he might think her likely to attack soon after I was gone. But, lying on the ground, I couldn't talk or move any of my limbs. I tried to think clearly. I remembered that he'd suggested he might attack Stratogaster with them, and that I hadn't told Suzeal this. In making this agreement to release me from the prador, was Suzeal's intention to save me? She knew about the thralled hooder, so still might bomb this place, or she might not – it all depended on how her further negotiations were going. But whatever she did, I had to remember her interests were always utterly mercantile.

I lay face down in the dirt. Flecks of organic matter went into my mouth and lungs. I had the overpowering urge to cough but simply couldn't and my lungs started bubbling. Then something droned and a shadow fell across me. A weird sensation passed through my body – feeling light and then pushed into the ground in waves. For a second I couldn't place the familiar sensation, then my mind and its store of data came up with the answer. An operating grav-engine had just passed closely over me. I heard the vehicle settle, then a moment later a hand reached down and flipped me onto my back. I lost it for a second again.

'They've done something to him,' said the woman with a shaven skull, on the side of which was tattooed the letters SGZ.

I could only see her vaguely because of dirt in my eyes but after a moment I blinked and cleared it. That blink, as events continued, occurred regularly every two minutes. She wore black and white combat armour with its Strato-GZ decals and other decorations and held some kind of heavy multi-barrelled weapon over one shoulder. She seemed improbably wide and, I soon found out, was very strong.

'Who cares?' replied a voice I recognized at once. 'She wants him and she'll get him. We both know what happens next.' Brack sounded very annoyed, and I thought about the interaction between him and Suzeal. I was sure they were lovers. Perhaps he didn't like his lover sending him into such danger? No, that wasn't it, there was something else here.

The woman reached down and, without taking her weapon off her shoulder, scooped me up with the other hand and held me under her arm. Something about that position took the pressure off my back and gave relief, but the pain surged back when she tossed me into the back of the grav-raft Brack was driving. She climbed in beside me and all I had was a view of her profile and the sky above. The raft took off and a steady breeze marked its progress. I felt no acceleration, since it operated on grav. Time passed and another of those pre-programmed body maintenance actions kicked in. I hacked, bringing up detritus, and swallowed. The woman looked down at me and I blinked.

'You conscious?' she asked.

Of course, I couldn't reply.

The raft slowed and dropped, then slid into a narrow bay. The woman climbed out and, after a moment, Brack peered over the seat ahead. He reached down and prodded me in the eye with an armoured finger. That eye began watering, then blinked once. He smiled nastily, looked over his shoulder for a second, then reached down again with both hands. He put one hand over my mouth and closed my nostrils with the other. All I could do was just lie there, suffocating. But then a hand came in from the side and slapped Brack across the head.

'Come on, Racher,' he said, releasing me and putting his hand up to his skull. 'I had to see if he's faking.'

'Yeah, sure you did,' the woman replied.

Brack climbed out after her and disappeared from sight. I didn't pant or take any deep breaths. My breathing continued as evenly as it had before, so it took some moments for the oxygen deprivation to pass. But then I thought I must be hallucinating as another face moved into view and peered down at me. I got the strong stink of garlic from it.

He had lost all his canines now and what had previously been a muzzle seemed to be collapsing back into his face, while the rudimentary shape of a nose had appeared. In this state Marcus looked even less human than before, but that would pass. His diet was doing its work.

''ith you,' he said, and moved away.

I heard something break and a clattering sound, then no more. How had Marcus got aboard what I presumed to be the ship Suzeal had sent to collect me? He didn't reappear, and I wondered again if I'd imagined him. I just lay there breathing evenly and blinking with machinelike regularity, drifting mentally until I heard the distant roar of fusion engines. We'd probably taken off before that on grav but I didn't feel the ship moving until those engines kicked in. A while later, the woman returned and heaved me out of the raft. She leaned me against it, holding me up by the neck and looked into my face.

'I'm putting you in my cabin,' she said. 'I don't know how much you understand but know this: Brack would like to see you dead, there's no honour in him, but I'm SGZ and do what Suzeal tells me to do.'

She slung me over one shoulder and I wanted to scream. All I saw then was her arse, legs and corridor floor as she carried me. A door opened and she threw me down on a bed, straightened me out and departed. Still I could do nothing, locked inside my own body. I spent time thinking through events and kept coming back to Suzeal. From the start, she hadn't seemed too concerned about whether or not I survived yet, in that last conversation with her, she'd suddenly appeared anxious to stop me dying. Also, from the recent memory that had arisen, I'd begun to realize that the connection between her and the original Jack had . . . complications. Right then I just couldn't parse them. My mind began wandering. How might Marcus have hidden himself? Perhaps in the air ducts? No, this wasn't a prador ship. A hooder sliding past in the corridor outside terrified me, the device on my back jerking in response because they were akin, while droon acid raised a steam all around me as it burned through the floor. Only retrospect told me I had slid into a state somewhere between the nightmares of wakefulness and those of sleep, until finally I did sleep.

12

The woman called Racher picked me up off the bed and put me on a gurney, run by grav, while Brack watched from the door. As the thing followed her out, slaved to her control, Brack stared down at me, his hand straying to the handle of his machete. But he did nothing. I mentally replayed what Racher had said before she dumped me in her cabin and it struck me that it'd been a precaution. She thought I might be able to talk again and didn't want to be associated with Brack's open intentions to harm me. This made me realize how absolute a ruler of the Stratogaster station Suzeal must be, feared by those who worked under her and, perhaps, worshipped.

Racher took me out of the ship, then down through a dropshaft and out into bright light. I saw two other tough-looking individuals walking along with the gurney. They wore uniforms of black and white, and carried weapons I recognized as slammers – guns that could fling out a bolus of metal dust to devastating effect on a human but didn't have much penetration. Perfect weapons for keeping order in a space station where you didn't want to make holes. A moment later I got my first glimpse of the hub of the station. A geodesic glass roof ran above, and through it I could see the curve inside the hub where spaceships were docked, perhaps including the one I'd been inside.

We entered a much wider dropshaft and the journey down this seemed interminable. A boulevard ensued and I could hear people all around me, with someone peering down at me before one of the guards pushed him away. We carried on down corridors, then arrived in another room.

'Put him in the frame,' said a man's voice.

As they did this, I felt my hopes rising on seeing the autodocs, scanners and other medical equipment all around. Racher heaved me up.

'Some help here,' she said.

The frame sat inside gimbals. They clamped my arms and legs spread-eagled, putting a strap about my waist. I noted then that there was no grav below the gimbals as they turned me horizontal. A mechanical arm unfolded from one of the pillars over to one side and inserted a sensor head and, as it traversed my body, I felt the wave of heat I'd felt aboard the King's Ship when first deep-scanned. It withdrew and folded up against the pillar again once it was finished. The gimbals then turned me upright to face a man who'd just come in through the door – the others had gone now. This odd-looking homunculus didn't seem to have any eyes, just flat skin there underneath a sensory band running an optic plugged into his skull. He grinned maniacally, exposing snaggle teeth stained by some red chemical.

'No bombs,' he said.

'I doubt even they would be so unsubtle,' said Suzeal, presumably through an intercom. 'There might be something else.'

'Not as far as I can see,' he said, tugging at his bottom lip. 'But I can only see so far. There's some nanotech distributed throughout his body, attached to his vagus nerve, but it just looks like quantum storage, so it's not a weapon.' He shrugged, loose boned. 'I don't think that's anything the prador made.'

'Never mind about that,' said Suzeal. 'As you said, just information storage.'

He nodded and continued, 'No other nanotech beyond what

a thrall usually produces, and no concealed compartments in its hardware. There might be a virus somewhere in him, but no chance of detecting that since I'm not a forensic AI.'

'So what else can you tell me?'

'His back is broken, just as Racher said, but the damage should only have paralysed him from the waist down. Vrasan used what maps as a segment of thrall hardware to stabilize his injury and keep autonomics running, but also to paralyse him above the waist too.'

'Higher functions?'

'Oh he's conscious but unable to respond to anything. Doesn't seem to be any brain damage.'

'So tell me what you can do.'

'I'll have to go in from the front to get to the spine. If I go in from the back I'd have to take off that segment and that might kill him. I'll need to repair the damage while detaching the thrall fibres – only once they're all gone can I remove the thing itself.'

'Can you reprogram the thrall now?'

'No – I'm familiar with normal prador software but Vrasan used his own version of that. I've no idea what he's put in there.'

'Could the thing still kill him?'

'Maybe.'

'Ensure it does not.'

The man rubbed at his mouth. He looked agitated. 'Okay.'

'Is there anything else I need to know?'

'Not that I can think of.'

'Keep me updated.' An artificial click ended the conversation.

The man moved closer to me. Just for a second, bright blue light blinded me, then as it faded the air seemed full of white shifting cobwebs. This then blanked out and I smelled burning.

'My name is Bronodec Variclear Schultz. I'm going to repair your spine and remove that thrall. Vrasan made an effort to ensure you continue to feel the pain of your injury, but I think I can shut it down.'

I put together 'think I can shut it down' with 'go in from the front' and panicked but, of course, none of this was visible to him. He walked over to a pedestal autodoc nearby – I could see him just out of the corner of my eye. There he opened a hatch and unravelled an optic. Reaching up, he pulled out the one plugged into his skull and inserted the new one before returning to me. Then he sat cross-legged on the floor. With a low hum the autodoc moved in, then another came from the other side. The one on the left reached in with one glittering arm and pushed something against my neck. Sharp grinding pain arose there as an object cut me.

'Sorry about that,' he said. 'The neural blocker cannot overcome Vrasan's programming until it makes its attachment.'

It shortly seemed to find a switch, and all my pain then went blissfully away. Further arms swung in, attaching dishes and other containers to the gimbals, extended on brackets so they could be close to my body. Still others began inserting tubes: into my neck, my forearms and torso.

'I think you should see this,' he stated. 'I like people to appreciate my work and this chore is going to be complicated.'

Something pressed against the back of my head, tilted it forwards and with a sucking click held it there so I was looking straight down at my torso. This was just in time for me to see the autodoc on my left use a glowing scalpel to slice me from crotch to neck, sizzling as it went.

Thanks, I thought.

Did he really want me to appreciate his work or did he have a ghoulish impulse to torture someone under his power? I realized he was probably loaded with pride and all sorts of other problems. His appearance, in an age when people could look however they wanted, indicated so. Also, if he'd wanted to torture me, he could have neglected to turn off the pain.

Hooks came in and pulled back the skin and muscle over my intestines, then heavier arms with spatulas on the ends sank into my chest, where it was apparent the scalpel had gone through the cartilage. The scalpel, meanwhile, sliced across the top of the first cut to form a T. The spatulas pulled open my chest and I gazed down at my insides. I could see my heart pumping, blood flowing in the veins, my intestines shifting like great worms. Blood and other fluids began to pool and a small suction head started to vacuum them up.

'It's a fascinating engine, the human body,' he said. 'Now to disassemble it while maintaining its function.'

More cutting ensued. Cage hands lifted out my intestines, severed behind the anus and still attached higher up, and deposited them in a big dish. Other things began to go, tubed and wired as they went. My breathing abruptly stopped and then my heart, but I felt no discomfort from this beyond a mental one – the blood droning in my skull was propelled by some other pump. The docs took out my heart and lungs along with other paraphernalia and inserted them into a tank of fluid. My liver into another. The machines then scattered my stomach and other organs in various containers, all artificially attached by tubes and wires, small pumps intervening. Out of the corner of my eye, I saw my heart start beating again and my lungs breathing, the trachea hissing above the fluid they sat in and looking like a leech mouth.

'In a previous age infection would have been a problem,' he informed me. 'However, perhaps you noted the light display before I started work?' He nodded as if I'd replied positively. 'First was a spectral flash that kills most bacteria and viruses, followed by nanolasers that kill off anything more rugged. I am also running a surgical nanosuite through you to hunt down and kill anything you yourself brought in. Also, you need have no worries about anything on me, since my nanosuite maintains me utterly free of foreign microbes.' He paused thoughtfully. 'Within limitations.'

Finally, Bronodec Variclear Schultz had everything out of the way. I lay there utterly eviscerated down to my back muscles and spine. He then cut away muscle to expose fully a section of spine. There I could see the inward dent of my vertebrae with pieces of broken bone and, on either side of this, silvery metal lines like rows of staples. Bigger surgical heads, but with smaller protruding instruments, now moved in, thankfully blocking my view. All I could do was listen as they worked: the slither of cutting, the hum of a bone saw, sucking and sizzling. I did, however, see pieces of flesh, broken bone, along with a mixture of blood and spinal fluid, sliding up a transparent pipe.

'You cannot see what I am doing at the moment,' he continued. 'I have exposed the damage to your spinal cord and am now making temporary fixes while I detach Vrasan's hardware.'

I drifted off into a half-sleep as the procedure went on and on. At one point it all ceased and Bronodec abruptly stood up. He detached the optic from his skull and plugged the one from his sensory band back in, then wandered over to the door and out. I'd slid back into half-sleep by the time he returned with a cup of coffee and sat on the floor again. The light flash and the ensuing operation of the nanolasers woke me up fully. I wanted to ask him why he didn't have a chair, but couldn't.

The sounds continued while he drank, then ceased. He picked up the optic on the floor while unplugging the other, and reattached himself to the hardware. The surgical heads abruptly retracted, exposing the work they'd done. I gazed down at my spine, its vertebrae opened out to expose the cord and all the metallic staple things of the thrall folded back. I suddenly felt as if the room was spinning, then realized the gimbals were flipping me over. Numerous tubes and wires shifted round me in a seemingly chaotic tangle, but none of them detached. I noted a lid closing down on my detached guts to stop them spilling from their dish. I supposed a grav side-wash from the floor plates might cause that.

'Now to get that nasty thing off!' said Bronodec.

He put on a pair of silky-looking gloves which were mottled with quadrate patterns and veined with black wires. He then set to work at something apparently in the air in front of him and I felt the autodocs busy on my back – their tugging and cutting and sizzling, but no pain. I felt the thrall part company with me and, in the open cavity of my torso, saw the metal sink out of sight. He meanwhile took the invisible object from in front of him and put it to one side. Telefactor gloves, I realized. Afterwards he moved his hands back and held them upright. A new sound started from behind me – a low buzzing and droning. As this continued, he just sat there with his hands held up as if in some strange meditative pose. Eventually the sounds stopped and the gimbals revolved me back into position. He set to work again, bringing his fingertips together and down. New heads moved in, which I recognized as bioprinters. They had decals on their main bodies behind the long black spears and objects like chromed sea urchins. There I read 'Cellweld™' and 'Boneweld™' and knew that he must now be permanently repairing the 'temporary fixes'.

'Repairing nerve damage is always intricate,' he explained. 'I like to be hands-on for this while others usually leave it to a program. I find they tend to miss out on excising some of the scar tissue.'

I could hardly see what the things were doing to my spinal

cord, other than that the kink in it slowly disappeared and swelling deflated. The bone welders folded the pieces of vertebra back in and deposition welded them whole again. They filled various gaps with artificial bone too, and then retreated.

'The rest we can leave to the program,' he said, stripping off his gloves and returning them to his belt.

The machines speeded up. They wove muscle back around my backbone and cell welded it. My lungs and heart went back in next, with the Cellweld head blurring around and in them. I watched my heart begin beating again, even as cage hands transferred over my liver and other mechanisms attended to its plumbing. I breathed a liquid breath, fluid coming out of my mouth only to be sucked away before it got further than my chin. My lungs continued to bubble, but only briefly, as long thin needles penetrating them drew off the fluid. I saw my intestines running through a pinch, snaking down to my torso and welded at the anus. The machines intricately coiled them, welders working all the time.

'Putting it all back, surprisingly, is not the greatest task,' he said conversationally. 'Getting everything aligned, and working as it should, is difficult. Autonomics must be retuned while bacterial and vagus nerve signalling must be re-established. I find it easier to establish new bacterial colonies.'

The smell was pretty disgusting as a worm of shit and half-digested food exited my back-inflated stomach. A mist of astringent arose around the whole process, while needles injected what I presumed were new bacterial colonies into my intestines. Through the blur of machine movement, I saw my torso steadily refilling, even as hooks closed across my folded-out ribcage. More long needles went in, perhaps dealing with the damage caused to the rib attachments at my spine and the bonewelder came in to close the sliced-open cartilage. In layers, the machines closed across the muscle and skin.

239

'Not much fat there,' he said. 'High gravity combined with malnutrition.'

I wanted to reply, and now found that suddenly I could.

'Was it . . . necessary for me . . . to be conscious?' I asked.

He looked up with a delighted smile made grotesque by his lack of eyes. 'Why, of course it was. I am not without sensitivity to the psychological effects here. You will note that though the procedure is apparently traumatic, you do not feel it. The neural shunt has maintained you in a state of calm. I would normally have taken a patient down to minimal function, a form of biological stasis, but, unfortunately, that would have interfered with the readings required to deal with the thrall segment.'

'You've removed the thrall segment,' I noted, now able to talk with a lot less bubbling. I turned my head and looked, clenched and unclenched one of my hands. The thrall segment sat in one of the dishes, seemingly pinned by a series of glassy rods from one of the many limbs of an autodoc.

'Would you prefer unconsciousness now?' he asked.

'There's no need for it,' I opined.

'This I understand.' He grinned again. 'However, a period of autonomic and bioshock adjustment indicates the necessity.'

I finally saw my torso almost closed up again, but for the outer layer of skin, then the world simply went away.

I awoke naked in a bed and felt very strange. As I thought about what'd just been done to me, a surge of panic rose up, but this liar slunk away as I peered down at my perfectly intact body. Still, I lay scared to move, with some deep, almost unconscious expectation of pain. And another effect kept me immobile. I felt as if a thrall would still deny me physical movement. After remembering I'd moved in the gimbals, and just recently tilted my head to look at my body, I knew this to be a lie too – wholly psychological. I started by opening and closing my hands, curling my toes, then lifting up an arm. This last felt incredibly light – lower gravity here. I battled for the motivation to sit up, since this would require my stomach muscles and I'd only recently seen them sliced open and peeled aside like the inner skin of some fruit. Finally I managed it.

My body was light again and my head swam. The tumultuous activity in my torso felt similar to when I'd suffered food poisoning. My mouth watered as my stomach bubbled, while from neck to groin I felt tender, fragile. My loosening bowel got me quickly into motion, just managing to make it to the sanitary unit and sit down before it opened, emptying me of a blue chemical-smelling fluid. Thirst hit next and I drank from the tap in there because I dared not move from the toilet. But then I had to, as I vomited it all up again into the sink, emerald green with bile, the acid burning my throat. The thirst didn't go away so I drank again and this time it stayed down, sinking into me like water into arid ground. It seemed to settle my other problem too and, only after being sure, I stepped out of the booth.

The apartment resembled those aboard the ship Vrasan and the prador had used to get here, only everything worked in this one. I started to explore, opening cupboards as though I was searching for useful survival items once again. I did find clothing and personal items just like in those other cabins and it seemed this one had another occupant besides me. I discovered that the mirror turned into a screen when I touched it, giving me numerous touch controls, and voice control, if I wanted it. A food fabricator set in the wall flickered on when I tapped its screen, but I didn't feel ready to use it just yet. Returning to the personal items, I examined the clothing but was disinclined to help myself to things which belonged to someone else. Returning to the sanitary unit, I examined the controls there.

The touch screen seemed easy enough and I sent the toilet back into the wall. Another control retracted the taps and the sink. I hit the shower control and the unit protruded a series of spigots and a tray with a soap stick on it, then bombarded me with hot water from every direction. Following my surgical procedure, I probably wasn't particularly dirty, in fact likely aseptically clean, but I revelled in those jets and the soap. I enjoyed this for some while, before exploring further. The depilator was a single rod with a comb on the end to set for depth, while a touch on the control turned one wall into a mirror – frictionless and devoid of water drops. I trimmed my hair and beard down short, the hair falling as dust to the floor. Then I reset the thing to take off the remainder of my beard. Another brief shower washed the debris away. A tooth-cleaning bot inserted in my mouth gave a strange but not unpleasant experience as it travelled around inside, following a cleaning routine. It paused and vibrated as it removed tartar – gritty in my mouth – then an ache I only noticed at that moment disappeared in a rear tooth, and I realized the thing did more than cleaning. Afterwards my teeth were bright white and my mouth felt the cleanest it'd been in some time. I stepped out, pulled a towel from a long cupboard beside the unit, and dried myself. Then the door opened.

'You recover quickly,' said Bronodec.

I studied him.

He was wearing a toga belted at the waist, and sandals on feet that looked twisted by some joint complaint. He stepped in, the door swinging shut behind him on a carpeted corridor, a wide window directly opposite briefly giving a view to another distant wall which had more windows glittering like slabs of mica. As he walked up to me, I backed away but he caught my shoulder.

'Stay still.'

He looked me up and down with the sensory band of his, and

I felt the heat flush of scanning, matching the progress of his gaze.

'Surprisingly good.' He released my shoulder. 'You have no nanosuite and no enhancements but your health is tip-top despite your adventures. And your physique, from the high gravity and your activity down there, is strong. If I didn't know better, I would say you've been boosted.'

'That's good to hear,' I said.

'The muscle development is useful and healthy, but you'll lose it here unless you find some way to maintain it. Have you considered boosting?'

The guy apparently had no idea about my history. Fighting to survive aboard prador ships and then on a hostile planet, I hadn't exactly had much opportunity for high-tech body adjustments and cosmetics.

'No problems from the thrall removal?' I asked.

'It was tricky and Vrasan had left booby traps, but their extent was limited. You'll be fine.'

'Booby traps?'

'A power surge to burn out your nervous system and brain. Numerous other connections that would have resulted in convulsions and body death.' He waved a hand airily. 'I'm guessing he didn't have time to do anything more substantial.'

'Will I have any other . . . problems?'

He walked across the room to the food fabricator. 'Not that I am aware of.' He started working the panel and, behind a glass window, printing heads deposited something in a cloud of steam. 'One of her security detail will come for you soon so I suggest you dress. You'll also need to eat.' He stepped back from the fabricator and waved a hand at it. 'This should be right. Your stomach and intestines will be delicate for a while.' He moved to the door and opened it.

'I can use the clothes here?' I asked.

'You can use anything – the former occupant no longer will.' He exited, closing the door behind him.

So the previous occupant had either left the station or was dead. It struck me that the latter seemed likely and this station was clearly a dangerous place to be. It was also where I needed to be, if I was to have any chance of getting closer to Suzeal and shutting down her operation here. Though, right then, that seemed a misty future aim. This place, I decided, was perhaps a microcosm of the Graveyard entire: full of mercenaries, salvagers-cum-pirates and others whose business the Polity frowned on, like those involved in coring and thralling. Thinking on that, I wondered where Marcus was at this moment.

The fabricator window opened and the smell hit me. Suddenly ravenously hungry, I stepped over and pulled out the tray, which held a big beaker of liquid and a steaming pile of variously coloured vegetables. Some I identified as broccoli, carrots and tomatoes, while others I had no idea about. I cautiously sipped from the mug – some kind of protein soup – then, using a chain-glass spoon as cautiously, I tried the vegetables. A moment later, I was shovelling them in and had soon finished everything. I wanted more, but decided further prudence was a good idea.

Clothing. One of the black and white uniforms hung in the wardrobe but I wanted nothing to do with it and instead found cotton underwear, a shirt of some towelling material, combat trousers and jacket in desert colours, and enviroboots that adjusted to my feet. I studied the other stuff. There was coded comp hardware I couldn't use, but I did find a large ceramal combat knife with a belt and sheath, and put them on. When I saw a backpack, I wanted to fill it with items which might be useful but, no longer fighting for survival as I had been before, I realized other techniques would be necessary. I took the belt off again, removed the sheathed knife and tucked it inside my clothing. I then sat on the bed and thought hard, and was still doing so when Brack and two heavy-set guards arrived.

'Get up,' he said.

He no longer had armour on, but still looked a hulk, wearing just casual clothes similar to my own. As he studied me, his expression was resentful. There were undercurrents here I had still yet to parse. From the memory I had had while Vrasan tortured me, it seemed my original self had betrayed Suzeal. But there was more to it than that. Brack's dislike of me seemed to go beyond my being the image of a previous betrayer. I stood up and he glanced at the two guards while resting a hand on his sidearm.

'Looks like you're back to health,' he said. 'Come with us.'

He made no threats about what might happen if I attempted to escape, or in any way disobeyed, probably because he would have rather liked me to try. I had no doubt at all that, given the chance, he'd kill me. I walked forwards as he gestured me towards the door. He moved round behind me and gave me a shove, making me stumble out between the two guards. I didn't react but just stayed between them as they set off down the corridor. No doubt he also itched to use the stun baton that was on the other side of his belt.

The corridor curved round, windows on one side and the doors into apartments on the other. A vast internal space lay beyond the windows. Lines of windows divided the far wall too, while the floor seemed to be occupied by a park. I could see the curve to it, sloping up ahead and narrowed by perspective. A glance up helped me locate myself, for the interior of the hub lay visible through a geodesic glass roof. The two guards walked me to a dropshaft, then, each gripping one of my arms, stepped in, towing me after them. We rose, feeling the side tug of grav

245

as we passed ten floors. Our ascent slowed as we passed sensor heads and weapons, whereupon we came to a halt in mid-air. I glanced down at Brack below me, just before the field tilted and slid us into a new corridor. He came out behind a moment later, fingers against his aug and a nasty look on his face.

The luxurious corridor beyond had a floor coated in thick carpet moss and statues of various zoo creatures in alcoves. Watching the expression on Brack's face, I reached into my clothing and took out the sheathed knife, holding it out to the guard on my right.

'Here, best you take this,' I said.

He snatched it away, fear writ large in his features, then both guards slammed me against the wall. The barrel of a gun pressed against the back of my neck.

'You come here armed,' said Brack tightly.

His stun baton hit me in the back and I shuddered. The barrel of his gun retracted. The stun baton, I realized, hadn't been at its highest setting. He wanted me to do something, react violently. I kept utterly still.

'I thought I told you to clear Hunstan's cabin of weapons,' said Suzeal through some intercom. 'Seeing as you didn't, why're you surprised he picked up the knife, after all he's been through? Lower that fucking gun right now and search him. If he doesn't get here alive, Brack, you'll be joining his body in the composter.'

They searched me thoroughly, then Brack shoved me into motion again. In my ear he whispered, 'A lot can happen here – you'll be mine soon enough.' And so they brought me to the door of Suzeal's apartment.

Soft fabric upholstered the wide door and was secured with silver buttons. It opened with a swish and the guards propelled me inside, but gently. I suspected they were unsure of my status, whether prisoner or a guest.

'We're here,' said Brack.

Large throne-like wooden chairs, nine of them, were scattered on a dais at the centre. Some were placed around a large circular table while others clustered about a couple of pedestal tables. Various consoles and screens stood against walls, while a far window, consisting of hexagonal pieces of glass framed by old wood, overlooked the area I'd seen earlier, but with the geodesic roof much closer now. I'd expected a larger apartment, but doors did lead off into other rooms. The mess surprised me too. Opened plasmel boxes lay about the floor, clothing had been tossed over chairs, while eating trays, cups and glasses and other detritus occupied the tables. Over to one side of the dais, wheeled tool cabinets and benches clustered at an antiquated heavy weapon which, after a moment, I identified as an ancient large-bore machine gun, of the kind once mounted on a land vehicle. Tools and containers lay scattered there too.

'We're here!' Brack repeated, louder now.

One of the doors swung open and Suzeal called from inside, 'I'm aware of that. Get out and get back to your harem. Leave the other two outside.'

'That's not a good idea. You know who this shit is,' Brack protested.

'I know exactly who he is,' she replied. 'And when did you get the idea you could argue with me?'

Brack swore, then whirled to the door and headed out, the two guards following him. Once the door closed, I moved further into the apartment. I could use the tools as weapons but made no move towards them.

'Get yourself a drink or something else,' Suzeal called.

I looked around and walked over to a circular shelf jutting

from one wall, loaded with bottles and other items. Suzeal had a colourful taste in alcohol and an inclination to other mind-altering substances. Beside and amidst the bright bottles lay drug vaporizers and a dispenser for mouthpieces, drug patches, tubes of pills, some with the glint of active internal hardware, snorters and ultrasound injectors and other things I just didn't recognize. I poured some bourbon, got some ice from a dispenser and raised the glass to the window to toast Marcus, who had to be out there somewhere. I then went over to put my drink on a pedestal table, and heaved round one of the heavy seats next to it to face the open door. As I sat down, she finally appeared.

I don't know what I'd expected, but not this. The last time I'd seen her she'd been clad in combat armour, but she had dressed to kill in another way now. I noticed that she'd done some work on her face, emphasizing her eyes, a touch of gloss on the lips. Emerald studs glinted in her ears, another in her nostril. Her hair, now completely blonde, was piled up on the top of her head. She wore tight black trousers, almost spray-on, flat sandals, and a diaphanous top in a green leaf pattern, semi-transparent, cinched at the waist with a belt of wooden links, and hanging down over her hips; it was plainly evident she wore nothing underneath it. She was large, muscular and tough-looking – and very definitely all woman. My feelings towards her started to become confused. She had sold me, and others, to the prador. Her regard for human life sat at nil unless it could profit her and I had vowed vengeance against her. But she was a *woman* and elicited a sudden intense sexual response which I had never felt before – it was almost an awakening. I guessed a lack of nutrition and constant danger had kept it in abeyance before.

Rather self-consciously, I thought, she walked over to her collection of drinks and poured herself a glass of bourbon too, perhaps because I was drinking it. Without looking round, she said, 'I bet you thought you'd never get here.'

'I had to work on the basis that I would, but it never looked good,' I said, sipping my drink.

She turned around and leaned back against the drinks shelf. Something fell off and clattered on the floor. With a flash of irritation, she moved away from the shelf and came over. She looked at a chair nearby for a long moment, then went to sit on its arm, facing me.

'I was of two minds about whether to drag you out of that pit,' she said.

'That was apparent when you used me to locate the prador.'

She waved a dismissive hand. 'Yes, you were just an asset at that point.' After pausing contemplatively, she continued, 'But when it seemed I was about to lose you, that resolved something for me.'

I contemplated this, then said, 'You knew him.'

She winced a brief smile. 'You're talking about the one I took your DNA from. Yes, I knew him.'

'So what was he like?'

She obviously didn't like this subject and her gaze strayed around the room as if seeking to escape it.

'Not what he appeared,' she said eventually.

'How did he appear then?'

Again a flash of irritation: this wasn't going how she wanted. She put her drink aside and gazed at me.

'He looked very much like you, of course, though not so muscular and with more lines on his face. Apparently ex-ECS, he'd become a salvager in the Graveyard seeking to up his game and make a fortune. He was excited about what he intended to do with the wealth. He wanted to start a company specializing in meta-material tattoos – etching computer hardware into people's skin. This has been done before, and there's a major concern in the Polity that does it, but he wanted to venture away from AI-controlled hardware and make something more . . . amenable for sale in the Graveyard. He was very enthusiastic about it and very believable.'

'Believable?'

Her expression turned bitter. She waved a hand towards the window as if she could see my erstwhile self out there. 'Everything about him was convincing. He had an extensive knowledge of trade in the Graveyard. He was good company and sociable, and sometimes seemed to lose control of himself. I believed him when he said he wanted in on the coring trade. I believed him when, apparently stoned on Arotophen, he all but admitted he loved me.' She looked at me with a challenging glare.

'But that, of course, wasn't true,' I said.

'He blinded me. But Brack, for reasons of his own, was suspicious and kept a close watch on him. He found evidence of a brief U-space exchange with someone.' Her tone turned flat and factual as she continued, 'When I questioned Jack about this, he told me he'd talked with his underworld contacts there. Severing some ties, he said. Then he tried to drown out my concerns with that charm of his, and I saw it was false.' The flatness broke at this point and I heard something else in her voice. 'He realized at once and tried to kill me, and even though I'd prepared, he nearly succeeded. I brought him down with stun rounds from an autogun – it took six of them and by then he'd broken my leg, ribs, an arm, and taken out one eye. We put him through intensive scan and found his gridlink, and attached the quantum storage. That storage proved to me what he really was: a Polity agent. I erased him there.'

There it was: love and betrayal.

'You erased him?'

'Yes.'

'You erased his backup personality,' I stated.

'Yes – the personality but not the knowledge, which I thought might be useful.'

'Then you should have known I couldn't be him.'

'I could never be sure – quantum storage is . . . complicated.'

'What did you do with the living man?'

'I disposed of him.'

There was much more she wasn't telling me, and I should have been surprised by how much she'd now revealed. But I wasn't. Right from when she'd contacted me aboard Vrasan's ship she had been more forthcoming than entirely necessary, considering the circumstances. And now I was beginning to understand why.

'But then you made clones from his DNA . . .'

'Yes, and in one of the clones I embedded what I could recover of the quantum storage, wishing then that I'd not been so hasty in erasing his recorded consciousness. It was a kind of vengeance that went beyond merely disposing of him.' She looked at me very directly. 'Only with events proceeding as they have did I realize it could be something else.'

Now I understood my presence here perfectly. She had loved a man who'd betrayed her, and getting rid of him should have been the end of it. Instead, in extending her vengeance beyond his death, she had created me. At first I'd just been an asset, as she said, but she'd now started to see me as Jack reborn, without the history that made him a Polity agent. I could be Jack the way she wanted him: her lover returned without the training of an agent, or the inconvenient morality of the man. I considered what I'd said to her the last time from down on the planet and knew I couldn't pretend to be as she wished. This too, apparently, came to her mind.

'You said you don't like what I do and hoped my negotiations with the prador would fail,' she said.

I thought hard and fast. 'I was dying, and you seemed to have once again used me to locate the prador.' I knew that wouldn't be enough. 'No, I don't like what you do. I was one of the humans you traded and I saw what happened to the other clones aboard the King's Ship.'

'And morality?' she asked.

'Survival, as I've learned, is the only one.'

'Convenient.'

I met her gaze directly, and smiled. 'You had to have been there. But coring and thralling? I've killed to survive and understand that the rules of the game in the Graveyard are not the same as those in the Polity, to which I have no reason or inclination for loyalty.'

She made a dismissive gesture. 'Coring and thralling is irrelevant now. That trade is coming to an end with the king cracking down on it. It'll be about the hooders now.'

'Trading in insentient beasts I have no problem with,' I said, pretending to be offhand about it all. She'd made a concession to me regarding the previous trade because, I thought, she wanted to believe me. I'd heard the regret in her voice earlier about what she'd done to the original Jack. She was hoping for a second chance but would still be utterly wary and suspicious of me.

'The coring trade is ending,' she affirmed, staring at her hands like an addict sure to give up her favoured drug. She looked up. 'It's a time for new beginnings.' Her response didn't seem quite right, but I had to run with it.

I reached out and took hold of her hand. 'I hope you mean that.'

She leaned forwards and I kissed her gently, noting that more than just Jack's knowledge resided in my mind. It was as if he was there, coldly spectating and approving. I felt attraction to her, but also self-disgust, leavened by the need to survive, which meant, in the end, the need to manipulate her.

We stood, mouth to mouth, and I tried to pull her in close, but her hands went down to the stick seam of my trousers. I reached in and tugged at her belt and it fell away, slid my hands up inside her top and squeezed her breasts. As I pushed her down to the floor, the passion didn't feel false. She pulled off her trousers while I shed my clothes and there was no foreplay the first time. I just did what my body directed me, quite urgently, to do. She made little sound, just heavy breathing in my ear as she clung on with rib-crushing strength, then she shuddered and pushed up into my strokes, and I came, feeling the world draining out of me. As I lay there, with her legs wrapped round me, I wondered if, should it be necessary, I'd still be able to kill her.

13

We stayed in bed for a time that might have been night or day. My naivety seemed to give credence to her belief that I was different to Jack Zero, and that I'd had a change of heart. Meanwhile, as we talked and I told her of my adventures, I felt again that her need for a new Jack, fitting her own specifications, was making her credulous. Or perhaps I was the credulous one. I wasn't completely cold and the idea of vengeance, of finally taking the life of someone who had sold me and other clones to the prador, became much more confused and diluted in my mind. Could I still hate her, after this? I knew I couldn't stay here and be her lover, though. Despite the vulnerability she had revealed to me, I couldn't forgive the things she had done, nor countenance her selling ancient war machine biomechs to the prador. On a fundamental level I did not, and could not, agree with her moral code. Did this mean I *was* the old Jack reborn, getting close to her to betray her? No, I was something else, and would find my own way.

Finally, because of my exhaustion and not hers, the lovemaking came to an end. I fell asleep cuddled up to her, woke briefly as she turned over and thrust her backside against my groin and wriggled it. When I couldn't respond she said, 'You need some alterations.'

I agreed sleepily and drifted off again, then woke with my stomach growling. Food stayed off the menu for a while, though.

When we were finally done, she gave me a robe from the wall wardrobe in her messy bedroom. I noted other men's clothing in there which, I suspected, would fit me exactly.

'I think you're hungry,' she said, looking down at me with an expression I can only describe as possessive.

'That would be an understatement.'

'Then we will eat.' She stepped through a door and a moment later a shower started up. I lay there calculating. Should I follow her in and have sex with her again? Would she expect that with our newly discovered 'passion'? No, I felt drained and could put that down to not being 'adjusted'. I lay there examining my feelings and how they'd changed during lovemaking. I knew plenty about sexual bonding and all its hormonal aspects and recognized it in myself. When my body, driven by that old urge to pass on its DNA, wanted sex, I had stopped focusing on the idea of her as my enemy. Now, sexually replete, the thought had come back. I found myself thinking not only about her immoral actions, but also the kind of people she had around her. Like Brack.

His threat that I'd be 'his again' made me wonder if Suzeal often had brief and fiery affairs she didn't maintain, and which always ended in disappointment if not disaster. I needed to plan my escape, after I'd first ensured my freedom of action. I had to turn myself into a character Suzeal would trust, and be utterly alert to my behaviour. I thought again about joining her in the shower but my refractory period, brief as it was, had yet to pass. I also ached from head to foot, my torso feeling especially sore. Sex, I knew, was not the answer. A physical, animal thing, sex could sit apart from the intellect and I surmised how people could make love passionately while hating each other. I needed to do things and behave in a manner that suggested intellectual acceptance of her *morality*.

255

She returned a moment later, naked and drying herself with a towel. She glanced at me and frowned, slid her fingers between her legs and started playing with herself. I pulled myself wearily from the bed and sat on the edge of it.

'Tempting,' I said, 'but I'm merely human. You may also recollect that it's not been long since Bronodec had me opened up and spread all around his surgery.'

She took her fingers away. 'You need that upgrade, and a nanosuite, and some hardware.' Her hand wandered to the aug behind her ear, then away again as if that wasn't the right choice. 'I want you up to speed with me.'

And so it seemed she already wanted to change me – standard behaviour in any relationship and almost obligatory in a possessive one. Of course my earlier self had known this too. As well as how to manipulate people.

I went into the shower and washed, dialling up the heat to drive away some of the aches. The tooth-cleaning bot sat in a sanitizer so I used it, noting the spotless cleanliness of the bathroom overall. I put this down to the resident of a hole in the bottom of the wall, who stuck out his sensory head as soon as I stepped to the door. Why she didn't use cleaning bots in her apartment I couldn't fathom. Perhaps she didn't trust them wandering about while she slept.

'The clothing will fit.' She gestured towards the wardrobe I'd seen her open earlier. I selected new underwear, black jeans, a high-collared white shirt and a combat jacket with numerous pockets – mainly because I might find something in them – as well as high-ankle training shoes with gecko function. Meanwhile, she dressed herself in a tight green bodysuit, white jacket and thigh-length white boots. I saw her watching me cautiously as she picked up a wide belt with a sidearm and other items attached to it, and strapped it on. I pretended nonchalance, but had noted her use a palm-coded lock on the cupboard she took them from. After her story of her encounter with the other Jack, I guessed that it had happened here and that the apartment concealed automatic weapons she doubtless controlled with her aug.

'Let's go,' she said with a tight smile.

We headed out, two guards falling in behind us as we left the apartment. They weren't the ones who'd brought me here with Brack, and I wondered if she had guards at her apartment door constantly. We entered the dropshaft and dropped down twenty or more floors to step out into the park I'd seen from above.

'There used to be a population of half a million here in the time before the war,' she told me. 'Now it's below a hundred thousand. Many of the original inhabitants went to the Polity during the evacuation, and the population is mostly from the Graveyard now.'

The green areas consisted of Earth grass, cropped down by dilapidated robot mowers in some places, but in most standing tall and scattered with weeds. Bubble grass grew low elsewhere but had spread across paths of crushed stone. Copses of trees, like those I'd seen below on the planet, had been planted evenly. Some of them had fallen, while others were standing dead. In one area a banyan had taken over and would, given time, occupy the entire park. I saw fountains overgrown with vines and vomiting out small quantities of oily water, broken-down robot gardeners frozen in the midst of some task, steadily being lost under the foliage. Animals lived here too. Groups of rabbits made a better job of keeping the grass down than the mowers and I watched them scatter as a creature like the louse-hunter in the prador ship flowed up out of a hole. Weird red flying monkeys screeched from a tree at a pure white lion squatting patiently below, with some sort of hardware attached to its head.

'Anything dangerous here is controlled.' She studied me with an expression I couldn't read, and I could sense she was becoming distant again.

'It all looks a bit rundown,' I noted.

'Simple economics,' she replied shortly. 'With a lower population and income, we can't afford to keep everything going.'

'That's a shame.'

As we crossed the park, she hooked an arm through mine and pointed out animals and plants that had once been part of the zoo. 'No hooders or droons here, though we do have one siluroyne still in its compound. There are mud snakes too, but no bigger than Earth snakes and not a threat. Some like to believe that a gabbleduck occupies deserted levels of the station too.'

The far wall came into sight and along its base were various shops, restaurants and cafes. People lounged or worked there but nowhere near enough to fill the number of concerns. Some I could see looked fairly normal, though I could hardly judge. Many wore black and white uniforms like the two guards with me, and others were types I could only describe as 'mercenary'. They had the look of Brack and those others who'd delivered me to the King's Ship: armoured or military-looking clothing in a variety of styles, envirosuits too, and all armed. I noticed a mixture amongst them too – some wore black and white or had Strato-GZ decals on their garments, some didn't. We walked along beside these small businesses and, as we strolled, the SGZ gave salutes – a flat hand against the chest just below the throat – some even standing to salute and bow. I wondered again at Suzeal's power here, and the strong loyalty and deference she seemed to have engendered in these people. I could only assume she'd established it over a long period.

★　★　★

She brought us finally to a place with circular stone tables out front, surrounded by chairs seemingly made of wrought iron but actually light composite. After bowing and saluting, the guards moved off to stand a short distance away, carefully surveying the crowd. Others looked over at us. I could see them sitting up straighter and wanting to respond in some way, but desisting and returning to their meals, drinks and conversation. A crab drone flew out and hovered over our table but Suzeal dismissed it with a peremptory wave, even as a human waiter hurried out.

'Madam,' he said, with a bow.

I noted the metalwork on the back of his neck. The flat object resembled the device I'd torn from my neck all that time ago in the King's Ship. Suzeal clearly controlled more than animals here. She saw me looking and met my gaze with a blank expression.

'Steak, I think, with the vegetable medley – we need to build you up.'

I tipped my head and smiled acquiescence.

'Also some sparkle with psychedelic ice,' she added.

'What's that?' I asked.

'A relaxing and liberating drink,' she informed me.

I didn't want it. Sparkle was a strong carbonated wine, while the ice contained a drug that diminished inhibitions more thoroughly than alcohol and could also bring about some lurid hallucinations. I needed to maintain my self-control here, with her. But if I refused it she'd probably suspect the truth behind my refusal.

'Sounds good to me,' I said.

I could see she still didn't trust me at all and wanted to trip me up. So I decided to go on the offensive, and nodded towards the departing waiter.

'I take it some aren't as well behaved as they should be.'

'You mean?'

'He has a thrall on the back of his neck – or rather some lesser iteration of a prador thrall. He doesn't look as if he has the virus.'

She sat back and waved her hands towards a table nearer to the restaurant front. Two of the mercenary types sat there, clutching tankards close and talking low and face to face. 'Many of the people here aren't the original inhabitants and haven't necessarily been inducted into the SGZ. They're an unruly bunch who have lived most of their lives outside any system of law. It's necessary to be strict and sometimes harsh to maintain order.'

'What did he do?' I stabbed a thumb towards the restaurant.

She tilted her head for a moment, obviously accessing her aug. 'He assaulted two of the SGZ and both ended up being put back together by Bronodec.' The statement was a challenge.

'Better than many alternatives, I guess,' I said, then continued as if dismissing the whole subject from my mind, 'What is it with that Bronodec? Surely he could apply his skills to himself?'

The drinks arrived on a floating vendor tray and we took them. In tall flutes, they bubbled steadily, the ice iridescent and packed in right to the bottom. I took a careful sip as she replied, 'He's an unusual man. He was born in the Graveyard on a moon colony descending into primitivism. Inbreeding, combined with high radiation due to a failing EMR shield, resulted in him and his brethren. We raided the moon for bodies before we got our cloning facility up and running and found him in charge of their medical tech, where he held his position because of his unusual intelligence and facility with it. I kept him. He's never said why he prefers to stay as he is.' It was another challenge and again she was looking for the wrong response.

'What happened to the rest of them?'

'We infected them with the Spatterjay virus and cored and thralled them.'

And again. I felt my anger rising, and had to quell it. 'Did you have to offer a discount, if they were as fucked-up as him?'

She smiled and nodded, taking a gulp of her drink.

'Was he involved in that – the coring and thralling?'

The drink was obviously already affecting me because I should've moved away from that topic to continue speculation on why he'd refused to change.

'Not in our earlier trade, when we stuck wholly with prador technology on virus-infected humans. But he is a very clever and technically adept man. He developed the technology later to produce thralls which could be easily installed on uninfected humans – as you have seen.' She gestured towards the restaurant. 'And as you have experienced.'

'He had no objection to it?' I damned myself as soon as the words were out of my mouth.

She gazed at me steadily. 'He had no objection to it. Though he worked on the people of that moon, he was all but a slave there.'

I wondered if he understood that he'd exchanged one form of slavery for another and saw the benefits of both acquiescence and making himself useful. I only just stopped myself asking that and realized the drink was having the very effect she required of it. Luckily the food arrived soon after, again on two floating trays, the waiter walking out behind them. The trays settled on the table and we took off the plates and cutlery to allow them to shoot away again.

'Will you require anything more?' asked the waiter.

Without looking up, Suzeal waved a dismissive hand. I looked at the slab of meat on my plate, the vegetables being more of a decorative trim than anything substantial. I noted a slight halo around the meat and, looking up, saw other objects had acquired this too. My stomach bubbled loudly and Suzeal snorted laughter. I assumed she must be getting as high as me, and I dug in, hoping that the food would kill some of the effect. I had another reckless impulse to ask how long a person ended up under the thrall for assaulting her SGZ. I suspected no limitation on the time. Having polished off half the steak and beginning to feel a bit less as if I might say something stupid, I searched around for a safe subject.

'The prador,' I said.

'What about them?' she asked.

'You're still in negotiations with those on your docking moon?'

She ate a lump of meat and scribed some shape in the air with her fork. 'Not with them – I've been speaking through a relay to another prador in the Kingdom. It's going slowly. He doesn't believe I've given them all the families I traded with – and I haven't. He's dickering over the prices on the hooders and methods of delivery and wants Vrasan overseeing all of that. Negotiations stopped when I hit the facility from orbit.'

'You killed him?'

'Apparently not. I completely destroyed the facility but the little shit had tunnelled up from underneath. No sign of dead prador or hooders.'

'But still no negotiation?'

'Oh that's continuing – more demands have come now and he wanted my promise not to try hitting Vrasan again.' Her eyes narrowed thoughtfully. 'I think he's either deliberately delaying or has to run everything past the king.' She looked over to one side. 'Time for the show.'

I peered into the park and felt as though the drink was screwing with me again. A shimmering wall had appeared. I realized that a lot more people had arrived, all sitting at tables and looking towards the wall. A bright spot appeared at the centre of it, opening out into another place. Holographic projection. There tall walls enclosed an area like one I'd crossed with Marcus. Flute grasses grew in abundance, but in a different state of growth from those on the planet – large wiry branches from them were covered in flower buds of red, yellow, violet and white. A platform stood in the centre of the grasses, just a few feet off the ground. All stood clear, then clearer still as the view focused in on that platform. A transparent cylinder descended from above, and down through this dropped a shape. I only saw the man as the cylinder ascended again. Down on one knee, he wore body armour and a breather mask. He stood up abruptly, holding what looked like a quarter staff.

'I'm betting on seven minutes,' said a familiar voice from nearby.

I glanced over to see Brack sitting at a table with the man I'd heard called Frey when I was first sold to the prador. They were with others of a similar type. He had women on either side of him clad in strappy creations of black leather and metal that concealed very little. The blonde on his right had a black eye and bruises all up one arm. The brunette on his left turned her head to look at the display, revealing a thrall unit on the back of her neck like the one the waiter wore. He gazed at me with some amusement, then away again to watch the projection.

'Ten minutes and he's free,' said Suzeal, her gaze fixed on me.

'What's this?' I asked, trying to keep my tone casual.

'Hunstan was not sufficiently obedient,' she stated.

The man whose apartment I'd woken in after my operation whirled around to face movement in the flute grasses. My gaze strayed away for a moment, taking in the others now gathered here and I saw that many people were wearing thralls – not the mercenary types but servants, slaves and the like.

'A couple from Brack's harem?' I asked, indicating the two women, and staying away from the subject of the man in the projection.

'Yes,' she said contemplatively. 'He probably has the right idea. It's difficult to trust a partner when you're in our trade.'

'Very difficult to get close to anyone when they're slaves, though?' I suggested.

'That is not a necessity,' she said.

Rapid movement in the grasses drew my eye back. Something tried to get to Hunstan over the edge of the platform, but it was difficult to see. I got the impression of a transparent bulk, briefly etched by the fading impression of flute grasses, and then I realized. Hunstan swung his staff and it connected with a red flash. As the shape dropped away, I got a clearer look at it. In two deep dark eye-pits glittered eyes like faceted grey sapphires. Its huge head had the appearance of a bovine skull patterned with flute grass stripes and trailing two flat-tipped feelers from its lower jaw. The teeth, when exposed, had no camouflage and gleamed like hatchets of blue bone. Its long wolfish body had clawed forelimbs similar in structure to those of a gabbleduck. This was Suzeal's captive siluroyne.

'Harsh punishment indeed,' I commented. 'Wouldn't it be better to thrall him?'

Suzeal shot me a puzzled glance. Maybe at last I was making some headway.

'He knew my laws and, as a free citizen and candidate for the SGZ, knew he'd be subject to harsher punishments.'

I contemplated 'free citizen' as the monster bellowed and reared, its multiple forelimbs opening out in silhouette against the background like a huge clawed tree. Hunstan hit it again and red fire flashed down its body, revealing its heavily ribbed torso. It grunted and dropped, but didn't completely abandon the platform. He struck it on the head as its legs scrabbled in the grass and mud behind, then rolled aside as it surged onto the platform, dragging the tip of his staff down its side, sparks and burning matter flaring away. The thing next rolled on its back, simultaneously flicking great clods of mud and flute grass rhizome at him. He staggered back and its foreclaw flashed out, closing around the staff. The creature shrieked, as fire flared around its claw, but it still pulled the staff away and sent it arcing into the grasses.

'Four minutes,' Brack noted.

'He's not dead yet,' Suzeal returned.

Hunstan backed to the edge of the platform as, hissing and snapping its jaws, the siluroyne stalked towards him. He looked over to where his staff had landed, jumped, but the siluroyne jumped too. It caught him in mid-air and slammed him down in the flute grasses, then dragged him by the legs back onto the platform. He fought hard as it sat back on its haunches. For a moment a knife flashed in his hand and he delivered a series of stabs into the forearm of the claw holding him. But the thing reached in, snapped his wrist, and the knife fell away.

'Who gave him that?' Brack called.

This raised much hilarity.

The animal then started to tear off his armour, like a glutton peeling a prawn. He shrieked in pain and terror; he was obviously a tough man to have remained silent until now. He continued fighting, flailing at its looming head with his broken arm. It caught this in its teeth and stripped off the flesh, then turned him, naked now, and began stripping the skin off his legs. I watched in numb silence, aware Suzeal was watching me. After the thing had eviscerated him, Hunstan finally died. The siluroyne began crunching up his bones, biting down on his head and feeding on his spine. Once finished, it scoured the platform for any bits it might have dropped. I just sat still, knowing I couldn't pretend nonchalance or acceptance.

'That probably doesn't provide it with all it needs,' I managed.

'We give it necessary supplements,' said Suzeal. 'Also required antihistamines to prevent a reaction to human flesh – too many oxides in it.'

'Perhaps you could provide it with what it needs,' said Brack at my shoulder, and I felt something cold against my neck. Peering down, I saw the blade of his machete there.

'When I no longer have a use for him,' said Suzeal, gazing at Brack severely.

I wondered again at the distance she'd reimposed since we left the apartment, and I knew I'd failed some kind of test. Any hint there'd been of her starting to trust me seemed gone completely. Something touched the side of my head. The charge from his stun baton convulsed me as he took the blade away, and everything turned red, laced with white lightning. My knees hammered up under the stone table then I fell from the chair into blackness.

I woke in a cell feeling sick, aching from head to foot and naked, strapped down on a bench. Bronodec stood over me, steadily sponging down my body. Nearby, on the floor, lay a pile of my clothing, the smell of shit and piss rising from it.

'I told him not to use the stun baton,' said Bronodec conversationally. 'Luckily there's nothing the nanosuite won't be able to handle. It's an illusion that modern surgical techniques leave no damage. The repaired tissues can be quite delicate for a while.'

He continued washing me down until, finally satisfied, he stood back, dropped the sponge into a bowl on a trolley and from there picked up a multiple needle injector. The large thing, with its chromed finger grips and glass body, looked almost antique, and a metallic fluid swirled inside. He pressed it against my neck and triggered it. I felt the needles go in, then further movement as they sought out the correct veins and arteries. A moment later the injector hummed and the fluid drained away.

'Of course, this is not the nanosuite entire. The solute contains micro-factories wrapped in cell membranes, with attached guide vesicles, programmed RNA, immune suppressors and reprogramming viruses. They have to find the correct locations in your lymphatic and vascular systems, and in your liver.' He paused contemplatively. 'In fact I can't think of anywhere the micro-factories don't seat themselves.'

'Why?' I asked, voice hoarse.

'She doesn't want you dying of something easily preventable, and she wants you fit, healthy, and sexually at a peak far above standard. She also likes the muscle you acquired on the planet so boosting has been programmed in.'

'She wants me alive?'

'For now . . . Right, as I was saying, once the micro-factories attach, they begin producing, as some would have it, the nanotech that floods out into your body. The description "nanotech" is a bit of an artefact from the days of the pure nanotech revolution. In reality, the factories themselves are partially organic and produce a lot of organics. These update your immune system to cover most maladies. They destroy senescent cells and promote autophagy and apoptosis, as well as recognize just about every pre-cancer and eliminate them, promote stem cell renewal and much else besides. Once the nanosuite is in operation in a couple of days, your lifespan is potentially limitless. Isn't that wonderful?'

'My impression,' I managed, 'is that my lifespan will be as long as Suzeal's interest in me.'

'True,' he said, 'but we can't have everything.'

I lay there trying to sense the effect of the injection, but only felt the constant ache and nausea. Bronodec stood shifting from foot to foot as if uncomfortable.

'Is there anything you would like to ask me?' he finally said.

'Boosting?'

'Oh yes.' As ever a question delighted him. 'It used to be done over a period of weeks and often surgical techniques were required to weave in dense artificial muscle and sometimes electromuscle. Now, with the modern nanosuites, the changes can occur in situ. The suite promotes the growth of dense muscle fibres that are immune negative, so they won't be rejected by your body. They cause a similar toughening and densification of bone and cartilage. Other alterations are of course necessary for the support of these: increased platelet count, a mitochondrial upgrade, faster processing of ATP, nerve optimization and oxygen transport. Over a period of a few weeks, you'll get markedly stronger. You will put on bulk but not so much as you see in the older versions of boosting, a lot of which were really cosmetic.' He rambled happily but stopped when he saw my reaction to what he said next. 'Of course these will not be necessary for fitting – just the nanosuite establishing will be enough for that.'

'Fitting?' I asked sharply.

'Your thrall. They do cause a degree of trauma and a standard human being can have a bad reaction from the nerve connections and flood of nanomachinery, though my design is not the death sentence the usual prador version would be.' He paused, again lost in thought. 'It was interesting to see that Vrasan used some of my techniques, though I did have to deal with a lot of damage from his procedure.' He focused on me again. 'But the nanosuite will be programmed to ameliorate most effects.'

'Thrall,' I repeated.

'You won't be cored,' he continued hurriedly. Then he paused. 'Well, not at present – you would need to be infected with the Spatterjay virus for that to happen and I have received no instructions in that regard.'

I tested the straps holding me down but couldn't budge them. After a moment, I turned my head away from him and closed my eyes. I tried to persuade myself to be positive. I wasn't dead yet, after all.

'I'll leave you to it,' said Bronodec. 'The suite should take a day or two to establish.'

'Yeah, you do that,' I replied.

I lay there listening to him shifting from foot to foot still. Then he moved off and the door opened. After a short pause he said, 'Oh!' then something crashed into the room. I whipped round to see the trolley over on its side and him lying on the ground, clutching at his head. Blood ran from a wound in his skull and his visor had been torn away. At the door stood a big mercenary clad in a patchwork armoured suit, visor closed down. He stepped in, dragging one of Suzeal's SGZ, whom he deposited on the floor before heading out to drag another in. He stood upright and closed the door, inserted Bronodec's torn-away visor into a belt pouch and then raised his own.

'Hello, Marcus,' I said.

His face had almost returned to human shape, but the skin was still blue and webbed with red veins, while his nose was a beak and his eyes deep set and black. He walked over and tugged at one of the straps holding me, then, after a moment, began to undo them. Perhaps his steady return to humanity had lost him some of his strength because I would have expected him to break them. I sat up, head swimming, then swung my legs over the side of the table.

'Clothinzzz.' He pointed at the guards.

I got unsteadily from the table, tottered over to one of them and began stripping off his uniform. Slowly my head began to clear and I dressed, pulling on the boots. Marcus ducked out for a second and returned with two pulse rifles. I strapped on a sidearm, took the other sidearm from the other guard and then searched their pockets. Bronodec groaned and rolled over, and Marcus quickly stood over him.

'No,' I said, 'let him live.'

Marcus turned to me, an odd look on his face I finally interpreted as a smile. He took a short cylinder out of his pocket and pressed it against Bronodec's neck. The man slumped, breathing heavily, and Marcus hauled him up and slung him over one shoulder. Holding a pulse rifle in his free hand, he gestured to the door.

'We go,' he said.

I moved ahead of him to ease the door open cautiously, realizing that Marcus had had no intention of killing Bronodec. Remembering he'd put the man's visor in a belt pouch, I saw that Marcus's being here might have nothing to do with me at all. I reconsidered. It had perhaps been his intention to grab the man and my presence had motivated him to do it in this place and at this time. What did he want the doctor for? Perhaps to return him further to his humanity?

We moved out into the corridor and Marcus led off at a swift pace. I looked around for some way we could move Bronodec less conspicuously and, when we entered an area where a wheeled gurney stood, I pointed them out.

'No.' Marcus shook his head.

He led the way around a corner where two personnel, both clad in white hazmat suits with the hoods down, were moving someone on a grav-gurney. They stopped and stared, but Marcus marched straight on past them.

'He'll be fine,' I said.

They didn't seem particularly troubled and, glancing back, I understood why: both of them had thralls gleaming on the backs of their necks. Another corner and then another until two of Suzeal's SGZ stepped out of a dropshaft. Almost with casual indifference, and not slowing his pace at all, Marcus opened fire. His shots traversed the chest of one then the visor of another. They staggered as armouring in their uniforms deflected some of the energy. Marcus kept firing until they dropped and he marched straight past them, with smoke and the smell of burned flesh and plastic filling the corridor. One of them was groaning rhythmically and scrabbling at the floor with burned hands, the other inert, his headgear burning.

At the dropshaft, he input the destination quickly. We descended, whipping past floor after floor, decelerating, coming to a stop, then dropping abruptly about ten feet to land on a net stretched across the shaft. Marcus grabbed rungs on the side of the shaft and directed me to do the same, then sliced the net with pulse rifle fire. He shouldered the strap of his rifle and, releasing Bronodec, though keeping him balanced on one shoulder, climbed down through the hole. As I followed, I realized the grav felt lower, and different, and slightly at a transverse to us. I could feel the spin of the station.

Two floors down, we entered a dilapidated corridor. The walls were scratched by the transit of people and their paraphernalia, the floors worn, rubbish strewn here and there, and many of the light panels out. Shrugging Bronodec to a better position, Marcus raised a hand to his ear and only then did I see the small coms unit inserted there. He gave a brief nod and marched on. We took many turns, went through a series of bulkhead doors, climbed down through deactivated dropshafts and deeper into darkness and areas of the station obviously unused. At length, we halted at another corner and Marcus listened to his coms unit again. When we rounded it, I saw two mosquito autoguns sitting in a corridor in front of a bulkhead door. The door opened, a woman with cropped black hair peered out, then she gestured us in.

14

The woman was their leader, that seemed evident. Her soldiers filled the section of the station they had temporarily fortified. They addressed her as 'Commander' and saluted when she passed.

'Ankhor, get the autos packed and on the move right now. Molotor, one mile spread and proxies to our rear. They'll be after us in a big way soon.' The two were both thickset men, probably boosted. They had their long hair tied back in pony tails, beards tightened with metal rings and, over the usual attire I had seen on the mercenaries above, wore chameleon-cloth sleeveless jackets, presently set to a mottled red. Molotor stepped over and passed a similar jacket to me. It was white when I put it on, then changed to match the colour of the rest as I did it up. Only now, glancing at Marcus, did I see that he already wore one.

'Colour changes on random – we don't want them matching us.' I presumed this referred to the jackets and I guessed it a good idea to be able to distinguish friend from foe. Though some of the foes of these people were easily identifiable by their black and white uniforms or armour, others were mercenaries yet to be, or disinclined to be, inducted into the SGZ.

I couldn't count how many troops surrounded us because we weren't in some open space but a maze of corridors, shafts and rooms. We moved off, a group of four soldiers in the lead, then Marcus, me and the woman next. Others came in behind, with mosquito autoguns walking delicately behind them, barrels facing backwards.

'Who are you people?' I asked.

The woman grinned at me without humour. 'The revolution.' She waved me on.

'Your name?' I asked.

'Salander, but you can call me Commander. No talking now.'

More corridors and dropshafts ensued, then we came to the floor of a vast factory, where giant matter printers squatted like pondering giants over mile-long conveyors. Only now, as we travelled through it, did I think about the scale of the Stratogaster station and its population. Suzeal had told me that a hundred thousand now occupied it, but even that number seemed very small in a thing fifty miles across. As I didn't know the exact figure, I estimated its depth at ten miles, which meant a total volume of nearly twenty thousand cubic miles. The population wouldn't be evenly distributed throughout it either – people tended to cluster together – leaving lots of empty volume. More than enough for a revolution to hide in. But how much of the station was unoccupied? Perhaps a lot of it didn't have air and power? I noted a great deal of dilapidation as we passed, but at no point did we move through areas without at least some lights and other signs of power usage. Fusion plants would be scattered throughout, some of which could be as small as a coffee mug. Super- and ultra-capacitors, laminar batteries, ninety-nine per cent solar panels outside, gravity and torsion generators since the station spun over a gravity well – all linked with superconducting cables. Plenty of power available, evidently. That left atmosphere, a question soon answered when we trooped along a suspended walkway wrapped around a giant bioreactor atmosphere plant.

'Mask up,' Salander instructed, as we came to a huge door but went through a human-sized airlock inset in the thing. A breather from the collar of my uniform went into my mouth, supplying air stored in its layers. Marcus lowered Bronodec to the floor and strapped a breather mask on his head, checking its security over his mouth before picking him up again. We stepped through into a familiar landscape: flute grasses stretching for miles, but with multiple electric suns in the sky.

'The siluroyne?' I queried.

'Not here,' she replied, and now seemed more chatty. 'This was where he kept his hooders and mud snakes. None of the latter here now – bacterial infection. The former were all transported down to the planet – the Polity didn't want them breaking loose during an attack.'

Paths had been trodden down through the grasses and we headed across at a steady trot. I struggled to get going, with my body one big ache, but then, as I pushed on, something happened. A weird fizzing passed throughout my frame with an accompanying hot flush, and shortly all my pain disappeared. Maybe the nanosuite had begun its work. Bronodec had said it would take a couple of days but the extra activity could have accelerated it.

'We planted crops in the old droon pen in the early days, but Suzeal poisoned them,' said Salander. 'We now keep hydroponics scattered throughout.'

'Surely that's not enough?' I asked.

Not enough for a civilized existence at least, I thought.

'We have our factory units. There's more than enough equipment here from the old days and we trade. She tried to stop that too but the blockade started to affect her own business. So we've been in a kind of truce for decades . . . until now.'

'And what's changed now?' I asked.

'Prador, the space dock out of commission, and him.' She pointed, but I wasn't sure whether at Marcus or Bronodec. 'Also Suzeal's steady attrition of us. She hasn't conducted an outright attack over those decades but her people come on hunting expeditions. If our people aren't killed, they're taken back to be put under the thrall. We kill lots of them, but more always come to replace them.'

After crossing the flute grasses, we entered further corridors, old boulevards, massive pedestrian and grav-car ways, and we used working dropshafts. These finally brought us, I assumed by the armaments everywhere, to the base of the revolution. Here apartment towers stretched between floor and ceiling of a large space. Grav was low. Crop areas covered the floor and were also up on what was the ceiling from my perspective. As I studied the sides of the buildings more closely, I saw grav-plates had been utilized and crops were there too.

Most of the troops and autoguns scattered to head off to their own destinations. Just Salander, Ankhor, Molotor, Marcus and his burden and I entered the cabin of a glass tube lift which took us up. In the interior of the building, we marched along corridors with peaked ceilings and a lot of old decoration.

'You know where to take him,' Salander said to Marcus.

He nodded and walked on. I moved to follow him but Molotor's meaty hand came down on my shoulder and Salander turned to open a door to one side. 'You and I need to have a talk.'

Molotor propelled me firmly after her into an ornately decorated room. There were even bookshelves containing paper books, though I felt they must just be part of the decor. The two men disarmed me and pushed me down into a deeply upholstered chair below a crystal chandelier, while Salander took a seat in the chair behind a wide wooden desk.

'One of his apartments.' She gestured around her. 'He had a taste for the lurid.'

'You're talking about Stratogaster?'

'Yes.'

'Is he still alive?'

'Somewhere in the Polity, last I heard.'

'What do you want from me?'

'I want you to tell me your story, right from the beginning, not missing out any detail,' she stated, caging her hands before her, elbows on the desk. I felt keenly aware of the two big men standing behind me and half expected this to turn into an interrogation, but then Molotor walked over to one side and grabbed a couple of composite chairs and took them back to the door. He and Ankhor sat on either side of it, arms like hams crossed.

'I presume you've heard some of it from Marcus?' I asked.

She just stared at me.

'Or perhaps he's still not talking much. I don't know how the virus affected his brain.'

'Marcus,' she repeated. After a long pause she added, 'It's surprising he has any brain left at all. This is something I must ask him about when he does start talking more, rather than making his suggestions.'

Her hesitation confirmed something for me. She'd been stumped by the name Marcus until I elaborated. As I'd suspected down on the planet, this wasn't his real name. I considered asking her about that but, since she'd run with the fiction, I decided to leave it for now.

'Okay,' I said, 'It starts, obviously, with when I first woke up . . .' I told her it all. At one point Molotor came over with a tall glass of some fruit drink, and later on Salander pointed me to a door over to one side when I needed the toilet. I eyed the shower longingly as I used the toilet, then returned to her to relate the rest.

Her curiosity climbed in the latter stages of my story and she leaned forwards. 'So Suzeal told you she wants to switch over to selling hooders to the prador? Do you think it's a certainty?'

'No I don't.'

'Elaborate.'

'She wanted me to be a new version of the Jack she knew before. I think she just said it to move away from the subject of coring and thralling. I don't see her abandoning any enterprise until it ceases to be profitable.'

She nodded. 'You're correct. Her cloning facility is still running and she has eight hundred prisoners locked down, all infected with the Spatterjay virus. Even if the king does manage to close down her trade with the Kingdom, which I doubt, she's still expanding her trade across the Graveyard.'

'Trade across the Graveyard?' I asked, not sure what she meant.

'Do you think it is only prador who like to have human slaves?'

I felt a bit sick. 'And I suppose Bronodec's thralls make the process easier and more attractive to some.'

She nodded. 'She already has people coming here with prisoners of their own: enemies usually, though sometimes family, very often people to be thralled for prostitution. Suzeal makes plenty of money off that.' She shrugged. 'She even sells to rebel prador in the Graveyard – they're much more inclined to use human blanks than those that remained in the Kingdom.'

I continued my story but suspected Salander of only half listening. However, her interest came back when I related what Suzeal had said about her negotiations with the prador.

'She thought they might be delaying, that they have another agenda?'

'Yes. Seemed like it.'

'They probably have. Prador are not inclined to just roll over when circumstances change. And you can bet the king knows she has no intention of stopping her coring and thralling trade with the Kingdom. It'll continue, even if only through intermediaries in the Graveyard.' She paused thoughtfully. 'Perhaps your Marcus is right.' Before I could ask about that, she continued, 'Tell me again about Vrasan's intentions with the hooders he thralled.'

'I told you it all, but not my own speculations on the matter,' I replied. Until then I'd just related events as they'd occurred.

'Go on.'

'I think their mission here was in two parts. They wanted to shut down Suzeal, certainly, but their prime objective was to use Stratogaster. They wanted it as their base here to gain access to the hooders.'

'So you don't think their method of attack was all about preserving information about the Old Families she traded with?'

'That's part of it . . .' A new thought occurred to me. 'But they could have brought heavier weapons to break up the station, grabbed survivors for interrogation and surviving memory storage for forensic analysis, if that were their intent.'

'Seems more their style,' she agreed. 'Tell me the rest.'

I did so and it was a brief tale thereafter. She stood up as I finished. 'She does like feeding people to that siluroyne.' She gazed at me steadily. 'That was her idea in the first place. It wasn't left here during the war, but is one of a very small number she took from the surface. That was after numerous failed attempts to capture a hooder, which tells you something about her idea of selling those creatures to the prador. Come on.'

At the door, Molotor handed back my weapons. I nodded my thanks and we trooped up the corridor.

'So what are your plans now?' asked Salander.

Until then my only plan had been to remain alive. I took a long time before replying as I thought things through. Suzeal's business here had to end and I'd do anything I could to facilitate that. This, after all, had been my original objective. And, as I replayed the scene in my mind of Hunstan's death, with her, Frey and Brack watching, I wanted payback.

'I think it depends on what your plans are,' I said.

'To kick the scum off this station, shut down Suzeal's trade and feed her to her siluroyne,' she replied.

I considered the brief feelings I'd experienced for Suzeal, how my motivations became confused and how I'd thought that killing her might not be necessary. I recognized them as stemming wholly from the part of my brain I could call the mating ape. However much she'd opened up to me in our encounter too, she'd since confirmed her heartless brutality.

'Seems like a good plan to me,' I replied.

They'd put Bronodec in a small cabin with guards outside the door and he was awake when we entered, standing in the middle of the floor with his back to us. When he turned, I saw that Marcus had returned his visor. But of Marcus there was no sign.

'Sit down,' said Salander, gesturing towards the bed.

Bronodec made a good attempt at a grin then went over to the bed and sat down. Salander grabbed a chair and sat astride it facing him. It seemed I'd been consigned to the position of Ankhor and Molotor, the lurking heavies. I noted Molotor walk off to one side, fingers against a small circular aug or coms unit behind his ear.

'You know your situation,' said Salander. 'Your chances of rescue or escape are close to zero. If it looks even remotely as if Suzeal might get you back, I'll kill you myself.'

'She may try hostage exchange – I am valuable to her,' said Bronodec.

'Too valuable to her and too much of a danger to us.'

He nodded as if expecting this. 'Then why am I still alive?'

'Because of your thralls.'

'Ah, I see.'

'Do you really? Okay. Here's how it is: Suzeal has tens of thousands of my people under her control. You are going to help me release them or you're going to die.'

Bronodec wrinkled his brow, which looked odd with him having no eyes. 'A difficult proposition because it is difficult to break the linkage between thrall and host. Most nerve linkages are physical while those that are not, such as the radio, red laser and ultrasound links to nanites and separate system-ware incursions, are tightly controlled by the coding.'

'You must have a back door into the code,' she said.

He winced. 'I tried to make one and it was there in the earlier versions, but Suzeal is paranoid and when she paid an expert to review my work, I closed it. Despite the fact that much of the code was my own design, the holes were a little too obvious.'

Salander glanced round at us, puzzled. It seemed she'd never encountered Bronodec before and had yet to understand him. I did, however. He occupied the world of intellect and stood distant from human emotion. His work was everything. He hadn't tried to keep silent or lie or bargain because he really did understand his straits and, perhaps unlike the kind of people Salander surrounded herself with, knew nothing of loyalty, camaraderie and human interaction.

'But of course,' I interjected. 'This presented you with the interesting problem of how to maintain access to your thralls.' I shrugged. 'Not because you wanted some kind of safety net or some tool you could use to your own advantage, but simply because it was an interesting problem.'

Bronodec smiled at me. 'You understand.'

I glanced at Salander and she waved me to continue.

'Of course I do – the work is important and problems must be solved. Order must be imposed over matter and information. So what did you do?'

The door opened now and Marcus stepped in. Bronodec gazed at him – no fear, just curiosity – then returned his attention to me. 'With the back door into the code closed, I looked at the EMR methods of access. Unfortunately, because my coding is tight it will respond to any interference there – it makes adjustments at any attempt to gain access, then finally, once things get outside set parameters, it knocks out the subject. I thought a virus might work, feeding back through the red nanolaser to expand those parameters, but the variance caused a loop that killed the subject.'

Salander grunted then looked away from the man to me and nodded for me to continue again. Evidently Bronodec had experimented. I wondered how many people he'd killed to satisfy his need to solve this 'problem'.

'So what was the answer?' I asked, sure he'd found one.

'Their nanosuites,' he said, obviously delighted by the memory. 'The addition of a reprogramming nanite has their nanosuites attacking the physical connections. It is quick and breaks the protocol which ensures unconsciousness, while launching a viral attack on the thrall itself. The whole system collapses in just three minutes.'

Salander swung back to look at him. 'And what happens to the subjects?'

'My sample size was not sufficient to be sure, but based on that, six per cent die, forty-three per cent suffer debilitating pain for a minute before being free of the thrall, the rest experience no discomfort at all.' He paused contemplatively. 'It'll be difficult to get to a hundred per cent problem-free disconnection because the thralls adapt to the varying types of nervous system.'

'Six per cent,' Salander repeated.

He swung to her and demonstrated that he wasn't a complete robot. 'I think those presently under the thrall would be prepared to take the risk.'

'What would you need to make this nanite?' she asked.

'Structor tanks, nanoscope, LZD124 nanofactory . . . I could give you a list,' he said helpfully.

'How long would it take?'

'About a week to get set up, then a further week till first product. Thereafter it would be two days to produce enough for dispersal.'

Salander turned and looked round at the rest of us, her expression flat. 'Suzeal will never give us that time.'

'You're right,' said Molotor, fingers at his aug again. 'Large numbers of SGZ and mercenaries are heading our way right now. I'm told about twenty thousand. The traps will slow them but they'll still get here.'

She closed her eyes, breathed through her nose for a moment, then with a flash of anger turned back to Bronodec. Before she could say anything, Marcus moved forwards, quickly past her. He grabbed the front of Bronodec's toga and hauled him to his feet, then up until he hung a foot above the floor.

'Where?' said Marcus. 'The nanite you . . . made.'

Bronodec struggled for a moment and slumped. 'In my laboratory. Coded drawer B122 and inverting this is the code you put in.'

'Distribution,' Marcus slurred.

Bronodec looked up. 'Air dispersion.'

Marcus dropped him and turned. Salander leapt up.

'Let's move,' she said, slapping her hands together. 'Molotor, get to the defences. Ankhor, get the non-combatants out to the rim and prep escape pods.'

Ankhor tilted his head. 'Really?'

'If this goes to shit, there's no way Suzeal will stop this time. The old escape pods still have working cryonics and there's room for thousands – it's a chance of survival.' She turned to Molotor again. 'When it hits, I'll ensure those who are freed of their thralls know to head our way, and will route them to Ankhor.' She turned to Marcus. 'I reckon the outlet of Atmos One will be the place. How many people do you need?'

Marcus gazed at her for a moment, then reached out, bringing his hand down on my shoulder.

'You're sure?' she asked.

'Easier to sneak . . . not attack,' he said.

'Okay . . . okay, let's move like we have a purpose, people!'

She headed for the door with her two heavies in tow. Marcus held me back from following. The door swung shut. He turned back to Bronodec.

'Prisoners,' he said.

'She keeps them in the old inspection pens. Uses the hooder grabs to collect them. It causes a lot of damage but she only does it when they're ready.'

It took me a moment to realize he was talking about prisoners ready for coring and thralling. Only such virus-toughened people could survive a 'hooder grab', which didn't take much thought to visualize.

'She cannot win, you know,' said Bronodec from behind us, pointing to the closed door. 'Suzeal tolerated her while she didn't affect business, but now—' He gestured to himself.

Marcus looked round. 'I know.'

He stepped out and I followed, the door lock engaging with a clonk behind us.

'Come,' he said, setting out at a swift jog.

★   ★   ★

We took a dropshaft down a few floors to enter another corridor. He pushed open the door into a sparsely furnished room with a drip feed set up by the single bed. The red liquid in the suspended bottle was surely a derivative of sprine. Marcus had been working on his condition.

'Food.' Marcus pointed to a pile of packages standing on a side table. I walked over and recognized supplies we'd obtained down on the planet, but other stuff too. I opened a container full of mixed fruit in syrup and practically inhaled it while he pulled out a long flat chest from under the bed.

'What's the point of us getting this nanite, supposing Bronodec didn't lie about it, if Salander can't win?' I asked, next munching my way through a slab of protein I'd unwrapped, the thing veined with fat.

He glanced round at me. 'She can save lives,' he said. 'And some will have a chance to save themselves.'

'The escape pods,' I said.

He nodded while punching a code into a small console on the lid of the chest. 'They will disperse to the rim. Many will die. Many will escape.'

Picking up a cup, I headed over to his sanitary booth and filled the thing twice. Despite draining it both times, that didn't seem enough, so I drank two more cups and returned to the food.

'Why are you sure Salander will fail?'

Compressed figs, a packet of salty dried fish, packaged fruits I didn't recognize, pastries and biscuits. I ate so fast I bit my tongue. Why so hungry? Yes, it'd been a while since I'd eaten, but this seemed over-compensation. The boosting and other changes in my body, perhaps?

'Numbers,' said Marcus. 'And Suzeal is ruthless.'

He could talk a lot better now, I noticed. I peered into the chest as he opened it. Weapons and equipment were packed in neatly and he began taking them out. He picked up a heavy weapon with multiple barrels and a large pack from which he plugged an armoured power lead into the weapon, as well as armoured pipes and ammunition feeders and a hinged arm. He had a kind of multigun which would normally be mounted on the tripod he left in the chest. Next he strapped on a bandolier loaded with a variety of grenades and spare power packs, along with other instruments I had no idea about, but which I felt sure were lethal. He finally donned the pack, hinging the gun out in front of him on its arm. He'd told Salander we'd be sneaking to Bronodec's lab. This didn't look like sneaking at all.

'Prisoners first,' he stated.

'Why?' At last I seemed to have reached repletion, in fact felt a little bit sick. I stepped away from the table.

'Disruption.'

'What're we doing, Marcus?'

'Suzeal,' he said, cutting the flat of his hand across before him, 'must end.'

I couldn't see how releasing prisoners undergoing mutation, and those under the thrall, would end her operation. It would disrupt things for her for a while, but she could survive it and carry on. It seemed to me this could only result in death and destruction.

'The prisoners will attack everyone,' I said.

He shook his head. 'They not like me. Infection only to level for coring, not beyond.'

'Okay, so they'll still have their minds, but I don't see how this can end her operation.'

He gestured to the chest. 'You.'

I stared at him for a long moment, then said, 'One moment.'

I stepped inside the sanitary booth, opaqued the walls and just managed to get my trousers down. It felt as if my insides were coming out, and kept on coming out. Finally, when done, I cleaned myself and headed out. Marcus stood by the table, feeding himself almost as fast as I had. His expression showed a hint of amusement as he pointed towards the chest again.

'I'm only human,' I said, walking over and stooping down.

Despite all my questions about intentions, I trusted him and would go with him. Whether or not he could stop Suzeal, the release of prisoners either incarcerated or under the thrall was only a good thing – now I also understood the virus-infected ones weren't monsters. I looked at the weapons. I had a pulse rifle on its strap across my back and two pulse gun sidearms – one in its holster and one tucked into my belt. The chest contained all sorts of other delights. I assumed it to be his, which raised some interesting questions too. It seemed he'd been here before, for how else had he contacted the rebels so quickly and become embroiled with them?

I took out one large package, studied it briefly, then stripped off my weapons and my outer clothing. The combat armour suit pulled on like heavy garments and fitted perfectly. It was likely his, but could no longer fit him, hence his motley armour and combat clothing. As soon as I had it on, it powered up, and those areas where movement wasn't required stiffened as its meta-materials meshed or filled with shock foam. I checked its action. The concertinaed hood snapped up quickly from the back collar, the visor extruding at the front and clicking into place against it, a head-up display coming on. Though similar to the envirosuit I'd worn, this thing had many more functions. Judging by Marcus's pacing, I didn't have time to test them all right then. However, the suit felt utterly familiar and I knew my earlier self would provide answers. I pulled on a bandolier, equally as loaded with lethality as the one Marcus wore. I hung the pulse rifle on my back, put on my uniform belt and reinserted the sidearms, then picked up another weapon and stared at the thing. Pulsed laser carbine with underslung grenade launcher – short and compact. Almost without thinking, I picked up its spare grenade clips and attached them to my belt, plugged its power and data lead into the suit belt port and got targeting on the HUD. This was a massive upgrade from a pulse rifle. I was ready.

Marcus stooped down and picked up the colour-change jacket and handed it to me. Annoyed with myself, I detached the carbine cable, shed my rifle and the bandolier, and put the jacket on before returning them. He nodded once, briefly, and headed for the door. As we jogged through the corridors of the rebels' building, we got some strange looks. But the people moved on urgently, for now the floor was shaking, and I could hear the rumble of explosions and the distant crackling of weapons fire. As we took the lift down, I wondered why Marcus had chosen me to come with him. Others here surely would've been more adept with the equipment he'd provided. I felt sure, though, that somehow he'd known I would understand and quickly familiarize myself with it. Even as we descended, I checked out the suit's systems, its weapons connections, its tactical data, logistics and numerous other readouts. I *did* know how to operate all of it. Only one doubt remained in my mind: could I? Yes, I had killed, but only mindless clones and maybe one or two distant prador. I didn't believe I had the casual facility with it that he had.

We came out in the crop areas and quickly crossed them to the nearest wall. Here people – non-combatants loaded with belongings – crowded through bulkhead doors. These I guessed were heading for the rim and for safety – a temporary safety if Bronodec and Marcus were to be believed. I folded down the helmet and visor.

'Do you intend to kill her?' I asked.

He tapped his ear. I knew what he meant at once and took

the coms units from my suit collar and pressed them into my ears. The visor came up, offering connections in its HUD. Clearly marked at the top was 'Marcus'. I stared at it for a moment to acquire, then blinked, enabling the connection.

'If necessary,' he replied, his voice close and clear.

We circumvented the crowds and headed for a ladder running high up the wall. I pressed my weapon against a bond patch on the front of the suit before climbing up after him. I found the climb easy in the low grav, while the suit didn't hinder me at all, and it got easier still as grav dropped and then the plane of it began to turn. A short while later, Marcus stood and walked on the wall. I followed until we came to what had looked like a tube access from below, and now became the mouth of a drop-shaft. It was non-functional so we climbed down the side, entering a short corridor that transformed into a walkway over a complex of factories. I felt the familiar loss to my sense of direction that I'd experienced aboard the King's Ship.

The walkway took us into a series of corridors. As we approached a junction, Marcus held up his hand and made a signal I recognized: be ready. I hit a pad below my throat and my visor and hood closed up with a snap. Then we stepped around the corner.

Three of Suzeal's mercenary types stood in the wide corridor ahead. The fighting was about to start before I'd resolved whether I was ready for it. They were poring over a tablet, heads bowed, and then one spotted us. I just stood there gaping, not sure what to do. She yelled, swinging a pulse rifle towards us, opening fire before lining up on us and spraying shots along one wall. Suit linkage hardened and target frames dropped over them, the shooter negated because she was Marcus's first target. Without thinking, I aimed at the one to the right, while the one on the left struggled to bring a heavy laser carbine to bear. Marcus's single shot picked up the shooter and flung her back through the air, but not before a shot ricocheted off my shoulder and another hit me in the chest. The shooter's chest exploded mid-flight, spreading open her armour and her ribs, and she hit the floor bonelessly. I went down on my arse, losing targeting, then reacquired and fired. I hit the one on the right in the legs and he went down yelling, with my next hit on his visor just as the other one staggered back, armour debris, blood and flesh exploding out of his back. Another function of the multigun: rail beads. Only someone as strong as Marcus was able to handle the recoil. He reached down, grabbed my arm and hauled me up.

I inspected the damage and saw small smoking craters in my armour already closing, healing up as if the suit was a living thing, but it was a limited repairs system. Shots had traversed Marcus's chest too and burned through armour at one point. The flesh underneath steamed but he hardly seemed to notice. We moved forwards. The two he'd shot were plainly dead, while the one I'd hit lay making horrible snorting sounds. His visor was gone – the chain-glass turned to a white powder. I stood over him and saw a face of charred ruin, his nose and top teeth gone and the burn hole right down into his sinuses. With the medical technology here he could be saved and go on to lead a practically limitless life. But he would never have thought the same for me and would probably have left me bubbling out my life on the floor, not wasting another shot. As one of Suzeal's people, he thought little of turning other people into slaves or, after tearing out their brains and part of their spines, into organic robots. He was also probably one who sat making bets on how long the next victim would last against the siluroyne.

I drew a sidearm and shot him twice through the forehead. He jerked, raised a hand then dropped it and lay still. This was the first time I'd killed a thinking human being. Right then I felt very little about it at all; only as I hurried after Marcus, who'd not stopped, did it hit me. I halted, my legs losing strength, and dropped to my knees, knocked down the visor and puked against the wall. After a moment I stood up shakily, but something began to harden inside me. I caught up with Marcus.

'Quicker, next time,' he said.

More corridors, more walkways, and then we came to a dropshaft. The arrow beside it was blinking red and, even as we faced it, someone sped down past the entrance. I closed up my helmet again as we moved forwards. The arrow went out, just for a second, before coming back on again. Marcus snapped a grenade off his bandolier and we waited. More troops swept past the entrance, heading down, and as the last went past he tossed in the grenade then waved me to one side of the entrance. A moment later, fire and debris gouted out and I heard the screams from below. The red arrow went out and he hit the up arrow, which came on green. Next he ripped off the panel beside that arrow, reached inside and pulled something out, discarding it on the floor. The arrow stayed on green as he tossed in four more grenades. We moved off to the right to find another way.

A steady climb up an inactive dropshaft brought us out into a park. This one was little like the one I'd walked across with Suzeal. Dead trees stood peeled of bark and shedding branches, while other plant life lay brown or black, damp and decaying. I had my visor down but the smell of rot wafted in. Life hadn't completely failed here, though, and the place avoided being monochrome. Toadstools scattered the ground – mostly white but some blue and some yellow. Bracket fungi clung to the dead trees – multiple shelves of them with either the pink of new skin or like great yellow and brown agates. Most of the lights set in the ceiling above were out and it would have been dark, but for the gunfire and explosions.

Salander's soldiers advanced behind a barricade of armoured shields that ran across the ground on treads. Their jackets were all now a pale green and only then did I notice that Marcus's and mine matched the colour. Even as we moved into the park, a missile streaked down from high up and blasted two of the barricades, scattering smoking bodies all around. Other barricades had begun to fail under a constant heavy onslaught, whittling them away until some parts of them looked like metallic lace.

'Run!' Marcus instructed, accelerating past me.

As I followed, another missile streaked down and hit the dropshaft we'd just exited. The blast threw me forwards and I rolled, coming up behind a barricade where four soldiers crouched. They glanced at me and I could see their desperation. Doubtless they thought they should be retreating, while the barricades were advancing. Marcus came down on one knee, shouldered his weapon and fired a missile, the shot jerking his shoulder back. High up on the far wall it hit below a balcony. The intense hot blast burrowed into the wall and the balcony tilted, spilling a launcher and three bodies.

'Stupid tactics,' I heard him say over com. 'Salander. My location. Fast advance.' He waited a moment, then looked around. The soldiers behind the barricades began to look in his direction and he switched his attention to me. 'We go.'

He stood, bounded forwards and leapt the barricade. Just for a second I froze and saw other soldiers were undecided. I stood and rounded the barricade to run after him, glancing back to see others joining the charge. A group of Suzeal's SGZ were behind a tree, so I threw three grenades there. Two blasts flung them through the air while a third had the tree toppling over.

Movement right. Target and fire. A man pirouetting through flame. A grav-car tipped on its side ahead. Shots from there hit my leg, but I only stumbled and the suit clicked into assist, righting me quickly. Marcus railed the vehicle, the shots going in with a horrible metallic sound and seeming to have little effect on the side I saw. Debris exploded out from the other side and the firing ceased, a pulse rifle thudding to the ground. A missile struck just behind me, blasting up the earth, and I tumbled through the air. Suit assist again as I went down, rolled and came upright. Grenade off the bandolier. Three seconds with one press, and into a tangled mass of dead briar. It blew with a sharp crack, filament shrapnel going through the briar like a hedge cutter, and revealed someone screaming with both hands severed away. I spun to further shots from behind another tree, then saw the shooter staggering back under the convergence of two streams of pulse rifle fire. A glance back showed me that the others had all followed. We were really in it now.

Marcus held someone above his head while strafing others flat on the ground. He then tossed that person and shredded him in mid-air. People leapt up before me. It was close shooting now, and hand to hand. I stuck the carbine to the front of my suit and drew both sidearms. Shot to one head and the knee of someone heavily armoured, stamping on the back of a rising figure and spinning to kick the one in the armour. One grabbed my arm and tried to swing in a slammer but he fell away with most of his face stuck to his visor. I saluted a thanks to one of Salander's soldiers, but then saw her spun round, with pieces of flesh and armour shredding away.

'On me,' said Marcus calmly.

He'd reached the far wall, back briefly against it beside a freshly cut entrance. He then stepped round and opened fire with the numerous functions of his gun. The place beyond filled with fire and explosions, and the sharp waspish sounds of fast-moving metal on metal. He turned, fired again, and two swinging towards me went over, one coming in half at the waist. A beckoning hand. I moved up beside him and we ran into the ruination, leaving the main battle behind. Burning wreckage lay everywhere in a place that might have been some sort of shop. Bodies lay there too. Someone screamed rhythmically far over to the side, while nearby another dragged along the tattered remains of his legs. I jumped him, shooting him in the back of the neck as I did so. I knew how to kill now without hesitation.

I was good at it.

15

Beyond the battle, we encountered Suzeal's soldiers once more, in the park where I had walked with her. These unarmoured individuals moved a grav-sled towards what I presumed were the front lines. We hardly slowed, dropping them all with a series of single shots, perfectly coordinated. More corridors, tunnels and walkways and dropshafts brought us to a deserted apartment overlooking the park I'd first seen, the geodesic dome close above giving a good view into the hub chamber.

'Take off your jacket,' Marcus instructed.

It seemed we *would* be doing some sneaking about. I put down my weapons, stripped off the bandolier and then the jacket, inspecting a large burned hole in the back, before folding and stowing it. The thing had changed to a dull yellow now, as had Marcus's.

'Logistics and damage check,' Marcus stated briefly.

I set my suit to run it, while he stripped off his jacket and then did the same check manually with his weapons and ammunition. My grenade launcher ammunition was low and I replaced the cartridge, loading up other cartridges to overfull with the remainder from the one that was nearly spent. Carbine power had dropped to half. I swapped out the power supply but retained the first on my bandolier. Suit diagnostics told me of armour damage on the leg, on the back, and on the helmet, which would no longer close down. I looked at quick fixes, but realized the helmet would have to stay up since its ribs had been fused with a laser shot. The other damage required patches which I carried in my belt. I stretched and shaped the first patch, initially circular and of a dough-like consistency, until it matched the hole in my leg armour, then pushed it into place and pulled off the tab. It shifted like a black amoeba, filled up the hole to a level with the surrounding armour, then hardened, its colour changing to match the armour's present grey. Marcus put the one on my back for me.

Further diagnostics took me a moment to understand. I realized they were for me: grenade splinters in my leg, a first-degree burn on my back the size of a hand and a crack in my skull. I stared at the readout, then focused on the measures being taken. Numbing agents had been infused, artificial skin had been printed in, and the grenade splinters had been stabilized with an injection of Tufgel to stop their sharp edges cutting further. Bone composite had also been printed into the fracture, and a programming link had been established to my nanosuite to speed healing. I'd felt nothing at all and my head was clear. The military medtech of the suit didn't want soldiers compromised and I wondered just how much damage I could take and still remain on my feet.

'All good?' Marcus asked.

'Some injuries,' I replied.

He shrugged and turned towards the door.

'It should be easier now,' he stated.

We were soon walking through inhabited parts of the station and, even though armoured and loaded with weapons, we didn't stand out particularly. Groups of mercenaries headed here and there, others just idled about, while still others guarded various areas. When we reached the park, I noticed quite a few of them around the dropshafts leading up to where Suzeal had her apartment. I kept my visor up and set it to mirror, as some around here might recognize me. Marcus did the same. We came to the line of restaurants and bars where I'd eaten with Suzeal. Here the expressions of those who'd been thralled were notable. Most looked worried as they carried out their allotted tasks, but wore bland faces when dealing with Suzeal's mercenaries. Some looked happy – perhaps those who didn't know Salander's slim chances of success. I noted numerous holographic displays and simple screens here too, showing the action going on in the station. I could hear the mercenaries betting on people's lives again and restrained the urge to spray them with my carbine.

'Here,' said Marcus.

An alley cut between two establishments. It was open hundreds of feet above for the first hundred yards, then turned into a tunnel. Holo-posters decorated the walls along it, showing hooders, droons, gabbleducks and other monsters. Inspecting the variety of creatures, I felt happy with having encountered so few. It occurred to me that swift natural selection must have occurred down on the planet, wiping out many of the other horrors depicted.

The tunnel next opened into a long boulevard. Here further establishments including shops were clustered, mostly empty and abandoned. Travelling along the centre of this, in the opposite direction to us, came further troops, hundreds and hundreds of them. All were armoured and heavily armed, which seemed standard here, but they had other items with them too. The robots weren't AI drones, or at least I liked to think they weren't. They looked like heavier versions of mosquito autoguns, walking on four thick legs and protruding more barrels than seemed feasible. Amidst these were also others, not armed but carrying recognizable shield generators.

'Salander,' said Marcus, 'cam visual.' He paused to run his gaze along the length of the column. I couldn't hear Salander's reply, but I guessed she wasn't happy. Marcus nodded then said, 'Pull to the rim – I will . . . solve this.' He shrugged and replied to her obvious query, 'You will see.' We moved on.

'So, what are you going to do?' I asked.

'Stop Suzeal,' was his only reply, despite my badgering him for a further few minutes. In the end I gave up. It occurred to me that Marcus's terseness had little to do with his viral mutation and a lot to do with his personality.

Ahead a sign hung above the boulevard telling us we had reached the entrance to Stratogaster's Zoo – a row of broken-down turnstiles were below it. Beyond these lay a large chamber with numerous tunnels leading off it. We went through a turnstile and took a right to a heavy round door. Marcus turned the wheel at the centre and heaved it open. Judging by the creaking sound and chunks of decayed seal falling all around, it hadn't been opened in a long time – Suzeal's people must have used some other access. A series of high corridors and stairs, all in brushed metal, led us up. We passed an opening where a catwalk extended over a large cylindrical chamber, but I couldn't see what lay below. Then another one, until Marcus turned into the next one.

When I dropped my visor, the smell hit me immediately: human sewerage, other decay and a weird spicy tang. On the platform stood pedestal-mounted weapons that looked like harpoon guns from ancient whaling ships, but their business ends were more a combination of harpoon and grapnel. Marcus moved out ahead of me on the suspended walkway and, following him out, I looked down.

The chamber floor consisted of muddy paths worn through a mixture of standard and bubble grass, with patches of thick briar gathered here and there. Hundreds of people, mostly gathered around feeding stations, were down there. Many wore ragged clothing while others were naked. It took me a moment to figure out what was wrong with this scene. The colours looked off, like a virtuality given a sombre monochrome tint. I then realized this was due to the skin hue of the people, resembling that of humans who'd been asphyxiated – bluish and pale. Thin as famine victims, they began looking up, and their expressions showed hatred and aggression. Some sped away from the feeding areas and scrabbled at the base of the nearest wall, even managing to climb a few feet up before sliding down the polished surface. Others protruded tongues which were open at the ends in leech mouths.

'She put me in here for a while,' said Marcus.

These were the eight hundred prisoners Suzeal had captured and infected with the Spatterjay virus. Glancing across at one of the pedestal-mounted weapons, I realized how she took them out of here. The harpoon grapnels ran from drums of monofilament, with a coating mechanism that sheathed the filament on firing. I visualized the scene of mercenaries firing on those below, snaring them like fish and hauling them up, probably then shocking them into submission before dragging them off for coring and thralling. I imagined the mercenaries laughing and placing bets.

'How long—' I began, and that's when the missile hit.

The explosion tore through the walkway between us. The section Marcus stood upon twisted, and the weight of the weapons pulled it down. Marcus slid off, then fell as the collapsing piece of walkway dragged down the section I stood on. I managed to stick my weapon to its patch on the front of my suit before sliding too, scrabbling for handholds. I caught one of the rail posts as the walkway sank to twenty degrees, then got the fingers of my other hand into one of the gaps in the grating. As I started pulling myself up, another missile hit above and I found myself hanging by shreds of metal. Adrenalin and suit assist kicked in and I grabbed the rail which remained intact, then scrambled up that.

The wreckage of the walkway offered further handholds and I pulled myself up into the doorway. Glancing back, I saw the tangled mess of metal reaching down to the floor of the chamber, Marcus struggling to his feet with all the residents down there crowding in towards him. When I dragged myself into the corridor beyond the doorway, I saw that my own troubles had only just begun.

SGZ and mercenaries crowded in at one end. I snatched at my weapon, coming up into a crouch, as slugs hit me. The impacts sent me skidding backwards along the floor, then tore up a line of splinters as the firing tracked past.

'Don't kill him!' someone yelled.

A pause ensued as I tried to stand and bring my weapon to bear. Pulse gun fire hit my arm and error messages scrolled in my HUD, then a blast opened up the floor beside me, chunks of metal zinging in every direction and underlying bracing bars sprouting like plants. The carbine clattered from my grip. The slug thrower hit me again and I fell back, over the wreckage and crashed to the floor. I saw a bulky shape moving forwards, cleared the HUD and realized it was someone in a heavy power suit. I tried to rise, drawing one sidearm, but the figure closed horribly fast and slapped the weapon from my hand. A motorized and heavily armoured claw then reached down, grabbed my upper arm and hauled me up. The figure's visor slid down.

'I'm not going to enjoy this as much as Brack would, but still . . .'

I merely registered who faced me and calculated that I didn't stand a chance against this powered suit. But he'd made himself vulnerable. I jabbed my fingers towards his eyes, driving one into his right eye, though not deep enough. He tried to push me away but I grabbed the edge of his helmet and extended a forefinger into his eye again. The visor shot closed on my fingers as I kept trying. Its power was stronger than expected and trapped the end of my middle finger then, after a brief hesitation and an audible droning, it closed with a crunch. My hand fell away and I couldn't reach him again. I felt a brief pain and then numbness. The end of my finger was missing and bloody impact foam was oozing from the severed tip. He hurled me against the wall.

I hit it hard, headfirst, and collapsed to the floor. I rolled, as his heavy boot smashed down where I'd been, leaving a dent in the floor. He swivelled, kicking me with his other boot and slammed me into the wall again.

'You're so going to pay for that, clone,' he said.

His visor stood open again and blood had cut a runnel down from his eye. He reached into his helmet and took out my fingertip, inspected if for a second, then tossed it behind him. I groped for my other sidearm, but it was gone. I had no weapons. No, that wasn't right, there was something else . . . He stooped over me and closed a hand around my neck.

'Do you want to try that again?' he asked nastily.

His look of surprise was satisfying as I grabbed the edge of his helmet and jammed my fingers in between it and dropped my package near the side of his face. The visor snapped up again, forcing them to the top, but this time I managed to extract them without losing part of a digit. After a brief pause, precisely three seconds long, a dull whumph ensued and his armoured form shuddered, then smoke and a fine red spray issued from every joint, and his armour froze. A moment later, his visor slid open again, and a minced smoking mass of flesh, shattered bone and cooked brain dropped out.

'Hey!' someone yelled.

I struggled to free myself from his hand but the damned thing had locked solid around my neck. I now had a view into the chamber where they kept the prisoners. Marcus stepped into the corridor: he must have climbed the fallen walkway and opened fire with every function of his multigun. The end of the corridor, where Frey's companions had clustered to watch the show, simply disappeared. Fire and wreckage blew back towards us, Marcus standing in its midst. Then other figures appeared, running heedless into the tangled ruin down there. The prisoners had followed Marcus up and were after some payback. They picked up human remains then hurled them aside and moved on. I just lay watching as they swarmed in from the chamber, filling the corridor in both directions. Marcus shouldered his way through the crowd over to me, pausing to snare my carbine from one of them, then stooped down and set to work on the erstwhile Frey's armoured hand. He had to snap off two fingers before he managed to get it off me. That somehow seemed appropriate.

'I told them to head for the rim,' he told me, as he helped me up. 'I don't think they will, just yet.'

I leaned against the wall.

'Are you injured?'

My body ached and my missing fingertip burned, but I dared not reinstate the HUD display to tell me how badly Frey had hurt me. And even then, the pains began to diminish. As the crowd cleared, I searched for my sidearms, but they were both missing. The prisoners might have been under the influence of the virus, but they hadn't been so far gone as to neglect useful weapons.

'I probably am,' I replied.

He shrugged, as he had before, then headed towards the wreckage, waving for me to follow. I paused and looked back at the gore-lined helmet of Frey's suit. It had been a long and roundabout route but I'd come full circle, fulfilling one of the promises made to myself shortly after I'd climbed out of that cold coffin aboard Suzeal's ship.

We made our way through wreckage, body parts lying where he'd fired his weapon. Beyond it, we found two more corpses and they were in pieces too – the prisoners had already begun exacting their vengeance. We finally reached the entry door to the sounds of a fire fight off to the right. I followed Marcus close along the wall to the turnstiles. The whole area beyond was in chaos and a number of the prisoners lay just beyond the turnstiles. Most were in fragments but one, having merely lost the top of his head, was still managing to crawl slowly along the floor. The soldiers hadn't kept the prisoners back, and they were now swarming them. Close-quarters combat. Figures struggling. Weapons fire peppering the walls and ricocheting off the floor. Amidst all this, the robots stood unmoving, yet to be given instructions. I saw two prisoners with a mercenary between them, each hanging onto an arm, then tearing one of the limbs off. An armoured man lay nearby, screaming as one of the prisoners eviscerated him. Such scenes played out everywhere, while towards the other end of the tunnel the bulk of the force was in disordered retreat, the prisoners leaping amongst them.

'That will keep them occupied,' Marcus stated.

A side corridor lay clogged with mingled mercenary and prisoner corpses. Shrapnel grenades had been used there, turning the floor into a bloody swamp. Around a bend at the end three hid. I opened fire without thinking, following Marcus a moment later, and we left them smoking behind us.

'Where to now?' I asked.

'Bronodec's laboratory.'

As we worked our way towards that destination, the sounds of fighting continued throughout the station, but we managed to avoid it. As we stepped out of a working dropshaft, Marcus remarked, 'Suzeal has recalled her forces, and Salander has the first of the prisoners coming her way.' I supposed some of them might not be as intent on vengeance as the rest. Finally the style of the corridors here became familiar. Marcus brought us to a coded sliding door, put his hands against it then dug in the nails of his clawed hand, heaved at it for a moment until something snapped and opened it. He paused at the door.

'Salander's retreating,' he said. 'She has at last understood she cannot win.'

'So she'll use the escape pods?' I asked. 'And go where?'

'Anywhere that's not here,' was all he said.

We stepped into the laboratory.

Bronodec had been provided with every facility. Equipment packed the place: suitcase nanofactories, nanoscopes, micron and sub-micron manipulators, and nanoforges, as well as matter printing units standing like iron-cowled monks over shifting platens. A casting unit ran out gleaming items I recognized as the covers for thralls. He also had prador thralls racked, each in a chain-glass box. And here too lay their victims.

Amidst this panoply stood surgical slabs and chairs, autodocs and more complex autosurgeons like upright beetles rendered in chrome and white bone. Three tables occupied one space with three naked people strapped onto them, face down – their skin hue matched those released from the zoo. They'd been cored.

The backs of their skulls had been cut open, each section hinged over on skin. The backs of their necks and part of their upper backs had been opened too, the vertebrae split and held apart by a series of silver rods. A brain and section of spinal column sat in amber fluid in a clear polymer cylinder beside each table. It puzzled me why they'd been retained. Movement then drew my eye and I saw one of the corpses straining against its bonds. Life continued, but mindlessly.

'I will kill him,' said Marcus. He turned away and headed over to a wall of storage lockers and began inspecting the numbers.

I just stood there staring at what had been done to the three. Another movement drew my eye to one cylinder. A length of spinal column flicked like a tail. I felt sure nerve tissue had no muscle, so the movement had to be due to the virus and any alterations it had made. I thought about Marcus's ruggedness and how the virus preserved life. I also remembered Vrasan's head gaining independent life in his bathing pool and, more recently, the escaped prisoner crawling across the floor with the top of his head sliced off. Vrasan's brain hadn't been in that head but in his main body, while the prisoner might have been alive but not necessarily a conscious thinking being. But still . . . these brains and spinal columns had independent life. Would they retain intelligence? I acted without considering the matter further.

I flipped the lid off the first cylinder, reached inside and grabbed the brain. There would surely have been a better way to do this using the surgeons, but that would take time and expertise I did not possess. As I lifted the thing out, the spine coiled about my wrist. I pulled it off while reinserting the brain into the skull cavity I presumed it came from. A transparent jelly oozed out all around as I pushed it in, and it seemed to bed itself in there, shrugging and shivering as it did so.

'What the hell?' Marcus began, standing by an open drawer holding a squat silver cylinder. He inserted the thing into a belt pouch and walked over. He'd found the nanite.

The length of spinal nerve trunk writhed over the open section of spine like a snake trying to force its way to cover. I pulled out the rod in the first vertebra and pushed a section of it into place, and then the next and the next. The thing kept popping out and I swore. Marcus came over with a gun-like device which trailed a cable and feed tubes to one of the surgeons.

'Hold it closed,' he said.

I pinched a top vertebra together and he applied the device.

The bone weld wasn't neat, but it held. He handed me the bone welder and stepped over to one of the other slabs. Once I'd welded all the vertebrae, I took out all the hooks holding the flesh and skin back from them and looked round for a cell welder, but found no need. Skin and muscle meshed even as I watched, blue fibres wriggling in it like thread veins. I closed the skull lid and held it in place until it firmed, then went over to the next one. Once Marcus had finished the same procedure with the one he'd gone to, he came over to help me. After we were done, he drew a large commando knife and began cutting the straps.

'Do you think it'll work?' I asked.

He shrugged. 'Maybe.' We headed out of there.

We negotiated our way through an area of the station where, by its dilapidation, it seemed few people came. As we moved away from the sounds of fighting, he said something I didn't quite understand, 'I would not have thought of that.'

'Thought of what?' I asked.

'Those three, back there.' He stabbed a thumb behind.

My turn to shrug. 'Seemed like we could give them a chance.'

'You're different.'

I didn't ask what he meant by that. Weren't we all different from each other?

The atmosphere plant sat in a large open area cut through numerous station floors. The thing measured a couple of hundred feet from pole to pole – a sphere of metal fed by numerous pipes and power lines. Various decals and mechanisms covered its surface. The thing was biotech. It was filled with modified chloroplasts in a support gel, run through with microtubules for feeding it and carrying away wastes sieved out by meta-material membranes. Optics would supply light throughout the interior to complete the process. At the top of the thing sat a huge extractor fan that drew off the constant bubbling up of oxygen, while linked to it stood a mixer for adding surrounding air – mainly to cut down on fire risk.

We climbed a ladder up the side of the thing to the steady thrum of the upper fan, then walked along a pipe standing ten feet wide from that and clambered over the mixer. Beyond this, the pipe fed into a huge junction box with smaller pipes running off, into the station to feed the ventilation system. This wasn't all of it. There would be CO_2 scrubbers and crackers throughout, recyclers and filters, plants for producing nitrogen and other gases from compounds, and of course hydroponics and gardens adding their product to the mix. From here came the main breathable air to keep the station topped up, since no doubt a place as old as this leaked like a sieve.

'Here.' Marcus gestured to an inspection hatch in the top of the pipe.

I squatted down and tugged at the thing. The clip holding it down simply broke and it hinged up with a rusty creak, shedding corrosion. The air blast from it hit me in the face, redolent of those forests on the planet below. Marcus took out the cylinder of nanites he'd recovered from Bronodec's lab.

'Primed for atmosphere distribution.' He showed me the small fan in the end of the thing. 'Perhaps I won't kill him after all.' He placed the cylinder down in the pipe where a switch activated a gecko pad and stuck it in place. Holding his finger against another control set a fan running. Vapour spilled and once he'd extracted his arm I closed the hatch. The thing kept flicking up in the air blast until he put his foot on it and I used a low setting on my weapon to melt part of the edge into the surrounding rim. We were done. The procedure seemed singularly lacking in drama considering what we had gone through to get here.

'What now?' I asked, standing.

'Now it's time to talk to the prador,' he replied.

Marcus leapt down from the pipe, dropped almost two floors, landed on another narrow pipe and walked out of sight.

'What the fuck do you mean, talk to the prador?' I shouted. I got no reply. I looked around for a way down but saw only the route he'd taken. I jumped, hurtled down and landed on the pipe. The impact jarred up through my body, and suit assist kicked in belatedly. I fell off but managed to grab it and swing into the next floor. Marcus was still in sight, heading towards a bulkhead door. I ran after him.

'What the fuck do you mean?' I shouted at his back again.

He turned towards me and waited until I'd caught up.

'Your suit has a map you haven't used,' he said. 'You can head out to the rim and join the rest of them.'

He had become noticeably more eloquent now.

'I won't do that.'

He nodded, turned to the bulkhead door, spun its wheel and opened it, stepping through into an aged and non-functioning pedway.

'What do you think will happen here now?' he asked.

This had been on my mind for a while.

'If Salander cannot win,' I said slowly, 'then the best we can hope for is the innocents here escaping the station, just as you said.'

'Correct. Then what happens?'

'The escape pods don't have U-space drives. They either head down to the planet or out-system with those inside in cryo.'

'No.' He shook his head.

'No?'

'The prisoners we released will keep Suzeal occupied only for a little while – even supposing they stay and fight and don't head out to the rim. The same applies for those who are freed from thrall control. Salander will try to get people into the escape pods, but that will take time. I calculate that most of them will still be at the rim when Suzeal attacks. She has thousands under her and most are heavily armed, hardened killers.'

It was the longest speech I'd ever heard from him.

'So there's no hope?'

He continued relentlessly, 'Most will be killed, though Suzeal will capture some for the coring trade. She may let those in the pods escape. More likely she will kill all those aboard the station and recapture the pods, since it'll be easier for her to take the people in them as prisoners.'

'And talking to the prador will make this better how?'

He glanced at me, his expression almost pitying. 'There is no easy solution here. It is possible that some agreement between the Kingdom and the Polity will allow rescue ships in. But, even if that were the case, this would all be over before they got here.'

'All I'm hearing is negatives.'

'If the prador were to attack, they would go in at the hub. Suzeal would have to keep her forces there to counter them. This would give Salander time to get the refugees away.'

'But they cannot get here.'

'Not yet.'

'The railgun . . .'

He pointed to his pack, which until then I thought contained only the ammunition and power for his multigun. 'I have the solution to that. Yield of one kiloton.'

I didn't know what to say. It all sounded perfectly logical but the idea of allowing the prador here seemed crazy.

'What of the refugees when the prador get here?'

'They'll be off the station . . . mostly.'

'That wouldn't have kept them safe from Suzeal and will not keep them safe from the prador.'

'I told you, there are no easy answers.'

I fell silent as we traversed the station. In time I began to recognize our surroundings again and then finally the door back into the empty apartment overlooking the park. The sound of gunfire was still evident, but it had waned.

'We have to be ready,' said Marcus. 'This is going to be a hard fight.'

'What do you mean?'

'See to your suit and see to yourself.'

'What fight?'

'See to yourself,' he instructed tersely.

He shed his pack, cleared a table of debris and put the thing on it. I headed straight over to the apartment's sanitary unit and luckily found the plumbing still working. I felt utterly dehydrated. With that tended to, I stepped out and went over to look down into the park. Bodies scattered the ground, and medics moved about with grav-gurneys as fighting had ceased there. I noted many bodies were of prisoners. They weren't moving, yet they didn't appear highly damaged, which was odd. Weapons flashes and occasional explosions lit up the far end. I returned inside, reluctant to find out my condition. Then, angry with myself, I put up my visor and turned on the HUD.

Suit diagnostics first. The program highlighted numerous holes and burn craters and I set to work on them with my supply of patches. I used all of them up wherever reachable – a standard procedure since the front always took the most damage, unless you were inclined to retreat.

'I've run out of patches,' I said.

'Here.' Marcus waved me over.

Out of the mess of items from the pack, he picked up a box of patches and repaired the damage on the back of the suit. He next picked up a cylinder with FA 5.1 stencilled on the side. I knew the letters meant 'Field Autodoc'.

'You'll have to take it off,' he said.

The readout in my visor listed my damage. Besides the earlier injuries, I had a bullet in one leg, fragments of metal in my guts, shin splints and damaged knees, broken ribs and a broken arm. I looked at the arm concerned and opened and closed my hand. I'd felt nothing at all but now I could feel something shifting inside, or perhaps that was just psychosomatic. Further readouts showed how the suit had kept me mobile. It'd pumped in exotic cocktails of drugs, printed open wounds closed and isolated the bullet and metal fragments. It had also injected drain tubes here and there and made some serious alterations to my nanosuite's functions. The bone breaks were being held together by internal wrap-around splints of linked nanites. Using the wrist console, I ordered the suit to break its link with the nanosuite, extract the tubes and curtail the drugs. I shut down suit assist and ordered detachment at every joint, and immediately collapsed on the floor.

Lying there, weak limbed, I began to remove the thing in sections, exposing bloody underclothes, smears of analgesic paste and seeping punctures. Large areas of bruising were evident but difficult to distinguish from the staining of antiseptic and antiviral solutions. I got one arm section off as I lay flat on my back, leaving the broken arm till last, then tried to sit up. Harsh grating in my chest and horrible stabbing sensations ensued. Marcus, who until then had been observing me dispassionately, finally decided to step in and help. Soon he had me stripped of suit and underclothes and lowered me carefully back to the floor.

311

The effect of the drugs still in my system had begun to fade. I felt as if I'd been run through a rolling mill.

'Just lie still,' he said, uncapping the cylinder.

He tipped it and the field autodoc slid out, like a folded-up nymph only rendered in chrome, bone-white plastic and grey composite. As it dropped to the floor, it unfolded, landing with a clatter on its gleaming feet. The thing resembled a scorpion, with far too many legs and other manipulators. It immediately scuttled over to me and, in a fog of aseptic spray, climbed onto my chest. It felt very heavy; technology packed it near to the point of ultimate 'dense tech'. It hummed while it sat there, and I felt the hot flush of active scanning traverse me from head to feet. When it moved again down to my leg, I couldn't help but feel a flush of horror, with it looking so similar one of the lice aboard the King's Ship.

My leg numbed where the bullet had gone in. I tilted my head in time to see the thing slice me open, spray a coagulant, then delve inside. After a moment it lifted out the bloody nub of a bullet and discarded it, reached in again and threw aside fragments, then, with the hiss of a cell welder, sealed up the wound. It came up to my torso again and I suppressed the urge to knock the thing away. As that numbed, I decided not to look, but could feel the slicing of its scalpels, the tugging of its manipulators and hear the metal fragments hitting the floor. After these sounds stopped I made the mistake of tilting my head and looking down again. It had skin and muscle folded back in two large flaps and was concentrated on my ribs, shoving breaks together and welding them, laying in composite splints where necessary.

'Imagine how this would be in pre-Quiet War times,' said Marcus. He sat on the floor working on my suit with a small deposition welder. Yeah, before the AIs took over running human civilization, before nanosuites and autodocs, in the time when a body mostly relied on its own resources for healing.

I lay back and closed my eyes. 'I really don't want to use my imagination right now.'

The autodoc traversed my body further, dealing with my injuries in order of importance. Finally it sat on my chest again and gave me another scan. It clambered off and scuttled across the floor to its cylinder beside Marcus, folding up as it inserted itself inside. At the last, it reached out with two manipulators to grab the lid and popped it back into place. I felt no urge to move, but Marcus walked over and held a hand down to me. I grasped it and he hauled me up. I ached, felt sore and my thirst had returned along with a ravenous hunger, but that was all. It seemed somehow wrong for injuries to be repaired so easily, yet I didn't understand why I felt that way. It perhaps extended from some understanding of those ancient times Marcus had mentioned.

'Put your suit back on,' he said, turning away to head back to his table.

I instead found a plastic bowl on the floor and went to fill it, more than once. As I stepped out of the booth he said, 'Here,' and tossed me something. I caught one of the food blocks we'd used down on the planet and munched it down. He unwrapped one too and began eating.

'I forget your needs,' he said.

'And your own,' I replied.

16

Once I'd finished eating, I squatted over the suit, noting the thing had self-cleaned inside. I put it all on again and ordered the joints to reattach, which they did with a series of clicks, foam cushions expanding inside to tighten it around me. A system check revealed that Marcus had repaired the helmet as I went over to pick up my gun.

'You said there would be a fight,' I said.

He nodded contemplatively.

'Suzeal's paranoia has meant she's set up a net of jammers and blockers around the outside of this station,' he said. 'So getting a signal out will be difficult. To speak to the prador, we'll need to break into Suzeal's coms centre. It'll be guarded, of course, doubly so since it's just above her apartment.'

He'd refilled his pack and now slung it on his back, then picked up his multigun to reattach its feeds and support arm.

'Let's go.'

Numerous soldiers occupied the park, clustered closer together around the dropshafts that led up to where Suzeal lived. Others were working in the park, including the thralled who were collecting up bodies and the debris of battle.

'The nanite didn't work,' said Marcus.

I considered that for a moment then said, 'Bronodec gave us no time frame on its penetration. We also don't know how it'll distribute through the ventilation, and whether it's even got to this part yet.'

He nodded agreement.

I eyed the number of soldiers we would have to get through to access those dropshafts. I had no doubt that we wouldn't be able simply to walk up and use them without being checked.

'There has to be another way,' I said, looking up.

'All access from elsewhere in the station is blocked by armoured doors. Triple-layered ceramal with impact foam between, so' – he held up his multigun – 'even this won't make a dent.'

'Have you got a grav-harness in your pack?'

'No.'

'Look.' I pointed from where we crouched in the banyan.

'Balconies,' he stated.

'Seems she hasn't covered that access.'

He stared at them for a long moment, then stood and headed back the way we'd come. Turning my visor to mirror, I followed him out of the banyan. We left the park between two shops and took a dropshaft up, stepping out into the deserted section above them. Thereafter, for no apparent reason, stairs took us the rest of the way up. At the highest point, this volume of the station was once again inhabited, but most of those we saw were thralled. We finally reached the top floor, found an apartment with its door missing and, by the rubbish strewn about the floor, obviously unoccupied. Marcus stepped out onto a balcony and pointed up.

The geodesic construction ceiling lay just ten feet above. Did he have a way we could get through it without causing a major atmosphere breach, since on the other side lay the interior of the hub? When I transferred my attention back to him he'd stripped off his pack and dropped it to the balcony. He put on his colour-change jacket and worked a small panel at its hem. A moment later, its colour changed and his torso all but disappeared. In the places covered by the jacket, it was as if he'd become transparent.

'I'll move fast so there's a good chance I'll not be seen,' he told me. 'You'll be slower, though. Perhaps you should stay here.'

'Not fucking likely.'

'Then initiate your chameleonware and turn on your map – it'll show you where her coms centre is.' He paused, then continued, 'The 'ware is power hungry, so be careful.'

He stooped down and took a large, heavy handgun out, but left the pack and multigun at his feet. 'This will have to do – with the pack I'm more likely to be seen and I don't want its contents damaged.'

'You still haven't told me how we're going to get across there,' I observed.

He pointed up again. 'Rails for maintenance and inspection robots.'

The geodesic consisted of hexagonal panes of chain-glass held in a composite framework. A bar half an inch thick hung suspended around this framework. I visualized working my way across near half a mile clinging to that thing.

'Suit assist,' he reminded me.

'Right,' I said.

He nodded, squatted, then leapt up and grabbed a bar. He swung his feet up and it looked as if he clung with his toes too, then he began scuttling across the roof like a harvestman spider. He reached almost twenty feet out, looking like disconnected arms and legs moving independently, before I snapped back into focus. I raised my visor and, using a combination of wrist console and blink control, pulled up the suit's main menu. Assist was still on automatic response whereby it intelligently kicked in when required. I set it to continuous at fifty per cent. I found the chameleonware and turned it on. I looked down at myself but could still see every detail. I lowered my visor – it paused to deliver the warning that I would not be fully covered – then looked at myself again, or rather where I should have been. I then reached out to the balcony wall and by feel rather than sight snared up my weapon. Once in my hand, it immediately disappeared. I stuck it to the patch on the front of my suit, then closed up the visor again.

It all made sense. The warning about lowering the visor had been because people would see my disembodied face floating in the air. That I could see myself with the visor closed was a necessity for hand–eye coordination. By now Marcus was forty feet out and moving easily, with the suit amplifying my strength by half, I estimated I might be able to do the same, but felt a more cautious approach would be better. I climbed up on the balcony wall and from there could reach a bar. As I grabbed it, magnetic feedback stimulation gave me the strength of my grip. More confident now, I hauled myself up, taking a grip with my other hand and bringing my feet up for a further stabilizing grip either side of the bar. Ever so slowly, I released my hold and reached further along, then again and again, my feet sliding along the bar with me. I grew more confident and travelled faster. Halfway across, pausing to dangle by my hands, I felt utterly secure, and gazed down at those in the park far below. I then looked across to see Marcus dropping onto a balcony on the other side, drawing his sidearm and entering the apartment there. As I swung up again, a flashing bar appeared in the bottom of my visor, warning me that I'd used up half the suit's power. I moved fast and econom-ically then, having no confidence that I'd be able to cling on, supporting the weight of the suit, if the power ran out.

Finally, I reached the other side and dropped onto the balcony. With suit power now down to a quarter, I cut the chameleonware. Someone clearly lived in the apartment within but luckily wasn't home. I headed over to the door, calling up the map in my HUD, then I had to stop to work out how to read the thing. First it showed my location as a red dot in the station entire. As I zeroed in on that dot, the station expanded as a semi-transparent hologram. I had to orient the thing to my perspective by swinging it round a hundred and eighty degrees. Closer still, I got a 3D schematic of the complex I stood in, but without labels. Pulling out of the map and starting again gave me those and I zeroed in once more. The coms centre lay two floors below and a few hundred yards to my right at the end of a large oval tunnel labelled 'The Hall of History'. I opened the door and stepped out.

Fifty feet along the corridor, two of Suzeal's people stood over two thralled technicians who'd taken off a wall cover to work at something inside. I quelled my immediate instinct to turn on the chameleonware, since I might need it later and power was limited. I also had to factor in that I probably didn't have enough power to make the return journey. Instead I set my HUD for projected display so the map would at least partially conceal my face. The two looked up as I approached but showed no interest, instead returning their attention to the technicians. I saw that one of them had uncovered an air duct, while the other was programming an open case packed full of seeker spiders. Disaster-response teams used the small robots to seek out victims of building collapses. I should have kept going, but feared that somehow the nanite had been detected and Suzeal was now doing something about it.

'What're they doing?' I asked.

One of the guards looked up. 'We want to make sure the fuckers don't get in again.'

'Sorry?'

'Check your updates,' said the other guard dismissively.

But the first guard was more amenable.

'Been asleep, have we?' he asked.

'Yeah – five hours – needed to get some stuff out of my system.'

He smiled understandingly. 'That Salander bitch released the prisoners. A few managed to crawl through the ventilation system and get in here. Don't know how they managed it, I couldn't get through those pipes.'

'They been dealt with?'

He slapped his sidearm. 'Sprine ammo now. Takes 'em down fast. The survivors are running for the rim.'

'I better get myself some,' I said, and moved on.

'You'll need it later when we head out there,' he called after me.

I gave him a thumbs-up, now knowing why I'd seen dead prisoners down in the park.

A stairway took me down to the curiously named hall, passing other soldiers I acknowledged with a nod or occasionally some brief comment. Walking confidently around a place where they didn't expect an enemy to be worked better than chameleonware.

The Hall of History turned out to be lit with holographic displays. I found myself walking through the ancient buildings of Earth. The art of Michelangelo slid overhead, next displaced by ancient beams, then patterned plaster. Under my feet passed carpets, cobblestones and tiles, but I felt none of them. In occasional sections, the display had gone out, exposing grey glassy tube. Halfway along I thought for a second I could hear sound effects, but then recognized gunfire ahead. Chameleonware back on, I moved to the edge of the tunnel where the floor curved up into the wall, but I kept walking. A few minutes later, my map indicated a turning ahead, just as a group of Suzeal's soldiers spilled out of it. With weapons held ready, they gazed suspiciously along the tunnel in both directions. Suzeal walked out. I froze, wondering if my suit was managing to match the shifting hologram around me of some luxuriously furnished palace.

Next came four people clad in overalls similar to those of the technicians I'd seen earlier. They too were thralled and walked along with a grav-gurney. Suzeal turned in my direction, the soldiers falling in around her. I shrank back against the wall and put my hands on my gun, loath to pull it from its fixing for fear it would somehow become visible.

'How did you know?' asked one of the soldiers.

'I knew he'd want to get a message outside the station at some point, and this is the only place he could do it.'

'Didn't kill him.' The soldier looked back, and I recognized Brack. I wondered if he knew what had happened to his companion Frey.

Suzeal glanced back also. 'He's infected with some version of the virus the prador altered, and he's been infected for a long time. Seal him in the pens and we'll deal with him later.' She paused directly opposite me. 'And search up here thoroughly; there might be others.'

Now I could see the figure held down on the gurney with heavy ceramal bands. Marcus had been riddled with gunshots and was shifting as if in extreme discomfort. Even as I watched him, a bullet dropped out of one wound and clattered to the floor – a sprine bullet. So what should I do now? I pulled my gun off its fixing and pointed it at them. They couldn't see me . . . I lowered the weapon as even more soldiers came out of the tunnel, and marching amidst them was one of the heavily armed robots we'd seen earlier. No. If I opened fire now, I might well kill many of them, but only before they killed me. Meanwhile the lives of thousands of people out at the rim depended on the plan Marcus had made, and I had to carry it through to completion. Anyway, Suzeal had ordered him to be thrown into the pens and I knew where they were. I could get to him later.

As the gurney slid past and then the other soldiers came, I questioned whether my decision was based on self-preservation, but dismissed the idea. I owed Marcus a lot and would do my best to save him, after completion of the plan. I also considered whether killing Suzeal would stop her going after the refugees, and dismissed that too. Doubtless there would be some disruption, but their attack was already underway and someone in her command structure, like Brack, would fill her shoes. I also reasoned that Suzeal needed to be in place for Marcus's plan to work – to order her troops back to the hub. They moved on past, and as they disappeared into history, I moved on.

Coming round a turning, I saw that the holograms were down and this smaller tunnel was a grey glassy tube, peppered with slugs caught in some form of polymer. The tube ran into a square corridor with doors down one side. There was a lot of bullet damage here too. I came to the third door along, the one for the coms centre, according to the map. It stood partially open with a line of bullet holes down it, and I opened it all the way then stepped inside, still with my chameleonware on.

Four people occupied the room, two sitting at consoles and two guards. The guards swung towards the opening door, bringing weapons to bear, visors slamming down. I moved aside and just waited. After a moment one of them headed over to the entrance, peered outside, then stepped back and closed the door.

'They should have hit him before he got here,' she said.

'He moved fast,' said the other.

'Still.' She indicated the damage on the door.

I studied the room. The consoles had numerous controls while screens all around the walls showed various scenes. This was all unnecessary. There was no need for a designated 'Coms Centre' when people possessed cerebral hardware and could step into virtualities. It was the result of some antediluvian thinking and Suzeal's paranoia. My gaze fell on one of the many screen scenes – most of them showed fighting aboard the station – and I realized with a start that I was watching myself. There I was, observed from above, approaching the sleer and driving it down the valley. As the past episode played out, one of those working a console computer mapped the scene and swung it round, giving the viewer a better angle on the action. Suzeal had been quite right about my ventures down on the planet being entertainment here.

What to do now?

I studied the guards, hoping to find some way to deal with them which meant they'd survive, but I could see none. I walked up to the nearest of them, raised my weapon to his head and pressed the trigger once. Even as he staggered back, with a smoking hole through his forehead, I turned to the other and shot him through the visor too. The first hit the floor. The second went over, burning a line of holes along the ceiling. One of the two who were seated leapt up, so I stepped in and slammed the butt of my weapon against his head, felling him, then pressed the barrel against the neck of the other, who'd been about to rise.

'Stay completely still,' I said.

He did as instructed, hands frozen above the console, then said, 'Chameleonware?'

I looked over his shoulder at the console and realized I understood the thing just as well as I understood all the weapons and the suit I now wore. Without replying, I quickly reversed my weapon and thumped it into the side of his head. He collapsed out of his seat onto the floor. Grabbing his collar, I pulled him clear, sat down and gripped the single ball control, which was all I really needed. One press cleared the screen ahead. I turned off my chameleonware and opened my visor. Another press brought up a menu. Right turn on the control slid the menu over to the next screen along. I found U-comlinks, selected and pressed, and brought up a list on the screen before me. 'Prador emissary' sat right at the top of the list and I selected it.

The screen blanked and at its centre the icon of a Klein bottle began simultaneously filling and emptying itself. I waited, rattling my fingers on the console. The bottle froze for a second then winked out. The lights then came up, revealing a prador, clad in chromed armour intagliated with what looked like a Greek key, squatting before me, yellow eyes gleaming behind its visor. Its mandibles shifted and rattled against each other.

'Who are you?' enquired a flat accentless voice.

'That's not something you need to know,' I replied.

The prador paused for a long moment, then said, 'Speak.'

'Tell Vrasan and your other prador here to be prepared for their assault on the Stratogaster station.'

'Why?'

'Because I am going to destroy the railgun here.'

'A ruse.'

'Keep watching the station – it will become obvious that it's not.' I paused for a second then continued, 'They should begin their attack as soon as possible – the longer they leave it the more organized Suzeal's defence will be.'

'Why would you, a human, do this?'

I thought quickly, knowing some things I couldn't say. 'There are those aboard this station who rebel against Suzeal's rule. They cannot defeat her but want to bring her down.'

'We shall watch,' said the prador.

I nodded, clicked down the ball control and banished him. I was sweating. I'd been about to be utterly honest about the escape pods and the refugees, but at the last moment realized the prador would probably have liked all the humans killing each other at the rim, while they waltzed into the hub. Also understanding prador psychology, I knew they could accept the idea of rebels being prepared to give the station to one enemy to be rid of another. With nothing else to do here, I stood – I now had to put into motion Marcus's plan to destroy the railgun.

Back out in the Hall of History, I reactivated chameleonware, with an eye on the power bar. I had about an eighth of total power left and not enough for crossing the roof with the 'ware on. If I headed down, I'd need more power for that too. I couldn't turn the 'ware off either, for groups of soldiers were now, on Suzeal's orders, searching the building. I climbed up, while watching the power bar steadily diminish. A man rushed out of a door beside me and, as the door swung shut, I darted through the gap before it closed.

'It hurts!' someone exclaimed.

Two people lay on the large circular bed: a young man, little more than a boy, and a pubescent girl. They both wore tight strappy costumes of brown leather and brassy metal that did nothing to conceal their nakedness. The youth was writhing but for a moment glanced towards the door. He grunted, having sensed me there but, seeing nothing, coiled up around his pain again. The girl lay flat on her back, eyes rolled up in her head, hands poised above her stomach clenched into fists. The youth clawed at the thrall on the back of his neck – there were scratch marks in the skin all around it.

'Betan!' he yelled, then slumped, unconscious.

I had no doubt this was the result of Bronodec's nanite. The one hurrying out had doubtless gone to get help, with something he couldn't explain happening to his bedroom slaves. Noting a power point set in the wall above a side table, I headed over.

Checking through the HUD menu gave me the suit's schematic. Its cable sat coiled in a box on the belt and its universal bayonet slid into the socket beside a microwave emitter that probably powered the bedside lamps and other devices in the room. A charging bar appeared below the discharge bar and rose up to fourteen per cent. I stepped to the side of the table and sat with my back against the wall. A further search of the recharging menu gave me other options and I keyed into microwave emission first. Then I discovered more ways of drawing on emitted radiations and I turned them all on. A warning came up telling me that this option made my chameleonware less effective. I didn't worry about that just then.

'Betan,' said the youth, abruptly sitting up.

He sat there looking around the room, then reached up to his thrall. 'Yes,' he said, and dug his fingers in. He wrenched at it, like pulling at a large scab, and tore the thing up to reveal the fibres penetrating his neck. Blood welled out and it obviously hurt, but he kept pulling until the thing snapped away. He tossed it down on the bed.

'Betan?' he asked again.

The girl sat up.

'It's gone,' she said.

'Pull the fucking thing off,' he said.

She reached up tentatively.

'No, don't do that,' I said.

The youth looked around wildly, while the girl seemed numb as if just out of a deep sleep. I debated with myself for a second, then turned off the chameleonware and lowered my visor. The youth leapt off the bed, took a step across the room and grabbed up a stun baton lying on a nearby chair.

'Who are you?' he asked, all aggression and fear.

'I'm the person who introduced the nanite into the

325

ventilation system which has shut down your thralls. What's your name?'

'Tanis,' he said. Lowering the stun baton, he asked, 'Polity?'

I decided against standing up since that would've been more threatening. It had been foolish of me to reveal myself. I now felt I must help these two and, while my power supply had reached twenty per cent, not even at full power could I get them out of this building and across the roof.

'Are you able to move about freely in this building?' I asked.

'All who are . . .' he began, then reached up to the seeping wound on the back of his neck. He looked down at the thrall he'd torn away.

'You need glue,' I said. 'Clean up your neck, pull the thrall fibres off and stick the thing back in place. Do it quickly now.'

He gaped at me. I guessed I'd given him too much to process.

'Here.' Betan came off the bed, pulling the sheet with her, and held it out to him. He threw the stun baton down and began wiping away the blood while she went off into another room. She shortly returned with a first-aid kit and sat him down on the bed. I stood, seeing my power was now up to a quarter. She sprayed a coagulant. He picked up his thrall and began pulling out its internals. The coagulant also worked as glue and in a moment he had the thing stuck back in place. He looked at me questioningly.

'Some clothing,' I suggested. 'And perhaps some kind of scarf.'

Betan opened a wardrobe and began pulling out items. With a bitter look on her face, she shed her leather garment. Tanis went over to get clothes for himself, just as the door opened. I closed my visor, and turned my 'ware back on.

'Here too,' said a woman. She turned to the man I'd seen earlier, 'I would bet you have cuffs or manacles,' she added with a wry smile.

'Damn.' He reached for his sidearm.

I stood up and stepped away from the wall. Betan and Tanis had moved back from the wardrobe, clutching the clothing to themselves and looking over to where I'd been sitting. I waited until the door had swung shut before I stepped in closer.

'No need—' began the woman.

I shot her once through the throat, blowing a mess of smoking flesh in a crescent across the wall behind her, then turned to the man and shot him through the back of the head. Tanis, spattered with brains and bits of skull, screamed. Betan stood in shock for a moment, then whirled, caught hold of him and clamped a hand over his mouth. He sank to the floor and she went down with him. After a moment, she released him and he sat there gasping. How old were they, I wondered? Probably only just teenagers. I turned off the chameleonware again and plugged the power cord back in, belatedly remembering that they were technically older than me.

'It'll be dangerous out there now the thralls are going offline,' I said, leaning back against the table. 'But here will be dangerous too.'

They both watched me wide-eyed. I was preparing to abandon them to their fate, I realized, then as quickly understood that I couldn't.

'Put those clothes on,' I instructed them.

The power climbed to halfway as they dressed. I unwound the cord further and stooped down by the corpses, relieving them of weapons, ammo and power cartridges. One sidearm I kept, the other I hesitated over for a moment, then held it out, with spare clips, to Betan.

'Conceal this.'

They both now wore loose shirts and tight trousers. She put the weapon in her waistband and covered it, then went to search out some shoes. Tanis, with shaking hands, picked up the stun baton and concealed that under his shirt. Finally, after finding some suitable footwear, they were ready.

'Now what?' said Tanis, trying to be brave.

'We wait until I've recharged my power supply, then we walk out of here. You will be my prisoners.'

'Are you . . . Are you Polity?' he asked again.

I thought about this for a long moment, considering who and what I actually was.

'Yes, I am Polity,' I replied.

Tanis and Betan walked ahead out into the corridor. Behind them I kept my visor closed and ran the map display for exterior broadcast, concealing my face. I hoped it would be enough, though I felt pretty damned sure I was making a big mistake trying to rescue these two.

'Take the shortest route down,' I instructed.

We only got a few hundred yards along the corridor when four of Suzeal's soldiers charged around a corner. One of them immediately brought a pulse rifle up to his shoulder, but another slapped it down.

'You good?' the second asked me.

I waved a hand. 'They're no trouble, but I'm told Suzeal wants them all out of here.'

He nodded and the four ran on.

'The dropshaft,' said Betan a moment later, pointing.

She looked ready to run.

'Only walk,' I said. 'If you're running they'll just bring you down.'

At length we came to a dropshaft entrance. Tanis stepped forwards to enter it and I caught his shoulder, stopping him at the lip.

'Look.' I pointed at the red cross on the console beside the shaft. 'It's been shut down. We'll climb down. Can you do that?'

Tanis nodded mutely, reached inside to grab a rung and began to descend. Betan hesitated at the edge.

'Tanis seems okay,' I commented.

She got into the shaft and, after clinging for a moment, began to descend. I followed, counting floors. When they stopped below me, I reached across to the other side of the shaft, found the rungs there and descended past them. Tanis clung to the ladder, peering in through one of the shaft's entrances. Three corpses lay in the corridor beyond, still smoking from pulse rifle wounds. All of them were naked and thralled.

'Keep going,' I said. 'All the way to the bottom.'

I moved ahead of them, finally seeing the bottom of the shaft. Another thralled corpse lay there, body broken by the fall. Beyond the entrance was a foyer, soldiers scattered here and there, some standing armed over thralled workers who were loading corpses onto sleds. The fact the guards were so attentive told me the nanite must be continuing to do its job, as well as the sound of gunfire, which I could now hear again. I stepped out and waved the two youngsters ahead of me.

'Just head for the exit,' I said.

Nobody took any notice of us, until we stepped out of an entrance leading into the park, and a woman turned towards me. I felt my stomach drop when I recognized her.

'Where to?' she asked.

'The pens,' I replied.

'Bit young for that, aren't they?' she commented, frowning.

I thought fast. 'Suzeal's instructions,' I said, poking Betan in the back with my gun. 'These are Brack's.'

She grunted and turned away.

'Keep walking,' I instructed the two.

329

We crossed the park, heading down an alley between restaurants and finally out of sight of prying eyes.

'Do you know how to get to the rim from here?' I asked.

Tanis nodded, but Betan said, 'But our dad?'

'Salander is at the rim and that's the only place you'll be safe. Your father will head there if he can. Now go.'

'We can help you,' said Tanis.

'You'll die if you stay with me. Go.'

Finally, and hesitantly, they headed away. I felt bad about it, but had to stay with the larger picture. I guessed that would be how a Polity agent acted. They disappeared out of sight at the end of the alley and I turned to a nearby door, planted my boot against it and entered. I needed the backpack that had been left on a balcony above.

I took the CTD out of the pack and studied it. At once, I understood the workings of the console attached to the end of the matt black cylinder. I was about to take it and go, but then had second thoughts and pressed my weapon against its stick patch, picked the pack up, and hung it on my back. Swinging the multigun ahead, I grabbed the leads Marcus had detached and plugged them back into the thing. A second later, following a series of instructions that came up in my HUD, I detached the optic from my carbine, where it plugged into a belt socket, and switched its weapon control over to wifi. There was a danger of hacking with this option, but it should be fine for a secondary weapon. I then uncoiled the optic of the multigun and plugged it in. A firing list came up, selection of options by blink control and firing by the main trigger. A series of buttons behind the main trigger also gave me the same options, only slower. I familiarized myself with them, then checked on how much ammo and power remained. After some thought, I cancelled the rail-bead function, since it drank power and the recoil would either put me through a wall behind or require full suit assist.

Finally ready, I exited the apartment, reducing the weapon options to a series of dots down the side of the HUD, having memorized them, and called up the map again. This building was part of the designated hub rim, with no access to the station railgun from here. I needed to go down, head along the park to its far end, where cargo and personnel shafts led up into the space dock transfer area. No doubt the security would be heavy. On the way down, people who'd been thralled startled at the sight of me and ran. They mistook me for one of Suzeal's people and this became evident again a few floors down when the suit alerted me to danger behind.

I dropped and turned as something streaked overhead and exploded at the end of the corridor. A man shouldering a short launcher fired again. I targeted him and could easily have taken him out with one shot, but instead engaged chameleonware and leapt to one side. The floor erupted where the missile struck, then it bounced on down the corridor in a series of secondary thermal explosions. Pulling out of a half-collapsed wall, I went full suit assist and hurtled forwards through the smoke. He'd backed up against a wall and was trying to insert another missile into his homemade launcher when I reached him. I pulled the thing from his hand and tossed it aside, then caught him by the throat and pushed him back against the wall, slapping from his hand the sidearm he attempted to draw. I cancelled the 'ware.

'I'm not going to kill you.' I lowered my visor. 'I'm with Salander.'

He carried on trying to fight me.

'I'm with Salander!' I shouted in his face and finally he desisted.

'Okay, then let me go,' he said.

I did so and stepped back. He eyed his launcher, but made no move to pick it up.

'What's happening?' he asked.

'I released the nanite that freed you.' I gestured to the dressing on the back of his neck. 'Salander has retreated to the rim. Tell everyone to head there – you'll be safe.'

'Safe?' he repeated viciously. 'And what exactly does that mean?'

'You, and as many people you can tell, need to head out there.' I didn't elaborate on what more was to come, since if he told others and Suzeal's people caught and interrogated him, chances were she would realize her railgun was a target. 'We have nerve gas mines in the ventilation,' I lied.

'She said nothing about that,' he said. 'She just told us on the sub-net to get to the rim.'

I turned away. 'Perhaps you can understand why she didn't want to spread the news?' I headed off.

'Where're you going?'

'Not your concern,' I replied.

Unavoidable casualties, I thought. So Salander had managed to contact those who'd been thralled and told them to head to the rim and what safety she could provide there. Many would do that but some, like the man behind me, would stay to exact payback. Most of those would end up dead at the hands of Suzeal's soldiers, or die when the prador arrived. I could do no more than I had done in telling the lie about nerve gas. Perhaps Salander should do something like that too, but Marcus hadn't provided me with a comlink for her so I couldn't suggest it. I tried to think of other ways to get the people here to flee, as I walked out of the alley and back into the park. I then realized secondary considerations had begun to bog me down. I needed to stay focused on my objective. I couldn't save every life.

Bodies still littered the park, as well as clear-up teams and armed thugs. I fitted in perfectly and nobody took any notice as I headed out to the central path towards the far end. I passed a large sled loaded with bodies – the lower layer prisoners while the upper layers were those who'd been thralled. Then I saw something I couldn't ignore: two soldiers were shoving two men out of a restaurant onto the fading grass. Only as I saw them doing this did the nearby tree finally come into focus. Two corpses hung by the neck there, and the soldiers were driving their prisoners towards it.

I walked off behind a tangled briar and stooped down, engaging chameleonware. I knew I shouldn't allow this to distract me and, had Marcus been in my position, he would not have allowed it to. I ran out just as the two men were forced down onto the ground, with one of the soldiers uncoiling a length of high-tension cord. I slowed as the other soldier turned towards me, his expression puzzled – he'd heard me running. I shot him in the face, then turned and shot the other one, but this rebounded off his closed visor. He dropped the rope and squatted, grabbing for the carbine hanging from a strap over his shoulder. My sidearm would do no good against his heavy armour so I selected option two and fired. The multigun emitted a glaring blue particle beam that struck his front. He leapt up yelling but I kept it centred. He staggered back, armour smoking and peeling away, then the beam stabbed through, blowing a fountain of smoking flesh out of his back. The two prisoners were up now. Without shutting down my chameleonware I shouted at them.

'Run for your lives! Head for the rim!'

They didn't even pause, breaking into a sprint back towards the restaurant. Other soldiers now took notice. Shots cracked in from the side and one of the men cartwheeled then simply exploded into rags. The other reached cover, but whether he survived the fusillade that destroyed the front of the restaurant

I couldn't say. A big pulse shot then hit the ground just a few yards to one side of me, fountaining earth. Then another struck an equal distance over to the other side. I looked up, as the source was high up in one building – but surely I was invisible? A mini-gun opened up from a nearby copse, hitting the ground twenty feet behind me, then tracking across towards me. I fired two explosive shells back at that copse and broke into a run. Something hurtled out of cover with multiple legs thumping against the ground just before the shells detonated, bringing down a couple of trees. The robot fired a particle beam that scored past me. I went full assist and changed course just as an explosive shell detonated where I'd been.

How the hell was it, and the shooter above, tracking me?

I realized in an instant, even as the particle beam scored across again, briefly touching my leg with hellish heat. I dodged, stumbled and rolled, and came up looking for cover. Over to my right stood a fountain. I swerved towards it, heavy pulse gun fire still tracking me from above. Soldiers were now running towards the area and firing in my general direction. Obviously relay to their HUDs from the robots, but I hadn't yet been properly targeted. As I reached the fountain, it exploded and tumbled me through the air in rubble and fire. It had been obvious cover for me. I hit the ground hard, broken stone raining down around and on me. The impact stunned me, though the suit absorbed most of its effect, but I had no time for that. I reached for my wrist console to call up the EMR recharging options and quickly cancelled them. Stupidly I'd left them on and so opened myself to detection.

I was up and running again as shots rained down where I'd been. Soldiers all around fired on anything that looked remotely suspicious. A pulse shot hit my thigh, I stumbled, another hit my pack, throwing up error warnings in my HUD, and a laser carbine beam swept across my chest. I was heavily armed and capable of delivering a devastating reply, but the moment I did that my position would be located. I just kept running, finally entering a banyan and taking cover deep inside. I lay there, down beside a trunk, and gasped for breath.

Stupid stupid stupid!

I should not have intervened. But how could I walk casually past murder being committed? I shrugged off my pack to inspect the damage. The shot had mostly been dispersed by armouring in the pack itself, but it had seared an energy canister. I inspected the thing and checked diagnostics. Brief overheat but again stable. The CTD was undamaged. I put the pack back on, even as soldiers began searching through the trees. Moving on, and freezing any time anyone came close, I eventually came to the edge of the banyan. The end of the park lay ahead with its cargo and dropshafts, but now many of the robots were gathering there.

'High-phase scanning,' my suit informed me.

My way was blocked.

17

The building beside the park presented a blank wall above a slot-like space at ground level. Just inside, the floor dropped away and, before me, a cluster of massive pipes extended up towards a distant ceiling. Checking my map identified this as a fuel and supplies feed to the space dock projecting into the gap in the hub. The railgun sat on the other side of the hub from me, almost lined up with that dock. Time, I felt, to get a bit more inventive about my course towards it. I moved round the lip of the drop, looking for a way up, and eventually found a rail for an inspection robot running up one wall. Grav was low here, mostly being station spin and a side effect from the park. Setting my suit to fifty per cent assist, I began to climb.

Some fifty feet above park level, I paused to watch soldiers move in below to search the area with hand scanners. My suit delivered its warning again and I climbed faster. If one of them pointed a scanner upwards I'd be in trouble. A short while later they departed, but three of the robots moved to take their place, facing outwards. Perhaps they thought they had confined me to the park. Most likely, from Suzeal's point of view, one person in chameleonware wasn't a major problem. Some of her soldiers might end up dead but I would bet she had heavy protections and scanning around her. I intended to at least disabuse her of the idea that I wouldn't be a problem.

Two hundred feet up, the rail turned horizontally to run along a pipe leading into the mass in the centre of the shaft. I climbed along it and then up on top of the pipe where it joined the main mass. Here I ran a diagnostic on my suit. It needed repairs yet again but had not been breached. I began looking at its suitability for vacuum and found all I needed to know under 'Sealed Combat Mode'. The suit could seal itself completely against vacuum, but was intended for general combat where bio or nanoweapons might be deployed. It possessed a CO_2 scrubber and cracker, and an oxide substrate in its layers could activate to produce oxygen. I'd be able to last in vacuum for one hour on this, on condition that the combination of that and the 'ware didn't deplete the power supply.

My stomach rumbled and I felt a surge of hunger and thirst. This confirmed that my earlier starvation was due to boosting – my body was rebuilding itself whether I wanted it to or not – but I'd have to ignore that need for now. Okay, I had to find a way through above and, I hoped, one that didn't involve explosive decompression. The rail now ran round the mass of pipes and clambering along it only brought me back to where I'd started. I headed out again to a gap between two pipes and pushed through. Here a hatchway made for maintenance robots gave access inside a shaft. Flicking to light enhancement in my visor revealed rails running in parallel all the way up. Beetlebots ran on some of them, with wheeled feet against the walls, stopping occasionally to stab their probosces into readout ports. There would be detectors here, I knew, so kept my chameleon-ware running while I climbed.

And I kept on climbing. A slow transition ensued, grav waning until I only had to catch the rails to propel me on or stop me. Grav then began to impinge again from the side and soon I was walking along a shaft transformed into tunnel. When it became apparent I'd travelled further than needed, I stopped to check the HUD map and focus on my position. Suspiciously, the map didn't show this maintenance shaft and I wondered then about other concealed access ways. The suit had probably downloaded this map from station computing, perhaps after Suzeal or some other paranoiac had altered it.

The map showed the pipes extending into the hub, taking a right-angled turn over the geodesic roof of the transit area, then taking another turn to run along the back of the dock that extended into the hub. It had my position just after that first turn, so the grav holding me in place must have issued from the transit area plates. The next turn revealed itself more by the slow reorientation of grav rather than by any physical indicators. Soon I was climbing a shaft again, but the grav grew weaker, so I could do it without suit assist. I kept going, marking the various hatches in my mind. Eventually the end of it came in sight with a hatch there, so I carried on until I'd reached it.

Circular and quite small, the hatch had a manual latch on the side. Being a pressure hatch, it might open into vacuum on the other side. Still, it hinged towards me, so the air pressure in the shaft would make it impossible to open without assist. I decided to give it a try, first sealing my suit. The latch clonked open easily, but thereafter seemed stuck solid. I braced my feet either side of it, initiated assist and tried again. It began to lift on a simple seal then air started hissing through. Vacuum on the other side, I thought. If I opened this all the way, the air pressure would blow me out and clear with no way to get back to any solid surface. Then abruptly the hissing increased to a sucking whoomph and the thing flew open with me dangling from it. Air pressure had equalized with a small compartment behind, and in there sat a maintenance robot, all folded up. I could only see the back end but it looked just like the one Marcus had pulled out of its hole on the planet.

I scrambled up, reached inside and tugged at the thing. It felt solid for a moment, but it seemed my action had woken it because it extended rear limbs out, around the hatch, and heaved itself out. As it slid clear, it released all but one of its limbs and flipped over onto the surface around the hatch, coming down and gecko sticking. It gazed at me with a collection of sensors, shifted mandible manipulators, then shuffled round and opened a hatch in its side towards me. I stared, puzzled for a moment, then realized that even maintenance bots needed their own mainten- ance and this was sometimes conducted by humans. It waited for me to repair or reprogram it.

Ignoring the thing, I pulled myself into the space it had occu- pied. Another hatch lay at the far end and this one doubtless opened onto empty vacuum in the hub. Reaching down, I closed the other one behind and, in the cramped space, worked the hatch above, ensuring a firm grip on the lever because of what would happen next. It opened with a bang, tugging me out, and the air pressure behind finished the job, so I ended up seemingly hanging over some vast abyss. Grav was even lower here, almost undetectable. I swung my feet down and engaged gecko function, released the hatch and stood upright to look around.

I was standing at the far end of the dock. The thing was just a square bar a few hundred yards across leading back to the inner surface of the hub. Over on the far side of where it attached, the geodesic glass ceiling extended over the transit area. On this side of the dock ran the mass of supply pipes I'd climbed, branching off at intervals to enter the dock until few remained at the end. I walked over one of these pipes onto the dock proper, up the side, then out along the top. Now I could see spaceships and shuttles latched on down its length, like aphids on a stalk. Turning, I surveyed the inner ring of the hub – its acres of geodesic, its various protrusions and other docks, engine nacelles for station correction, and then, of course, the railgun.

The massive structure extended up from a ball coupling a hundred yards across in the hub. I could see no rails because a cooling jacket with pipes and power feeds cloaked the weapon, making it look like a tree overgrown with vines. I needed to get to the thing but, checking my suit, I found it didn't have the kind of steering thrusters of a proper spacesuit. I damned myself for coming this far out without checking earlier, and looked back down the length of the dock. The walk back to the hub inner rim of over half a mile didn't look tempting, nor the walk round to the railgun, which would make it a further three miles. Could I do that in an hour, the limit of my air supply? On a planetary surface wearing normal clothes, no problem, but walking on gecko function was another matter entirely. Also, who knew what detectors or watchers might be there? I turned back and looked towards the railgun. It stood a mile and a half away. I walked along to the far end of the dock, stepped round and walked out on that, the railgun now above my head. I considered the possibilities of variable grav from the station diverting my course, then dismissed the idea because the hub rim was very wide and I'd aim for the centre of it. I squatted, disengaged gecko function, and leapt.

I sailed through vacuum towards the area of station behind the ball socket of the railgun. I seemed to be travelling fast but knew, any grav effects aside, I should land with the same force imparted by jumping. Swivelling over had me apparently falling feet first towards the thing. I turned gecko function back on, then took it up to its highest since I didn't want to bounce away again. With that done, I'd reached halfway across and now began to feel as if I was falling from a great height. Suddenly I felt a surge of panic. I'd not accounted for the spin of the rim – my departure point was travelling in one direction but my destination would be travelling in the opposite direction. My landing might be very hard and some distance off target. I let the panic rest there in my mind and circumvented it. It was a bit too late to worry about that now.

I sailed on down, legs straight and ready to absorb the impact. I ramped up suit assist to maximum since it also operated a dampening system. Around the ball socket spread acres of armour, scattered here and there with inset sensor dishes and mobile ones on pylons. I found myself coming down at an angle towards one of these, hundreds of yards off target, and as it seemed to stab up at me, I slapped my hands against the edge of its dish, slightly diverting my course and slowing my descent. Landing at its base, I bent my knees to absorb the impact, the shock juddering through my legs. I bounced up again, my boots tearing free to send me tumbling. Hull sped beneath, then another pylon zipped towards me and I slammed into it, bending metal, but I managed to reach out and grab hold. I lay there gasping, apparent motion seeming to disappear. If this pylon hadn't intercepted me I would've ended up floating out into vacuum again (and probably trying to figure out how to make a hole in my suit to use its air pressure as a jet to bring me back down to the surface). I had arrived.

With a mental shift of perspective, I untangled myself from wreckage and walked across a plain of armour towards the protruding dome of the cooling jacket which enclosed the railgun ball socket. It took half an hour and as I drew closer, gaps in the jacket revealed the teeth of racks on the socket surface, no doubt driven by cogwheels in the hub to position it. The gun itself stood on the other side of this, pointing out into clear vacuum. The arc of the planet I'd fought to survive on was visible just to the left of it and slowly moving right with the station's spin, while the dock moon lay clearly in its sights and remained there, the gun moving slowly to track it. Estimating the movement of these objects, I realized that the gun could keep the moon in its sights with only slight adjustments because the station and moon orbits were matched.

Where to put the CTD? Anywhere here should wreck the weapon, but I walked round until the gun itself sat poised overhead, then I continued into the cooling jacket, and there unshouldered the pack and multigun. Even as I did this, I realized that floating in vacuum wouldn't have been a problem, for I could've used the recoil of the rail beader to send me where I wanted to go. I took out the CTD, sorted through its program, then paused to plan what I'd do after I'd set it. I couldn't go back through open vacuum, since the blast wave might send me away from the station. I needed to get to cover a good distance away from the detonation. I gave myself twenty minutes, wifi linked the timer to my HUD, then gecko stuck the thing below the railgun. I then put my pack on and set out at a clumsy lope across the armour and around the hub rim. A hundred yards away, I damned myself for not similarly connecting the thing to my HUD so I could just remotely detonate it. I wasn't quite as precise and efficient as a real Polity agent.

Two hundred yards away, the armour ended at a geodesic chain-glass roof. Down below, people were scattered through a maze of buildings, and soldiers and robots arrayed in what looked like a central square. Ten minutes passed as I circumvented half of the roof and had yet to see any airlocks inside. A right turn took me towards the face of the station disc. When I reached this and peered down from my perspective across the face, I realized that progress there would be difficult, as the further I went in that direction, the more centrifugal force would throw me outwards. One mistake with gecko stick and I'd fall across that face. So I continued around the hub rim. Eventually another protruding weapon came into sight. This particle cannon pointed into the space at the centre of the hub – obviously used for security there. Pausing, I studied the rim and saw a number of such weapons dotted all around it. The prador would find entry here a bit more difficult than I supposed.

Fifteen minutes passed as I loped around the thing, looking for the maintenance robot hatch, as it seemed likely there'd be one here. Instead I found an airlock for humans. The thing had a manual purge and lever but it occurred to me that somewhere in the station someone would be alerted if I opened it. Only five minutes remained, though. I hesitated, looking towards the particle cannon and its surrounding structure. That thing could give me cover from the blast. The need to see the imminent destruction of the railgun informed my decision. I moved away from the airlock and crouched behind the cannon, finding a couple of struts to grip when necessary. Next I checked functions in my HUD. The visor would react to glare but could be set to react faster – in fact it had a setting to cover nukes and CTDs, and I selected that. I gripped the struts and watched the railgun, the timer ticking down in the corner of my HUD.

It hit twenty minutes. The flash blacked my visor for a couple of seconds then it slowly returned visibility in time to reveal the expanding fireball and the rapidly approaching particulate blast front. I ducked back as the latter swept past. My HUD alerted me to radioactivity, but within the parameters of my suit's shielding. I felt the vibration through my hands and the station shuddering underneath me. Another look revealed a debris cloud and the business end of the gun tumbling across the hub gap. It clipped one of the docked ships on its way past, hit the edge of the chain-glass roof of the transit area and tumbled on over the face of the station and away. I focused on the roof, but couldn't see any explosive decompression. Chain-glass was all but impact-resistant and the frame holding the sheets no doubt consisted of a complex interweaving of meta-materials which allowed deformation and retention of seal. A smoking line cut across past my helmet, sending me ducking back. All around, debris was blowing small hot craters in the inner rim. Larger objects slammed home as well, sending shudders through my feet, and a chunk of jagged ceramal stabbed into the composite just over to one side of the airlock. All of this, of course, occurred in absolute silence.

I watched and waited, seeing the flash of debris impacts all around the rim. Here and there the blasts of brief explosive decompressions bloomed, and I hoped at least that these hadn't killed anyone who didn't deserve to die. Eventually, when it felt safe to do so, I came out of cover and headed over to the airlock. Any watchers would now be dealing with numerous faults. They might not notice the lock being used, and they might even put it down to damage here. I opened it, taking one last look towards the docking moon. Was it my imagination or had I seen a swarm of brassy bees departing it already? I climbed into the lock and closed the outer hatch.

Incredible noise filled the station and the whole structure was shaking. Crashes and booms echoed through the corridors and distantly the clamour of people shouting. I located myself on my map and began heading back around the station, back to where Marcus had been incarcerated. What I would do beyond finding and freeing him I didn't know.

The journey back passed without incident. I kept encountering troops and robots in a big hurry, but they had rather larger concerns and ignored me. I also looked like one of them – either responding to Suzeal's orders or, like many others, running for cover. A dropshaft finally took me up a couple of floors into the transit area, and no one guarded the shaft. Even as I exited, one of Suzeal's troopers shouldered me aside and stepped into the shaft, with a long line of others crowding in behind. Above, ships were on the move and others undocking. Understandably, those who could depart were doing so. Still many people occupied the area, both soldiers and thralled citizens, and they were running for the exits. Here and there bulkhead doors were closing on the corridors and larger tunnels extending from this place. I broke into a run, sure that after they closed, the shafts would be sealed next. It might be that the chain-glass geodesic roof was tough, but it was still weaker than the rest of the station and would be a likely entry point.

'They're coming!' someone shouted.

I paused to look up. Now all the remaining ships on the dock parted company from it, in some cases tearing away supply tubes and airlocks. Explosions bloomed out there, and decompressions flung suited figures out into vacuum. Two ships collided, one tearing a chunk out of another, which then slid out of sight. A moment later the floor bucked and a firestorm tangled with debris spread overhead. I ran again, now only glancing up occasionally. Particle beam defence guns began opening up and further blasts shuddered the station. One glimpse revealed a weapon firing from the other side of the hub, then erupting in a big blast, putting out its beam. Other shapes then became visible – the prador had certainly arrived.

A crowd crammed into the dropshafts, entering them in packed streams I realized I wouldn't be able to get through and it was probably too late to try. Swinging to the right, initiating atmosphere seal on my suit, I headed towards a side wall where people crammed through a steadily closing bulkhead door. Even as I reached this, someone fell away screaming, his arm off at the elbow. A low roof jutted over the entry to a parking area for cargo drays further on. I ran in and towards the back, but found the single bulkhead door there closed too. Then grav went off. I had no time to engage gecko and found myself flailing through the air. I grabbed for a dray to alter my course, and ended up catching hold of a support I-beam. Wrapping my arms around it, I looked out with my hands locked together and full suit assist engaged. A blast on the far side of the geodesic blanked my visor for a second. As it cleared, a hollow roaring filled the world. The effect took a moment to reach me, but then the massive decompression took hold and my legs flailed towards the hole the prador had just blasted in the roof.

People and masses of debris swirled upwards. The screaming became a one-voiced beast, behind the noise of things breaking, clashing and the hungry sucking of the wind. Many were thralled and I could no longer comfort myself that my actions hadn't killed innocents. The wind roared on and on and I half expected to see the drays sliding out below me. One did, in fact, but safety clamps rooted the rest to the floor. Then, gradually, the pull waned and the noise diminished. People no doubt still screamed, but were issuing their last breaths into vacuum. Then the prador entered, swarming down through the hole. Lasers and particle beams stabbed up at them and missiles too. They juddered in flight, shedding shattered slugs from their armour. One, struck by a missile, spiralled into the far wall then bounced away, gutted by fire. But the defence, consisting as it did of a few robots and those who wore suits or armour that could retain atmosphere, dissolved when the prador opened fire in return.

Lines of Gatling slugs chewed up the floor, particle beams lanced out to nail suited figures. Prador and humans swirled in an incendiary dance. Two soldiers ran as fast as they could on gecko towards my hideaway, then simply fragmented into clouds of shattered flesh, blood and pieces of armour. The visible firing lasted perhaps ten minutes, though it seemed longer. I supposed other firing wasn't audible or visible in vacuum, but at the end of that time it seemed only prador and the broken remains of Suzeal's soldiers remained. Belatedly I remembered to turn on my chameleonware.

While the bulk of the prador force hung above the floor in the centre of the transit area, others set about tasks elsewhere. Unlocking my hands, I pushed over to a dray nearest to the outside and crouched behind it. A group of five prador were up by the hole in the roof. Two had large tanks on their backs and wielded gun-like devices, reminding me of the flamethrower the prador had used against Marcus aboard the King's Ship. Others outside were manoeuvring a large cylinder towards the gap, shifting it until it protruded halfway through. They folded across struts from the thing, then the flash of welders secured them. The three inside, without the tanks on their backs, unwound some mesh into the gap between the cylinder and roof and fixed it in place, then the first two opened fire with jets of white fluid. This spread out along the mesh and around its edges and, by the time they'd finished, a great dripping white mass, like mucus, filled the hole around the cylinder and bulged out into vacuum. I checked my readouts and saw atmospheric pressure rising. One of them tossed an object into this mass. From the point where it landed, the substance retracted to the mesh, smoothed, turned yellow and hardened. Pressure continued to rise, though very slowly. I guessed most of the ventilation ducts to here had closed, and the air was only building up from faulty ones which hadn't. But why did the suited prador require air?

A glance along the transit area told me why. Groups of prador had set to work on the larger bulkhead doors. Of course, they wouldn't want explosive decompressions perpetually slowing them. The air was for their convenience, and no altruism was involved here. They retreated from one door and explosives detonated behind them. The door blew inwards on hinges, bent out of shape, then the pressure beyond swung it back. The air shrieking round its distortions came as a distant wail. The prador advanced on it and as one steadily pushed it open again, welders flared for them to fix it against the wall of the tunnel beyond. The wail grew in volume as greater air pressure in here began to transmit more sound. Another door blew, and then another and the pressure began to climb steeply. They only opened the larger doors. It made sense to concentrate on those they could actually get through.

Then grav came back on. The prador juddered in place but didn't drop. They must have used some kind of EMR weapon to knock out grav and had now shut that down. Next they descended and assembled into neat ranks. One of the Guard landed before them – I recognized him by his armour as one of those who'd entered Vrasan's sanctum to find him . . . injured. He began pacing before the gathered troops to clatter and bubble instructions at them. Above, weapons fire flashed all around the inner rim of the hub, so it was likely the force here was just a small part of the whole I'd seen aboard Vrasan's ship. Suzeal's reign was at an end, and the time had come for me to achieve my next limited objective, namely, rescuing Marcus. I moved out from the dray and over to the wall. Even with chameleonware on, I used available cover to head towards one of the blown-open bulkhead doors. Then all the prador paused in their tasks to tilt and look up with their main eyes. I looked up too.

Prador were still outside but now others had arrived. Something black snaked above and across. The inner door of the large cylindrical airlock opened to reveal a shimmershield within. The hooder nosed through the kaleidoscope of light, then, like a giant parasite dropping out of some fruit, it slid down into the transit area. It snaked across the air as if across a solid surface, unaffected by gravity, and seemed to have brought some of that shimmer with it. Lines of light, or energy, or some kind of force field, traversed its length as it began to settle towards the floor. The prador below scattered, either running or firing up the grav-drives in their suits to get out of the way. Just a few feet above the floor, its lights went out and it dropped with a heavy thump. By now another was coming through from above and yet another queued up behind that. I watched rapt, scared and horrified. Prador were bad enough, but this?

They didn't seem completely under control, for one of them darted at a prador and sent him tumbling through the air to crash down against one wall. Another whipped round, the shimmer spilling from its front end and an odd pink meniscus shooting through the air to hit another prador. The victim simply disintegrated, coming apart at every joint and its main carapace flying open at a horizontal break, then everything inside the armour spraying out in a glutinous fog. Prador opened fire on the creatures, Gatling slugs rattling and zinging off them, a particle beam stabbing in and splashing against another meniscus. Orders clattered in the air and, after a few more shots, the prador retreated all the way to the walls. Then, through the airlock above came one I recognized: Vrasan. The moment he entered, the hooders dipped their spoon-shaped heads against the floor and froze in place.

What have I done? I asked myself. But then I tried to harden my resolve and dismiss the question. I'd brought war to force Suzeal to concentrate her troops around the hub, and given those who'd reached the rim a chance to escape. I couldn't control it and shouldn't feel guilty about making a choice that allowed the greatest number of innocents to survive. It was precisely as Marcus had said: no easy answers. It seemed an appropriate reminder when, moving on, I stepped over the bloody and bulging-eyed corpse of one of the thralled, still holding on with his death grip to some pedestal-mounted coms terminal. I'd killed him, and had yet to see any of those I had perhaps saved.

The nearest door opened into a tunnel twenty feet across, ribbed down its length like some reptile's gullet. Two prador crouched before it, utterly focused on the three hooders. My suit warned me of high-phase scanning just for a second, then that faded out. A moment later, it offered me 'Anomalous Energy Signatures', which presumably came from the hooders. I crouched behind the terminal watching the things. The thrall technology affixed to their bodies stood clear and it seemed Vrasan had restored some, if not all, of their war machine past. They'd already used field tech that no part of me recognized. What else were they able to do? Could they see me? I comforted myself with the idea that Vrasan's control of them seemed rough at best and that he'd now shut them down to stop them killing his own kind. I ran for the tunnel. One of the prador flicked his stalked eyes round, perhaps hearing me or detecting an air disturbance, but did no more.

I entered the tunnel and kept running, after about fifty yards slowing to a walk. Atmosphere pressure was now high enough for me to unseal my suit. Checking the power supply showed me that it was down to below half, and that was being eaten away as the suit recharged itself with air. Shutting that down, I opened the visor, huffed at the thin air, and a strong smell of something like burned electronics hit my nostrils. A little further ahead, smaller atmosphere doors had slid into place in the tunnel wall. The console beside one of these showed its safety setting still on. It wouldn't open while the pressure on my side remained lower than on the other side. However, with a little reprogramming to show a human was operating the console, and that it hadn't developed a fault, I'd be able to open it. My fingers froze over the touch screen as a hissing clattering movement reached my ears.

I turned. The hooder had approached without me hearing it and halted just ten feet away. Perhaps the sound was of its feet contacting the floor? Vrasan stood at the far end of the tunnel. Could he see me? Or could he see me through whatever access he had to this creature's senses? I gazed at it, rapt. If it could see me then no time remained to alter the programming of the console, and running was no option either. The fact it had halted here told me it must have seen me. Its armour now looked slick rather than the matt of those on the planet. Waves of iridescence ran over it and it emitted the hum of power as of a large fusion reactor. The burned electronics smell grew stronger and now I realized its source. The creature shivered, briefly, then in one slow smooth motion raised its spoon head from the floor.

The nightmare underside revealed its manipulators, terminating in the kind of tools usually found on an autosurgeon, writhing black tentacles and two rows of hellish red eyes. I reached back in motion equally slow and pulled the multigun forwards from its position beside its pack. Was I trying not to startle the beast? I had no idea. Only then did I realize that of course the thing could see me because my visor was still open. I made no effort to close it, and again didn't know why. Only one option could help me in this situation. I felt my way down to the bottom button behind the main trigger and pressed it. The hooder shivered again, as if in pleasurable anticipation. I raised the weapon and aimed by sight, then pulled the trigger.

351

Suit assist kicked in immediately, with computing obviously linking it to this option on the gun. The rail beader emitted a long sonic cracking and down at the end of the tunnel Vrasan, my target, disappeared in a cloud of hot impacts, pieces of his armour fragmenting. Even with assist working, the weapon's recoil picked me up and flung me backwards, spraying both tunnel and hooder with further shots. I landed on my arse as the hooder went wild. It thrashed from side to side, smashing great dents in the wall, pink menisci shooting away from its body and, where they hit, turning composite into embered explosions. I doubted I had killed Vrasan and felt sure he would soon reassert control. I turned, still on my backside, and fired on one of the smaller doors. I watched it fold up and tumble into the corridor beyond as recoil slid me up against the further wall. I leapt up and ran for the door, diving through as the hooder's head knifed into the wall just beside it and with a wrenching crash slid across, tearing out the door frame.

Shoulder rolling to come upright, I ran along a corridor too narrow for the beast, hoping the surrounding structure would slow it. The crashing continued behind me. One glance back showed it twenty feet into the corridor, a mess of twisted beams and wall panels on either side of it. Then it stopped, and I stopped too at a junction. The beast wavered where it was, then lines of light sped up its body to converge at its nose. I turned down the side corridor and ran on as a blast ripped up the corridor behind. The shock wave sent me stumbling and molten metal and burning composite rained past. I kept going, not inclined to stop again until utterly sure I'd got away.

Half an hour later I rested, gasping against the cowling of a fusion reactor. I was shaking and felt as if I wanted to throw up, but it seemed the boosting process hung onto the food in my guts. I closed up my visor to check for damage via my HUD.

And that was when the comlink menu of the suit came up. I stared at it in bewilderment, sure that when I last checked the only link available to me had been Marcus. Now another had appeared. I hesitated over allowing it, since while such a link remained open the sender could locate the receiver. But curiosity won out.

'Once again,' said Vrasan, 'you have interfered in my plans.'

His appearance showed the damage to his armour, but there was something odd about the image too. He hung in what might have been a virtuality of black and red movement, ghostly carapace segments revolving and sliding in and out of each other. He shouldn't have been able to obtain the link address to me by conventional means, yet he had. Somehow he'd worked through the hooder technology to send a link request. This worrying development bespoke a degree of com penetration of which I had no knowledge.

'I also destroyed the railgun so you could attack the station,' I replied.

He paused for a long moment, then snapped a claw in comprehension. 'I see, you draw Suzeal's forces back to the centre so the other humans can escape at the rim.'

He was annoyingly percipient.

'Now you are here and, from what I've seen, will soon control the station,' I said. 'Your plans are reaching fruition.'

'They are, but that does not change the plans I have for you, Jack.' He began to fade out. 'I will, as you say, soon enough control this station. If you survive what is to come, I will find you, for I've now decided you have become a very special project for me.'

'Surely you have more interesting concerns?' I replied.

'It is good to hate,' said Vrasan, and closed the link.

I pushed away from the reactor cowling and ran. I didn't think he would hunt me right then, but wasn't sure. There could be no escape. Once Vrasan controlled the station, he controlled this system, and he could hunt me down at his leisure.

I stepped out onto the balcony with my chameleonware back on, after resting it for a while and allowing my suit to recharge on my route here. There was too much activity in the park, and in the air above it, for me to step out here unconcealed. The prador were advancing on the ground behind shield generators, occasionally rising into the air to try and get something in over the shields of Suzeal's forces. They only occasionally risked this option because launchers on two of the robots were high-powered railers spitting out armour-piercers. One hit a prador, with the flash of impact, then, after a brief pause, the creature's armour parted horizontally on an explosion. The prador armour was toughened with exotic metals that couldn't be found on any old elementary table, so the missiles had to sport equally exotic nose cones, high-temperature vaporant and an ensuing metallized hydrogen charge. Such things I knew.

The remains of the prador fell out of the sky – a victory for Suzeal's troops – but then one of the human-controlled shield generators blew and two prador zoomed forwards, Gatling cannons shrieking and particle beams stabbing. Over twenty human fighters turned to bloody and burning mist before another missile streaked out and tossed one of the prador across the ground – the charge detonating outside its armour but making a dent deep enough to crush it to pulp inside. Next, BIC lasers stabbed down from the balconies opposite and the prador opened fire at them, rubble raining down. Voices in the building behind me drew me back inside. A man, heavily armoured, came opposite the open door.

'In here,' he said.

I moved to one side as another soldier came in, towing a sled loaded down with a pulse cannon and heavy power supply. They headed for the balcony and began to set the device up. I'd gone out through the door by the time the missile struck. The apartment filled with fire and the wall I dodged behind bulged out as the fire spewed from the doorway. I moved on down the corridor as the two men staggered out swearing, smoke pouring from their armour.

'I think it's time to leave,' said one.

'Nice idea, any plans on how?' said the other.

'The only way we have left,' came the reply.

I moved on to the stairs and down. After they ended, and with the power out, I used the ladders down the sides of the drop-shafts. In an alley beyond, my suit immediately alerted me to scanning. I'd seen a few fights before this one, mainly skirmishes in the main tubeways of the station, but had yet to see anyone using chameleonware. It could have been because of the scanning – no one wanted to take the tactical risk of relying on something that could fail at any moment. But it still struck me as odd. Perhaps it was one of the foibles of the troops who'd signed up with Suzeal, but more likely her paranoia didn't allow it in the station. The prador of course didn't have anything to do with such cowardly technology. They wanted to see their enemies and their enemies to see them. They also tended to have a highly disposable attitude towards their troops.

I shut down my 'ware since, being behind the human lines, anyone would assume me on their side. I headed out at a walk, fired a few shots towards the prador for form's sake, then set off at a steady trot towards the rear. I tried to put on the appearance of someone with an important task to perform. Others weren't bothering with that and were just running as fast as they could. Two of them went over in a hail of pulse gun fire from their own side, and I halted, raising my hands towards the shooters, then pointing back behind me urgently. After a moment, I banged a hand against my helmet. Obviously I had a com malfunction. They hesitated, but turned away because bigger problems than deserters had just arrived. The hooders. I accelerated and used suit assist too.

Even from behind, the light intensity of the weapons fire darkened my visor, while the noise ramped up so high my suit started to dampen it. Blast waves buffeted me and sent me stumbling, chunks of hot metal raining down all around. The suit reported numerous shrapnel hits then one on my thigh sprawled me face down, just ten yards from the dropshafts at the end. I rolled over and looked back.

Two hooders writhed in front of the human lines, beating against hardfields and fending off a constant fusillade of missiles, slugs and beam strikes. The combination of pink menisci and amber hardfields gave the impression of them being caught at the centre of giant, ever-turning gems. A hardfield generator eventually exploded and one of the hooders took advantage of the opening with a weapon I had not seen before. White beams stabbed down from every segment of its body, slicing through soldiers and machinery with equal ease. Where they tracked, the floor boiled and exploded, flinging up dismembered fighters and chunks of robots. Another hardfield collapsed, its generator bouncing towards me emptying its molten interior. It came to rest fifty feet away and even at that distance I could feel the latent heat collapsing it into a lambent pool that melted a hole through the floor. I watched all this for longer than necessary, then got up, ran to the hole and jumped in. Twenty feet down, I hit another floor where the molten metal spread and cooled. That gave way underneath me and I dropped again, but slower now in a rapid reduction of grav, and hit another floor in a rain of red-hot gobbets. I hurled myself aside. Coming up into a squat, I shrugged at my delay in escaping. I'd watched for so long because the scene, as horrible and destructive as it had been, had also been startlingly beautiful.

The far wall contained a row of shaft mouths too small for a human being, while I stood between two of the rows of conveyor belts leading to them. Glancing at the items on those belts, I saw squat cylinders of polymer, their ends rounded and interiors packed with goods by the multi-armed robots, now stooped over dead, at the far ends of the belts. This stuff was manufactured by the city of matter printers and other fabricators lying beyond. I'd effectively fallen into one of the station's supermarkets. The people who lived here, or had lived here, ordered their goods at a terminal and they arrived just a little while later by pneumatic tube.

In long low-grav bounds I headed between two belts and out onto the massive factory floor space. A long aisle stretched ahead of me. Many of the lights were out and the air tainted with smoke, so I couldn't see where it led. Nevertheless, picking up my pace, I all but flew when the far wall came into sight. Lying amidst a waterfall of feed pipes leading into the factory stood a single riveted door. I slowed a little, but still hit it feet first with suit assist kicking in. The door sprang open in a shower of corrosion and I shouldered into the far side of a corridor. I turned right, now about on the level of the pens where Suzeal had incarcerated Marcus, and headed towards them.

Even as I ran, a few floors down from the park, the effects of that combat continued to reach me. A crash ahead blew out a cloud of smoke, which cleared to reveal the corridor peppered with holes, actinic light glaring through them from above. Further on, an energy beam stabbed down like none I'd ever seen before, and of which my previous self had no knowledge. Bright green and about an arm's width, spirals and shifting patterns traversing its length, it bore some resemblance to a BIC laser informational warfare beam. But it had cut through metal and composite, leaving no debris and generating no heat. It then changed, its surface scaled with black diamonds, like a rolled-up sheet of animal mesh, and tracked across the corridor, then through the wall. The section I stood on slowly dropped a couple of feet, exposing a perfectly clean and shiny cut. I leapt up over that and moved on. Just how much of the space station would remain before Vrasan subdued the opposition?

The corridor next spiralled up and ended against a deactivated dropshaft. I climbed this, pausing partway to check the map, and then to activate chameleonware. Three floors brought me out in a stairwell, for there seemed no lower access to the pens. Eventually I entered the corridor Marcus and I had walked before, with its accesses to suspended walkways over the pens. I passed a couple and finally came to the one where the walkway had fallen. I presumed Marcus would be in this pen, where the prisoners had been held.

'You know,' said a voice I unhappily recognized, 'those who use chameleonware become arrogant and forget simple tricks like floor pressure plates and air disturbance monitors. I've killed many like that, who thought they were undetectable.'

At the far end of the corridor, the wall exploded and the air filled with fast-moving metal. The weapon was noisy, so in that respect inefficient, but heavy slugs slammed into me at a rate, if my brief realization was correct, of two thousand rounds a minute. The fusillade picked me up and flung me backwards, shedding hot metal as I flew through the air. I hit the edge of a doorway into the pens, spun down onto the ground and tried to bring my weapon to bear. It was gone – just the broken arm protruding from its pack. I reached up for the carbine but saw only its remains in the shattered ruin of the front of my suit. Warnings and damage reports scrolled down the side of my HUD, then blinked out when the stream of projectiles picked me up and sent me tumbling down the corridor again. I didn't need them to tell me my chameleonware had failed, suit damage at critical, and that I was probably about to die.

As the shots blew me into the stairwell and took my visor away, I glimpsed, through the eaten-away wall at the end of the corridor, Suzeal sitting behind that old tripod-mounted machine gun from her apartment. The firing ceased as I slid backwards down the stairs and out of sight. I tried to get up and run, but nothing seemed to be working right – I felt as heavy as lead. Percussions followed and a number of metallic balls, each a couple of inches across, bounced into the stairwell. I had time to see lights revolving under their metallic sheen just before they all detonated. The flashes blinded me and waves of heat passed through my body. The leaden feeling increased as the suit now lay dead on me after the series of EMR bombs. I'd be going nowhere until out of the thing, but I had some reluctance to remove it, since it might be all that was keeping me alive.

18

'Okay, we've got him,' said a voice. 'Now let's get the fuck out of here.'

Brack stepped into the stairwell to peer down at me. Others crowded in too, weapons pointed at my face, then came Suzeal.

'Strip him,' she said.

'We haven't got time for this!' protested Brack.

She whirled towards him and delivered a gauntleted blow hard to the side of his helmet. He staggered back.

'I will say when we leave!' she spat. 'It may all be over here but don't forget only I can get us into the shuttle and only I control the defences around it, in it and on it. And only I choose who comes aboard.'

He raised a hand. 'Okay.' He waved two of the others ahead.

They grabbed my arms and dragged me up into the corridor. Pain shuddered through my body, in between the patches of familiar numbness. After dumping me on the floor, they proceeded to take off my armour, having to use an atomic shear at one point to get past the damage. Soon I lay naked and, seeing these armoured figures looking down on me, and feeling my complete vulnerability, I realized her comments about arrogance had some truth. A lot of truth, in fact. I tentatively tried to move. I ached from head to foot and could see blood and burns all over my body, but my arms seemed to operate without any bones grating inside. Putting my hands against the floor, I heaved upright.

'That was some suit,' said one of the soldiers.

'Polity manufacture,' Suzeal replied. 'Higher spec than anything you'll find in the Graveyard.' She stared at me with utter hatred. 'And it's good it's gone, isn't it, Jack, because now you'll be able to entertain us.'

I didn't comment, just continued testing my body. My ribs ached but none of them seemed broken. Nothing was moving in my legs in any way it shouldn't. Burns, contusions and cuts seemed to be all of it. Yes, it had been a hell of a suit. I looked up and listened to the sounds of battle. I reckoned the fighting was now down in the entrance to the zoo – some of those explosions sounded very close.

'Pick him up.'

The two stepped forwards again, but I held up a hand and stood by myself, swaying with momentary dizziness, then steadying. One of them shoved me from behind and I continued walking in the direction of the shove. No need to say anything to Suzeal. I knew where this was going and felt no inclination to give her the satisfaction of some verbal exchange. Her gauntleted hand came down on my shoulder, halting me at the entrance to the pen with the fallen walkway.

'I would have liked to have fed you to a hooder,' she said, 'but this will have to do.' She paused in thought for a moment.

I just turned and looked at her.

'Yeah,' interrupted Brack, his fingers up against his aug. 'You might get your wish with the hooders. The fuckers are right down there.' He stabbed a thumb towards the stairwell.

She turned, drew a sidearm and poked it straight in his face. He staggered back with a yell. 'One more word,' she warned.

He nodded then looked towards the end of the corridor as a blast blew smoke and debris up the stairwell. The other soldiers here were getting nervous, shooting glances down that way too. She turned back to me.

'Nothing to say? No questions to ask?'

I shrugged and turned to the doorway, moved to the edge and peered down. I could see that Marcus already lay down there on the ground, unmoving.

'Climb down,' she instructed.

The walkway the prisoners had climbed up still hung to the floor. I reached out and took a hold of a rail and began to work my way down. I took my time about it since they were in such a hurry. The sounds of battle grew in volume so I couldn't hear what they were saying up there, but voices were being raised in anger. Finally reaching the muddy ground, I headed over to Marcus. He lay flat on his back, breathing raggedly. He turned his head and looked at me, moved his mouth but only wheezing sounds came out.

'Here!' Suzeal called. 'You get the same chance as Hunstan!'

A knife with a chain-glass blade thudded into the ground beside me. I stooped and picked it up, then looked up just in time to see a blast blow a hole in the ceiling, raining down molten metal that thankfully fell nowhere near me.

'Go!' Suzeal commanded, and the others moved out of sight. She peered down at me for a moment, then fired a laser carbine at where the walkway was attached. Metal flared and showered sparks, then the thing crashed down into a pile on the floor.

'It's not very hungry today!' she shouted at me. 'That means it will play with you for longer.' She headed away.

Marcus wheezed again, managing to lift a hand and point. A doorway, ten feet square, stood open in the far wall. Through it lay a brightly lit area, as if the door opened onto a planetary surface, in this case being the surface of Masada, since flute grasses grew in there. The knife and the mention of Hunstan confirmed what Suzeal had intimated above: a nasty death. For that doorway opened into the place where she kept her siluroyne.

I studied the knife, having a more urgent use for it now than self-defence. Ignoring the open doorway, I moved closer to Marcus and inspected the bullet holes all over his body. He shifted, rolling one shoulder, and a bright nub of metal squeezed close to the surface. I dug the tip of the knife in and flicked the bullet out, then moved to another hole and probed down into it, finding the bullet a couple of inches down and easing it to the surface and out. Marcus, being infected with the Spatterjay virus, would have healed by now if these had been normal bullets. His body would either have ejected them and healed, or just healed over them. But the sprine in them killed the virus, weakening his ability to recover. Luckily the consistency of his flesh remained the same – woody and tough. This made it easier, once I'd loosened a bullet, to then lever it out of the hole. I'd removed five of them by the time the hole left by the first one had closed up. After another five, I began shooting panicked glances towards the door. This seemed endless, his body a pepper pot, with apparently hundreds in just the one side of it. Then he reached up and took the knife from my hand.

'Find . . . something,' he gestured with the knife towards the debris of the walkway then, grunting and wheezing, heaved up into a sitting position.

I ran over to the mound of debris and began scrabbling at it, feeling horribly vulnerable in my nakedness. Sharp edges and still-smoking metal threatened. Everything still seemed connected together until I turned my attention to one of the harpoon guns. Where its pedestal had torn free from the walkway, it had freed up a series of strengthening struts. These were two-inch I-beams, mostly as long as the width of the walkway – six feet in one case with brackets at each end, four feet in another with the bracket only at one end. They were both light, though the brackets were of a heavier metal. I dragged them out and inspected the weapon itself. No. Severed power leads had rendered it unusable. Maybe the monofilament? No again, since I had no way of handling it. I didn't fancy making the effort and leaving my fingers on the ground.

Marcus had by now opened a flap of skin and muscle down his torso and was flipping out bullet after bullet impacted on his ribcage. Hoopers were more resistant to pain than most but he grimaced as he did it, so I guessed it wasn't pleasant. I squatted beside him, watching the door. He eventually closed up the flap and held it in place, then, when it had sealed itself there, set to work on his right leg. Something shifted in the pile of debris. Surely metal that'd been disturbed during my search? My gaze strayed to what I had earlier thought to be heat haze rising from the metal Suzeal had cut through. But it wasn't heat haze.

I gaped in horror as patches of flute grass colour began to etch themselves out of the air. The thing had been there all the time I'd been searching through the debris, just ten feet away from me. The patches of beige and green, striated like the fronds of the grasses, spread and began to take on different hues: bone white, and red shading from that of fresh blood to the black of old. In a moment, the siluroyne squatted in full view, its night-mare head like a bovine skull poised six feet above the ground. Why had it revealed itself? The thing was an ambush predator that used its camouflage to come unexpectedly on its prey. But, according to Suzeal, it also liked to play. In revealing itself, I felt sure it was doing so, but this also suggested it understood the fear its prey would feel, which bespoke some degree of intelligence. All this went through my mind as I kicked the larger strut over to Marcus and held the smaller one in readiness. Meanwhile, the siluroyne began shrugging itself and squirming as if excited, like a cat watching a pair of mice.

'Unpleasant-looking creature, isn't it?' he said.

I didn't look round at him, but his coherence was reassuring.

'How strong do you feel?' I asked.

'Stronger than you,' he said, 'but much weaker than I was.'

'Suggestions?'

'Stay alive?'

He moved up beside me, leaning on his makeshift weapon as he continued to dig bullets out of his leg. The more he managed to remove, the stronger he would get. He, I knew, was our biggest chance of survival, so I needed to give him as much time as possible. I don't quite know what came over me then because the injustice of it all came crashing down on me and I suddenly grew very angry.

'Right, you fucker,' I said, raising my weapon, and charged.

The siluroyne tilted its head to one side and froze in position, obviously intrigued by this strange behaviour. I just kept going, right up to the damned thing, and swung the length of metal as hard as possible. The bracket at the end went straight into what looked like one of its nostrils with a crunching sound and jammed there, transmitting a brutal shock down through my hands. It roared and hissed nasally, spraying me with mucus coloured by its purple blood and jerked its head back. I hung onto the bar as it lifted me ten feet from the ground. It raised a claw to its face, scrabbling at the bracket jammed into its nostril, and it whipped me from side to side. A moment later, I ended up sailing through the air to land hard on my back.

I got up quickly, in time to see the thing fade out, and to trace the shimmer of its movement as it ran off to my left, circling round. I lost track of it over by the door into its own area. Had I driven it away? The prey can sufficiently put off a predator if the latter is well fed, but I doubted this creature would be deterred for long. It had become accustomed to feeding on people and, as I had seen with Hunstan, people who fought back.

'Well that probably annoyed it,' said Marcus, 'not that whether or not it's annoyed is germane.' Much better. I glanced back at him, still digging out the bullets. He waved me over and held up the knife. 'I need you to dig them out of my back. I'll keep watch.'

'Over there.' I pointed to an area where terran grass hadn't been trampled down around a patch of briar.

'Good idea.'

I didn't need to explain to him that, though we couldn't see the thing, we had a better chance watching out for it in a place where we might see movement. We headed over, warily checking our surroundings, and waded into the grass and up beside the briar. With that at my back, I set to work with the knife, careless of inflicting damage as I levered out bullets. One patch over his shoulder blade was full of them. I sliced down the side of it and levered up a big flap of tissue to get to the slugs, all imbedded in bone as tough as combat armour. As I pressed it all back, bullet free, and held it in place, the grasses shifted ahead of us. The siluroyne appeared with squid-like waves of visibility traversing its body, then began to pace around our refuge.

'Just keep digging,' Marcus instructed when I paused.

He turned to track it and I kept working, as quickly as possible. The two bullets in the back of his skull came out easily, while the ones in his thighs required deeper work, with some I simply couldn't get to. However, when I completed one leg and looked at them again, they'd come closer to the surface and I was able to lever out a few.

'Don't stop,' said Marcus.

'I understood you the first time,' I snapped back.

The siluroyne made one complete circuit and we turned with it until we were back in our original position. It grew utterly still and disappeared. It next issued a low rumbling growl and the ground kicked up as the grass parted. Marcus shoved me away, swung back the strut and, timing to the movement of the grass, swung it back so hard and fast that it made the kind of sound one would expect from a whip. It seemed to stop in mid-air, impacting with a soggy crunch, and Marcus's feet left the ground, the force telegraphing through him and flinging him aside. The monster reappeared briefly with a dent in the top of its head, leaking fluid, and pieces of bone or carapace sticking out. It rounded on him, tearing up grass as it shot back in. He stooped into its charge, wedging one end of his strut against the ground, the other end directed at its chest. They slammed together, then the siluroyne went over him, flipped by the length of metal and crashing down on its back. By now, I was close enough to bring my weapon down hard on its translucent body. The bracket sank in then bounced out. It was like hitting rubber, but it obviously hurt, for the thing rolled away from me hissing. It faded to near invisibility again as it beat a retreat through the grass.

'Bullets,' Marcus snapped, picking up one half of his strut and tugging the other half from the ground. The two halves now had vicious jagged ends and he held them like swords.

I grabbed up the knife and set to work again as the siluroyne reappeared. Its purple blood dripped from its face and, where Marcus had struck it, a bulbous swelling had risen. I noted it probing its lower body with one claw. I continued to dig out bullets as Marcus noticed this too.

'The head is least vulnerable, but for those eyes,' he said. 'Heavy bone or whatever.' I worked down his other leg just as fast as I could. He glanced over his shoulder. 'That's a chain-glass knife. It won't break and it won't lose its edge. You go for its belly.'

'Go for its belly?' I repeated stupidly.

He stepped forwards, brandishing his weapons. 'Come on, you bastard!'

The siluroyne snarled, going down on its foreclaws. He broke into a run towards it and I hurried to catch up. They slammed together and it grabbed him, ploughing him into the ground and jamming a leg in its mouth. Seemingly oblivious to this, Marcus stabbed one half of a strut straight into its eye and, using it to brace himself in place, used the other one to stab at its other eyes. It howled as I ran round and then in at the side. At the last moment, I discarded the strut and slid feet first underneath the thing. I stabbed up with the knife and sliced, then sliced again and again, doing as much damage as possible. Blood spattered down on me, unexpectedly cool. I tasted its acidity in my mouth and saw something gaping and pulsing out a stream of it. Then a great mass of liver-like organs and ropy objects studded with sacs fell on top of me. I sliced across that and blue fluid squirted out, just before its back claw dug forwards and flung me away.

I landed on my face, rolled over and leapt up – no pain, just adrenalin. The creature reared up, Marcus still clamped in its jaws and now cursing and yelling. He'd lost one of his weapons, but was trying to drive the other deeper into one of its eyes. The creature came down again and tried to run, but it stepped on its own viscera and howled, releasing its hold on Marcus. He clambered up, ragged skin hanging from his leg, and wrapped both legs around its neck then, bracing there, drove the half-strut deeper and deeper. With a low thudding crunch, the metal went through, poking out the front of its neck. The siluroyne crashed to the ground, flinging him clear, and lay there shivering.

It was stupid really, considering the situation, but I felt terribly guilty for having played my part in its slaughter. I staggered then, suddenly feeling very dizzy.

'I didn't know if its brain was in its head,' said Marcus, climbing to his feet and holding down a flap of skin and muscle on his leg. 'Seems it was.'

'Seems so,' I agreed, mouth dry, eyesight kinda fuzzy.

'That doesn't look so good,' he said, pointing at my torso.

I looked down at the claw slice extending from my chest down to my right hip, and at the streaming blood and loop of intestine protruding. It felt just, somehow, that the creature had done to me what I'd done to it, then I collapsed face-first in the mud.

Consciousness came in brief flashes. I dangled high above flute grasses and looked down at my body. A twisted rope of grasses ran from armpit to armpit, holding me up. I guessed that was the reason I was having difficulty breathing. Further grasses wrapped my torso, soaked in blood. I reached up to try and relieve some of the pressure of the rope, but my hand fell away, weak as dough.

'Chain-glass,' said Marcus. 'With the strength to drive, it can cut anything.'

'That's good,' I managed, noting how his speech no longer slurred or hissed, before I went away again.

I woke in agony and tried to knock away the thing digging at my body. Aboard the King's Ship again, a metal ship louse feasted on me, making horrible grinding sounds and stinking of burned metal. But I couldn't move my arms, which were clamped up above my head. When I tried to kick, legs wrapped around mine and Marcus's face loomed close.

'Keep still,' he instructed.

His face surprised me for a second because there seemed little of the viral mutation remaining in it, but still I couldn't obey him. The pain was too much. Nevertheless he kept me clamped there . . . now I was on Vrasan's table and the prador just kept on cutting. I screamed into blackness, then saw walls sliding by to the sound of metal on metal.

I looked down at the autodoc attached to my torso. The thing had been burned and partially melted but had various pipes inserted around a long wound stitched together with wire, and I understood. At least I could no longer see my own guts sticking out. I became aware of a travois under me made of a floor grating but, after a short time, that awareness went away again.

When my consciousness returned the next time, it stuck around. I didn't feel delirious and quickly understood my location in time and place. Certainly the room had to be somewhere in the Stratogaster station, and certainly some hours had passed since a siluroyne had attempted to repay me for eviscerating it. I lay on a piece of foam in a small room. A couple of light squares, in a row of them along one wall, cast a dull illumination by which I could see a pile of containers, weapons and other equipment. A low bench and a couple of chairs stood to one side. On that were food packages and bottles. I really wanted to get to them but as yet didn't dare move or even look at myself. A near-empty drip feed hung from a piece of ratty string attached to a hook in the ceiling, with the tube running down to enter my forearm. By the colour, the thing certainly didn't contain saline. Just a couple of feet out from my forearm lay the autodoc. It had been damaged and now lay partially disassembled. I then braved a peer down to my torso.

My gut looked bloated – straining against the wire stitches holding it together – and my body ached horribly. Fluid had leaked out to leave a worrying yellow crust. I tried to ease upright, got a little way, but then a terrible cramp in my guts froze me in place. I groaned, wondering what repairs my movement might have broken, then my anus signalled intent before opening. With a horrible sputtering of wind and squirting fluid, my bowels emptied. The stink was foul, a combination of shit and rotting meat. The foam darkened beneath me, with new wetness spreading amidst old stains. Even so, my guts noticeably deflated, bringing huge relief, and I finally sat up.

Had Marcus done what he could for me and then, seeing the task as impossible, abandoned me? The smell worried me. Gangrene? No, I shouldn't think so negatively. By now my nano-suite should be up and running and any infections were highly unlikely. Also, the pain wasn't the agony I would have felt had my guts been rotting. Marcus had obviously collected the equipment here and perhaps gone off for more. The stuff in that feed must be some form of medication too. I recollected the moments of lucidity. He had bound up my wound with flute grass and hauled me out of our prison. I now realized the walls in one of the enclosures must have been some material softer than ceramal, because he'd been able to cut handholds in it with the chain-glass knife. Thereafter, he'd done what he could with a damaged autodoc before bringing me here, to some form of safety.

Even as I took a step towards the table, my belly rumbled and intense hunger and thirst made themselves felt. I hesitated. Was it a good idea to eat so soon after seeing my guts exposed to the air? Closing my eyes for a moment, I concentrated on the know-ledge of my erstwhile self. Even if my bowel had been opened, the nanosuite would have worked fast to seal it up and that would have been after what the autodoc had managed to do. That suite would be clearing toxins and infections, accelerating repair at a cellular level. Meanwhile it was also boosting me. In both cases, it needed energy and materials to work with. I pulled the drip feed needle from my arm, went over to the table and opened packets containing fish in oil, protein slabs, dried fruit and a dense chocolate and cherry fudge. I gulped them, washing them down with a drink from a large bottle of mint-flavoured water. On finishing, weariness hammered me, but I didn't want to lie down on the stinking mattress. I sat on a chair, rested my arms on the table and lay my head on them.

'Wash yourself.'

I jerked awake. Sleep had hit me like a bludgeon and I had no idea how much time had passed. A man stood over me, clad in a neat envirosuit. He'd placed a bucket of water by the chair, and now put a bottle of antiseptic soap on the table and a rough sponge beside it. I eyed a nearby bottle of wine as a potential weapon, but a moment later realization struck me.

'You're much improved,' I said.

'Though it wasn't her intention, Suzeal did me a favour filling me with sprine bullets,' Marcus replied. 'They regressed the virus enough for . . .' He waved a hand at his face and his body. 'This.'

The only difference between him and somebody uninfected now was a slight bluish tinge to his skin, as well as a pointiness about the ears and the claw-like fingernails on one hand. His face did not look right – it seemed too long and bony and the eyes too sunken – but it wasn't alien. He could now pass for human and, in reality, there were plenty of 'humans' who looked a lot more exotic, through cosmetic and adaptogenic alterations.

'How strong are you?' I asked, sliding out of the chair and standing. I felt stronger and practically buzzing with energy after my feed. Glancing down at my front, I noted that my belly had shrunk further and the wound, though still wired shut, looked as if it had sealed nicely.

'About the level of a hundred-and-fifty-year-old hooper,' he replied. 'Perhaps straying up towards the strength of an Old Captain.'

Knowledge came to my mind of Spatterjay's Old Captains. They were residents of that world and hoopers, with a legendary strength and durability. It took centuries of being infected with the virus to make them the way they were. I didn't know how long Marcus had been infected but certainly not that long. Then again, the prador had altered the virus in him, and it had likely undergone stressed, accelerated growth.

He pointed down at the bucket. 'Deal with yourself.' He stepped over to the amassed equipment. Now I noticed the smell again and saw that while sleeping on the chair, I'd had another involuntary bowel movement. I moved the chair over to one wall then kicked the foam mattress after it. I felt embarrassed, but that was rather foolish. I imagined Marcus himself had gone through worse in the King's Ship.

I washed standing on the end of the mattress so it could soak up the spill. By the time I'd finished, the water remaining in the bucket had turned filthy red. He tossed me a towel to wipe off the remainder with it. I discarded it on the chair when he handed me a neat cellophane-wrapped envirosuit and even some underclothes. I dressed.

'You've been busy. How long have I been out of it?' I asked.

'Twenty hours.'

I looked up. 'Really? What's happened?'

'A lot. Finish getting dressed and I'll show you.'

I closed up the envirosuit. Its tech was pretty good: power storage in graphene and other meta-material layers that also acted as a temperature regulator and recharged themselves from movement, with heat differentials and EMR. A wrist unit threw up an interactive control hologram. I discovered a fabric hood that slid up over the head, and then the face, at the touch of a finger control – the front of this also turned transparent, offering a HUD – while gloves clad the hands in the same manner and retained touch sensitivity. Once I understood its operation, I checked out his other supplies, attaching a gas-system pulse gun in a blood-specked holster to a stick patch at my hip, as well as selecting a twin-barrelled carbine that fired pulses of ionized aluminium from one barrel and a selection of projectiles from the other. Ammunition too. I then eyed the packs and other items.

'Food, drink and ammunition,' said Marcus. 'Once I've shown you what's out there, we'll head straight for the rim.'

I let that 'out there' slide and asked, 'What's the situation in the station? Salander?' I hurriedly filled a pack with items, hesitated between protein bars and a couple of sticky bombs that lay there, then chose the bombs. There were prador on this station; dealing with them had higher importance than the demands of my stomach.

He set off out through the door into a ratty, rubbish-strewn corridor. 'The prador are in full control now. Salander kept her forces at the rim, and some way in, to get refugees to the escape pods. Hundreds of those are already out in vacuum. She had a fight with the remnants of Suzeal's soldiers but that soon ended – they were anxious to get away from what was behind them and surrendered. She's disarming them and dispatching them in the pods too.'

'You're in contact with her?'

'Not just her.'

'Who else?'

'You'll see.' Marcus grinned, which was something he hadn't really been capable of before.

He led me through the station via corridors and powered-down dropshafts I had become tired of seeing. Remnants of battle lay all around: bullet holes and beam burns, walls pulled down or melted, areas torn open by explosions, and corpses everywhere.

Most of these were Suzeal's soldiers but I felt sickened on seeing those that weren't. Breach sealants snowed in some areas, occasionally we had to close up our suits where smoke boiled thick. At one point we came to a tunnel cut through the station without regard for walls.

'Hooder,' said Marcus, and we moved on.

Eventually we came to a pipe devoid of grav. We propelled ourselves along this to where it came up like a well mouth in a circular floor paved with bricks of green and red gemstone. As we pushed ourselves out onto this, grav slowly engaged to bring us down on our feet. Marcus had brought us out to one face of the station disc, for we stood under a dome of chain-glass. I gazed at the immense view, finally bringing my attention to the station itself.

'Fuck!'

I ducked down to try and get some cover behind the opaque ring of material that supported the dome, but couldn't get low enough. Prador stood out there, on the face of the station, a line of them running in a curve that passed close by us, with the nearest only fifty or so feet away.

'Don't concern yourself,' said Marcus. 'The glass is one way.'

I stood up, annoyed because I should've realized that.

'What're they doing?'

'Watching and updating on events,' he replied. 'They were ordered out here in readiness to head for the rim, as it's the shortest and easiest route, but now circumstances have changed.' He pointed. 'Do you see?'

I looked to where he indicated and saw a lozenge-shaped object floating high over the planet. I recognized it at once but allowed him his moment.

'That's the Polity dreadnought the *Hamilton*. It has the usual complement of weapons, but also a large medical contingent, along with accommodation for thousands and cryo or gel storage for tens of thousands. It's eight miles long.'

'And those?' I pointed.

'The agreement between the king and Earth Central is for neither side to have an advantage. Apparently they wrangled for some time about what that meant. Those are reavers, four of them, whose firepower and tactical advantage are higher from being four separate ships, making them supposedly equal to that of the *Hamilton.*'

The four ships, bearing the shape of extended teardrops, gleamed orange in the glare of the sun. They stood arrayed just out from the Polity dreadnought, and I had no doubt some itchy fingers were on triggers . . . or rather claws.

'I detect that you don't think that's the case.'

'The *Hamilton* is run by AI, and we have a lot of weapons the prador don't know about.'

I noted that *we* and stored it away for later.

'The prador have weapons the Polity doesn't know about too,' I noted.

He turned and shook his head. 'If you're talking about Vrasan's hooders, that secret came out the moment he attacked here. Suzeal might have kept U-com under wraps in the station but she couldn't cut it in the ships at the docking moon. Someone contacted the Polity immediately – probably an agent – and that's why both the Polity and the prador are here. And that is also why the *Hamilton* is over there.' He gestured to the planet.

'You've been in contact with them too,' I suggested.

He tapped a comlink in his ear. 'Suzeal's jamming is dead now. The captain of the *Hamilton* has been speaking to me on occasion. He kindly waited until we got here before the fireworks start.' He looked back at the planet. 'And now they are.'

Lights flickered all over the dreadnought and just a moment

later hundreds of vapour trails appeared in atmosphere. These travelled round the globe. Next it seemed that the planet grew spines, all directed towards the ship. The first were missiles obviously seeking out targets that lay out of line of sight. The second were railgun strikes, already hitting before their vapour trails appeared. Then further spines extended out of the ship, actinic blue in vacuum, then turning royal purple as they punched down. Particle beams. Was there anything this ship *wasn't* firing? Below, the surface of the planet became spotted with red-orange glows, massive explosions and firestorms forming.

'I don't understand,' I said.

He looked at me. 'Do you think the Polity can allow the prador access to hooders that they'll weaponize? This, in the end, is why Vrasan is here: to secure a supply of them.'

I felt abruptly sad about that. The creatures weren't exactly cuddly but exterminating them seemed an unutterable shame.

'Shit,' he said. 'They've responded.'

Explosions now bloomed around the *Hamilton* across hardfields, like scales of amber glass flashing into existence in vacuum. The dreadnought jutted four long ribbed flames of fusion and shot out in a curving course away from the planet. The reavers moved as well, and then they too disappeared behind a firestorm and a sudden proliferation of defensive fields. Meanwhile, the prador on the skin of the station abruptly set into motion, leaping out into vacuum and firing up suit thrusters. A moment later, a scattering of them simply exploded and they were down again, pulling open large hatches back into the station.

Marcus stood there, head darting from side to side as he tried to take it all in.

'Railgun, close – something else here. Probably a black ops attack ship. Come on!' He leapt to the tube, dropping straight into it. I followed, unsure whether the situation had improved or not. Sure, the Polity had arrived and might make mincemeat of the prador, but that wasn't any comfort for anyone outside either that dreadnought or this supposed black ops attack ship. Space stations involved in space battles tended to have a short lifespan.

'Will we be any safer in an escape pod?' I asked as we headed at speed through the station.

'They have their own drive systems,' he said, 'and now things have blown up here she might escape.'

I didn't need to ask who the 'she' was.

'Where?' I asked.

'The docking moon,' he supplied.

19

The prador seemed as surprised to see us as we were to see it.
But it soon got over that and began spraying the tubeway with
Gatling fire. I froze for a second as the air filled with hot metal
slugs and metal splinters, then remembered my envirosuit only
had impact layers and dived back into the side corridor. Marcus
followed me a moment later and we got up and ran, shots
smacking and zinging through the walls around us until we'd put
the tubeway some yards behind us.

'Best we keep to the smaller corridors,' he opined.

'Seems like a good idea.'

We moved on. In retrospect it'd been a mistake to try and
use one of the quickest routes to the rim since, of course, the
prador were using those. I think Marcus realized that because
he looked annoyed. A moment later, our surroundings seemed
to jerk to one side and a deep rumbling vibration shook the
station.

'Debris probably,' said Marcus. 'Or a stray shot.'

He quickly threw up his wrist hologram and made some adjustments. In response, my suit made a buzzing I recognized from
the planet and I flicked up my control hologram to see a comlink
request with two subsidiary links attached. If I accepted the first
I accepted all three. I glanced at Marcus.

'That's me,' he said.

I accepted the first link from 'Suit 0098G' and the rest established. They were 'Salander' and '*Hamilton*'. A moment later, as Marcus worked his own suit hologram, the suit designation changed to 'Marcus'.

'If I get killed you'll be able to talk to those others,' he explained. 'I made a mistake cutting you out before. I've made too many mistakes.'

I didn't think so, but then perhaps didn't have his expectations. The fact he'd done this a moment after that hit on the station, whatever it might have been, didn't reassure me. I felt our survival expectations had just plummeted. I pulled one earphone from the collar and plugged it into my ear.

'You know they're heading your way?' he asked.

I was about to ask what he meant when Salander answered him – he'd included me in the exchange.

'I know. We've blocked the large tubeways and established mosquitoes and other autoguns in them,' she replied.

'That'll only delay them.'

'I know that too, but if we can hold them for maybe four hours we'll all be out of here.' She paused for a second. 'Supposing some stray shot from out there doesn't destroy the station.'

'You won't have four hours. Mosquitoes might inconvenience them but won't get through their armour.'

'Other autos have armour-piercers and I have four rail beaders in the main tubeways. I've also got units in the side tunnels with sticky mines and iron-burner missile launchers.'

Marcus grunted an acknowledgement. Obviously Salander knew what she was doing.

'Why are they attacking the rim?' I asked. 'The people are leaving and they have what they want. It doesn't seem rational.'

Marcus glanced at me, about to reply, but Salander got there before him. 'I don't think Vrasan is entirely rational and, anyway, why expect rationality from the prador? They're pissed off because the ship out there just tried to wipe out the hooders, which it seems likely were their main reason for coming here. And right now, a Polity dreadnought and four reavers are knocking the shit out of each other.'

'Okay, right,' I said, feeling stupid.

'We're heading for the rim now,' said Marcus. 'Tell your people I want to take an escape pod – no passengers.'

'That's a waste,' she replied tartly. 'We're overloading them now.'

'Suzeal took her shuttle to the docking moon and I'm going after her.'

After a long pause she replied, 'Okay I've relayed that. Do you know where and when you'll reach the rim?'

'Sector Seven, unless we have problems – a couple of hours hence.'

'Right, I've told Trecannon. Now I've got a bag of sticky mines I want to make use of. Confine contact to the necessary.' She cut com, but the link remained.

'Do you think she'll be able to get everyone out?' I asked.

'Probably, but her problems won't end then,' Marcus replied. 'They'll be out there defenceless, and if Vrasan wants to start taking pot shots at them . . .'

'There's the black ops attack ship,' I noted.

'Which the captain of the *Hamilton* has neither confirmed nor denied.'

'Does that matter now?'

He shrugged. 'I doubt the prador are trying to destroy the *Hamilton*. They just want to stop it wiping out the hooders. And there'll be fast negotiations between Earth Central and the Kingdom. Neither side wants war.'

I still didn't feel reassured.

'So surely, with everything else, the presence of a black ops ship is irrelevant to the prador now?'

'It wasn't in any agreement between Earth Central and the king. Its presence, if revealed, may be one push too far. They'll keep it under wraps for now.'

'I see,' I said, not sure if I did. However, on that premise it occurred to me that the shots the black ops ship had taken earlier were deniable – they could have come from the *Hamilton*. But if it started hitting prador and their weapons on the station, to defend the escape pods, it would soon become obvious it wasn't the *Hamilton* firing. It might be that it wouldn't leap to their defence at all.

Travelling via the smaller tunnels, we had no further encounters with the prador. We did, however, traverse a corridor with skylights in the ceiling, and it was like passing under working arc welders as the ships out there fired on each other. I put up my hood and visor and searched the suit's system, eventually finding a map of the station which gave our position. Thankfully we were past the halfway mark between hub and rim, but that still left us about ten miles to travel. We could speed up through sections without grav, but would have to take diversions.

'Another caller,' said Marcus shortly after my map reading. 'Take a look.' In retrospect, I wondered if it was my use of the map, which might have been downloaded from station computing, that gave our location. I called up the comlink menu in my visor and eyed the name that had appeared there: Vrasan.

'Probably not a good idea to answer,' I suggested.

Marcus shrugged. 'Comlinks will give away your location if you open one you already have to someone. But for someone to send you a link, they must at least have a vague idea of where you are in the first place.'

I knew that. Or rather, after he'd told me, I realized I knew that.

'Should we reply to him?' I asked, just as the station shuddered again from another impact.

'You can, if you wish. He has nothing to say that interests me now.'

We moved on through a narrow tube, then out of that into a chamber with a fusion reactor sitting at the centre, like a pinned bacterium. I thought back to my previous exchange with the white-armoured prador. He'd told me he would find me and do something nasty to me. It seemed like a good idea to talk, since maybe he'd give away something further about his intent, which we could act on. I opened the link.

'Vrasan,' I said.

He appeared in my visor but I banished the image so I could see where I was going. I belatedly included Marcus in the exchange too.

'Jack Four,' said the prador.

'Things are not looking good for your plans right now, but you can't blame me for interfering this time,' I said.

'I can and do blame you. You are a clone from a Polity agent so represent that organization. I cannot reach the ship out there but I can reach you.'

'So that's all this call is about: another opportunity for you to threaten me?'

'You survived the siluroyne, but mainly because you had the experiment there with you. He interests me. He was more resistant to control than he should have been and has returned to human form quicker than seems feasible.'

Marcus interjected, 'If you had me up close you wouldn't enjoy how interesting I can be.'

'But I do want you up close to examine. There is a mental

component involved in the transformations caused by the Spatterjay virus. The extent of your mutation should have wrecked your mind and a change in diet and sprine bullets shouldn't have brought you back to your present state.'

'How interesting,' said Marcus.

'I will capture and kill Jack as slowly as the feeding of a hooder can be made, but you I must study.'

'Go fuck yourself,' said Marcus.

'And now I see you better, I can make comparisons,' said Vrasan.

Marcus turned to me and drew his finger across his throat. I hesitated for just a second then cut the connection.

'Hooders coming,' he said. 'We have to move fast and without distraction.'

He accelerated into a run and I hurried to catch up. Much about that exchange bothered me. I too had suspected that Marcus's recovery was unusual and now it had been confirmed. It would have to wait, however, because as he said, hooders were coming.

We kept going at this fast pace for a few miles. I expected the exertion to hurt, but instead ran easily with my breathing only slightly heavier. The boosting effects, along with the increased muscle and strengthened bones, were greater lung capacity and oxygen transport. Then the station began to vibrate all around us and a distant crashing grew closer and closer. A few minutes later, one of the hooders tore through the wall a hundred yards behind us then turned to follow the corridor, tearing out the walls as it came so it could fit through. As we ran I glanced back repeatedly. The relentless thing almost kept pace with us despite the station infrastructure in the way.

I threw up the map in my HUD, then the control hologram.

Using these slowed me, but we could not keep up this pace right to the rim, and eventually our pursuer would catch up. A few alterations to the map gave me the station schematic and I started hunting for what we needed. *There.* I dismissed the hologram but kept the schematic in place, managing to study it and at the same time not fall on my face.

'Second left,' I said to Marcus.

He glanced at me, and instead of asking what I planned, simply gave a brief nod. We passed the first left and swerved into the second. A short corridor took us to a walkway with a stair leading down into a small factory.

'We don't want open spaces,' said Marcus, pausing at the sight.

'Keep moving!' I snapped, hardly seeming to touch the steps as I flew down the stairs. He followed because he had no choice and we sprinted across the factory floor. Behind us the crashing noise increased in volume, then with a final loud bang and sound of falling debris, the hooder flowed over the walkway towards the floor behind us.

'There!' I pointed at another stair going up to a similar walkway on the other side. Even as we reached it and began to climb, a pink meniscus hit the stair and walkway above us like a flying wall. It folded up, crushing and twisting the metal but then faded out. Still a way up, the wrecked stair remained and we scrambled up it. At the top, I ran along to a circular bulkhead door. I struggled with the wheel but Marcus stepped in and grabbed it, easily turning it, and yanked the door open. Once we were on the other side, he slammed it shut and spun the wheel.

'Good idea,' he acknowledged, briefly studying the bulkhead wall in which the door had been set. 'But that won't hold it for long and we don't know where the others are.'

The wall was part of the strengthening of the station: ceramal and I-beams, bearing metals and compression foams. A structure of this size, turning next to a gravity well, needed such things to hold it together. We ran on as behind us the hooder hammered against that wall. A glance back didn't even show a dent and soon the wall fell out of sight.

'We need to get to the rim.' Marcus took us to the right and then after a couple of switches, back on course. On the schematic I studied his likely course and looked for bulkhead walls, rows of strengthening I-beams and other heavy tough structure we could put between ourselves and these things. By now, even though beginning to pant, I felt no urge to slow down. While I kept checking the schematic, Marcus got ahead of me, then he skidded to a halt and swore. Catching up with him I saw the problem.

The corridor we'd been running along now ended at a gulf. A section of the station had been hollowed out – its materials compacted on a nominal floor – though when I waved my hand beyond the ending of the corridor floor, I felt no grav.

'There.' Marcus pointed.

A hooder lay coiled at the far end and, even as we watched, it began to uncoil and quest outwards. Marcus turned to go back, but I caught his arm.

'Wait.'

'What is it?'

I kept watching the creature, sure something here wasn't right. The things didn't normally coil up. In fact, I suddenly felt utterly sure this was something they did when injured. Also it wasn't moving very fast – as hesitant as an arthritic old man. I flipped up the control hologram, found visor magnification and focused in on the thing. Its body looked generally as healthy as before, but something odd impinged about its thrall hardware. It looked battered, which one would have expected since the thing had been in battle and crashing about in the structure of the station. Then I saw it. The hardware wasn't quite moving in consonance with the beast itself. Pieces of the chain of ceramal had ridden up and come partially detached.

'He's losing control of them,' I said, running a few paces back then forwards again, hurling myself into the gulf.

'This was something we should have discussed,' said Marcus through the comlink.

As I flew across the gulf, I looked back. He'd followed, of course.

Directly ahead lay the continuation of the corridor, but it steadily began to drop away as my course diverged, either because of the initial leap or the surrounding grav effect. The hooder still moved hesitantly, but then it thrashed, lines of light passing down its length and the chain of thrall components on its back breaking. It dived down, straight into the wreckage, smashing and wriggling through it, then coming back up again. As it surfaced, I saw it had peeled away half of the device. But now it lay much closer and I had yet to reach the other side.

'This was not a good idea,' Marcus commented.

The creature briefly oriented towards us, then it turned, releasing a fusillade of the white beam shots from down the length of its body. I closed my eyes, expecting to die, then opened them when I hadn't. The shots were passing underneath us and burning through wreckage far to my left. The hooder slammed through the wall we'd departed, a hundred yards to one side, and flowed in. It wasn't coming after us.

'Lucky,' said Marcus.

I glanced back at him as, behind him, the wall of the gulf peeled open and another hooder flowed out. This one had a complete, though partially detached, thrall and I guessed it was the one that'd been following us originally. The next moment I slammed into a buckled wall section above the corridor, just managing to grab a skein of optics to stop bouncing away. I scrambled down, grabbing available holds, and swung into the corridor. A second later Marcus followed me in. Rather than run straight away, I used the selector on my weapon and chose mini-grenades and opened fire. Avoiding the hooder's head, I instead aimed along the length of its thrall hardware. Explosions ran in a line down its back. Most had little effect but one hit underneath one of the loose segments and lifted it, tearing free a couple more further along the chain. But the hooder kept coming.

'Run!' Marcus shouted.

With grav out in the continuation of the corridor, no running would be possible. We propelled ourselves fast along it as a meniscus hit behind, then travelled down the corridor towards us. It would reach me first and Marcus just a second later. Would it crush us, burn us, or what? The thing faded out just a few yards behind me, shorting into the walls. This confirmed what I'd thought with the other hooder.

'They're fighting Vrasan's thralls!' I shouted.

'They still might kill us if they catch us,' he stated.

That was true. Vrasan had returned the things to their prior iteration as war machines and they apparently didn't like his control of them. But they were alien war machines who'd been vicious predators. In this case, the enemy of my enemy might not be my friend. The hooder continued its destructive progress towards us as we rounded a corner. Another bulkhead door lay ahead, but that was just luck since there'd been nowhere else to run. Marcus opened it and we paused at the threshold, for another big tubeway lay before us.

'No prador,' he stated.

'Worth putting some distance between us and it?' I suggested.

'Not much choice,' he said. Checking his map, he added, 'Two hundred yards ahead.' By this time we bounded along the low-grav central strip. We'd nearly reached the point to leave the way when the hooder came through the wall where we'd departed it. We turned in, Marcus working the console of an atmosphere-sealed door just as a meniscus sped past us, raising the hairs on the back of my neck. Dammit, the thing had deliberately missed us! I shrugged off my pack, a stupid and crazy idea occurring. I dragged out the two sticky mines. The things were designed as prador killers, their blast focused by planar explosive to a single point behind a tetrahedron of hyper-diamond.

'What the fuck?' Marcus said, as I dropped my rifle and bounded towards the hooder.

As with my attack on the siluroyne, I'd not given myself any time to think about it. But while running, I began to, and understood the difference between this and a crazy attack on an animal. The hooder didn't seem to know how to respond, its head weaving from side to side. It turned and emitted the white beam from behind its head, but not straight at me – it tracked along the central path towards me, burning through the floor like a thermic lance. As the beam drew close, I threw myself to one side. With grav only on the path, I shot straight towards the wall, flipping over as I approached it. The hooder came opposite me as I absorbed the impact in my legs and propelled myself away, flying towards the middle of its body. It began to turn towards me as my feet hit its side and I fell forwards across its back. My hands went down, bonding the two sticky mines to two thrall segments which seemed firmly attached still. I then spun over the top of the thing, tumbling towards the further wall of the tubeway, which I slammed into, back first. From there I got a good view of the two mines detonating. Two blinding flashes blanked my visor for a second, and the two segments of thrall shattered and exploded away. The hooder bucked at that point, then thrashed, its spoon head knifing into the wall just twenty feet along from me. It carved back towards me, raking up a mass of debris. By now I had my feet underneath me and launched again, tumbling over the thing and falling down towards the walkway. The moment my feet touched, I set out at a run without looking back.

'Are you ready to do that again?' Marcus enquired.

He ran towards me as another hooder came through the wall behind him, where he'd opened the door. The hooder I'd mined was still going crazy, writhing like an electrocuted snake. It smashed against the walls and tied itself in knots – just a great balled mass of segmented carapace turning like a series of conjoined wheels. But the one ahead showed neither hesitation nor inclination to shoot off target. It spat a pink meniscus that hit Marcus like a sheet of lead and slammed him against the side of the tubeway, pinning him there. A moment later, it turned towards me. I immediately felt as if I was running through porridge, the air turning rose hued all around. The meniscus picked me up and threw me against the wall too, just a few yards away from Marcus. As the creature flowed clear of the wall, I saw it was one with all its control hardware intact and firmly attached. Had I now, through delaying us here, just killed us?

The thing reared before us and, despite the cacophony in the tubeway, I heard the comlink chime and saw the request come up. I couldn't move to answer it and felt little inclination to talk to Vrasan. Then the meniscus over me loosened, and I had second thoughts – the longer I could keep Vrasan talking the better.

'What do you want?' I asked.

'Again you interfere!' he raged. The translation to Anglic was very good because his human voice did sound angry. Or perhaps he could speak it, not strictly having the physiognomy of a prador.

'You mean I had the temerity to try and survive?' I enquired. When he didn't reply, I continued, 'If you're calling me to talk about further dire punishments I think you've mined that one as deep as you can go.'

'Interfere,' he managed, then, 'human.'

His image appeared in my visor in a chaos of turning red carapace shot through with blue lights. I gathered the display reflected his problems with the hooders in the real world. Even so, I should have been terrified but wasn't. I'd been through so much damage and pain by now, and so many near-death experiences, that this all seemed to be the inevitable termination of my brief life. Because he'd caused the hooder to release some of its hold on me, I reached down to my sidearm, managing to draw and point it inwards and up towards my heart. But my hand froze and the force around me tightened. It pushed the weapon out again, then flicked it from my hand.

'Not so . . . easy,' he said.

Another crashing sound issued from my right, past Marcus and, peripherally, I saw the third hooder had arrived in the tubeway. I also noticed the racket to my left had died. The hooder before us turned its spoon head in the second direction, just as the hooder whose thrall I'd damaged speared in. They crashed together hard – it was like standing just a few paces away from a train wreck. The force holding me in place died and Marcus reached over to grab my shoulder, pulling me. We scrambled along the tubeway, just as the edge of a hooder body dug into the wall where we'd been. The two were in a knotted mass fighting each other. Then the third one hammered in too. In a moment, the whole area turned into a slow-motion explosion. The tubeway disappeared and debris surrounded us, the writhing hooder bodies entangled together. Marcus grabbed me again, his hand a hideously strong clamp around my upper arm. He launched himself hard, near dislocating my shoulder, and we fell into a space surrounded by sharp metal, with chunks of insulation snowing through the air. He quickly jammed us into a smaller space under some I-beams as two hooder bodies, wound together like a DNA spiral, drilled through the previous space. As this happened, I saw a thrall segment tumble clear, and another one. Then the hooders were back where, nominally, the tubeway had been, tearing at each other. We just crouched, hoping the things wouldn't come our way again. It occurred to me that perhaps this scene had already played out once – in that gulf where we'd seen the first damaged hooder. Then, as if someone had hit an off-button, it ended.

A great chunk had been torn out of the interior of the space station. At its centre sat the three hooders, all knotted together but now slowly unravelling. Chunks of metal, composite and other items fell through the air all around, then, abruptly, all this debris started orbiting the hooders. A giant flash bulb ignited at their core and the creatures turned translucent, like pink glass, as they continued to separate. I was riveted. The danger here was horrifying, yet the scene so utterly beautiful.

'Oh fuck,' said Marcus, as one of their spoon-shaped heads appeared and then swung round towards us.

I scanned around for some place to run, but compacted wreckage closed everything off. It slid towards us, the light going out, all the hooders returning to their oiled machine appearance. The hood turned up to cover the top of the space we occupied. I looked up into the face of hell as the rows of red eyes observed us. Heat grew at the centre of my body, spreading in a wave. The thing was scanning us. It then suddenly pulled away, paused for a second, and speared into a wall of wreckage and through it. As its tail disappeared from sight, I realized it was the last to depart. No hooders remained nearby.

It took us half an hour, and the application of one of Marcus's sticky mines, to get into a station corridor. We travelled along this until we found a turning towards the rim. All the while, rumbling movement and then distant explosions and sounds of weapons fire reached us. I assumed the hooders had headed straight back to Vrasan and hoped they would give him serious trouble. The rumbling grew to a steady vibration as the corridor turned right ahead of us, after a short distance ending against an atmosphere door. As Marcus worked the console on this, I put my hand on the thing and felt it vibrating.

'What's the situation?' Marcus asked.

Again he included me in the conversation and, checking the links, I saw the *Hamilton* highlighted.

'Temporary truce,' replied someone in a slow drawl.

'Why?'

'The king wanted his hooders but now it seems Vrasan has lost control of those he had, and the king is no longer sure they're worth the price.'

'For now,' said Marcus.

'Oh, you humans are so cynical,' said the voice. 'Catch you later.'

'The *Hamilton* AI?' I asked.

'Yes,' he said tartly, returning to the console.

I could still feel the vibration through the door, and now realized it wasn't due to anything happening outside the station. The door slid aside and revealed the cause.

Beyond lay another tubeway, along which a force of prador were moving fast. Amidst them, a heavily armoured tank bristling with weapons ran on sticky treads. I recognized a prador implant tank which, at a stretch, compared to a Polity war drone. Since the prador didn't like AI, they used the excised and flash-frozen ganglions of their children to control such devices. As I identified the thing, one of the accompanying prador swung towards us. I threw myself aside as a particle beam lanced out, smoking the air and melting a hole through the wall at the turning. Marcus hit the control and the door slid shut, in time to bulge with multiple dents from Gatling slugs, then peppered with holes from those that punched through. We hit the floor as further slugs cracked through the walls. I began to crawl away, ready to get up and run.

'Wait,' said Marcus, holding up a hand.

The firing ceased a second later.

I nodded. 'Recalled?' I suggested.

'Looks that way,' he agreed, standing.

We'd shown our faces and one of the prador had responded as expected. However, it seemed likely that Vrasan had recalled his forces to the hub to deal with the hooders. They'd be under strict orders to get there fast and very likely none would be coming after us.

'What's happening there?' asked Marcus, again including me in an exchange with Salander.

'They're withdrawing,' she replied.

'Trouble at the hub,' said Marcus.

'The Polity coming in?' she asked.

'No, my friend here disabled a hooder's control thrall with a couple of sticky mines, which led to them attacking each other and disabling all their thralls. The hooders are headed back towards the hub. I think they might be unhappy with Vrasan.'

Salander laughed, long and hard, with a hint of hysteria in it.

'Well thank you, Jack Four,' she said finally. 'You just saved thousands of lives.'

'My pleasure,' I replied, feeling a bit of a fraud since my actions had resulted in the prador being here in the first place. But this had also been Marcus's plan originally, which I'd followed through.

'Trecannon is ready for you,' she added.

Over the next twenty minutes the immediate noise and

vibration died away. I finally put my eye to a split in the door to see the tubeway beyond standing empty. Marcus stepped up and inserted his hands in that split. He heaved and one half of the door broke away, falling with a crash to the side. We went through.

The tubeway now lay empty in both directions and my map showed that it led directly to the rim at Sector Seven. Grav was out, even on the central walkway, so we propelled ourselves along the near wall, ready to dart back into available side corridors should any more prador put in an appearance. None did, and we travelled for a couple of hours into the eye of the tubeway before we saw signs of action at the rim. Here the walls had been shredded by weapons fire. An implant tank sat with its top blown away, revealing a mass of electronics and thawing organics, while the remains of prador armour floated about, further organic slurry painting what remained of the walls. Movement over to one side attracted my attention. There lay a prador with all its legs gone and only half of a claw limb remaining. It kept pointing the stub of a limb at us and, I had no doubt, had its Gatling cannon or particle beam weapon still been attached, we would've been paste.

'Still alive,' commented Marcus.

The prador, it seemed, weren't much inclined to collect up their wounded. The humans, however, were. As the barrier came into sight, we saw doors open in the side of the tubeway and people loading others onto grav-stretchers.

'Trecannon?' Marcus asked.

A woman in a hazmat suit soaked with blood waved us towards the barrier. 'He's down there.'

The barrier consisted of slabs of ceramal and I-beams welded across the tubeway. At regular intervals, the barrels of heavy weapons protruded, while a row of mosquitoes squatted in front of it, along with a larger mobile weapon I identified as a rail beader. Salander's troops were here too, welding up breaks in the barrier, shifting debris, cutting weapons from gutted suits of prador armour. One bulky man floated high on the face of the barrier overseeing all this. Marcus must have recognized him because he launched up towards him. I stayed surveying the wreckage. The barrier had obviously held but the walls of the tubeway all around were utterly shredded and tunnels had been blasted into the surrounding structure of the station. No doubt the barrier would have continued to hold while the prador went round it. A flash of data arose in my mind of an ancient war on Earth where people had made a similar mistake depending on their armoured defences. I jumped and sailed up the barrier to catch hold of a protruding barrel beside Marcus and the man.

'So this is him?' The man turned towards me.

'Yes,' said Marcus. 'This is Jack Four.'

Trecannon wore an armoured spacesuit. His head was hairless and his skin an unnatural pink, with whorls in it as if covered in scar tissue from deep burns. More knowledge, not my own, surfaced and I recognized him as an adapt known as a krodorman. He grimaced at me and shook his head.

'I don't know whether to thank you or put a bullet in your head,' he said.

'That's not reassuring,' I replied. 'Why?'

'You destroyed the railgun and let the prador in. That gave us more time to get people out when Suzeal recalled hers. But maybe we could've held against Suzeal's lot – we certainly couldn't have continued to hold against the prador.'

'He did what I was going to do anyway,' said Marcus.

'Good little soldier, eh?' Trecannon continued to study me as if he wasn't quite sure what to make of me.

'He did what was necessary.'

'Up to and including attacking a hooder with a couple of sticky mines?'

Marcus shot me a glance. 'That was an interesting tactic.' He swung back. 'Now, that escape pod?'

'Just go through to the ring corridor and head right. EP234 is the one you can use.' He pointed down to the right of the barrier. 'There's a way through down there.'

Marcus nodded, inverted himself and kicked against an I-beam, sailing down in the direction indicated. I moved to follow but Trecannon caught hold of my shoulder.

'You don't have to go,' he said. 'I know you did what you thought was best in the circumstances and, really, we could use anyone who would even think of attacking a hooder.'

'Suzeal . . .' I began, not sure what to add.

'He can probably take her down without your help. You stay with him and he'll likely get you killed.'

'You saying I'd be safer here?' I asked, loath to point out that it didn't sound like it, if I was the kind of man he could use.

'A lot of people have died because of him.'

'But did he kill them?'

'Some, but it's not that. His kind don't think like soldiers. They look at the big picture and sometimes little people get lost in the paintwork.'

'Thanks for the warning,' I said, and propelled myself after Marcus.

It was then that some knowledge and speculations about my companion, which had been fermenting in the back of my mind for some time, began to surface.

20

Refugees crowded the ring corridor and rooms on the station side. We walked to the sound of announcements telling those with certain numbers to head to variously numbered escape pods. Some officious-looking types with orange armbands organized the queues leading to circular inward bulging hatches, checking numbers printed on their hands and taking away large bags of belongings.

'How many times do I have to say this?' one of them was saying. 'You've got room for one small bag, and not your fucking wardrobe!'

Piles of such bags lay on one side of the ring corridor and, even though this was a matter of survival, some were prepared to argue the matter.

Windows sat between the doors leading into the escape pods and I paused by one to take a look out. The pods were brick-like objects, with a slight curve to them to fit them to this part of the station rim. One of them detached with a blast of air and fell away into vacuum. There it fired up thrusters to stabilize and slid into a formation steadily receding from sight. Putting my face up against the window, I got a view towards the planet and there saw hundreds of black dots silhouetted against its face. Should Vrasan decide to fire on them they would make easy targets.

'Where can they go?' I wondered.

'Salander has told them to move around the other side of the planet,' said Marcus. 'Problem is she has no control once they've left. A lot have gone for the space dock and many are just hanging around the station in the hope that things improve.'

I stepped away from the window. 'You talked to her?' I couldn't help but feel a bit of resentment that he hadn't included me this time.

'I wanted some idea of what we're flying into,' he explained. 'It's good that a lot are heading for the dock – that'll give us cover if Suzeal is watching.'

I reflected on my brief talk with Trecannon. Those pods were heading towards a place that might still be occupied by prador – a dangerous place where civilians could end up dead. Since Marcus was aiming to kill one individual he held a grudge against, I didn't see this cover the civilians provided as part of any larger picture. Then again, perhaps Suzeal represented so much of a danger that casualties were permissible to prevent her escape. It might not be all about vengeance, I thought sourly.

Finally we came opposite one of the circular doors with EP234 stencilled on its surface. Two guards stood before it remonstrating with one of the armband crew and a group of people.

'It's not to be used,' said one of the guards.

'Saving it for more important people, are you?' sneered a woman in seared clothing supporting an arm in a reactive cast.

'It's for us,' said Marcus peremptorily, walking up.

'Just two of you?' said a young woman. 'That doesn't seem fair.'

'Life isn't,' he told her.

The young woman turned to me and I recognized her.

'You,' said Betan.

I felt a surge of joy in seeing her smudged face. Then a tightness in my stomach when I saw she was alone.

'You made it . . . Tanis?'

She gestured vaguely. 'He's around here somewhere. We're waiting for our pod.'

Since Marcus didn't seem inclined to diplomacy, I decided I should be.

'We're heading for the space dock to apprehend Suzeal,' I told them all. 'She's there with some of her soldiers and prador are there too.' I didn't know whether that was true but thought it a good idea to throw it in. 'Meanwhile the prador here are retreating to the hub – they're being attacked by their own pets.'

'Hooders?'

I looked round at Tanis.

'Glad you made it,' I said.

He stared at me without reaction.

Meanwhile Marcus had gone up to the door and as he drew it open, the crowd surged forwards. The woman with the broken arm reached him first and tried to push past, while Tanis and Betan weren't far behind. The two guards shoved a few back while Marcus caught the woman by her jacket and casually tossed her back into the rest. Then he opened fire with his pulse rifle into the floor, the guards moving in either side of him.

'If you want to die I can help you right here,' he said, stepping forwards.

The crowd shrank back from him. In that instant, he didn't look human. He gestured to me sharply and I moved past him and the guards, through the door. As he stepped in behind, I got a last glimpse of Betan and Tanis and saw only anger in their expressions. I felt sick, empty. He closed the door.

'You misread that,' he said, walking along the short entry tunnel.

'They want to escape,' I said.

'Like crowds pushing at the door in a burning building,' he said.

The analogy didn't really apply and I questioned whether us taking this pod for ourselves was right. But the reactions of Betan and Tanis gave me a feeling of betrayal. He opened the next door into an airlock whose inner door stood open and we entered the pod. No grav in here but my boots automatically applied gecko function.

'You wonder if we're doing the right thing. You wonder if I'm doing the right thing,' he said.

Four acceleration chairs occupied this level of the pod, with another two in front of a control console and screen, for pilot and co-pilot if necessary. Presumably, by its dimensions, it had two other levels with a similar number of seats. Gel stasis tubes lined the walls, so maybe there was room here for a hundred people.

'Yes, I question it.'

He took one of the two seats in front of the console and I took the one beside him. He strapped in, so I did too.

'Suzeal has been responsible for thousands of deaths. She's the prime mover of the coring and thralling trade in this sector of the Graveyard and she didn't just run it from this station. If she gets away, that trade continues.'

'You're telling me it won't continue if we stop her?'

I was conflicted and understood that the earlier simplicity of Jack Four the clone and his search for vengeance had, for a while now, been breaking up against hard reality. Things had ceased to be simple once I stepped beyond plain survival.

'No, I'm not telling you that. But the trade will fragment and there'll be infighting between wannabe replacements for her. That will make it easier for agents of the Polity to take it down.'

'Agents like you,' I said.

He nodded once, but said no more, instead taking hold of a joystick and thrusting it forwards. The screen came on as, with a thump, the pod detached. A formation map came up on the screen overlaying what we could see, with our position indicated within it. He cancelled that and swung us away. Thrust punched me in the back. Slowly a distant dot swung into sight and began to grow: the docking moon.

'We may face prador there,' I said.

'Which is why we're not going to dock where expected,' he replied, a slightly twisted smile to his face I wasn't sure I liked.

The dot steadily expanded. The moon had been mined and reformed so it no longer looked like a moon. Structural rings wrapped around it to attach the long protrusion of the dock, making it resemble the vast head of a stone mace, bound to a long metallic handle. Along this 'handle' ships had attached like buds along a branch and reminded me of the King's Ship.

'Do you see – at the far end of the dock?' Marcus asked.

I did see. Even now, escape pods were attaching to a section there – hundreds of them side by side, forming series of segmented lines along the dock.

I also began to see damage and debris floating around the dock. Large patches were dotted along it, doubtless covering the holes the prador had cut to gain access. I noted its weapons emplacements, and others that looked like recent additions. One huge turret had to be the particle beam weapon the prador had been using. I reached forwards to the console and threw a frame up in the screen to give me a view back towards the station. It lay tilted to my perspective, so I could see the rim where escape pods were still departing, as well as part of the hub where, even now, a blast blew a plume of air and debris into vacuum.

'I wonder how long Vrasan will try for?' said Marcus.

'Try?'

He glanced at me. 'Try to recapture and thrall the hooders.'

Now I understood. 'Until his own life is sufficiently threatened, I should think.'

'My reading of it too,' said Marcus.

'Of course it is,' I said.

He gave me a speculative look and continued, 'You know, by pissing off Vrasan and being a reachable representation of the Polity, you saved further lives.'

'Really?'

'Vrasan sent his prador against the rim barriers. How long do you think Trecannon would have held up against even just one hooder?'

'Not very long,' I replied. 'But Vrasan didn't make any tactical errors since he had achieved his objectives. Human lives are a matter of irrelevance to him.'

'True enough.'

'Which is why,' I added, 'he won't leave the station until he's made every possible effort to regain one of those objectives – the hooders. I expect he'll lose a lot of his troops during those efforts.'

'I expect so too.'

It seemed pointless continuing the conversation, so alike did we think.

He called up another view of the dock moon with its fuel silos, warehouses, accommodation units and other facilities built up on the bands of composite which surrounded it. On the screen he sketched vectors, making calculations. After a moment, he grunted with satisfaction.

'She kept this place supplied with pure water, deuterium, cracked oxygen and hydrogen and even hydrocarbons. A lot of ships came here and she had fuel for all kinds, even some ancient relics, for which she charged a premium,' he commented.

'I'm not seeing any docking circlets down there,' I said.

'There are none. The fuel ships just mated here with injectors to offload their cargo.'

'I presumed you were looking because we're docking there.'

He swung the view back to the dock. 'Suzeal's ship is here.' He put a frame over the dock halfway along and expanded it. Attached there, belly down, was a sleek-looking craft, like a spike, with two large U-space nacelles to the rear and what looked like weapons pods protruding halfway along. He changed the view, again bringing up where the escape pods were docking, and set our course in towards there.

'I thought we weren't docking where expected,' I commented.

'We aren't.' He unstrapped and stood up. 'There are a couple of spacesuits below provided for external repairs of the pods. We need to get into them.'

I unstrapped and followed him down. 'I suppose you're going to use the usual dramatic technique of telling me as little as possible until the last moment?'

He stopped and looked at me. 'Yes, I suppose I am.'

The lower deck had similar seating and gel stasis pods as above, but a sliding wall revealed two vacuum shell suits we could don over our envirosuits.

'She's stuck here at the dock until she can find a window for escape, but she'll be dug in inside her ship. And she'll have her people installed in the station itself to snipe at anyone who gets close. The ship itself will have its sensors looking out into space for any attack and weapons ready to be deployed.'

'So pretty invulnerable to attack from just two men,' I suggested.

'Pretty much,' he agreed. 'But there's a slice in between where she might be vulnerable. She'll have antipersonnel weapons trained along the outside of the dock, but might not expect something bigger via that route.'

The spacesuit was a hollow iron man which I stepped back

into. It folded closed around me and immediately gave me a HUD detailing its assist, suit jets, atmosphere readings and all the other requisites of vacuum survival. I stepped out wearing it at about the same time as Marcus, and we headed back up. I felt safer now because the suit's armouring offered a bit more protection. Very prador of me.

'The airlock sits at the back, where the main thrusters of this pod are,' he explained, now over com.

The screen showed us drawing in towards where all the other pods were docking. Marcus strode forwards and began punching in new instructions. He grabbed the joystick and swung the pod round. Crosshairs came up on the screen, wavering until he locked onto a distant object along the dock. Thrust then sent me staggering, as the pod accelerated. He gestured towards the airlock and, picking up his pack, took out a sticky mine. I began to understand his plan, but would've preferred some discussion of it first. I picked up my weapon and pack and secured them to belt links on my suit, hurriedly opened the inner door of the lock and we stepped inside.

'I calculate,' he said, 'that the atmospheric blast should slow us down enough for our suit jets to deal with the rest of the speed we'll reach in . . . twenty seconds.' He slapped the mine against the side of the outer door over the hinge. 'You ready?'

'Little fucking choice in the matter,' I said.

'True.'

I didn't like being this close to the mine, despite its blast being directed, but he didn't move, so I stayed put too. My mind went into accelerated overdrive as the twenty seconds counted down, but I found I couldn't even begin to get a handle on the calculations he must have made.

'Are there airlocks—?' I began, and the mine detonated.

*   *   *

My suit muted the explosion. The door swung out into vacuum, its hinge shattered, its locks tearing away. The atmosphere in the pod hit us from behind like a train and kicked us out. The door tumbled ahead and we tumbled after it. I got a glimpse of the pod departing, but relative to the dock we were still hurtling along only marginally slower than the thing.

'Pull out,' Marcus instructed.

Using blink control and a wrist console, I selected the dock itself as the relative point to stabilize to, and the suit thrusters took over, correcting my tumble till I flew along, feet down, towards it. Marcus moved out from the dock and I fired up the thrusters beside my boots to follow him out. He pointed down and I looked in time to see the pod hurtling along towards Suzeal's ship. A weapons nacelle on her ship protruded a railgun, which riddled the pod, causing it to leave a trail of fire. If any attackers had been inside, they'd have been be dead now. A miscalculation on Suzeal's part, since the attack was the pod itself. Belatedly a missile spat out and the pod exploded, but still large debris crashed along the dock and into her ship, jouncing it sideways and ripping off one of the U-drive nacelles. As we passed over this mess, I set my thrusters to take me back down. We would be easier targets out here, if anyone was looking, and anyway, I wanted to act before Marcus told me to do so.

'Ten seconds and then we decelerate, landing on the moon,' he said, much to my irritation. Then, before I could pose the question I'd been wondering about before the door blew out of the pod, he answered it. 'And yes, there are plenty of airlocks there.'

We went lower and soon the ships and structures on the dock came between us and Suzeal's ship, while the moon loomed before us. I fired up my suit's thrusters to slow me. Marcus sent over a map indicating an area ahead and I had my suit prepare for that. I held out my arms and the suit locked them in place. Wrist, leg and chest thrusters fired all at once and, despite the padding, the deceleration crushed me into the front of the suit. But I slowed and soon regolith surged up towards me. At the last moment the suit swung, its assist kicking in, and dropped me down on my feet. Dust rose around me.

'Come on,' said Marcus.

He stood just a few paces away, pointing towards one of the bands of composite that wrapped the moon. Standing on top of this were three large storage tanks and, running up the side of the composite, where he'd pointed, stood a ladder leading to an airlock. I set out in long bounds towards it, jumping at the last to take me halfway up its length. Grabbing hold, I scrambled up the rest of the way and headed for the airlock. Marcus arrived with a dusty thump beside me as I strained at the manual wheel. He'd used his suit jets. He grinned at me and punched a code into the console beside the hatch and it popped open. He gestured me in, since it only had room for one of us at a time. I stepped through the inner door onto a grated floor, no artificial gravity, just the light pull of the moon itself. Checking pressure, I saw it lower than ideal but manageable. A moment later he joined me.

'We'll keep the suits on for now?' I suggested, opening my visor.

'Yeah – they offer some protection.' He opened his visor too.

I huffed at cold air, felt the dearth of oxygen and then a moment later that faded as the oxygen transport effects of my boosting took over.

As ever I let him take the lead and followed him along a walkway curving into the distance. Scattered along the tube, windows looked out onto the moon's surface. It wasn't much of a view.

The corridor finally took a left turn into an area ringed with dropshafts and presumably bringing us to the base of the dock itself. Most of these were working, though in one section a wider and newer shaft had displaced two of them and I supposed the prador had come down here too. Of course they had – they would've wanted to ensure they were secure here. The shaft took us up just a short distance then out onto a curving grav floor, to bring us into consonance with the grav of the dock. We walked into an area like a great shopping mall, with corridors spearing on into the dock proper.

'No prador,' Marcus observed.

'That's good,' I said, not sure it was.

'If they all went to the station, you can guarantee they left something here to ensure this dock wouldn't be used against them.' Marcus confirmed my suspicions. We walked between malfunctioning fountains and ripped-up gardens dotted across a floor tiled with white and pale green pseudostone. Here and there I could see the results of Gatling fire and beam weapons, as well as human corpses. There weren't many, but of course the prador wouldn't have wasted such a delicacy. They ate human flesh and enjoyed it, not so much because it provided nutrients or, as I understood it, because it tasted any good to them, but because it came from intelligent enemies. I wondered if they'd killed everyone here, or just those who had resisted.

'There.' He pointed to one of the long corridors.

'How close?' I asked.

'A mile up that way. She would have wanted to stay covert but she will still have defences in place.' He grimaced. 'And you can be damned sure she knows we're here now.'

'Why can you be damned sure of that?'

'Because she would've wanted to see us die and then, knowing we didn't, be sure what we'd do next. Or at least, what I would do.'

408

Of course, she'd left cams in the siluroyne enclosure so she could watch.

'So what's the plan?'

'Her ship is damaged so she'll want another one,' he said. 'She'll be on the move along that corridor. We—'

Something hit me hard and sent me tumbling in a ball of fire. I slammed into a fountain, visor automatically closed, and fractured diagnostics scrolling in my HUD. I tried to sit upright, but assist had locked. My suit was smoking, its plates warped and some rucked up from their underlay. It'd offered some protection but it hadn't been a Polity combat suit. I looked around but couldn't see much because smoke surrounded me. I did, however, see Marcus lying over to one side. My HUD finished its damage report and offered its only suggestion, but I didn't want to take it because three figures were looming out of the smoke before me. I delinked my weapon from the suit, and just let it fall.

'Now there's a familiar face,' said a familiar voice. 'I'm going to enjoy this.'

Brack stood there, in all his boosted and armoured barbarian glory, a heavy pulse rifle cradled in one arm and his stun baton in his other hand. Using blink control, I initiated the option my suit had given. It crumped and folded open and I peeled up out of it, grabbed my weapon and threw myself sideways. A shot from a laser carbine stabbed into the empty suit just behind me, flaming the interior as I rolled and came up shooting. I just had time to see the stun baton turning end over end through the air before it hit my shoulder, numbing my arm.

'Don't fucking kill him,' Brack raged, slapping one of his compatriots across the back of the head. 'Find the other one – this one is mine.'

I hit the ground, grip sliding from my weapon as he strode towards me. He drew his machete and grinned evilly.

'This is going to—' he began, but I drew my sidearm left-handed and opened fire. The shots slammed into his armour, blowing pieces away and leaving smoking holes. I tracked up towards his face but he simply ducked his head away and turned his back on me. The shots in his back did little, so I aimed for his legs as I stood up. Then the clip emptied. I ejected it, stuck the gun in my right armpit, extracted another from my belt and inserted it. He stooped, picked something up, turned and threw. The tile hit me in the chest and I staggered back, the gun falling. I then turned and ran towards the nearest shopping centre.

'Coward!' he shouted.

Brack was armed and no doubt stronger than me. He'd just used a stun baton that put me at a further disadvantage and I needed a few moments to get the feeling back in my arm. Instinctively, after a couple of seconds, I dodged to one side, and pulse fire tracked across the ground. He was going for my legs. He didn't want to kill me with a shot in the back since that would be far too easy. He was the type who wanted me under his power for a while – that was his disadvantage. Glancing back, I saw him advancing confidently with the pulse rifle, machete sheathed again.

I ducked through an arch into the shopping centre. The place had been pretty torn up and it was obvious a prador had been through here. Aisles had been pushed over, robot shopping trolleys and goods were strewn all over the place. I needed weapons, a weapon, *any* weapon. This didn't look like the kind of place where guns would be conveniently shelved, but glancing at the signage, I did see a hardware section and headed straight there. More shots tracked up the aisle behind me. I dived into a gap between stacked boxes which, by the pictures on the outside, contained service eggs. As I crashed through the gap the boxes squawked, 'Error code! Error code!'

'I'm still here!' he shouted happily.

I glanced back to see him charge up opposite and start pulling out boxes. I scrambled through, fell out into the next aisle and ran along it. By now the feeling had returned to my arm. I flexed it, flexed my hand and ran into a room with short rows of goods. Here was the hardware. Round a turning, then another. Hand tools. Heavy wrenches, deposition welders, spanner and screwdriver sets, but nothing in the way of laser cutters or atomic shears. I picked up a wrench, my breathing settling as he tramped along the next aisle. Spotting something else, I gently put the wrench down and picked up an axe. The handle was duralumin and the head ceramal. Walking to the end of the aisle, I understood that such tools were available because those who came here often had old ships, or occupied primitive locations, where old technology had to be persuaded with brute force. I rounded the end of the aisle with the axe already swinging.

Brack looked briefly startled. I'd timed it just right. The axe slammed down on top of his pulse rifle, cracking the casing and shorting something inside so it showered sparks. Yet he still held the thing with rigid strength. I stepped back for another swing when the busted rifle hit me in the chest and sent me staggering.

'I didn't want to use it anyway,' he said, drawing his machete again.

He stepped in, stooping low and swinging at my legs, still seeking to disable and not kill. I jumped, kicked, driving a foot into his face and pushing away to come down into a squat. I swung at his legs as he came at me, getting in one good hit where I'd directed my earlier pulse gun shots. He staggered and winced, his visor snapping shut, and swung at my head. I simply ducked it and, squatting on one leg, sweep-kicked his ankle. He staggered again, but was too strong and heavy to go over. I came up, grabbed a shelf and pulled it over on him. He clambered out of the debris only to get my axe in the top of his helmet. It glanced away but I could see it jarred him. He looked angry now. He kept swinging at me and missing and didn't like that. Axe and machete clashed in a fast exchange, but seeing the deep cuts in the axe shaft I knew it couldn't last. His visor opened again.

'Prador metal,' he said, holding up the machete. 'Yours will break soon, then we'll see if you can dance without legs.'

Always the same, this thing with the visors. They all wore armour, just as I had, but kept opening up that hatch to the most vulnerable part of their bodies. It had been Frey's undoing when I shoved that grenade into his helmet. I noted my breathing was slow and even. I'd hoped to cause him some damage through what I'd already inflicted on his armour with the pulse gun, but that was too slow. If he got hold of me just once, or got in one hit with that blade, I was done.

I stepped in and swung at his chest. He blocked with the machete. I swung again and again and he blocked every time. I guess he assumed me that inept. The axe handle now looked close to giving up. Assuming a look of fear and defeat, I held it out before me to, supposedly, keep him back. He grinned and brought the machete down hard. With a high loud ring, a short length of the shaft and the axe head fell away. He grinned, and I drove the jagged shaft right at his face. I could have gone for one of his eyes but he would have closed his visor and, though hurt, would be all but invulnerable again. The jagged shaft struck his cheekbone and slid deep into his helmet beside his face, ripping through skin and flesh. His visor tried to close, but instead clamped the shaft. My fingers followed through, forefinger and mid-finger in one eye and the other two in the other. Hard, right down into the sockets. I hooked them and pulled, and he screamed.

Shaking the fleshy detritus of his eyes from my fingers, I stepped away as he swung his machete. He swung again and

again. Blind. Pulling a case from one shelf, I tore it open
and pulled out a memory metal screwdriver. On the handle were
the controls that set the kind of head it switched to, but they
were irrelevant, for all I needed was the long length of metal and
a suitable grip. He realized his danger and reached up to grab
at the axe handle, just as I thrust-kicked the back of his knee
with all the force I could muster. Going down on one knee, he
turned and swiped, but I'd moved to one side by then. Another
kick to his chest put him on his back. I followed him down,
within the swing of his blade and, two-handed, stabbed the
screwdriver into his eye socket. The machete clanged away and
he closed his arms around me, trying to crush me. I bore down
on the screwdriver as his arms began to bend my back and my
ribs felt as though they were about to break. The driver sank
with a crunch right to the back of his skull, but still it seemed
he would break me. He released his hold and hit my arm –
I heard the bone break. But, still holding with the other hand, I
wrenched the screwdriver from side to side, stirring its shaft in
his brains. He made a wet snorting sound, blood and brain tissue
coming out of his nose, and the pressure came off.

It took me a moment to free myself from his arms and finally
stand, shaking and nauseated. My arm was definitely busted and
my ribs didn't feel in much better shape. I stared down at him
as he jerked a few more times, or perhaps that was some remaining
function of his suit.

'I wondered when you were going to stop playing with him.'

Marcus crouched up on top of a nearby shelf. He dropped
down to land lightly in a squat and then stand. Blood spattered
his envirosuit and he now carried a selection of weapons. The
other two had obviously found him. Unlucky for them.

'Now,' he said, 'let's get him out of his suit.'

⋆   ⋆   ⋆

'They're abandoning it,' said Marcus, his voice not like his at all.

The window could be adjusted to show sensor data from any of the telescopes and other sensors positioned along the dock. It showed prador strewn between the Stratogaster space station and the distant reavers. I also noticed some heading this way and felt that didn't bode well for us.

'Vrasan has given up,' I suggested.

'The *Hamilton* AI says so,' he replied. 'And neither side will let the other get their hands or claws on those hooders.'

I nodded, then wished I hadn't because it felt as if Brack had cracked something in my neck too. We moved on from the viewing section which sat between the docking areas and airlocks and on up the tunnel of the dock.

Whether it had been his plan all along to make an approach like this, I didn't know, nor whether my presence was unnecessary. Had he watched the final moments of my fight with Brack or only just arrived as I finished it? I liked to think he would've intervened had he arrived earlier, but just wasn't sure. He prodded me with the stun baton and I stumbled. This kind of behaviour would be expected from Brack by the two guards who were standing behind the six-legged drone in the tunnel.

As we drew closer, the drone targeted us, but at a snapped command from one of the guards, it returned the focus of its impressive array of weapons to the tunnel lying behind us. I glanced back at Marcus. He had his visor closed and had smeared it, and the suit, with blood and other messy exudates. To add to the effect, he'd introduced a couple of malfunctions, so occasional sparks issued from one leg and smoke wisped from other joints. I hoped these distractions worked, because I had no confidence in the sidearm in the sling supporting my arm.

'Jeset and Dragim?' one of the two asked.

'The other one got them,' Marcus replied. 'Jeset stuck a mine on him.'

He'd explained to me that the one called Jeset had actually tried that, before Marcus broke his neck. He'd then laid out his simple plan, while adjusting the voice output of Brack's suit based on some of the recordings it contained. Now, with a lot of crackling interference, his voice matched Brack's. We walked straight past the drone to where an airlock stood open. Just beyond it, a loading ramp reached from an open hold door onto the dock. At the foot of this lay three bodies clad in grey shipsuits pulled over a variety of clothing. With her own ship damaged, Suzeal had taken another. I guessed them to be the previous crew of this ship and that others in a similar condition would be inside. I wondered how many more of Suzeal's soldiers would be in there too. It hadn't been something we'd discussed. As we reached the airlock, the ramp began to retract. Marcus halted and turned to the other two.

'Over here,' he said, giving me another prod so I stumbled into the airlock. The inner door stood open, with a body sprawled beyond. I was right about the crew. I looked back around as the two sauntered over. When they drew close, completely oblivious to their danger, Marcus snapped a hand out and grabbed the lower rim of the nearest one's helmet, while simultaneously shooting the other in the face. As the second man staggered back, his face a burned ruin, the first hit the wall beside the airlock. Marcus closed in and drove a fist into his now-closed visor. The thing smashed back into his face and the man slid bonelessly to the floor. Some suits were better than others, it appeared. The drone began to turn, but by then Marcus had entered the airlock and closed the outer door.

'Here.' He handed me the laser carbine he'd taken from Jeset. I held it one-handed but didn't think I'd be much use with it.

Besides the crew, who were likely all dead, I was the only one without armour. Marcus opened his visor and marched up the corridor.

'Suzeal just asked me what happened out there,' he said. 'I began to tell her about a drone malfunction, then my com, which hasn't been good since the fight, broke down.'

Was it really going to be as easy as this?

He continued along a corridor which presumably led to the bridge. A soldier stepped out of the door ahead of us, hesitated for a second, then spotted my carbine. He began to raise one of his own but I fired, flaming the front of his suit. Marcus's shots hit next, dancing him back along the corridor. A hand reached out and shoved me, making me fall through a doorway as pulse gun fire filled the corridor from behind. Marcus turned, shots sizzling on his armour, and launched grenades back towards those shots, then followed after them at a run. I pulled myself up and peered round the door jamb to see him barrelling into three of Suzeal's soldiers. They were all just rising, the grenades not enough to penetrate their armour. Grabbing the first one by the neck, he used her as a shield as he continued into the other two, and then threw her at them. He chopped the side of the head of one without a helmet, deforming his skull and snapping his neck. The woman struggled to rise with her back against the wall. He slammed the barrel of his weapon into her visor and kept on firing till it collapsed, meanwhile back-kicking the other soldier into the other wall.

Movement behind. I turned to see the one we'd first shot climbing to his feet so I fired on him, and just kept firing. I couldn't afford to let him get a shot off at me. He collapsed in flames, then some power supply blew in the side of his suit, throwing smoking guts up the wall. I turned again. Marcus had dropped his weapon and had his remaining opponent up in the air by his throat. That soldier drew a sidearm and fired into his chest. Marcus flung him face down on the floor, came down on his back with one knee, grabbed his arms and heaved. I don't know whether the horrible crunching issued from his armour or breaking back, but he folded up midway, the armour parting underneath, then lay there jerking when dropped. Marcus was a killing machine.

A shot hit my shoulder, spinning me round. I came down on one knee and opened fire. Five soldiers had now appeared from the bridge and I kept firing, even as I flung myself back through the doorway. Weaponless and roaring, Marcus hurtled past straight into the fusillade. The firing dropped away when he arrived and I heard yells, screams and the thump of bodies hitting the walls as I inspected my shoulder. The shot had penetrated my envirosuit and dug a lump of flesh out of my shoulder, while simultaneously cauterizing the wound. It wasn't too deep but hurt like hell. Then again, there weren't many parts of my body that didn't hurt, my broken arm especially. This brief pause gave me time to take in the contents of the room. Two cold coffins sat in a framework with feed and power lines extending to the walls. I quickly stepped over and peered in the viewing window of one. A woman lay inside, thin and blue. Her shaven head revealed a line where her skin, and probably the underlying skull, had either been glued or had healed together. I ducked back to the door and looked round the jamb into the corridor again.

One of the soldiers lay on the floor, legs bent away at the hips at an angle they should not have been able to achieve. Another tumbled head over heels in my direction and landed on his back, tried to rise and then slumped. I aimed at the others, trying to get a clear shot, but couldn't really manage it one-handed. Marcus then grabbed the helmets of the remaining two, heaved them both from the floor and slammed them together. A visor and pieces of segmented armour tumbled away. He stood there, his helmet, and plates of Brack's armour hanging loose, smoke rising from underlying flesh, clenching and unclenching his hands with a clicking, crunching sound.

'Where ish she!' he shouted at the five who, even if they were alive, showed no inclination to answer. In irritation he tore away his loose plates and shed the damaged gauntlets.

I walked out, worried about his slurring voice. He focused on me, took a step forwards and for a second looked puzzled, then grimaced and turned to head up the corridor.

'Where ish she?' he hissed.

I entered the bridge behind him to see a very frightened man sitting in an acceleration chair, spun round from the navcom. Marcus loomed over him, hands still clenching and unclenching. I took in the scene. The man wore a shipsuit just like those I'd seen on the corpses of the crewmembers. He also couldn't get out of the chair because someone had wound a band of reinforced tape around him and the chair.

'Marcus!' I moved up behind him quickly and, using the carbine, tried to push him to one side. It was like trying to move a tree. He whirled towards me, teeth bared in a snarl, but at least they were human teeth – the change never that quick. He grabbed my weapon and sent it crashing into a nearby wall. Then he just stopped, head tilted to one side as he looked at the weapon. After a moment, he stepped away from the acceleration chair, gesturing me towards the man.

'Do you have anything here I can cut that tape with?' I asked.

The man nodded gratefully and pointed over to wall storage. Stepping over, I opened a hatch and slid out a tool chest. From this I took some diamond-faced snips and cut through the tape. He pulled it away and stood, then looked over to Marcus.

'The bitch is in the hold,' he spat.

Marcus was gone in a moment, hurtling back down the corridor, leaving chunks of armour behind him. The man went over to another storage hatch, put his hand against a palm lock, then pulled it open to reveal three racked slammers. He pulled one out angrily.

'She killed them,' he said. 'She didn't need to kill them.'

'Wait.' I caught his arm as he moved to go after Marcus.

'She fucking killed them!'

I glanced over at my carbine and saw a definite bend to it as well as the energy canister lying to one side, so snatched up one of the slammers. The short weapon seemed apt for one-handed use, but the kick might be difficult.

'We'll follow,' I said, 'slow and careful. Best not to get in Marcus's way.'

'He's a hooper,' said the man.

I thought about Marcus as he'd been when hunting me down. He might have lost most of the visible signs of his mutation but he still retained a hideous portion of that strength. And now he had something else: a mad rage I'd never seen before.

'Yeah,' I said, 'something like that.'

As we moved down the corridor after Marcus, deep thumps transmitted through the dock and into the ship. From above came a metallic clattering, which then proceeded away from us.

'They're back,' said the crewman.

I didn't need any further explanation.

Gunfire echoed ahead then ended with a long wailing scream. More shots ensued, followed by crashes and thumps. My companion paused by one of his crew, turned her over and looked at the hole drilled through her forehead. He stood again, tears in his eyes.

'What's your name?' I asked.

'Galash,' he said woodenly.

'Why are you here, Galash?'

'Trade,' he said tersely, but I saw the brief shift in his expression. I thought about the two cold coffins I'd seen earlier. The short stock of my slammer hit him hard in the temple and he dropped to the floor. Gazing down at him, I contemplated a killing shot.

'Get another job,' I said instead and departed. Even while walking away, I wondered if really I should have killed him. Anyone who traded in thralled human blanks was either a murderer or an accomplice to murder. Yet, it seemed the Graveyard contained so many scumbags like that and I couldn't kill them all, could I?

The ship had become an abattoir. I passed the detritus of Marcus's passage, checking for life signs and finding them either fading or non-existent. A short spiral stair took me down; halfway I had to move a body out of the way that was near torn in two. Through smoke, stepping over ugly remains of humanity along a path that was easy to follow, I finally came to the racket of gunfire and hot splinters flying out of the hold. I paused outside the open airlock then, once the firing had ceased, risked a quick glance inside.

The hold contained a cargo of large plasmel boxes, many of which had been shredded by gunfire. Marcus crouched behind a stack of these. The reason for his sober retreat had begun to climb the ramp. The drone had all its weapons directed into the hold, and I jerked back, even as heavy slugs smashed and zinged through the airlock. Then the firing ceased again.

'She's run,' Marcus growled.

I eyed the control panel beside the airlock, rested the slammer against the wall, then pulled up its menu, searching through until I found what I wanted.

'Come back to me now!' I shouted.

'She can't get away!' he snarled back.

'And you won't get past that thing intact! Think! The ramp controls are out here!'

After a short pause, the gunfire started up again, throwing splinters of metal and shreds of plasmel through the airlock. A moment later, Marcus came rolling through, jerking as a heavy slug ripped into his bare side. I risked another look to see the drone was well up the ramp door, then hit the control. The firing continued, but now hit the hold floor as, with a steady whine, the ramp closed up. Marcus crawled from the line of fire. He was a mess, Brack's armour all but gone, and his body riddled with holes and burns. But even as he stood, his woody, virus-infested body shed pieces of metal and oozed clear fluid that quickly scabbed. The firing ceased abruptly. A scrabbling sound ensued, followed by a heavy crash. I looked in and saw the drone on its back, but even in that position, its legs folded right down to bring it up again, and it turned to bring its weapons back to bear.

'Come on!'

We ran into the ship, a missile streaking through the airlock then past us to explode ahead. I ducked down, metal fragments zinging all around me, then came upright again, amazed that none had hit me. We reached the stairs and climbed, a fire burning ahead of us. Another missile shot by below and exploded, but through the airlock the drone couldn't target us. As we reached the original ship's corridor, it began crashing against the airlock. I would say it was furious its prey had escaped, but I didn't think it bright enough for that.

We exited the ship through the airlock up from the now-closed ramp door. The drone must have been scanning for us because the door shuddered as the thing slammed against it. I don't know how Marcus chose to run left, but I followed him anyway. The tube doglegged ahead, which was handy because targeting lasers lit us up from behind just as we reached it. I glanced back, expecting to see the drone free from the hold, but instead saw prador coming up the tunnel. Why targeting lasers and not their usual fusillade of heavy slugs and sweeping particle beams? The answer seemed obvious: Vrasan had arrived and he wanted us alive. Clearly, in the brief time they'd seen us, they'd not been able to get a clear shot at a leg, or been able to deploy some non-lethal weapon.

Rounding the first turn of the dogleg, a view through a side window showed larger ships docked ahead. We rounded the next bend into a bigger tubeway, boiling with smoke. Targeting lasers flicked again and a figure appeared ahead with a launcher shouldered. I threw myself aside and rolled up against the hatch of one of the exterior maintenance airlocks, seeing the laser flare on Marcus as he broke into a run. The launcher cracked, flinging out a jet of fire behind. Everything seemed to slow down to me and I even saw the missile clearly as it sped towards him. The long, spear-like thing had a barbed point and flight fins to the rear. It struck him hard in the chest, punching right through and juddering him to a halt. He didn't go down. I expected it now to explode but it just sat there, skewering him. He reached up, grabbed it and tried to pull it free, but the barbs jammed in his back. When he released it, the thing snapped back into position, opened slots in its sides and folded out hooks to engage with his back and his chest. He groaned and went down on one knee, his head bowing over.

'We sometimes use them to bring down the virally mutated,' said a familiar voice.

I turned, back braced against the hatch and fired the slammer at the half-seen figure. She staggered back, dropping her launcher, while the recoil juddered me back against the hatch and put my aim off. Then she advanced. I managed to brace the weapon back against the rim of the hatch to deal with the recoil and hit her again and again. But her armour was simply too tough. For every pace I blew her backwards, she took another three forwards, smoke and the burning dust load of the slammer wreathing her each time. When she reached me, she simply stooped and wrenched the weapon away, sending it skittering across the floor. I tried to get up, pulling the sidearm from my sling and managing three shots at her visor before she slapped that away.

'Stay down or I will break your legs,' Suzeal ordered me.

I resorted to talk, because the longer that lasted, the longer I might live. 'I never saw that weapon used against the escapees.'

'Of course not,' she replied, standing upright. 'They're specifically for hunts. They're good at keeping my people sharp and always entertaining.'

'Sprine in them,' I said.

'And some other synergetic paralytics.'

Before I could reply to that, she turned away and said, 'I have them.'

The smoke, which had obviously been deliberate, began to clear, revealing further soldiers in the tunnel – all pure SGZ in black and white and strewn with decals and decorations. This was notable, since those aboard the ship had mainly been her employed mercenaries. She turned back to me. Three of them, I saw, had launchers like the one she'd used. If her shot hadn't brought Marcus down, then theirs would have. I glanced to the right and saw the two prador that had targeted us coming into view. I considered my location – my back against an airlock – and, using blink control on my HUD, opened up a comlink to give it access to everything I could hear and see. I just hoped Marcus had been right about what was out there.

'I was going to blow the dock, but the two of you suddenly became valuable,' she said, turning back. 'When you both entered the ship it became obvious I couldn't bring him down in such close confines.'

'You're telling me this because you want me to understand how clever you've been?'

She lowered her visor and now I could see her expression clearly. She didn't look victorious, but grim and just a bit worried.

'I set the drone to delay you.'

'It didn't delay us for long enough, did it?' I carefully eased myself to my feet, glanced at the rip in my envirosuit shoulder, then down at my belt where a patch kit was attached. I continued, 'You needed access to a vessel and you don't have that yet.' I glanced left and through the clearing smoke saw more than just the two prador approaching. 'One the prador might struggle to board,' I added.

'You think you're clever now,' she said, glaring at me. 'You destroyed my railgun and you brought hell to Stratogaster.'

I gazed at her steadily. 'Hell was already there.'

She took a pace towards me, bunching her hand into a fist. I couldn't survive a punch from her in that suit. But she paused, looked over to Vrasan, and stepped back. Forcing a smile onto her face she said, 'I gave him the rest of the Old Families I traded with but he wanted to be sure, so he demanded me too. This trade gets me off the hook. You'll be going back to the King's Ship and I expect you'll spend a long time dying there.'

I bowed my head as if in defeat, but with my head down studied the airlock console. A menu sat on the screen but I didn't need that, just a big green button below it. Looking up again, I studied her. It seemed, despite all the terrible things she'd done, she did have some code she lived by based on exchange, trade and a twisted form of honour that must have grown up over her years on the station building the SGZ. Perversely, it seemed she expected others to adhere to it too. But the prador lived by their own code: prador first and everyone else dead. How the hell did she think this would run?

'Vrasan!' She turned.

The white-armoured prador advanced out of the remaining wisps of smoke, reached out a claw and closed it around the dart through Marcus. With a wrench and a flip, he simultaneously pulled the thing out and flung Marcus aside. He crashed into the wall next to me, and I didn't think that coincidental.

'You have them,' he said, coming closer.

'And our deal still stands?' said Suzeal.

Vrasan seemed to mull that over. I meanwhile noted how his prador had positioned themselves. Suzeal sat in a trap, diverted with some hope she could bargain her way out. I looked down at Marcus and he looked back up at me, managing a slight painful flexing of his legs. I nodded my head back at the airlock hatch behind me. He blinked – I wasn't sure if he understood.

'I am, as I have always been, loyal to my father, my king,' said Vrasan. 'We tried to obtain hooders for advantage but now the Polity is here. Trying further to obtain them will result in war and, anyway, the ones I did obtain beat their thralls.'

'So a brief setback,' said Suzeal brightly. 'But that dreadnought didn't kill all of them on the planet and their young will still be hatching out underground. I'm sure we can find a quieter way to go about this.'

'Perhaps so,' Vrasan agreed cordially, 'but at present we must take what we have and retreat.' He turned towards me. 'You, human, have been a bane of my existence. You told me once that my king effectively informed you how to free yourself from your thrall, and now it seems his whims persist. You have one very small chance, then you are mine. Do I have to say anything more?'

I shook my head.

Suddenly a man screamed, high up and clamped in a prador claw. Gatling cannons fired, flinging bodies, with armour fragmenting in every direction. A particle beam sawed, tossing another back through the air. Vrasan snapped out a claw and closed it around Suzeal's waist. I hit the button and reached with my good arm down to Marcus, who'd just managed to get his feet underneath him. I pulled and it was like trying to haul up a tree root, but he came. We fell into the airlock and I kicked the door closed, managing to get to it and spin its wheel. Leaning against it, I peered through the chain-glass window. Suzeal had pulled a weapon from her back – some kind of rail beader by the sound, which was audible even through the hatch as she shot it into Vrasan's body. This didn't last. With his other claw, Vrasan plucked the weapon away, then he slammed her to the floor, hard, and brought a couple of his armoured feet down onto her. He turned then, looking directly at the airlock, and began to reach out with a claw.

'Damn, all the way,' I said, scrabbling at the patches on my belt.

I got one out and slapped it on the hole through the shoulder of my envirosuit. The thing wasn't made for vacuum but it could keep me alive at least for a little while. Marcus looked up at me.

'You'll survive this,' I said. 'You did before.'

He reached up and grabbed my belt as I turned to the console for the exterior hatch and overrode the safeties. Explosive decompression blew us out into space, tumbling end over end past a ship like an iron segment of an orange. My suit ballooned around me from its internal pressure. I looked at Marcus, jetting vapour from holes in his body, eyes freeze-drying.

'If you're going to do something, do it now,' I said into the open comlink. 'This suit will give me maybe five minutes of air.'

Horribly, there came no reply for long minutes, then seemingly out of nowhere, a black surface, shot through with weird glittering facets, came up to meet us. The surface parted and we fell inside, thumping into an explosion of crash foam.

'Gotcha,' said a voice I didn't recognize. 'Pumping air in now.'

Apparently the black ops attack ship had been hanging around the dock for some time. It knew Marcus and, as best it could, had been keeping track of him. And, of course, it knew me by very close association.

Epilogue

The autosurgeon was far in advance of the one Bronodec had used. I climbed onto the table and lay back, felt the touch of something against my neck, then after a brief hiatus sat up from the table clad in a white shipsuit, all my ills repaired. Looking round, I saw the surgeon folded back into two gleaming pillars. A door opened ahead.

'Go left and keep going till you reach the viewing gallery,' said the voice of the *Hamilton* AI. 'He's waiting for you there.'

I got off the table and followed the instructions. The interior of the ship – at least this part of it – was all aseptic and white. Only the carpet grass, inset decorations on the walls and the occasional weirdly twisted sculptures set in alcoves dissuaded me from spooky comparisons with the King's Ship. At the end of the corridor wide steps led up into a gallery with a panoramic chain-glass window. The gallery, and the window itself, curved round out of sight in both directions. Over to the right stood a group of people whom I presumed to be refugees from Stratogaster who had decided to take up the *Hamilton*'s offer to return with it to the Polity. A man in ECS uniform stood with his hands behind his back, taking in the view. I walked up and stood beside him.

Stratogaster station sat close below us. Much damage was visible and steering thrusters were firing to correct its position. Escape pods swarmed around it, coming in to dock.

'It's still there,' I said.

'Interesting development,' said Marcus smoothly. 'The AI was going to demolish the station with imploders to ensure nothing of the hooders remained. But they came out.' He raised an arm to the window and sketched a frame over the station, touched a slider along the bottom and drew it back. An image now showed me the station as it'd been some time ago; perhaps when the autosurgeon was bone-welding my broken arm. I saw particle beams flash down towards it – careful strikes that still demolished substantial parts of it near its hub. Then, out of fire turning to wisps and fizzling out, out of the spreading clouds of hot debris, the three hooders writhed. They moved through space, rippling with pink light and were soon well clear of the station. I expected some apocalyptic weapon to hit them but the light went out and they coiled up together in a single mass. This drifted across the face of the planet in silhouette. Marcus pushed the time slider forwards and we got a view of this mass kicking out a tail of fire, as the hooders fell into atmosphere.

'The AI let them go?' I asked.

'No indication of active Atheter technology on any scan.'

'Still, it is alien technology.'

He glanced at me. 'I don't try to second-guess the decisions of AIs.' He wiped his hand across to dismiss the frame.

'Salander and her people?' I asked.

'Going back to rebuild on the station,' he replied. 'She's got supplies going over from the *Hamilton* to help with that, but then we have to get out of here. This is still the no-man's land between the Polity and the Kingdom and even though there have been some . . . problems, the truce returns in force in just a few hours. That means no warships from either side here.'

I looked up past the planet towards the reavers. No doubt departure would be simultaneous, down to the second.

'And the hooders down there. What about them? They're still a danger.'

'Salander has agreed to keep watch and intends to establish bigger and more permanent bases down on the planet. The prador may try again, who knows?' He shrugged. 'This shit happens all the time. It'll be described as a brief police action – a swiftly resolved border dispute.'

'And what about you? What next for you?'

'A long holiday until I get bored, then the next mission.'

I nodded, nerving myself because something else still needed to be touched on.

'So what do I call you? I can't keep calling you Marcus . . .'

He looked at me with a slightly twisted smile. 'You know exactly what to call me. I don't intend to give up my name just because someone else has it. It is quite a common one, you know.'

I grimaced at that, uncomfortable with it. 'So how did you end up on the King's Ship?'

'After Suzeal had handed me over to Brack and Frey and they'd finished with me, they stuck a leech on me and threw me in the pens. I went with others to one of the Old Families, only it was one the king brought down shortly afterwards. He destroyed the slaves that had been cored, but kept me, handing me over to Vrasan. Vrasan tried all sorts of techniques to rid me of the virus, but the damned thing mutated stronger than ever. I saw it as torture and lost my mind. Vrasan controlled me with thrall tech but, well . . . You saw the result.'

'I thought Suzeal destroyed the recording of your mind inside you?'

'She did, but she didn't destroy the original or extract all the quantum crystals. My mind recorded back to them and kept reloading, along with the same knowledge base you had, and stabilized eventually.' He paused. 'So what about you? What will you do now?'

I thought about what had driven me in the beginning. Brack and Frey were dead and in Vrasan's claws Suzeal had entered the kind of hell to which she had consigned others. That was all over now, and it was time for a new beginning.

I shrugged. 'Up till now I haven't had the time to give it much thought.'

'I think ECS would be quite happy to take you on.'

'I'll think about it,' I said.

'You do that, Jack.'

'And you enjoy your holiday . . . Jack.'

He snorted a laugh, turned away and walked back into the ship. I didn't laugh but my amusement was similar, of course.